SWEET YOUNG Thang

A Theta Alpha Gamma Story

BY ANNE TENINO

I0637024

RIPTIDE
PUBLISHING

Riptide Publishing
PO Box 6652
Hillsborough, NJ 08844
www.riptidepublishing.com

This is a work of fiction. Names, characters, places, and incidents are either the product of the author's imagination or are used fictitiously. Any resemblance to actual persons living or dead, business establishments, events, or locales is entirely coincidental.

Sweet Young Thang (Theta Alpha Gamma, #3)
Copyright © 2013 Anne Tenino

Cover Art by L.C. Chase, lcchase.com/design.htm
Editors: Sarah Frantz and Rachel Haimowitz
Layout: L.C. Chase, lcchase.com/design.htm

ISBN: 978-1-62649-033-8

First edition
July, 2013

Also available in ebook.
ISBN: 978-1-62649-032-1

SWEET YOUNG Thang

A Theta Alpha Gamma Story

by Anne Tenino

RIPTIDE
PUBLISHING

For Justin and Matt. Any (superficial) resemblance to either of you is coincidental, I swear.

Table of Contents

Chapter 1

"**I**'m probably going to die, aren't I?"

Eric Dixon fiddled with his patient's IV for a few seconds, collecting his thoughts. Mr. Siskin was on a fair amount of pain medicine, but his speech seemed clear. Eric met his gaze. "Do you remember what I said the problem was?"

Siskin grimaced. "Uh . . . aneurysm in my abdomen, right?"

"Well, that's what I think, but we don't carry the equipment on the ambulance to know for sure." Not to mention he wasn't a doctor. Eric watched the pulsing swelling just below Siskin's navel and could only imagine that was one thing, though. "It's called a thoracic aortic aneurysm. It means your aorta—the main artery supplying blood to your body—is in danger of rupturing. If I'm right, and that happens, you'll bleed to death." So fast that even if he was already in surgery and opened up, they might not be able to save him.

"How much danger?"

Eric blew out a breath. "You hear the sirens?"

Mr. Siskin nodded tightly. Sweat beaded on his forehead.

Eric leaned forward to adjust the drip, giving his patient more medication. "We don't always go to the hospital code three, meaning with the lights and sirens on. Only when someone's in imminent danger of death or permanent injury."

Mr. Siskin nodded again, closing his eyes. Maybe he believed in the power of prayer. Eric hoped it'd work, because there was nothing he could do except keep the patient as comfortable as possible. This sort of call frustrated the crap out of him. In this case, Lincoln's job—getting them to the fucking hospital as fast as he safely could—was the more important one.

Lincoln's job was extra hard today, though, because the Siskins had been vacationing at their cabin up on the McKenzie River, right at the border of their ambulance service district. Eric glanced at his watch. Best-case scenario, ten more minutes to the hospital.

Crap, he should have fucking called for a helicopter. But no, it wouldn't have been any faster. He'd had Siskin nearly ready to go when the swelling in his abdomen had started. One of those cases where even though the patient had shown signs of a heart attack, the EKG hadn't backed up the diagnosis. Eric'd had a bad feeling, and he and Lincoln had to take the guy in anyway, so they'd been working fast.

Siskin flinched, grimacing again. Even though his eyes were closed, when Eric reached for the IV again, he said, "No."

Eric looked down at him. "How bad is the pain? Remember the pain scale? Give me a number between one and ten—"

"I don't care." Mr. Siskin waved him back. "I don't want to die while I'm stoned." He smiled for a split second. "More stoned, I mean."

"Gotta tell you, Mr. Siskin, in my professional opinion, you need to believe you're going to live." He'd seen some people who should be dead refuse to die, and he'd seen a few who had no medical reason to die go ahead and do it.

"Call me Bryson."

"I can only do that if you promise me you'll live."

Siskin's eyes opened again and he actually grinned. Not for more than a couple of seconds, but he met Eric's gaze and shared a moment of humor.

Humor is a good thing. Eric smiled back, trying to make it genuine.

"Okay, it's a deal." Siskin sucked in another breath. "What's your name again?"

"Eric. At work, people call me Dix."

"Okay, Eric, I'm a numbers man. My whole career is about numbers—I'm an actuary for an insurance company. What are my odds of living? Give me a number."

"I really don't know," Eric said, relieved he didn't have to lie. "We can't know how bad things are without a CT scan, and I couldn't guess how much time you have before it ruptures even if we did."

Siskin looked at him levelly. "If it ruptures while I'm still in this ambulance . . ."

Crap. He nodded.

Siskin closed his eyes again. His breathing had evened out. Eric thought their discussion was over, but Siskin asked, "Do you have any kids?"

He knew—and hated—where this was going. "No, I don't. I'd like some, but it hasn't worked out."

Siskin grabbed his hand and gripped it tighter than Eric thought he could. "I have a son, you met him up at the cabin. If I don't make it, you tell him having him was the smartest, best thing we ever did. Tell him not to wait to give his mother grandchildren, more than one. Then tell him to take all the damned money I'm about to leave him and do something stupid with a little of it."

"I will. Promise." He craned his head, looking through the front seats to see out the windshield. "But we're nearly there. You can tell him yourself."

Siskin scrunched his brow. "Well, I can't tell him if I don't die, because I'm not giving him the damn money then."

Eric blinked. "I meant tell him how you feel."

Siskin nodded, and Eric could read the pain in his expression. Not the physical kind—the kind that made his whole face draw in, as if fighting to keep something from getting out. "I'll tell him, I gue—" He gasped, eyes opening wide and face paling.

Fuckfuckfuck. There was nothing he could do. Eric leaned closer, still holding his patient's hand. All Siskin's fear of dying that he hadn't shown before now welled up. Looking into his pupils felt like staring out into space. "I'll tell him, Bryson," Eric said.

Siskin licked his lips. "Do that."

"It's okay." Death. Death was okay, if you accepted it.

"Seems l-like it might b—" Siskin sucked in another quick breath, shaking with it, but he wouldn't ever get enough again. He was so pale now that Eric could see the black-blue voids under his eyes. He sucked in air once more, and squeezed Eric's hand reflexively. His body relaxed, and for a split second Eric could see the whole universe in his pupils, but all the stars were winking out one by one, until they dulled. Eric couldn't see in, and Bryson wasn't there to see out anymore.

Thank fuck. One of the better deaths.

Chapter 2

C ollin held his cell phone to his ear, but was listening to the thoughts in his head rather than to his uncle.

For a young gay man like himself, college should be the best time of his life, right? He should do things with wild abandon; he should openly—publicly even—experiment with his sexuality; he should do stupid shit like light articles of furniture on fire and push them out of second-story windows; he should fail a class. Not get put on academic probation or anything, just flunk one measly economics class.

Which he was in danger of doing if he didn't pull at least a C on the midterm. And no, the first week of the quarter wasn't too early to start freaking out about that. He sucked at Econ.

He should have the freedom to flunk that damn class—to do all those things, and then laugh about them later (probably in some embarrassment) with friends who'd done equally stupid things.

Well, he had the friends part down cold; they came with the fraternity membership. Okay, and he'd made inroads on being a slut, but mostly in secret. But his stupid, overdeveloped sense of obligation had repeatedly kept him from pulling a variety of crazy, college-student capers. Obligation to his family, particularly his uncle.

The uncle he should probably be listening to, rather than daydreaming about throwing his desk through the window, soaking it in gasoline, and sparking it up.

"Now, Collin, I know you registered for that International Business Communications class, and I've been thinking it might make an excellent final project if you—"

Never mind, he didn't need to listen to Monty yet. He slumped further over his desk, resting his cheek on his fist, staring out at the gray, drizzly day. January was such a horrible time of year in Oregon. The month would totally benefit from a pile of furniture blazing merrily on the lawn.

Yeah. A raging fire would be an excellent way to dispel the current drizzle of life.

Instead, he had his uncle yammering in his ear about this term's courses and how each one was important to his future in the family business, including Econ. Or whatever.

"I think I've found a replacement for Sooty as liaison to the Alumni Weekend Committee," Uncle Monty said, snapping Collin back to attention. Well, for a moment, until Collin started wondering why they called the corporate realtor from Delaware "Sooty." Probably because at some Theta Alpha Gamma bacchanalia, he'd pushed a flaming sofa out a window.

Now Sooty was pushing up daisies, or would be in the near future.

Collin hadn't earned a nickname in college, not even once he'd joined the fraternity. It was probably for the best—he'd have ended up with a nickname like Jeeves, the Theta Alpha Gamma Butler. Or they'd name him after that kid in the Dutch fairytale that had held back the sea by sticking his finger in a dyke.

Not that Collin had any intentions of sticking his finger in any dykes. *Shudder*. But there was no denying he was the guy who always stepped up to the plate when no one else would. He felt like he managed the whole damn frat sometimes.

Okay, not the whole frat, but a lot of it.

Thank God Kyle had run for frat president for their senior year or Collin might not have escaped that fate.

"Collin, are you listening to me?"

He didn't even bother unslouching. "Of course I am, sir."

Julian acted far more like a frat butler than Collin ever had. Although, come to think of it, Jules's butlery was sort of a hollow performance. He posed as the guy who had his finger on the pulse of the place by answering the front door and dusting off random picture frames or the odd piece of furniture, but he was more footman than head of staff. If it didn't happen in the entryway, Jules didn't have a clue. He wouldn't survive a second belowstairs.

". . . I've made reservations for you to play golf with him on Saturday morning. Seven a.m. at the McKenzie Club."

Collin sat up straight and nearly dropped the phone. "What?" *Him who*? Jesus, not Saturday morning. "Is it necessary for me to meet him so soon?" But more importantly, was it necessary for Collin to meet him on Saturday morning? Everyone knew Saturday morning followed Friday night, and if things went as hoped, he'd be sticky, sated, and sleeping at seven on any given Saturday. "Isn't it disrespectful to Sooty's memory to replace him so quickly? He only died a week ago." He cringed at using a dead man as an excuse, but it was necessary. Hopefully Sooty would understand. Collin had never met him in person, but a man who lit furniture on fire must realize the importance of Friday night.

"Sooty would have wanted it this way," Monty intoned.

Collin rested his forehead in his hand—the one not occupied with holding his phone—and massaged his temples. Could he possibly find a way out of this? "I'm sorry, but what time did you say I'm meeting, um, him, again?" He could have heard wrong.

"Seven." Monty must have swiveled around to stare out the windows overlooking his olive groves, because Collin could hear his uncle's chair making that familiar squeak. "Collin, as you know, I have a limited amount of time and I would appreciate it if you listened to me so I don't have to repeat myself."

"Sorry, sir." It was better to apologize and move on; experience had told him that.

"It's only golf, son. I know how you are about your Friday nights, so I didn't commit you to a dinner, which is what Sparky suggested."

"His name is Sparky?"

Monty sighed, and Collin flinched.

"It's Donald, but he earned the name Sparky in college and it stuck. After all, Sparky Donaldson is obviously preferable to Donald D. Donaldson." Monty paused before adding pointedly, "And you'll be meeting him at the McKenzie Club."

Collin fell back in his chair, holding in a groan. "Um, yes, I caught that part. But thank you." *For taking time out of your busy schedule to repeat it.* He cringed at the thought—he shouldn't think such disrespectful things about the man who'd all but raised him.

It probably wasn't a good sign that Collin had started reminding himself of that every time they spoke. *I love my Uncle Monty. I love my Uncle Monty. I lo—*

"I'm expecting a lot of you, I know, but I wouldn't give you such responsibility if I weren't confident you were capable of it. Once you've finished this chapter of your education and you take your position within the company, you'll appreciate these experiences. It's why I wanted you as the Theta Alpha Gamma alumni liaison. The position is very high profile, and as principal organizer of Alumni Weekend, you'll have the opportunity to make many valuable business contacts."

"Of course," Collin said, nodding into the phone.

"Now, as I said before, Sparky is only going to be in the Eugene area this weekend, and since he's available, I think a meeting would be advantageous."

Collin knew his uncle was only warming up to the topic, so he needed to ask what he wanted to know now. "Do you know how he got that nickname?" He figured it was the most pertinent information about the dude. Nicknames seemed very telling.

"Well . . . I shouldn't spread this around since it's unsubstantiated, but I've heard he was a bit of a firebug when he was younger. I've had quite a few business dealings with him, and he seems perfectly normal to me. Now, let me give you some more background—he's a very successful stockbroker, class of '86."

Collin's head began to fill with images of loud plaid golf pants, an engraved hip flask, and endless stories of a youngblood's early days on Wall Street. *Groan.* He couldn't keep his mind from drifting off again while Monty droned on, giving the socio-economic background of Sparky What's-his-name.

The dude sounded like a great time. Saturday morning was really shaping up to be lovely, wasn't it? Instead of sleeping off his bout of semi-anonymous sex, Collin would be blurry eyed on the golf course in freaking midwinter. "Sir," he said suddenly, seizing on that, "I'm sure you remember what Oregon can be like in January, are you certain—"

"I checked the weather report, and it's going to be clear. Brisk thirty-nine degrees, winds from the northeast. You'll be fine."

Shit, he was going to freeze to death. Dying at twenty-one, seated in a golf cart next to a corpulent moneychanger, wasn't how he'd imagined his death. He'd never imagined it, but if he had to, he'd prefer dying in his nineties, lying in bed beside a sexy, naked stripper in *his* twenties.

Monty cleared his throat, signaling an uncomfortable change of topic—one Collin thought he might benefit from listening to.

"You should know Sparky is one of the alums who opposed the new membership policy."

Collin closed his eyes and counted to ten. "Uncle Monty . . ."

"I didn't deliberately set you up, Collin. He found out about Sooty passing on—they were friendly—and contacted me about taking the man's place. You know we need someone on that committee. The Alumni Weekend is coming up quickly, and you increase your chances of having a successful event if you work with more alums. And we both know the more alumni you impress, the better it is for you in the long term."

"It's not for twelve weeks. You can't give me time to find someone who isn't a homophobe?" *Oops.*

"Opposing the new membership policy does not make one a homophobe," Monty said curtly.

Oh God, headache. Right between the eyes. "Yes, sorry, sir." He needed to end this conversation, because he'd just implied that his uncle was a bigot.

"One might oppose this new 'open' membership policy because one feels, as do I, that it makes the fraternity a target. Especially since your friend is so publicly gay and continues to be an active member."

Collin sat up straight, matching Monty's tone and formality. "Please remember that, in fact, the fraternity has always accepted gay members because the policy didn't specifically exclude them. It was simply a tacit Don't Ask, Don't Tell system. We voted to codify the acceptance of those members, and show them that being out is acceptable and safe here at TAG." Monty could never seem to discuss just the policy; he had to make it personal by bringing up Collin's friend Brad. His uncle had been poking him with the pointy end of that argument since Brad had come out last spring, and it had worn right through his need to placate his uncle.

"That doesn't affect my opinion of it in the slightest. You persuaded me to accept this new policy by convincing me that it wouldn't alter the position of respect that generations of Theta Alpha Gamma brothers have worked to acquire at Calapooya College. I've placed my trust in you on this issue, and I interceded on your behalf with the Alumni Association members who questioned it as a favor to you. In return, I expect you and the other active brothers to ensure that TAG is just as influential on campus after this as it was before."

Collin swallowed, but used his "confident" voice. "I'm making certain of it, sir."

After an awkward good-bye, Collin sat staring out his window for a long time, imagining his cell phone ablaze in the front yard.

Chapter 3

At the hospital, Eric wrote a letter to Mr. Siskin's son, telling them his father's last words. He'd only ever had to pass on last words once before, but it had taught him that doing so while they were still in shock was pointless. Better to write it down so they could take it in later.

Lincoln went off to find some coffee while Eric finished the rest of the paperwork. When he was done, Lincoln met him by the emergency doors, holding two cups. "One's for you," he said before Eric could ask.

Eric took it. "Thanks, man." They started out toward the ambulance.

"Bad one?" Lincoln asked.

Eric shrugged. "Not really. Just so weird when they go that fast and they know what's happening. But he didn't get that terrified look they sometimes do."

"If they have to die in the ambulance, I'm glad most of them aren't conscious."

"Isn't that the truth," Eric said. Even though it hadn't been a "bad" death, it took something out of a paramedic when he or she lost a patient. "Kind of makes me wish I hadn't taken this shift for TimTam." Normally he worked C shift, but he'd helped out another paramedic in need (of a free night for a date) and taken a B shift also. Now he had to work a double and he'd lost a patient.

"Saw your ex," Lincoln said. "Couple weeks ago when Mandy and I got a babysitter and we were eating dinner at the Water Station. Jay came in hanging on some rich-looking fucker and he acted all surprised to see us there, but I watched him detour halfway across the restaurant to accidentally walk past our table. He made a big show of asking about you."

"When was this?" Eric asked, but he had to wait for the answer, because they'd reached the rig and split up, Eric walking to the passenger door.

Lincoln started talking as soon as they'd both opened their doors. "I just said it was a couple weeks ago. Since I switched shifts I don't see you as much, so I forget to tell you this shit. You should come over soon, man. Mandy'd love to see you, and you haven't seen Greta in so long she'll forget who Uncle Eric is any time now."

Eric snorted and pulled on his seat belt. "You're really starving for some male company, aren't you?" Lincoln and Mandy had two daughters; Greta was three and Cecily was nine months. He hadn't seen the baby in a while either. "Okay, I'll come over next week someday."

"Good."

Eric nodded and figured their conversation had wound down, but Lincoln wasn't done talking about Jay. *Crap.* He grinned over at Eric as he started the engine. "So Jay the other night, he asked me if you've found the right man yet."

Eric laughed shortly. "What, like he wants me back?" As if that would ever happen.

Lincoln grunted, checking his mirrors and putting the ambulance in reverse, starting the dumb back-up beacon noise. "Yeah, if you let him fuck whoever he wants on the side. I can't stand that bastard. When I see him—you know, if I don't manage to hide from him before he sees me—he acts all concerned for your welfare or something, but it's bullshit. Still kinda pissed Mandy wouldn't let me crawl under the table."

"He just wants you to tell me what he said. It's a mind game." Jay's way of getting all possible attention, even if he wasn't around to enjoy it.

"I guess." Lincoln started heading back to the station, quiet for a few seconds, fooling Eric into thinking the subject had finally died.

But it hadn't. "He also asked Mandy if you were 'over it.'"

"Jesus," Eric groaned. "It's been four years since I kicked that little prick out."

"Hey man, you know our deal: no details about your sex life or your dates' attributes."

"Ha. Ha."

"Anyway, you know what Mandy did—she says, 'Over what?'"

Eric laughed along with Lincoln. Mandy always had his back when it came to his love life. Thank God, because it had taken him a while to get over that asshole. He should have realized that it was a setup when Jay had said he didn't know if he could be faithful. Then when he did fuck around, he'd been able to say, "Well, I warned you." As if that had made it all right.

"Then he made that comment that really pisses Mandy off."

Eric opened his mouth, because he knew what was coming and he didn't need to hear it again, but Lincoln didn't pause.

"He was like, 'Oh, he finally found someone as domesticated as he is to settle down with, then?'"

Eric blew out a breath. As if it might clean out the bitter aftertaste that comment always left in his heart.

"So Mandy says, 'I think the word you're actually looking for is *domestic. Domesticated* refers to animals, and I'm sure we can all agree that Eric was never your pet.'" This time Lincoln laughed much more than Eric did.

Once back at the substation, they restocked and went back to bed. "Wake me up when the shift's over," Lincoln said as he stumbled off.

By some miracle, they slept the rest of the night without another call. When Eric woke up at 6:30 and made it into the crew kitchen, he found Val—his new partner on C shift—already there, sipping coffee. He kind of liked that about her, that she usually came to work early, just like he did and the opposite of how Lincoln operated.

When she saw him, she raised her eyebrows over her mug. It looked like more of a challenge than an invitation to talk. He'd worked with her just long enough to know what that meant: she was not in a mood to be bothered. *Heh.* As if she'd get away with that— they already had a habit of messing with each other.

"This fresh?" he asked, pointing at the coffee pot.

She grunted at him.

Excellent. "Does one grunt mean yes?"

She grunted again.

He opened the cupboard, looking for mugs and forcing patently false cheer into his voice. "Didn't stop for coffee on your way in, huh?"

She grunted twice.

"Does two grunts me—"

She grunted loudly, shoved her chair back with a screech of legs against linoleum, and stalked out of the kitchen.

Chuckling to himself, Eric poured two cups of coffee and went to harass Lincoln into consciousness. He set the cups on the nightstand in his partner's quarters and leaned really close to his friend's ear. "Hey!"

Lincoln flinched. "Go away," he mumbled.

He needed to get some new material. "Val's already here." Eric tickled Lincoln's cheek with a few strands of his hair. Lincoln slapped at his hand, but missed, hitting himself in the side of the head.

Heh. "You could go home," he singsonged, leaning over until his lips nearly touched Lincoln's ear. "Wake up your wife before the girls are up."

"Fucking faggots," someone said from outside the room. Eric turned to see Rod walking away from them toward the kitchen.

"Fucking homophobe," Lincoln called after him, suddenly awake.

Rod flipped them off over his shoulder.

Lincoln propped himself on his elbow, scowling out into the hallway. "Asshole. I'm not even gay and he's harassing me."

Eric sat on the edge of the mattress. "Yeah, well, apparently if you aren't my enemy, you must be gay too."

"Gonna sic my wife on him someday," Lincoln muttered, then sat up, struggling to untangle from his bag, kicking Eric in the process. "Just forget about him, man."

Eric nodded. Rod wasn't anything to get worried about, not really. He didn't need to go getting anxious over the few dickheads at the department. Most of the other firefighters and staff didn't have a problem with him or the few other members of the rainbow family.

Still, it didn't add anything positive to his morning.

"Hot Rod getting all uppity again?" Rudy asked from the doorway. He stood outside it, black hair corkscrewing up everywhere, in uniform pants but no shirt, scratching his taut, ribbed belly. *Drool.* He yawned after Lincoln nodded, then held up a hand to Eric. "Morning, Dix. You working your regular shift, too?"

Eric nodded. "Yeah, I'm working a double."

Rudy tipped his head, then smirked. "You checking out my chest, boy?"

Eric grinned. "Hell yes." Rudy was the opposite of a homophobe.

Rudy laughed at him, flexed his pecs, and walked on down the hall.

"Get off my bed, man, I'm trying to get up," Lincoln complained.

Eric ignored him. Well, at least he didn't move. "You going home early?"

"Since no one will let me sleep anymore," he grumbled, then kicked Eric again. Probably on purpose this time.

Eric was about to say, "Have a good time with your wife," but the station tones sounded over their radio system before he could. The dispatcher's voice followed. "For engine twenty-three, rescue twenty-three, medic twenty-three, and ladder two. Report of an explosion and possible bombing at 460 South Willow Street—"

"*Bombing*?" Lincoln repeated.

But it was the address that caught at Eric's brain for a second, until the drone of the dispatcher's voice demanded he listen to more details.

"—caller is advising of a twenty-year-old male victim with unknown injuries. Reports smoke but no visible flames. Police are responding, five minutes out. For engine twenty-three, rescue twenty-three—"

Eric stopped listening as she repeated the information, and he had to move so Lincoln could grab his boots and zip into them. "You gonna go?" he asked, standing up and heading toward the kitchen to grab his jacket.

Lincoln was right behind him. "Not if Val will go for me, I need to find her—"

"I'll take it," Val said, standing in the hall. "Go home."

"Thanks," Lincoln called after her—she was already walking away. He grabbed Eric, surprising him, and gave him one of those bro-hugs straight guys liked so much, then let go as if Eric had burned him. Must have surprised himself too.

Eric hid his smile. "Tell Mandy 'hi' for me, and give her a good time," he said as he hurried toward the ambulance bay.

It wasn't until he was in the rig, Val in the driver's seat (she always drove if she could wrangle it), and he was looking at the map info on the screen that he realized why the address seemed familiar.

The explosion was located at his old college fraternity house, Theta Alpha Gamma.

Chapter 4

On Friday morning, Collin woke up to the bed swaying and bouncing under him, and his first thought was that the last guy he'd picked up at the Slaughterhouse—before Christmas break—was here to rock his world again. He opened his eyes just in time to watch some books topple off his desk in the dim daylight.

What the fuck?

His next thought was, *I'd never bring a guy back here.* Not to Theta Alpha Gamma House, even though he didn't currently have a roommate, through some miracle of seniority.

"Hey! I think it's an earthquake!" Someone yelled from the hallway, then screamed, followed by a thud-thud-thud-thunk.

That thoroughly woke Collin up.

Holy shit, earthquake!

He half fell out of bed, expecting to feel the floor jolting under him, but there was no sound or movement—even the dust motes had suspended all motion. The sudden stillness stifled him, gluing his butt to the carpet. Like something had thickened the air to jelly, encouraging him to blink in stupefaction.

He heard a moan from outside his room. Possibly from the bottom of the stairs? He fought off his inertia and scrambled up, reaching for the knob and yanking hard a couple of times before the door would open. The air swirled sluggishly as he ran the three feet to the right that brought him to the top of the stairs.

"Help!" Someone shouted from the bottom just as Collin reached it. The railing had cracked in half a few feet down, and some spindles were missing, along with some of the actual steps. Seriously scary-looking wooden spikes were poking out above the foyer, and the whole thing hung in midair.

What the hell did that?

As he started down the staircase, it creaked loudly. He hugged the wall, but he could see far enough over the side to make out Julian crouched over a pair of legs. One of them looked really, really wrong—legs couldn't bend that way naturally, could they?

Even more alarming, he could swear he smelled smoke. "Oh, no," he whispered, back sliding down the wall past the broken part of the banister.

Jules looked up at him, face pale and eyes open wide. "It's Ricky, I think he's injured."

Uh, yeah. "Don't move him," Collin said out loud. "Do you smell anything?"

"What the hell?" Kyle's voice came from above him, and Collin looked up to see him and a bunch of other guys looking down the stairs, gape mouthed. Some stared at Collin and some peered into the foyer. "Shit . . . earthquake?" Kyle asked, looking uncertain. They all seemed as slow-moving as he'd been; being shaken awake had stunned the fraternity house occupants into a daze.

"I don't think that was an earthquake," Collin said. "Do you smell something burning?" He was past the break in the railing, so he gave up his caution and rushed down the last steps. He could hear Kyle and the other guys starting down the stairs. It sounded like a herd of very heavy lemmings rushing a cliff edge. One that creaked alarmingly.

Suddenly everyone was talking and moving in normal time. Jules stood up and waved Collin over, looking at him as if he could somehow fix things. Guys spilled into the entryway and under the stairs, shouted, moved into other rooms to check for damage. Collin knelt next to Ricky's leg, but he wasn't sure what to do next. He didn't want to touch the guy's knee—just looking at it made his skin crawl. He turned to ask how it felt, but Ricky's eyes were scrunched tightly shut and his skin was white and dotted with sweat.

He took a guess that it didn't feel good.

"Does anything hurt?" Kyle asked, coming up behind him and stepping over Ricky's feet to kneel on the other side.

"I think it's his leg," Jules said. Kyle reached to probe the knee, but Ricky hissed.

He yanked his hand back. "Okay, no touching."

"Dude, what the fuck is *this*?" Tank asked from under the stairwell, and out of the corner of his eye he saw a couple other guys join Tank. Whatever "this" was, they'd have to deal with it.

Jules leaned forward and gripped Kyle's shoulder, nearly pushing him over onto the mangled limb. "Can you do anything for him? Is he going to be all right? Is it his leg?"

Ricky moaned, and Collin barely stopped himself from telling Julian to stop being such a drama queen. Maybe he was in shock. Or just being his stupid self.

"How am I supposed to know? He needs an ambulance." Kyle shook Jules's hand off, turning to look up at him. "We need to call 911."

"Oh!" Jules nodded vigorously. "Someone should do that." Then he dropped down to kneel next to Ricky's head.

Kyle looked up at Collin, raising an eyebrow.

He was about to stand up and find the house phone when the door to the basement burst open, and Turbo and Danny spilled out into the hall off the foyer—they must have fallen asleep in the TV room again. They hacked and waved their arms around, like they were trying to clear something out of the air.

Possibly the smoke pouring into the house from behind them.

Turbo heaved in a breath. "Fire—" *hack, hack* "—Explosion. Furnace. Dudes!"

θΛΓ

In spite of lots of the guys being hungover, the frat house was evacuated surprisingly fast without a lot of wailing or freaking out. Collin even managed to throw on shoes and grab his jacket from the entryway. For once he appreciated Julian's insistence that they leave those things by the front door. Tank packed Ricky out over his shoulder—there was some wailing going on there, but it was totally understandable. Even Billings's pet chameleon, Snake, made it out.

"We really shouldn't have moved him," Kyle said, while he and Collin followed Tank across the street to the lawn of the Nu Omicron Mu sorority. "He could have a spinal injury."

"What else were we gonna do? Leave him in a burning building?"

By the time Tank set Ricky down on the lawn of the sorority, the dude was making enough noise to assure Kyle that he still possessed a fully functioning nervous system and was capable of feeling pain.

One of the Nu Omicron Mu girls had called 911, so Collin didn't have to after all. Instead, he ended up helping Kyle try to keep Ricky . . . well, "comfortable" seemed like a lot to hope for. They just aimed for no screaming. Crying was acceptable.

"The ambulance will be here soon," Collin said for the third time. This time he could hear sirens, though, so it wasn't a lie.

Ricky groaned, and more tears leaked down his cheeks. Maybe they should give him whiskey? Collin turned to ask the sorority girl talking to Kyle about it and heard her say, "—and I told them I thought it might be a bomb."

"What?" Kyle yelled, red in the face.

Why would she think someone had tried to blow them up?

"You seriously thought someone's that pissed off we have an openly gay fraternity brother? That they'd bomb us?"

Oh, no. Collin went suddenly cold all over, thinking about his conversation last night with Monty.

The girl planted her hands on her hips and leaned forward, right into Kyle's face. "Well, considering the *boom* I heard this morning and the way the last Greek Council meeting went, yeah, I think it's possible."

Kyle looked away, muttering curse words under his breath and turning even redder.

Collin stood up and asked calmly, "Kyle, how did the council meeting go?" And why hadn't he said anything? He knew Collin had a stake in this shit. They all did.

Kyle ran a hand through his hair and wouldn't look at him. "Not very well."

Collin gritted his teeth. "Kyyyyle . . ."

"Later, okay?" Kyle gave him a pleading look. "Let's get through this and I'll tell you later."

Collin pointed at him. "You better. I need to know." So much for all that work convincing Monty that Brad coming out and the new policy wasn't going to be a problem. This could be a fucking disaster.

Kyle's hand landing on his shoulder startled him, and he looked up from the grass he'd been staring blindly at. "We'll figure this out, I swear, but we gotta get through this situation first. Maybe she's overreacting." Kyle jerked his head slightly toward the sorority girl, who was watching them, arms crossed and shaking her head. Kyle lowered his voice. "I know how important this is to you."

Important? His uncle believing that gay was okay was absolutely *necessary* to Collin's own future.

"Does someone need a paramedic?"

Collin whirled around to see a man coming through the crowd toward them. A fireman in navy blue cargo pants and a white uniform shirt under a navy jacket, carrying an oversized, screaming orange duffle, another fireman—whoops, firewoman. Firefighter? Whatever, she was walking along just behind him.

The guy in front seemed to take in the scene, first looking at Kyle, then zeroing in on Ricky. Just as he reached them, he glanced at Collin, then away. When their eyes met, Collin absently noted that he was cute. More than cute. Sexy.

Suddenly, eyes widening in what Collin thought for sure was recognition, the firefighter looked at him again.

They didn't know each other. Did they? He remembered every guy he'd ever been with before. Didn't he? Collin shook off the weird momentary pang in his chest, whatever the hell it was. He couldn't afford to stress out now; Ricky still needed him and the frat was burning to ashes.

The firefighter—paramedic?—dropped his gaze and looked back down at Ricky. "So, I guess he's the patient?"

Chapter 5

At the fire scene, a group of guys wearing TAG shirts—one of them holding a wire cage with a lizard inside it—stood on the sorority side of the street and watched smoke pour out of the Theta Alpha Gamma House. Eric ignored the fire for now. He'd have to get all nostalgic and maudlin about the frat burning down later. When asked, the TAG guys directed him and Val to their patient, farther up on the lawn behind the crowd.

"I think Ricky has a broken leg, dude. Tank had to carry him out of the house," one of them said.

So weird to be back here; he'd spent some time at this sorority, pretending to be into girls. And it was a typical "Greek event"— people everywhere, watching the show. "Kind of a circus, huh?" he asked Val as they walked closer to the big white sorority house. Instead of answering, she poked him in the shoulder and pointed to a group standing around a figure lying on the ground. Eric pushed his ancient history to the back of his mind and focused on work.

Then he saw the boy with the sexy eyes.

They were amazing—huge and swirly hazel irises ringed with long, dark lashes, making him look almost as if he wore eyeliner. And they looked familiar. Like the eyes of a guy he'd gone to school with— been in TAG with.

Crap. He made himself look down at the very obviously broken leg of the guy on the ground. "So, I guess he's the patient?"

"Here," Val said, handing him the oxygen and taking the C-collar. "I'll get this on and then fetch the traction splint." She knelt next to the patient's head on one side while Eric knelt on the other, setting down the kit and the bottle of oxygen.

What had those guys by the street said this kid's name was? "Hey, my name's Eric. Can you tell me yours?" He started sorting out the oxygen mask.

He got a gritted-teeth, two-syllable grunt in return.

"His name's Ricky." Sexy Eyes knelt next to him.

Eric nodded in acknowledgment, but didn't look at him. "Hey Ricky, I'm going to put a mask over your mouth and nose to give you some oxygen. Just breathe normally, okay?" As normally as could be expected under the circumstances. He'd be light-headed in seconds. As Eric started the oxygen, Val stood and nodded at him when he glanced up, then headed back to the ambulance. He moved down to the patient's foot and dug the trauma shears out of his kit.

"Do you need me to do anything?" Sexy Eyes asked. Out of the corner of his eye, Eric could see him gripping his knees tightly, digging his nails in.

"Can you tell me what happened?" Not that it probably mattered, but it would make him feel useful. "Did anyone do anything to stop the bleeding?"

"Bleeding?" someone asked faintly. The guy still standing with the TAG sweatshirt on.

"Keep it together, Kyle," Sexy Eyes said.

Eric ignored them in favor of cutting into the hem of the patient's pajamas and ripping the shears up to the break. His radio squawked while he worked—dispatch responding to something from fire command. Were they going to have to call out more engines? If they went to a second alarm, he bet that building would be a total loss.

"We just got him out of there as fast as we could. We didn't even realize he was bleeding until we got him here and there was blood on Tank's—oh my God," Sexy ended in a gasp.

Not surprising—Ricky had an open fracture. Blood seeped out of the wound just above his knee, and the bone protruded obviously from it. Eric heard the sweatshirt wearer gag a couple of times.

Yeah, it wasn't pretty. "How far did he fall?" Grabbing a sterile gauze pad, Eric pressed down on the gash, keeping as clear of the bone as possible. Ricky stifled a scream with his hand. The guy who didn't like the bleeding whimpered. He grabbed Sexy Eyes's hand, ignoring the warmth of it. "Press on this for me, right here. Wait, put a glove on first." He had to let go of the hand to dig one out of his belt pouch.

The guy took the glove and did as he asked—he was pale, but he did it. Eric checked the pulse in the patient's foot while Sexy started telling him how Ricky had gotten into this state.

"He fell over the side of the stairs. Maybe twelve feet onto a wood floor. Um, is this hurting him?"

What? Oh, the pressure. "I'll give him something for the pain." The pulse in the patient's foot was strong enough, so Eric put a line in and started a saline drip, then gave him some painkillers just as Val made it back with the splint and the stretcher. Once he was in traction, Ricky's pain would lessen considerably.

"It's a fucking zoo here," she bitched. "There are a bunch of rubberneckers who brought lawn chairs to watch the damned spectacle, and everyone's *color coordinated*. Fire's almost out, I don't know what they're going to watch after the engines go home."

"Huh?" Eric asked absently, but whatever she meant, it caused the kid holding the dressing to start talking to the other guy. Something about keeping things friendly. He ignored it—as long as Sexy kept the pressure on, he didn't care, and the guy was. The other dude left, which was probably for the best.

Val pulled traction for him once he had the ankle cuff on. Eric watched the patient's face ease as the muscles in his quad stretched, stopping his bones from mashing together. He found his own muscles relaxing—that always looked so damned painful, when bodies got all messed up like that. Compound breaks were a bit of trigger for him, he didn't know why.

Val was prepping the stretcher when Eric finally looked at Sexy Eyes again. He was staring down at his hands, still applying pressure to the leg. His shirtsleeves were pushed up above his elbows so Eric could see all the corded muscles in his forearm, the veins sticking out, and how he shook from pushing down on the dressing.

"You can ease up, he's okay."

Sexy looked up at him, eyes wide, and his face looked so young. Way too young for a guy like him. If Eric had even been considering something, which he hadn't. Who picked up someone on a call?

That's how Lincoln met Mandy.

Still, this kid was just a baby. But Eric found himself brushing a clean bit of his hand across Sexy's forearm anyway—because he needed to get him to ease up, so it was totally a legitimate touch.

About half the tension shuddered out of the kid when Eric touched him, and he fell back on his heels. Still holding the gauze, but not so hard.

"What's your name?" he heard himself ask.

The boy with the sexy hazel eyes looked away and then back. "Collin."

He nodded, turning away to get something to bind the wound. "I'm Eric," he added like it was an afterthought, then he gently moved Collin out of the way, being careful not to get blood on him. More touching and that warmth he should ignore. "Has anyone informed Ricky's parents? We're going to need someone to do some paperwork, too." He bandaged the gash.

"Oh, shit," Collin muttered, closing his eyes and rubbing his forehead. "So much happened so fast. Um, I'll get someone working on the parents, and someone to help you with paperwork, I guess."

"Okay, great. Whoever it is can meet us at the ambulance and Val will get some info down."

"Sure. Um, thanks. Eric."

He smiled quickly at the kid, but focused on what he was doing, not looking as Collin got up and walked away.

The last thing he needed was to get hung up on someone who was half his age, even if he did look like a guy Eric had wanted to fuck twenty years ago. That wouldn't even be fair. Besides, he was thirty-six and he had no business jonesing after a twenty-year-old kid who may or may not even be gay.

Lecherous old fart.

Chapter 6

Not surprisingly, there was a sea of lawn chairs, Bloody Marys, mimosas, and guys from rival fraternities in the street, blocking the fire trucks. He wandered through lots of running fire engines, firefighters in heavy, smoke-stained yellow uniforms, and many, many hoses snaking into the house, catching occasional glimpses of light gray smoke wafting out of some broken TAG House windows. Earlier, he remembered seeing lots of black smoke, but he'd been dealing with Ricky and not really paying attention. The house looked even more dirty gray than usual now that things had died down a little.

It was much less of a spectacle than he'd expected, but it didn't seem to diminish the enthusiasm of the spectators. Some guys were cheering on the firefighters, while others seemed to be chanting for the fire to show itself.

Collin wondered if there was a betting pool. Then he decided he didn't want to know.

Someone—probably the Nu Omicron Mu girls judging by the "NOM" embroidered on the corners—had passed out blankets to the TAG guys who didn't have enough to wear. Oregon weather could be pretty mild, but in January, "mild" meant lower forties. The blankets were a blessing—a couple of guys who had no business being in public mostly naked had escaped the fire wearing only boxers, or in Danny's case, a thong. *Shudder.*

Too bad Tank had on sweats, though. He could wear a thong. Or nothing.

Someone must have called Brad because he'd arrived. Collin looked around but didn't see Sebastian anywhere. He didn't know if Brad had left his boyfriend at home because he knew the other frats were unhappy about them having an out brother, or if Sebastian didn't want to come, but Collin was relieved not to see him.

His relief led to a spike of guilt in his gut.

It was lame enough that he couldn't be out, and now he wanted others to hide it? He sucked, and needed a massive priority readjustment, but not right now. He made his way over to Brad, who stood with Tank on the edge of the NOM girls' lawn. Both of them had their arms crossed and were glowering at the excited mass of Greek brotherhood.

"Hey," Collin said as he came up behind them.

Brad turned and unhesitatingly grabbed him, pulling him into a hug.

Collin took it, Greek brotherhood be damned. He needed this hug. He'd just seen a friend's bone sticking out of his leg.

"This sucks," Brad said in his ear.

"Yeah, shitty wake-up call." Collin wrapped his arms around Brad and hugged him back, hard. For a few seconds, he let himself have a fantasy—Brad was his boyfriend, here to see him through this tragedy. Sebastian didn't exist.

Damn, there went that guilt again. He liked Sebastian, and he could see how good he and Brad were together. Besides, he didn't know if he'd want to be with Brad if he were available. He just wanted . . . something. Comfort.

Last night you wanted to watch furniture burn on the lawn. Collin tried to figure out if he felt guilty about that or not, but he couldn't decide.

After a minute, Brad let go of him. "Where's Kyle?"

"He had to go do some ambulance paperwork. Did anyone tell you about Ricky?"

"Yeah, Tank filled me in. Sounds bad."

Collin made a face. "Dude, you can't even imagine. I'd tell you about it, but you don't share shit like that with friends." He had to take a deep breath before adding, "I had to call Ricky's parents. They're coming up from Shasta."

"What? Why didn't Kyle do that?"

"We flipped a coin."

Brad reached out and gave Collin's shoulder a squeeze. "You can stay with us tonight. I'll call Sebastian, but I'm sure he won't care—it's my place too. Kyle can also, if his girlfriend isn't around. You might have to share a bed with him." Brad smiled.

Collin appreciated the attempt at a joke, however weak. He nodded. "Ashley's here. I saw her and told her where to find him—she was kind of freaking out. Guess she likes him."

Tank butted in. "How's Ricky? What happened?"

Collin grimaced and told him. He meant to only give spare details, but soon he heard himself saying, "—and man, the bone—his femur I guess—I could see it poking through the gash on his leg. The paramedic, Eric, he made me put pressure on it." He'd handled it all right at the time, but maybe he wasn't now, because Brad and Tank each took an arm and led him to a lawn chair they'd liberated from a Tri-Ups.

Tank shoved him on the back of the head once he sat down. "Face between your knees and breathe normally. It's okay, man. He'll be all right."

Collin stayed like that a while, soaking in the feel of Tank's hand on his neck. Could this need to be touched be a common aftermath of tragedy? Whatever, he tried to work his diaphragm "normally," not looking at the fire.

"Hey, can I have my chair back now?" Collin didn't recognize the voice.

"No," Tank barked, and Collin felt the loss of his hand.

Oh no. He knew that tone in Tank's voice. Best to keep his head down for now.

"You can't have your chair, and you wanna know why? Wait, I don't care if you wanna know or not. You can't have it back because we can't go get any of our chairs, they're currently in our frat house which is *on fire.* So if my friend needs a chair, you'll—"

"Take it easy, Tank," Brad broke in, and Collin sat up to see what was going on. Brad was standing between Tank and some guy—presumably the owner of the chair. He had on a sweatshirt with "upsilon upsilon upsilon" written across the front. The dude didn't look like he wanted his seat back anymore, which was fortunate because Tank looked like the only way he'd return anything was by oral delivery.

Well, it was preferable to anal.

The Tri-Ups took a couple of steps back. "Never mind, I'll stand. Over there." He indicated a spot somewhere on the other side of the nearest fire engine before he turned and scurried off.

After a few more seconds of staring over Brad's shoulder, then glowering at Brad, Tank blew out a deep breath. "Sorry."

Brad clapped a hand on Tank's shoulder. "S'okay. If I still lived here I might not have said anything. Just let you scare the shit out of that guy."

Tank nodded, taking a step back.

"Is Penny here?" Brad asked. Good move—Penny would be a calming influence on Tank. He was hard to rile, but once he was pissed off, it got ugly fast.

As soon as they mentioned his girlfriend, Tank hung his head, looking more like a needy kid than a pissed-off linebacker. "She'll be here this afternoon. I just called her—she went home early for the weekend."

"Maybe you should call her again?" Brad asked.

He nodded. "Yeah, probably."

Tank wandered off to a semi-secluded boxwood hedge, phone clutched to his ear. Collin looked over to the street at the various frats represented—a few sororities sprinkled among them—and it hit him that they were all being entertained by TAG's tragedy.

The Greek societies at Calapooya College had always been competitive, but the frats and sororities were friendly, he'd thought. TAG had a never-ending rivalry with "the other" sports frat, Eta Pi Pi, but it had never been ugly.

Yet this crowd felt ugly. There were Eta Pis standing and hooting, like they wanted the frat to burn. Collin had assumed they'd be okay with TAG having a pro-GLBT membership policy because they'd just had two openly gay members graduate last year. But maybe they'd been happy to get rid of Ty and Sloan.

"Did Kyle say anything to you about the other members on the Greek Council who have a problem with, you know, you?" he asked Brad.

Brad nodded, but didn't look away from the fire. "He mentioned it, yeah. Thought I should be aware."

Collin turned on Brad. "How come he didn't tell me? I had to bust my ass fall term to get the Alumni Association to accept the changes in the membership policy."

Brad shrugged. "I don't know, dude. Ask him." He turned suddenly. "There is one thing I know about the Greek Council."

Collin straightened his spine. "Okay, what?"

"They're all worked up because of the membership policy change. Like, some of them thought it was bad enough that there were openly gay brothers before me, but now they see it as us *inviting* gay guys."

Fuck. "Where in the hell is Kyle? I need to know this shit. How'm I supposed to do damage control with Monty if this stuff blindsides me?" He took off to look for Kyle but stopped short when he stepped into a stream running off from a fire engine and splashed his pajama legs. Dammit.

After he'd shaken off the water and some bits of grass, he looked up to find Kyle heading straight toward him. "Collin! I need your help. You were just appointed Interim Chair of Building Maintenance."

Wait. "What? Who appointed me?"

"Me." Kyle stopped right in front of him, breathing a little fast. His adrenaline had to be pumping.

"Why do I have to be the damned interim chair?"

"Because the regular chair left in an ambulance with his bone—" Kyle clamped his mouth shut, looking green.

He really didn't need this. "Why can't Tank be the chair?"

"Because Tank's currently chasing off all the other fraternities that showed up to revel in our demise."

Brad snapped to attention at that, standing up. "I should probably go help with that, huh?"

"Please." Kyle sounded relieved. Sort of.

Collin leaned forward, trying to look tough even though he only came up to Kyle's shoulder. "Why do we even need an interim chair?"

"Because a Calapooya College Facilities guy is here to order the frat off-limits for occupation. They're planning to condemn it." Kyle nodded in time with his words, then grabbed Collin's arm and dragged him along to the tête-à-tête with the college's building maintenance dude.

At least, tried to drag him. He resisted Kyle's attempts to pull him by the arm while he looked at the frat house again. "They got the fire out that fast? I thought . . ." Well, it *had* looked pretty calm the last time he'd noticed.

"We have a sprinkler system on the main and second floors, so when the fire started to move upstairs, the system stopped it. The firefighters did the rest."

Collin blinked. "We have a sprinkler system? How come we didn't have one in the basement? How come I never noticed the nozzles?"

"Maybe there wasn't enough in the budget when they put it in. And Jules says it was the kind that's hidden in the ceiling behind little round panels that pop out when there's a fire. C'mon." He yanked on Collin again.

Collin planted his feet, which sort of worked. "But what about the stairs?"

Kyle dropped his arm and turned to face him. "We were busy with Ricky, but Tank found a water heater and a hole in the floor under the stairs before we evacuated. It looks like that's what caused all that damage. It like, BLEVEed—you know, Boiling Liquid Expanding Vapor Explosion—something was wrong with the safety mechanisms and it basically took off like a rocket, shot through the basement ceiling and hit the staircase, then Ricky came along."

"Isn't that an episode of *MythBusters*?"

Kyle screwed up his face and nodded. "I think so, yeah."

"This is fucking insane. Did the fire set off the water heater?"

"They told me it might have," Kyle said. "They sounded doubtful though. They're still investigating, and it'll take a couple of days to figure out. Seriously, Collin, we have to talk to this guy because the faster the building is declared unfit for habitation, the sooner the college will come up with temporary housing."

This time he let Kyle drag him along, too struck by the thought of being homeless to resist.

"Temporarily homeless," Harold the Facilities Maintenance Man told them. Something about his gray coveralls with the named stitched over the pocket comforted Collin. People wearing coveralls knew practical things and could fix stuff. Harold the Facilities Maintenance Man was walking, talking chicken soup for the homeless frat boy's soul.

Things got even better when the Greek Life director, Diana Vargas, showed up. She took over dealing with practicalities like clothing from the Red Cross and asking Harold about when, exactly, they could get some personal items and clothing from the frat. She was chocolate mousse cheesecake to Harold's soup.

"It's going to be a bit. We have to get a structural engineer in there and make sure the foundation and load-bearing walls in the basement are still capable of holding the structure up." He turned to Kyle and Collin. "You guys are going to have to get a contractor in here to fix it, regardless. But I imagine at a minimum, people can go in a couple at a time and get some stuff from their rooms by tonight. I don't know for sure when the campus will come through on housing, but once it does, you'll be covered until the building is livable again."

"I can be a point of contact for today, you two," Diana added. "I'll help resettle anyone who doesn't have a place to go tonight. Tomorrow we'll meet and start looking at what needs to happen next."

Ohthankgod. Collin's mind had been close to gibbering in fear when it had hit him that not only was he homeless, but he was the go-to guy for the president of the homeless. He'd begun to imagine he and Kyle would have to deal with all of it—finding guys places to live, figuring out how to get people in thongs clothed, buying out the local drugstore's stock of toothbrushes. Oh God, and the electronics. All those ruined laptops and smartphones—how would they watch porn? Finding out he didn't have to be strong for everyone else made him so weak with relief he wanted to just lie down in the street and sleep.

Then Diana said, "But you two need to go deal with your angry TAG brother on your own."

Tank.

In unison, he and Kyle turned to look at each other, considering the possibilities. But it wasn't until they heard the yelling that they both took off for the crowd of onlookers. Skidding around the fire truck west of where they'd been talking, Collin immediately saw Tank, lawn chair raised over his head, yelling "What's'a matter? Get fucking moving!"

For a split second, with Brad standing next to Tank like that and the crowd of shocked faces staring at them, Collin was reminded of when Brad had come out to the whole frat last year at a Theta Alpha Gamma general meeting.

But then it all changed. People started moving, doing what Tank had said. Some of them were giving Tank dirty, distrustful looks, but most began gathering their seats and alcohol, packing up after finally appearing to understand the magnitude of what had happened.

Tank encouraged them. "Take your drinks and go back to your homes. Leave the lawn furniture, though, 'cause we need it. Some of us may have to sleep on it tonight." He spoke mostly to retreating backs.

The guys from the Beta Lambda Omicron fraternity were the exception. They seemed to take issue with leaving without their stuff, or maybe they'd just had enough of Tank yelling at them. Nearly the whole group of them advanced on Tank and Brad, with a couple of Tri-Ups lurking at the back—including the guy whose chair had been liberated from his possession. That's when Kyle and Collin came panting up behind their frat-mates. Which meant about twenty BLO brothers facing off against the four of them, arms crossed over their chests and glaring. As Collin felt the other TAG guys gathering around, he couldn't help thinking that, even if they outnumbered the BLOs, a bunch of guys in their pajamas—or worse, wrapped in pink blankies that said "NOM" on the corners in flower-bedecked script— just didn't give them the necessary intimidating look.

"This is a public street," the leader of the BLO frat pack, Cody, said.

"Which you're obstructing," Kyle shot back from behind Tank. Was that a power position for negotiations or not?

"So?" Cody asked.

They appeared to be at an impasse.

"Dude, just leave it alone and go home," someone said. Collin craned his body to see over Brad's shoulder, and could just make out half of Nelson Repp's profile. He dropped to his heels in relief, then leaned back to see past the other side of his friend. Yeah, a couple of the guys from Eta Pi Pi were backing them up. They hadn't been happy to see Ty and Sloan leave the frat after all. Probably.

The air was still thick with tension, though. He looked between Tank and Brad's shoulders at Cody. He could clearly see the guy grinding his jaw. With one more narrow-eyed glance at Tank, he stepped back. Then he spit at Brad's feet just before turning away.

Someone gasped. Collin stared at the gob of phlegm on the ground as the BLOs walked away.

It was just like a real rumble. In the street and everything. Cody should get himself one of those switchblade comb things for a more authentic feel. Clearly he felt as if TAG was from the wrong side of the tracks or whatever.

"You should probably start expecting more crap like this, now that you're the gay frat," Nelson said.

Tank swung around to face him. "What do you know about it? Are you saying this wasn't an accident? What the fuck, man, Ricky could have *died*, and we're homeless."

Nelson held up his hands. "I'm just saying BLO isn't the only frat that's all riled up. But c'mon, to do this as a prank? No one's that stupid, not even that asshole." He nodded in the direction the BLO guys had taken. "Just sayin'."

"Say it somewhere else," Tank grumbled. Nelson shrugged, and he and his buddies walked off.

Collin watched them until Kyle spoke up next to him. "I know you're worried about telling your uncle. Right now, all we know is it was an accident."

Collin shoved his hands in the kangaroo pocket on his sweatshirt. "What if Nelson's wrong and it's not an accident?"

"One thing at a time," Kyle said, but his voice sounded strained. Anxiety was his natural state. "If you tell him it might have been on purpose and it's not, he'll freak."

Collin shook his head. "I'm pretty sure he's going to freak regardless."

"Yeah, he'll probably freak when you tell him we need to break into the rainy day fund."

Collin snorted. "Monty *is* the rainy day fund. Let's look at the budget seriously before we start on the rainy day fund."

Kyle shifted his weight from foot to foot. "If this really was, you know, sabotage or . . . Jesus, a bomb or something, we're going to have a hard time convincing him there haven't been 'repercussions.'"

Collin swallowed and turned to look at Kyle. "It's my problem, don't worry. He'll support the frat. I'm pretty sure he loves it more than me."

Kyle smiled halfheartedly, probably thinking he'd been joking. "Yeah, but are you ever going to be able to come out to him like you want?"

That's what Kyle was worried about? Collin shook his head, not knowing what to say.

Kyle stared at him another moment, then turned to look at the house, so Collin did, too. After a few seconds, Collin felt Kyle's arm settle across his shoulders. Dammit, the big lug was going to make him teary, and he'd been trying so hard to butch it up lately. For some reason, after coming out to Kyle last fall, he'd been slipping more and more with that.

Whatever. Collin sighed and leaned into him, looking over the house. Kyle patted his arm. "Well, at least it can't get any worse than this."

But, being Oregon, at that moment it started to rain.

Chapter 7

B y the time Collin made it to Brad and Sebastian's, he felt ready
to drop, but also completely wound up. Kyle had gone to stay
at Ashley's sorority, and Brad had gone home hours before to cook
dinner and "make sure it's cool with Sebastian," so Collin was alone.

Brad answered the door when Collin knocked. "Hey, dude.
C'mon in. Want a beer?"

"God yes." Collin dropped his bag right in front of the couch.
He'd managed to get some stuff out of his room when they started
letting guys in a few at a time, with careful instructions about where to
walk and where not to. He'd had to go up the rear stairs, of course—
the main set wouldn't be useable until they got a contractor in to fix
them.

Brad called toward the back of the house to Sebastian, "Hey,
babe, you want a beer?" but Collin missed Sebastian's reply. By the
time Brad came back in with two bottles, Collin was sprawled out on
the couch.

"You get stuff out of the house?" Brad pointed at the bag Collin
had left on the floor.

"Yeah. Smells, doesn't it? And it's all wet from the sprinkler
system too. There are puddles all over inside the place, and everyone's
electronics are going haywire. My phone seems to work." He'd had
a hard time caring about his laptop so far, though. Being free of the
responsibility it represented sounded awesome. He had enough shit
to deal with, screw school and Alumni Weekend for a day or two.

"Wanna use the washer and dryer?"

Collin looked down at what he was wearing. Pajama pants, his
sweatshirt, and his shoes. Seemed fine. "Maybe later."

Brad laughed. "I'll throw it in." He picked up Collin's bag and
walked out again.

"Thanks," Collin called after him.

Brad poked his head back in from the hall. "No problem. So, have you called your uncle yet?"

Collin groaned and covered his eyes with his hand.

"If it was me, I'd just get it over with."

"It's not you, though, it's me." Dammit, he sounded bitchy. He uncovered his face and sat up a little straighter. "Sorry."

Brad shrugged. "S'okay. Hard day. Besides, there's plenty of shit I'm not dealing with, so just tell me to shut up." He left with the laundry, and Collin soaked in the silence and drank his beer. He was too drained to think about Monty, or much of anything at all.

Brad's voice broke his trance. "I told you about coming out to my family, right?" He came and sat in the chair next to the couch.

"Yeah." Collin almost managed a smile over the memory. "Your mom cooked a roast and you guys had a celebration dinner, then your sisters took you out for a night on the town."

"Freaks," Brad muttered. "But you know, I thought they were going to be pretty cool with it. It wasn't a big surprise they took it like that. Except for them already basically knowing and waiting seven years for me to tell them. That was fucking news to me."

Collin laughed. It surprised him when it burst out—even though he'd already heard the story, and he was stressed about the Greek Council, and nearly everything he owned was ruined, and he'd seen a friend's bone sticking out of his leg, he laughed. Not very long, and he could hear a note of hysteria in it, but he laughed.

Brad smiled. "You losing it?"

"Pretty much."

"'Kay, we'll talk about your homophobe uncle later."

"No, let's do it now. Just give me a minute."

"'Kay."

Collin sat up straight, pulling his feet up on the couch and resting his arms across his knees, trying to figure out where to start. "He's not exactly a homophobe. He's more like . . . ignorant. And he naturally distrusts anything he doesn't understand, so he doesn't like it." He turned his head until he could see Brad, resting his cheek on his hands. "I guess that's one definition of a homophobe."

"There are people who'd think that fits, yeah." Brad picked at some loose threads on the arm of the chair he was sitting in.

"He pretends like he's okay with it, but he's not. I know him pretty well. He was basically my surrogate father after my dad died, but when I got to high school . . ." He shook his head, not sure how to explain. "He started, like, *expecting* things from me. Monty has lots of plans for me and my future, and I don't know if I can meet his goals."

Brad snorted, poking at the small hole he'd made in the upholstery. "Sometimes you have to tell the people you love about your own expectations, dude. Tell them what *you* want. How come you have to meet his expectations?"

Collin shrugged. "I don't know, I just do. Because he wants me to."

Brad scowled, but Collin couldn't be sure if it was about what he'd said or because Brad's finger had torn a bigger opening. "Your uncle sounds like an uptight control freak."

Oh, then it wasn't the chair that had annoyed him. Collin wanted to defend Monty, he just didn't have anything to refute what Brad had said. He shrugged. "I guess."

Brad gave up his exploration of the furniture and let his head flop back on the seat. "It'd make it a hell of a lot easier right now if he wasn't the president of the Alumni Association. I don't think the majority of the old guys would have fought that 'gay people are okay' clause in the membership policy like he did."

Based on his dealings with some of the other old guys, Collin had to agree. He sighed.

"Sorry, didn't mean to make it worse. Dinner's almost ready. I'll get you and Sebastian when it's time to eat." Brad stood up. "If Sebastian decides to eat tonight," he added in a mutter, then walked into the kitchen.

That caught his attention. "Hey, I can find somewhere else to go, if it's a problem." Toby'd let him stay, he was certain.

"Nah, it's fine, dude," Brad said, waving him off as he walked out of the room.

Collin lay on the couch a few minutes, thinking about fires and the five thousand problems they led to. Like causing tension between Brad and Sebastian, possibly. Or had he misread that?

Ten minutes later, Brad called him in, and Collin was seated, eating the stew Brad had made, before Sebastian showed up. He seemed normal, kissing Brad quickly when he walked in, so Collin figured things were fine. He relaxed, just eating and letting the other two carry the conversation. Well, mostly Brad did that. Sebastian didn't seem to have much to say.

Brad snorted, looking over at Collin. "Did you see Tank when Penny finally showed up?"

"No, missed that." He'd missed a lot today, probably.

Brad huffed. "Dude, it was pathetic. He's all quivering, standing stock-still and staring at her like a pointer that located a pheasant, but he can't fucking go to her because it's not manly or something."

"After he spent all day aching for her to get back to town? So lame."

Brad nodded. "Yeah, but when she hugged him he lost it. I mean, I guess he might have fooled some guys into thinking he was sniffing her hair or blowing his nose in it or something, but it looked like crying to me."

"Straight guys have it so rough."

Sebastian shook his head in mock pity. "It's a tragedy. Thank God that as gay men we don't have to put up with all that posturing and posing. No, we all behave as men ought to, burping and farting our way through life and love without a thought to how we look or how others perceive us."

Collin watched Brad nodding in agreement. "Dude, haven't you ever been to a gay bar? I mean, other than the Slaughterhouse? Even there half the guys can't think of anything but how they look." And their local bar was pretty relaxed.

But Sebastian answered. "Well, you know Brad was a virgin to all things gay when I rescued him from that straight frat hell. As a matter of fact, he's only ever been with one other man. That I know of." He smiled tightly, then stood up from the table and took his plate to the sink. "I'm going to bed, hon. Don't stay up too late talking."

After Sebastian had walked out, Collin had a hard time meeting Brad's gaze. But when he did, it didn't matter, because Brad was staring down the hallway after his boyfriend.

"I thought you said he didn't have a problem with, you know, what happened between, um, us. I didn't even know about him then."

"I didn't think he did. You don't care if I go to bed also, right?" Brad had already stood up.

Collin snorted. "Uh, no. I think it might be smart if you did."

"Yeah, me too. Left blankets on the bed in the extra room for you. G'night," Brad said on his way out, heading straight after his boyfriend.

"Yeah, I'll be fine out here by myself," Collin told the table. It reflected a faint image of his face back at him. "It was just a blowjob," he told it. It didn't seem to care about that either.

Well, this sucked. He'd had a ridiculously stressful day, and he'd had some weird idea that Brad would spend half the night picking it over with him, preferably while they drank something alcoholic. It was his second favorite way to deal with stress. His favorite—and most effective—way wasn't really an option, unless Brad and Sebastian wanted a third guy in bed with them.

That seemed highly unlikely.

Besides, being some committed couple's third wheel for a night sounded lonely.

Shit. Collin finished eating and rinsed his bowl in the sink before he looked in the fridge. Plenty of beer, but did he want to drink alone? That sounded as depressing as being a third.

He needed comfort. Companionship.

A half hour later he found himself knocking on Toby's door. Obligingly, Toby opened the door with a flirtatious "you know you want me" smile on his face.

Toby had that expression down pat, and Collin didn't think he'd learned it; it just seemed to come naturally to him. He'd probably given it to the obstetrician when he was born. He was good-looking, had natural sex appeal, kept in decent shape, and never really seemed to have psychological issues.

Perfect casual hook-up material. As Collin knew very well, and had known for over a year.

As Collin stood on Toby's doorstep smiling back, he wondered if Toby ever wished for anything more. Somewhere, he'd gotten the idea that Toby's past was littered with the occasional boyfriend and lacked traumatic love affairs. Was that all Toby wanted out of life? What did he want from love? Anything?

"I heard you had a very stressful day." Toby stepped aside so Collin could come inside.

"Yeah."

"Looking to relieve some tension?" Toby shut the door and rubbed Collin's lower back in passing.

"You don't have to be my comfort fuck if you aren't into it," Collin told him.

Toby's brows pulled together and his smile dimmed slightly. "Why wouldn't I want to?" He turned, and Collin followed him to the bedroom.

It was weird. The whole time, Collin kept reminding himself this was just fun, for stress relief, but he analyzed the kisses—should he provide more tongue now?—and what he should take off when. Were they at the socks stage yet? Then when Toby said he wanted Collin to top, it took him long seconds of staring to recalibrate his ideas of the way things were going to go.

Usually when they hooked up, Toby topped him if they fucked. He couldn't help wondering the whole time he was lubing up and putting on a condom whether this was Toby's way of being extra comforting. Like, he was trying to—for lack of a better term—throw Collin the juiciest bone.

Honestly, the reason Collin liked to bottom was because it was easier to get lost in it. Topping required more thought, and he already had a hard enough time turning his brain off, even during sex.

Topping tonight would just make that worse.

He knelt on the bed, naked, condom on, and his dick started to droop. He stared at Toby, frozen in indecision.

"Oh, I don't like that look," Toby said.

Why did I want to do this again? Comfort.

He wasn't feeling the comfort.

And he may not have known if Toby ever wished for anything more, but in a moment of perfect clarity, Collin knew *he* wanted more.

"I take it this isn't happening," Toby said after a few seconds.

"I don't think so. Uh, I'm not up for topping tonight." They both looked at his deflating penis. Collin tried to laugh, but only a weak "heh" made it out.

Toby raised a brow. "You want me to do you?"

Collin swallowed. He didn't want to give offense, but . . . "No."

Toby watched him a moment longer, then reached out and grabbed Collin's dick, stripping the condom off and dropping it on the floor. Then he patted the bed next to him.

Collin all but collapsed onto his stomach beside Toby, resting his cheek on his wrist and staring at the wall.

Toby sighed theatrically. "I'd been hoping we could make some kind of a ruckus to pay my roommate back for all the times he's brought some girl here and had loud, head-banging, hetero sex all night long."

"Sorry." Collin squeezed his eyes shut. He might not be feeling the comfort, but he felt the shame.

"So am I."

He forced himself to look at Toby. "Really, I'm sorry. I didn't do much for you, did I?"

"I'm more worried about not doing it for you, babe. Besides, I've taken my revenge on him for the homo team before. By my count, I'm a couple points ahead."

He sighed. "Maybe we should have skipped trying the sex and you could have just held me."

Toby turned until he could rub Collin's back. "I can still hold you. If that's all you wanted, why didn't you just tell me?"

Guided by nudges from Toby, Collin rolled onto his side and let Toby spoon him loosely. "Would you have done that? If I'd come to the door and said all I wanted was someone to hug me?"

He could feel Toby huff into his hair. "Of course. I'm doing it now. Why wouldn't I?"

Collin shrugged. After a while, Toby leaned across him and turned out the light. He stroked Collin's arm. "You okay?"

"We're friends."

Toby ceased all motion—body language for "What? Where did that come from?"

"I mean, that's all we'll ever be, and I think the 'benefits' part of the equation is maybe . . . unnecessary?"

"Ah." Toby held him a little closer. "You mean you want the benefits to come from someone who's more than a friend."

Collin reached back and patted Toby's cheek, or somewhere in that vicinity. He felt scruff; close enough. "Yeah. Or maybe I want a friend with a different benefits package." Totally lame joke, and mildly offensive. But Toby didn't seem insulted, thank God.

"I've never had any complaints about my package before," he mused.

Collin squeezed Toby's hand on his chest. "First time for everything."

"I'm man enough to handle it. So, is this helping you at all?"

He yawned. "Well, I feel like I might be able to sleep now."

Toby laughed. "Wow, this is getting very insulting. First you disparage my package, and now you claim the mere thought of sex with me bored you to near unconsciousness."

Collin yawned again, so wide his jaw cracked. "I'm sorry."

"Nothing to be sorry for. I've been where you are now. I'll probably get there again someday."

He might have said something after that, but Collin didn't hear it.

Chapter 8

Eric couldn't remember the last time he'd had such a detailed dream.

The mouth on his dick felt real, as hot and humid as the genuine article. The lips kissing him and the tongue licking up his length felt authentic too. Quick flicks, barely perceptible. Since it was a dream, Eric added a couple of inches to his penis. More to feel with that way.

He didn't want to look and see who was (hopefully . . . maybe) about to suck him off, because that could sometimes be a nasty shock in a dream, but the lips were making him curious. They left his skin, and a broad tongue stroked up from the base of his dick to just under the head, then started all over again. He spread his legs to give the licker more room to work, and slid a hand down to bury it in the hair of whoever it was, pushing his hips up at the same time.

The licker hummed.

That was too much; Eric looked down. And his eyes met the swirling hazel of that sexy boy from the frat house call. *J.M. Montes*, his brain supplied. *That's who he looks like*. Eric banished that part of his brain from his dream before it ruined this for him.

"What are you doing here?" His voice sounded rough.

Sexy Boy smiled, then wrapped his lips around the head of Eric's cock and sucked it hard, making Eric strain upward into his mouth and the back of his head land with a thud on the bed.

"Fuck, that's—"

"For medic twenty-three, engine twenty-three, rescue twenty-three, car versus semi at milepost 19, highway 40. Caller is reporting multiple unknown injuries, one occupant trapped in vehicle."

What in the hell is dispatch doing in the middle of my blowjob dream? He was already swinging his legs out of bed while thinking it, shoving his feet into his boots, shaking off the last of his sleep and his erection.

"Good dream? You were moaning." Val was standing outside his door when he looked up. She had her jacket on already, waiting for him.

"No comment." He stood up, stomping his feet in the boots and following her down the hall when she turned to go. "It's your turn to be lead medic."

"Yeah, but I still get to drive there," she said just before walking into the vehicle bays.

"Fine, I just don't want to be the one scraping someone off the road this time." Eric's voice echoed around the cavern they kept the rigs in. He blinked to orient himself. They kept this place so damned lit up, even at—he checked his watch—2 a.m.

Val may have answered him, but he couldn't hear it over the growl of the engine as she started the ambulance up.

The car versus semi was about a nine on the grisly scale. One DOA, one guy with head trauma they had to fly to Portland who probably wouldn't make it, and a ten-year-old girl he and Val transported to Sacred Heart with minor injuries. She'd been asleep in the backseat, and hopefully that meant she hadn't seen much, because Eric was fairly certain her father was the DOA. She was conscious as he drove them to the hospital, and he caught occasional bits of conversation between her and Val.

Two dead patients in one twenty-four-hour period. That was unusual. And it sucked.

When they finally left the hospital to return to quarters at seven, Val let him drive. A sure sign that her patient had affected her. She stayed silent most of the way back to Station 2, but right before they got back to quarters, she broke it. "Tell me about your dream, I need something to focus on."

"She knew her dad was dead?" Eric glanced over quickly to see Val's tight-lipped nod. "Well, I guess you'd do the same for me . . ." *Not likely.*

"No way. My erotic dreams are my business. And so are yours."

"Heh. Funny." He hit the left blinker, waiting for a break in traffic to turn into the substation. "Not much to tell, the tones went off before it got good."

"Really? The way you sounded, your 'not good yet' is better than most of the sex I've ever had."

"Stop, you're making me blush," he said, trying to ignore the fact that he actually was blushing.

"I am, aren't I?" Val had a smile in her voice, but Eric couldn't look because he got his break in traffic right then. As he pulled into the driveway, she asked, "Were you dreaming about that boy from the frat house call yesterday?"

Eric stomped on the brakes a bit too hard, lurching to a stop before he'd backed all the way into the bay, the ambulance's front end hanging out in the wind. A lot like he felt right then about his back end. "What?"

Val laughed. "You watched him as much as you did the patient. I don't blame you, that boy was kee-yute."

"Oh my God," he muttered, pulling forward to back in more carefully.

"Of course, you're old enough to be his father."

"So, you're saying I provided substandard care to a patient in order to indulge in my pedophile urges?" He halted the rig.

Val laughed harder. "I feel so much better now. Thank you," she sputtered.

Eric rolled his eyes and yanked on the door handle. "Don't mention it." He left Val yukking it up in the rig to go do inventory. Their shift was over, so they had to get the rig back in shape before its next rotation. He yanked open the rear doors just as Val came around.

"You didn't provide substandard care, c'mon."

He gave her a squinty eye for a second. "You sure?"

"Jeez, sensitive much? Yes, I'm sure."

He nodded once. "Okay."

Altogether, Eric had a shitty double shift. He'd lost a patient, his old frat had burned down—and regardless of some not-so-great memories, he had some good memories of the place too—they'd run their asses off all day after that, and then the whole thing was capped off by transporting a kid who'd lost her father.

Hopefully that girl had had a great relationship with him. Eric didn't know, but he thought that might help with losing a parent, if you could look back and see the happy stuff. Not that he had any experience with that.

He hated shifts like that; they always made him feel deadened somehow, like his reflexes were off.

It probably shouldn't have surprised him that he got wrapped up in his thoughts while driving home and somehow found himself parked on the street next to the TAG House, staring at the yellow scene tape nominally barring entry to it. The whole scene looked dark, sad, and lonely. Deserted. Eric surprised himself with a twinge of disappointment, like he'd been expecting to find something there to help him out of his funk. Or someone.

He stared at the house a minute. That stupid gray color always had looked pretty dismal. Why the hell did they keep repainting the building the same color as the clouds? That shade should be called Oregon Winter. Maybe it was.

Well, since he'd drifted over here, he may as well make some more memories, even if he had to do it by himself. He grabbed his camera out of his gear bag and checked the batteries before walking over to look at the house.

It didn't improve on closer inspection. The windows all had that slightly dingy look that houses got after filling with smoke, and the front landscaping—if you could call it that—was trampled and muddy. The dented and scorched hot-water tank sat abandoned on the front porch right beside the door. None of it was pretty, but framed right, he should be able to get a cool urban decay–type image or two. He took a couple shots of the hot-water tank—going right up on the porch to get close-ups, carefully avoiding anything that looked like it might be evidence. He couldn't see how it would mess up Marshal Taggert's fire investigation for him to stand on the porch, but Mike would kill him if he saw him there without asking first.

When he got around to the back, it looked worse. The basement windows had black soot marks on the frames, and one or two had been boarded up, probably broken by the fire or the firefighters. One of those little ornamental maples (he could just imagine some hopeful landscape architecture student planting that) near one of the window wells had branches broken off on the house side, and the whole thing was leaning away from the building, almost like it had tried to flee the fire. It was next to one of the barricaded windows, and fresh particleboard didn't make much of a shot. He'd have to 'shop that part out, because the way the scorch marks framed the tree, like an aura of black flames, was too good a picture to pass up.

He stood there a few minutes, figuring out what angles he'd need to take it from to crop it right and still get the image he wanted. In the end, he got a bunch of pictures from different angles and decided he'd work it out later in his graphics program.

It was kind of a pathetic tree. Almost the only nod to landscaping in the backyard. It probably looked lonely at the best of times, but now it looked drunken and unkempt too. A sad little wino of a tree.

Eric was still standing there, spacing off, when he heard footsteps on the porch. It was probably Mike Taggert, but he went to check anyway. Not to mention if Mike found him first, Eric would hear about it. The fire marshal was one of those guys who'd worked for the department forever, and he felt free to be as curmudgeonly as he liked.

Eric came around the other side of the house and found Mike on the porch, cursing and messing with the front door lock. "Hey Taggert."

Mike jumped and dropped the keys. "Jesus Christ, don't sneak up on me like that! And wipe that smirk off your face. You didn't fuck with my fire scene, did you? Goddammit, Dix, all you guys think my job's not important, but—"

"Chill, I didn't go inside; it's locked anyway. I just walked around the house and took a few pictures."

Mike squinted at him, keeping Eric in sight the whole time he bent over, as if Eric might attack. Marauding bear with a camera. He scooped up the keys and stood, sniffing and hiking up his pants. "Well, all right then," he said. "Guess you're harmless."

"Pretty much, yeah. So the structural engineer okayed the building for you?"

Mike gave him one more narrow look. "Yup." Then, in typical Mike fashion, he got over his irritation and relaxed, smiling at Eric. "You on shift yesterday?" he asked over his shoulder as he attacked the lock again.

"Yup. Thought I'd come by and check it out this morning."

"S'a weird one all right. You ever been on a hot-water BLEVE before?"

"Nope, never even heard of one. You?"

"Not in twenty-five years on the engine, or after. Gonna have to look at it pretty carefully to figure out what made it take off like that."

"Seems like a small one for a house full of guys."

Mike turned away from his task, nodding toward the hot-water heater. "This isn't the main tank; that one's over 300 gallons. This is just for the kitchen, and I'm pretty sure it was added in a later remodel. Haven't checked yet. One good thing about a place like this, everything will be permitted and easy for me to look up."

They both looked at the dented-up hunk of metal for a few silent seconds before Mike turned back to the front door, working at it again.

"Heard there was an injury." The door finally swung open, and Eric could see most of the entryway. It looked the same as he remembered, except as lifeless as the rest of the place. Well, except for the drunken tree. "Wanna come help me?" Mike asked, all cheerful now.

Eric half smiled. "Not really. But could I look around inside?"

Mike went back to his surly fire marshal persona, squinting at Eric. After looking him up and down, Mike pointed a finger at him. "You touch nothing, is that clear?"

Eric held up his one empty hand in surrender. "Completely clear, Marshal Taggert, sir."

"Smartass." Mike turned and walked inside, his voice echoing back at Eric. "And stay the hell out of the basement."

"Sir, yes, sir." Eric took the front steps two at a time. He didn't know why he was so eager to see the place again. Most of the last fifteen or so years, he'd hardly even thought about it.

Inside the frat, he felt curiosity, and maybe some mild nostalgia. Most of the furniture was different, but everything else was the same. Well, except the smell. It was that overpowering charred-wood wet smell with the bitter note of plastics house fires typically had. But otherwise, yeah, it was the same. He glanced around the entryway, then made a slow circuit of the main floor. He couldn't go up to his old room unless he went to the rear stairs, but he didn't do that. Poking around in there would be violating some current brother's privacy. Hell, it could be locked; not worth it. He pushed away the random thought about trying to figure out which room was Collin's.

What am I doing here?

Not really very damn much. Checking out an empty, smoke-damaged frat with puddles soaking into the hardwoods for no good reason. "Huh." He turned around slowly in the kitchen, then looked down the hall toward the entryway. Whatever he'd thought in college, TAG House was just that: a house. Especially when it had no people in it.

Crap, he could have been home sleeping this whole time.

He headed back toward the front door, intending to stop and yell down to Mike that he was leaving when he passed the basement. But just as he got there, he heard Mike shout his name.

Eric pulled the door open to see a pale-faced fire marshal hauling ass up the stairs toward him. "Get the fuck out to my rig and get dispatch on the horn! I can't reach 'em on my handheld. Shit, I shouldn't have even tried, I coulda ha—"

"Mike! What the fuck is wrong?"

Mike had nearly reached him, panting a little, wide-eyed. "Bomb. Tell dispatch to send a bomb squad."

Chapter 9

Collin's phone rang very early in the morning.

"Wha . . .?" Toby's elbow poked him in the back, and Collin leaned over to find his pajama pants on the floor, hoping the phone was in them.

It wasn't there. He felt around until he found his sweatshirt, then considered not bothering to dig his phone out since it had stopped ringing.

But there was his damn sense of duty to contend with, and it was very early, judging by the lack of sunlight. What if something had happened to his mother or sister? The voice mail tone sounded. Collin searched until he found the dumb thing in the pocket.

"Hi Collin, this is Sparky Donaldson—"

Shit. He shot up in bed, fully alert.

"—I won't be able to make our golf date this morning. An unexpected situation has arisen, and I need to leave the state suddenly. I should return within the next month or so—my business frequently brings me to Oregon. I believe your uncle gave you my contact information, so please don't hesitate to reach out to me if you need any help with Alumni Weekend." He paused, and Collin could hear what sounded like a flight being called in the background. "I'm looking forward to meeting you soon." *Click.*

"Ohthankgod," Collin groaned, sinking back onto the bed.

"Good news?" Toby slurred.

"The best."

"Good news that means we can go back to sleep?"

"Yes."

"Thank God."

The second call came at almost nine, but Collin wasn't any more awake then. This time he didn't even bother looking for the damn phone. He'd check the voice mail in a few minutes.

Whoever it was called back immediately.

"Someone wants your attention," Toby mumbled.

Collin just caught it before the final ring. "'Lo?"

"There'sabombinTAGHouse," Kyle shouted in his ear.

Collin screwed up his face, trying to figure out what language Kyle was speaking. "What?"

"There's a *bomb* in *TAG House*."

For the second time that morning, Collin jackknifed up, but this time he made it all the way out of bed. "The fuck are you talking about?" He started pulling on his pants. Where was his underwear?

Toby sat up in bed, looking at him questioningly. Collin gave him the "just a minute" finger. Then he gave him the "where are my briefs?" wave, but Toby didn't know that one.

"The fire marshal went in to investigate the fire and he found a *bomb*. I need you over here as soon as possible. Like, now. Come down Locust Street, I'm on that side of the barricade. They have all the houses evacuated for a 250-yard radius." Collin had his sweatshirt nearly on, he just had to pull the phone away from his ear for a split second, but Kyle wouldn't shut up. "It's totally a bomb, the fucking bomb squad is here! These are *definite* repercussions. I don't know what we're going to tell your uncle about this, but we can't back down from that poli—"

"Kyle! Give me a second." He yanked the sweatshirt over his head. "Okay, just chill until I get there. Have you called Diana? Is the Facilities guy there yet? Make sure when you talk to Diana that she's not talking to the TAG Alumni Association, okay? I'll handle this." Somehow.

He heard Kyle take a deep breath. "Okay. Okay. Sorry, I just got excited. Um, Facilities isn't here, but Diana's going to be here in a while—she has something going on right now she can't leave, I guess. I'll call her. Aw shit, man. I can't believe this."

"Neither can I. I'll be right there." He hung up and looked at Toby, unsure what to say. "Nothing. Let's go back to sleep," was out of the question.

"Bad news?"

"The worst. More of it."

ΘΛΓ

"I cannot believe someone planted a bomb in our basement," Kyle said for the five hundredth time.

Collin sighed and kicked at a rock at his feet. He'd stopped responding a while ago. He really wished someone else would show up and take over not answering Kyle.

It wasn't that Collin didn't appreciate the gravity of the situation—God, no—it was that he didn't want to have to appreciate Kyle's appreciation of the gravity of the situation, also. They'd already been here two hours, appreciating the gravity, and he'd had about enough of it.

"Where's Ashley?" he asked. Kyle's girlfriend should be here listening to him blather.

"She said she was far safer staying at her sorority, and I agreed."

Ashley was clearly a master at avoiding Kyle's neuroses. Collin sighed. Apparently he was the designated appreciatior of the gravity of the situation.

Fuck my life.

He should spend this time drafting an acceptable script for his upcoming conversation with Monty. Would it be better to call now and present the bare facts? Getting into conjecture—who might have planted the bomb, why they might have planted it—had to be avoided at all costs. Would it be better to wait for more information? Information could be good or bad, but the right information could nip conjecture right in the bud. Maybe by some crazy coincidence, the bomb had nothing to do with TAG being the "gay" frat. Maybe someone was pissed off about that recent fencing team loss—Gomer had practically thrown that last bout.

Well, that's what Collin had heard. He didn't know fencing from poking his sister with a stick.

"Oh, there's Diana, finally," Kyle exclaimed.

"You should go talk to her. Over there, by her car."

Kyle scrunched his brow, looking at Diana. "I think she's on her way over here."

"Maybe she has something to carry. You should help her, it would be gentlemanly."

Kyle scrunched more.

"Ashley would be proud. Gentlemanly behavior is hot."

Kyle unscrunched. "You think so? Good idea." And he walked off.

Collin felt like collapsing from the relief. Except not. It was more of an inner collapse, softening just the muscles around his spine. He turned back to the frat house, of which he could only see the attic story. There were too many trees and emergency vehicles in the way. The fire engines, police cars, and ambulances were near the barricades, holding the line against the crowd and presumably unable to get any closer to the scene for their own safety. The emergency responders had their own crowd on the opposite side of the barrier, made up mostly of firefighters.

Most of the ones that Collin could see were in their usual figure-hiding outfits, which he didn't really think about until he saw a firefighter walking around without one. This guy only had on navy blue cargo pants and a uniform shirt. The pants looked familiar.

It was completely inappropriate for the circumstances, but Collin got hung up looking at those pants. The guy inside them filled them out very well, especially the thighs. Collin couldn't help it—he was a thigh guy, and those were some beefy ones, the kind that strained the fabric with bulging muscle while the owner walked.

Where did he know those pants from?

He was so absorbed in them he didn't realize they were headed his way at first. When he did realize it, his eyes flew up to the guy's face, and got stuck on the raspy, strokeable scruff on his chiseled jaw. And chin cleft.

As the firefighter got closer, Collin could see gray sprinkled liberally through the whiskers. A silver fox. He had never been into them, but he could certainly appreciate them. His eyes traced the planes of the man's face, and something wasn't computing. He had gray whiskers, but his face looked younger than it should. No wrinkles that Collin could see. Just some near the guy's light-colored eyes. Those looked gray too, actually.

That's when Collin recognized him. It was the firefighter—paramedic?—that had worked on Ricky.

The recognition had to be on his face, because the guy waved, a small one, only waist high or so.

Collin lifted a hand in reply.

"Hey," the paramedic said as he came up to the red–and–white striped roadblock. "Collin, right?"

"Yeah. Um, Eric?" He could swear that was it, but yesterday was a bit fuzzy. Which he found astonishing, considering how freaking hot this guy was.

"Good memory. Lots of people don't remember names when they're that distracted."

"Oh, yeah?"

"Yeah."

Eric nodded, and they stared at each other a second. Collin couldn't quite figure out what was happening. If they'd been in a gay bar . . . this would be the mildly awkward prelude to a pickup.

As Eric stared at him—not checking him out, just meeting his eyes, quirking a half smile—Collin upgraded mildly awkward to moderately awkward. But Eric didn't look like he felt awkward at all. After a few seconds, he ducked under the barricade and stood more to the side of him than directly in front.

"I guess it would be a dumb question to ask if you're a TAG brother." Eric shifted his weight, glancing in the direction of the bomb scene.

"I am." Collin nodded.

Eric nodded back. "Yeah, that was a shock I bet, seeing your frat on fire."

He relaxed a little, because he could handle this bit of the conversation. "Waking up that morning with the bed shaking was a shock."

Eric smiled at him, in on the joke. "I bet. It freaked me out when we arrived—TAG was my frat in college. I showed up on a call and the place I called home for three-plus years was on fire. Glad it didn't completely burn."

Collin barely stopped from gaping. "You were in TAG? You . . . I don't know, handled that well, I guess." He felt extra disoriented. He'd thought possibly this guy was interested, but could the eye contact and the smiles be just about the frat?

Eric shrugged one shoulder. "Part of my job. You never know when you'll go out on one of your friends, so you learn to shove it to the back of your mind and figure you'll get therapy for it later."

"Are you going to need therapy for this?" Oh, that might have been too personal. Except Eric had brought up the therapy first, so was it?

Eric laughed shortly. "Going out on a call involving your former home isn't traumatic, much." He made very direct, intent eye contact with Collin. "Maybe talking it over with you is my therapy."

A small thing fluttered in Collin's stomach, messing a bit with his breathing. "I'd be happy to offer you therapy."

Eric took a step closer to him. "I'd like that." He stood there, a few inches taller than Collin and less than a foot away. "I'd love to give you a little therapy too. Somewhere else." Eric took a step back, not far but enough to give Collin some needed fresh air.

Swallow. Collin glanced around from under his lashes. They were apart from everyone, but not very far. Yeah, they probably needed to back off from the flirting a little. But only a little. "Is that what you're doing here? Looking for therapy? I mean, other than it being your job."

"I stopped by this morning to check it out; I guess I had an attack of nostalgia or something. The fire marshal let me into the house." He nodded toward it, and they were no longer negotiating a potential hookup, they were back to the more serious matter at hand. "Then he found the bomb. What did they tell you?"

"All I know is they found a bomb in the basement." Could Eric tell him more? Something useful?

"That's pretty much what I know."

"Dammit." Collin deflated.

"You were hoping for inside info?" Eric quirked another smile.

"Sort of. It's just that my uncle is an alumnus and he'll want to know details. I haven't called him yet. Honestly, I haven't even told him about the fire yet." That was the truth, except for the extent of the interest Monty would have about who could have done this, or why.

"He must be a more involved alum than me. I barely pay attention to the newsletter, and I never come to those events."

Collin sighed. "Yeah, he's involved all right."

"The thing I don't get is, why would someone want to set off a bomb in the TAG House? I've heard of pranks, but this is over the top. Nobody did crap anywhere near this scale when I was in college."

"I guess you really don't keep up on alumni news."

"Not so much."

"We changed the membership policy this year."

"Must have been a hell of a change."

"We changed it to state that TAG accepted gay, bi, queer, and questioning members."

Eric raised his brows. "Huh."

"Yeah."

"What about trans?"

"Um, that's a continuing argument that we can't quite get the alumni to support. Actually, I can't even get all the guys to go for it, yet. So, um, is that something you'd support?"

Eric tilted his head. "I'm in favor of the rest of it, I don't see why not that too. Not like there haven't always been gay guys who joined."

Even though Collin had been certain Eric was interested in him, his stomach fluttered again when Eric said that—all but admitted he was gay. "Yeah," he agreed, meeting Eric's eyes.

Then they stood there looking at each other. Collin's whole body hummed with the electrical feeling he got right before someone asked him out or kissed him or maybe invited him to their house for a cup of tea and a blowjob.

Then he heard something squawk, and a voice that sounded like it was coming out of a tin can said, "Dixon, where the—" then something unintelligible.

Eric's shoulders slumped, and he reached for the radio Collin hadn't noticed he was wearing on his belt. "Dammit, I've got to get this." He gave Collin another very intent look. "I'll be back in a couple minutes. Don't go anywhere."

Collin bit his lower lip, nodding. He let go of it to say, "I'll wait for you," before Eric walked off.

But of course, as soon as Eric disappeared around the corner of the nearest engine, speaking into the radio, Kyle called out, "Dude!" Collin closed his eyes, wanting to ignore whatever Kyle needed. But the guy was right behind him, and he wouldn't shut up. "The cops want to talk to us."

Shit. He couldn't really ignore that, could he?

"Can they come over here?"

Kyle snorted. "Maybe, but I'm not about to ask them."

He sighed, finally turning. "All right. Let's try to make this fast."

Chapter 10

I t was actually a police officer and a firefighter waiting to talk to them. Something about the firefighter's uniform made Collin think he was a supervisor, but he couldn't say why. The policewoman looked like a regular officer.

"Collin, this is Fire Marshal Taggert." Kyle motioned with his hand to the man. They both looked at the policewoman next to him, but no introductions were forthcoming.

"Call me Marshal. Is this the someone you said you needed to find from the building maintenance committee?" He tilted his head toward Collin.

"Mmm . . . sort of." Kyle nodded once or twice. "Actually, our entire building committee was the guy who broke his leg yesterday. Collin's been appointed interim chair in Ricky's absence."

Both the fire marshal and the police officer nodded, sharing a look packed with meaning. Not that Collin had a clue what that meaning might be. He doubted they were making plans for an after-work drink.

Marshal Taggert turned back to them. "This is Detective Homes," he said, indicating the policewoman.

"Um, Sherlock or Katie?" Kyle joked. Nerves always brought out his dorky streak, which meant he was often in a state of dorkiness.

"It's Rebecca," she answered, not cracking a smile. "And it's Homes, not Holmes."

Marshal Taggert redirected them. "Now as you both know, I found a bomb in the basement this morning when I went in to investigate. I was in the building briefly yesterday evening when the mop-up phase of the fire was completed, and I'm certain that bomb wasn't there then. I'm hoping you two can tell us something helpful."

Collin couldn't think of much that was helpful. Kyle thought of a lot of things, but as he blathered on, none of it sounded particularly helpful. They'd all left the scene yesterday before the fire marshal had gone inside, yet still Kyle felt it necessary to explain all about having dinner with Ashley, the conversation they'd had, the fact that he'd slept at her sorority (with no gory details, thank God). He was well into the story of being awakened by his phone and learning about the bomb in TAG's basement when Marshal Taggert finally broke into his monologue.

"Mr. Daley, do you have any reason to suspect anyone has a grudge against your fraternity or any of the members?"

"Uhhh, a few, yes." Kyle nodded briskly.

Detective Homes raised her eyebrows. "And those would be?"

"Well, um, Gomer practically threw that last fencing bout."

Seriously? "And we're considered the 'gay' fraternity on campus, which seems to make some people unhappy," Collin said.

Both Marshal Taggert and Detective Homes lost their confused frowns and started taking notes. "And why is it that you're considered the 'gay' fraternity?" the detective asked.

Kyle took over again. "We voted to include gay, bi, queer, and questioning members."

"Now we're getting somewhere," Taggert said.

But ultimately, Kyle and Collin still couldn't tell them much, other than the incident from yesterday with BLO and Eta Pi.

"Oh, plus some fraternities and sororities made comments at the last Greek Council meeting," Kyle added.

Shit, he'd forgotten all about that. "Like what type of comments?" Collin asked, because it was about damn time he knew.

"Just like yesterday: we need to watch our backs because some people might take exception to our new policy. That's pretty much it. They were just made with, you know, varying degrees of threat in the commenter's voice."

Collin looked at Kyle from under his brows, but the dude wasn't paying attention.

"These comment-makers were all from sororities and fraternities?" the detective asked.

"Yes. Um, let's see, the people who said things like that were from Tri-Ups—"

"Tri-Ups?"

"Yeah, Upsilon Upsilon Upsilon." Taggert and Homes nodded, so Kyle went on. "Um, Beta Lambda Omicron and Delta Upsilon Mu were the other frats that mentioned it. Only one sorority said anything, Lambda Upsilon Phi."

Collin snorted. "They have room to talk. Half the women's basketball team's in that house."

Kyle turned to him. "You know, assuming they're lesbians just because they're tall and muscular—and yes, a few have facial hair—is the worst kind of stereotyping. I'd think you of all people would be more careful about saying things like that."

Collin scowled at Kyle, but Marshal Taggert spoke before he could. "Why is it that you of all people would be more careful?"

Collin's scowl was nothing compared to his glare. Kyle swallowed. "Just, he had a gay roommate last year and he's generally very accepting."

"I'm gay," Collin said, surprising even himself. "It's not general knowledge, and I'd like to keep it that way." And now he felt a little light-headed. "Please."

Taggert studied him a second. "So, you're gay, but you're not out even though you're part of this accepting, welcoming fraternity."

"Why is that, Mr. Montes?" Homes asked.

Collin took a deep, calming breath. "It's my family. I haven't told them yet, and it's going to be . . . complicated."

Taggert and Homes looked at him another second or two, then went back to scribbling on their pads. "I getcha. My last marriage was complicated too," the fire marshal muttered.

ΘΑΓ

When Collin went back to his appointed Eric-waiting spot, the whole scene was starting to break up. The barricades were down, and equipment was leaving. It turned out the bomb had been successfully defused before Kyle and Collin had been questioned.

He hung out a while, but it was a crazy scene, with tons of people milling around now that the public could get closer for their rubbernecking and intermingle with the cops and firefighters. Even if Eric had returned, Collin couldn't be sure they hadn't missed each other. He didn't want to give up, but it seemed too pathetic to wait for a potential hookup in a situation like this. No matter how sexy the guy's thighs might be.

By late afternoon, he found himself back at Toby's. He hadn't worked up to calling Brad to find out if he was still welcome at his and Sebastian's place, so it was Toby or a hotel.

He hadn't worked up to calling his uncle, either.

He spent the first fifteen minutes at Toby's slouched on the couch, staring off into space. Then Toby said, "You need to go out tonight; blow off some steam."

Collin looked down at his sweats. "I don't have anything to wear."

"Brad dropped your clothes by earlier."

That probably answered the question of whether he was welcome at Brad and Sebastian's. Collin sighed. "Fine, I'll get cleaned up and we can go out."

Toby nodded. "Excellent."

He took a shower and did his usual pre-bar cleansing routine almost automatically. He had no intention of hooking up with someone random, and what were the chances that he'd meet someone non-random? But still he behaved as if he might.

Dammit, if he'd been able to find Eric before he'd left the bombing scene, maybe he'd be with someone nonrandom right now. But what did he really know about the guy anyway? He could be just as random as someone Collin met for the first time tonight at the bar.

Even if his gut thought otherwise.

ΘΑΓ

The Slaughterhouse was a pretty typical gay bar, if a bit more relaxed. Nearly everyone who showed up already knew each other from campus, so in that way it was unusual.

Although, when it came right down to it, Collin didn't feel qualified to define an average gay bar. He couldn't help thinking that he should be familiar with one; he'd grown up within two hours of San Francisco, after all, but he'd only been of legal age for about a year (regardless of any fake IDs he may or may not have owned in the past). Collin had been a little too youthful-looking in high school to try getting into any, and then he'd moved to Oregon for college.

The quality of Bay Area gay bars was as much a mystery to him as it would have been to his grandfather if, say, his grandfather had ever even thought about them.

"Well, well, well," Toby drawled softly next to him, recalling Collin to the scene he was in, not the one he'd desperately wanted to be a part of when he was sixteen and jerking off to the underwear catalogs he'd kept between his mattress and box springs. "The bears have graced us with their presence."

Bears could be pretty yummy. Collin didn't look over toward the door, though. Instead he tried to judge the relative hotness of the bears in question by watching Toby. Toby had the balls or whatever it was to watch the entrance unashamedly, seeing who arrived next. He wasn't exactly predatory, just curious and opportunistic.

Collin had tried, but without about five drinks, he didn't have that same quality. Mostly he focused on letting guys notice him. He was successful enough. He knew he had nice eyes, and if he got in the right lighting it totally worked for him.

That space between the sex-toy vending machine and the men's room wasn't the right lighting; he'd tested that so thoroughly he was pretty sure he could write a paper for an academic journal based on his findings.

"Must be dead over at their bar, tonight," Collin said. Toby's face wasn't giving him much information.

"Or they're looking for fresh prey. And I think one of them has fixed his sights on you."

"What?" He spun around on his bar stool, surprise overcoming his reluctance to look. "Ohmygod, it's him." He spoke to himself, but Toby heard him, even over the noise.

"Him who?"

Collin could feel Toby's interest drilling into the side of his head, but he'd just made eye contact with Eric, and he couldn't look away. Eric did "intent" so well. Collin's stomach tightened into a hard ball of excitement and apprehension. The good kind of apprehension.

Eric had come looking for him.

Chapter 11

"What do you mean, you want to go to the Slaughterhouse tonight? That's a college kids' bar."

Eric had suggested they all meet at Winston's place and have a beer before going out because he figured he'd encounter this kind of resistance. He tipped his bottle toward the couch that Win had draped himself all over and delivered his preprepared answer. "I need a change of pace. You want to go back to Baggy's and hook up with one of the same three guys you always do, you go right ahead."

Isaac, slouched in the chair next to Winston, offered no resistance. "Count me in, man. If some twenty-one-year-old with abs and a goatee wants to fuck me senseless, I'm up for it." He snickered down at his beer gut, as if they were in on the same joke. Which they probably were, come to think of it.

Win made a pouty face. "I don't know, maybe this is the night all three of those guys will come home with me at once, but I'll never find out if we don't drop by."

Isaac turned his snicker on Win. "Yeah, and what would you do, watch? You're not up to taking on three guys at once anymore, old man."

"I'm younger than you, you old fart. You'd get off once, then sleep through the rest of it."

Isaac nodded. "Which is why I want to go to find a college kid. They're all premature—he'll probably get it up four times before I come, then he'll pass out with me."

"And sneak out at 2 a.m." Winston sniffed.

"Come and run? That's a bad thing, how?"

Eric tuned out their sniping while they hashed it out. He could go to the Slaughterhouse on his own, but he thought Isaac would win this argument. He usually did. Win's problem was that he got angry— Isaac just got amused.

This morning, when he'd gone back to that barricade and found Collin gone, Eric had started to think he'd read things wrong. Their conversation had seemed so obvious, and Collin's body language had been welcoming, but maybe it was wishful thinking brought on by his inability to get the image from his dream out of his head: Collin between his legs, licking Eric's dick like it was an ice-cream cone on a hot summer day.

Could the kid be so naive he didn't understand what Eric had been trying to say? Or that straight?

No way. That line about being happy to offer him therapy was too blatant. Collin had to know what that had implied.

Then Eric had seen Collin talking to the police and he'd realized Collin had had to leave. It had seemed like a good idea to back off for the time being—work wasn't really the best place to pick up a guy.

But the Slaughterhouse seemed like a perfect place to pick up that guy.

"Why do you want to go there anyway?" Win must have given up his bickering with Isaac because his attention returned to Eric.

"I told you. Change of pace."

Win stood up, probably to better look down his nose. "Uh-huh. I don't believe you. There are other bars with guys closer to our age we could go to for this 'change of pace' you're so set on."

Eric sighed and took a long drink of his beer. Fine. "I'm looking for someone in particular."

Win tilted his head. "A particular college kid?"

Eric nodded.

Win brightened. "Well, this I have to see. I'll get my coat."

After Win left, Isaac pushed himself forward in his chair and looked pointedly at Eric. Not that Eric looked back, he could just feel it. He took another sip of beer and feigned interest in Win's walls.

Isaac, while easily amused, wasn't very patient. "Well, now. And how did you meet this sweet young thang you're chasing after?"

"On a call."

"Is that ethical?"

He swung his head toward Isaac in surprise. "It's not like I came on to him during the call, or asked for his number. Or threw him into the back of the ambulance and shoved my dick in his mouth. He wasn't even the patient."

Isaac held his hands out toward him. "Sorry, man, only asking. Do you even know if this guy is gay?"

Eric shrugged a shoulder. "Let's say I have a very strong feeling about it." Okay, more than a feeling.

"Is it a feeling inside your pants or outside?"

He couldn't help it, he snorted a laugh. "Kinda both. And yeah, I'm pretty certain he's gay. I saw him again and it was pretty clear."

"Okay!" Win walked back into the room, rubbing his hands together like a gleeful villain. "I'm ready, let's go find Eric's boy. I'm really looking forward to this."

ΘΑΓ

College-aged guys packed the Slaughterhouse, but Eric could see a few older ones in the crowd. He stood with his friends by the door a few minutes, scoping the place out. It took him about two minutes of methodical looking to find Collin, seated sideways at the bar, speaking to the guy next to him. Eric decided not to worry about who that guy might be or what his intentions were. His own intentions didn't include letting Collin get away.

"I think I see a place to sit over there," he said, loud enough to be heard by his friends. Probably.

"Told you it's a bunch of college kids," Winston said.

Hadn't they been over this? "So?" He began to work his way toward Collin. Win and Isaac could follow or not; as far as he was concerned, they were on their own at this point. He lost sight of his prey for a few seconds when a tall guy stopped to flirt with someone and he had to step to the side.

"So do you see him?" Win must have decided to follow.

He got past a trio of nearly shirtless young guys with large muscles who looked well on their way to bearhood, and located Collin again. He nearly lost Win at the trio, but they moved off to dance before his friend could whip out a snappy pickup line or flex his own gym-cultured muscles.

"He seems very focused. I'm going to guess he sees this boy he's after." Isaac must have decided to follow too.

Eric did better than see Collin, he locked eyes with him when Collin swung around suddenly on his barstool. His startled expression quickly gave way to something Eric thought might be excitement.

Good. He refused to break eye contact as he walked the last few feet to the bar.

"Hey, I thought you said you saw a place to sit," Isaac complained.

"I lied." Collin must have heard that part, because his eyebrows scrunched together. Eric took the last step, bringing himself within a foot of Collin. "I found you."

Collin licked his lower lip, but it looked like nerves rather than flirting. It had the same effect on Eric either way. "You were looking for me?"

"I had to. Earlier, you said you'd wait for me, but you didn't."

"I wanted to." Eric had to lean closer to hear him, one hand on the bar, half caging Collin in. "I had to go talk to the police." They were only inches apart now, and Eric wanted to be even closer, and naked. Being only this close to Collin made his blood thicken and pound in his fingers and lips and groin. He took a chance and laid his palm on Collin's knee, sliding it an inch or so up his leg, following the inside seam on his jeans. Collin's lips parted, and he swayed toward Eric almost imperceptibly.

"Oh, this is better than theater." Win's voice recalled him to the fact that they were in a bar, surrounded by people.

"These are my friends." Eric tilted his head to the left, but he didn't look away from Collin. "Winston's the tall one, and the round one's Isaac."

"Oh," Collin nodded. He indicated the guy next to him with his own head, still staring at Eric. "This is my friend Toby."

"Okay."

"I'm sorry," Toby said, "but I don't believe I caught your name."

"You know," Isaac returned, "I don't believe we caught your friend's name, either. Our friend here is Eric."

"Ah, nice to meet you all. My friend is Collin."

"Splendid," Win said.

These douche bags were having too much fun at their expense. "We should leave these guys to get to know each other better."

Collin nodded. "Definitely." He turned away a second to set his beer on the bar, then stood up, so close his shoulder brushed against Eric's chest and his hip rested a half second on Eric's thigh. This close, Eric could tell Collin had shaved recently, and smell a hint of soap, and see the pulse beating in his neck.

"Come home with me."

"Please."

"We'll just find our own ride home, don't you worry," Win called as Eric left with Collin.

Chapter 12

Collin led the way out of the bar, but Eric brought him up short by grabbing Collin's arm as soon as they were outside the Slaughterhouse door. Eric pulled Collin into his chest, while his other hand gripped the back of Collin's head, lifting him up to his mouth. It was one of those hard, desperate kisses—all about feeling and nothing to do with technique. The kind that made Collin's lips ache and made him dig into Eric's shoulders with his fingers to bring himself even closer.

He nearly came right there in the parking lot.

"Sorry, I couldn't wait," Eric whispered after he'd ended the kiss, still just inches away.

Collin tried to slow his breathing. "I don't mind at all."

Eric kissed him again, this time slower and less frantically, filling Collin's mouth with his tongue, and pressing against his body until Collin could feel his erection and he knew Eric could feel his too. No guy had ever made him hard just by kissing him before. They had to get out of here so Collin could know what other unusual reactions his body might have to Eric's.

"I wanna go to your place," he whispered when that second kiss ended. He watched Eric's tongue run across his lips, and began to consider a third kiss.

"Did you bring a car?"

"No, Toby drove."

"Mine's over there." Eric nodded toward one side of the parking lot.

Neither one of them made a move, until Eric reached up to take Collin's hand from his shoulder, stroking Collin's palm with his thumb and making him shiver all over. "Let's go." Eric pulled him along behind as he headed toward his car.

They walked toward a compact hybrid under one of the lot lights. Collin looked at the semi-burly fireman with the shaved head in front him, and back at the tiny car. *Really*? Couldn't be. Then Eric hit a button on his key chain and the car chirped and flashed.

Definitely where they were headed.

In the car, Eric quirked that smile Collin remembered while reaching over and resting a hand on his knee. His fingers stroked Collin's inner thigh while he drove, and it made Collin want to squirm, partly with the sensation but partly with the novelty of being touched like that. It felt personal; the same as when Eric had caressed his palm earlier and held his hand. Like getting Collin home and getting off were secondary to these simple touches.

"I'm sorry if that was too fast. I kind of rushed you out of there, didn't I?" Eric gripped his leg a second, squeezing his muscle.

Collin shifted his hips down, closer to Eric's hand. "No, it's fine, it's flattering. You came looking for me." That's what he'd said, right?

Eric stroked down to Collin's knee, then up to mid-thigh and let his fingers dance there. "Yeah, I was looking for you. It was the best idea I could come up with, other than hanging around the fire scene hoping you'd stop by."

The heat from Eric's hand was melting his brain. "I wanted to wait for you earlier, but I couldn't." Did he just admit too much? Hadn't he already admitted that?

"I know, I saw you talking to Taggert and the cop. That was a dumb place to approach you, anyway." They came to a red light and Eric looked over at him, smiling and inching his hand up Collin's leg until he was millimeters from Collin's dick. "But I was afraid I wouldn't find you again if I didn't talk to you there."

Collin's breath was coming short, but he managed to ask, "You were looking for me this morning, too?"

Eric's fingers worked under his leg, digging into the back of Collin's thigh. "I had a dream about you."

He couldn't do anything but stare, quivering, waiting for Eric to move closer to his cock and squeeze it, maybe then undo hi—

The car behind them honked its horn, and Eric looked away, sliding his hand down closer to Collin's knee.

"You're killing me."

Eric glanced over, cheeks darker in the dashboard lights. "Sorry."

Collin put his hand over Eric's and gripped him. "You don't need to be sorry, you just need to get me to your place as fast as you can."

ΘΑΓ

Collin tasted sweet. Not literally sweet, but that was the best description Eric could come up with. It was more about how his taste felt than anything. Collin felt sweet.

It took ten minutes to get to Eric's place from the Slaughterhouse, and he spent the entire ride dying to kiss Collin again. For the first time since he'd bought this car, he cursed it. It was too damn small to do much of anything with the console between them except make out.

And pet Collin's thigh, and maybe other things. Halfway to Eric's, Collin had given up conversation and closed his eyes, head back on the seat and lips parted, gulping air. When he spread his legs wider and lifted his hips off the seat, Eric nearly pulled over and shoved his hand down Collin's jeans, but they were only a mile from his house and doing it on the side of the highway was so high school.

Eric couldn't catch his breath by the time he got in the driveway. He hadn't even touched Collin's dick, just stroked up and down his leg, kneading his inner thigh and wedging his fingers underneath, to the sensitive spot high up under Collin's buttocks. Feeling Collin's muscles quivering and jumping under his hand.

He hit park as soon as he turned off the road and then undid his seat belt, didn't even shut the car off. Leaning over the console, he grabbed the base of Collin's skull and pulled him forward, then kissed him with the same force he had at the bar, letting his fingers finally slide all the way up Collin's leg to fumble with the snap and zipper.

Collin said something into his mouth, but Eric didn't stop and ask him to repeat it. Instead, he suckled Collin's tongue and ripped his fly open, shoving his hand inside and finding hot smooth skin over hard dick to wrap his fingers around. It was rough and fast and unlubricated, but Collin didn't object when Eric stroked his cock. Instead he lifted his hips into Eric's hand, shoving his dick through Eric's fist while his fingers dug into the back of Eric's neck and wrist.

It only took a few minutes before Collin came in his hand, breathing convulsively and pulling Eric halfway over the console. Eric resisted the urge to yank open his own jeans, even though his dick was throbbing on the edge of pain. He wanted so much more than just a quick jerk in a car. That thing Isaac had said about old guys who couldn't come forever had stuck in his head. He needed to make this last.

Collin's breathing started to slow, and Eric let go of him, pulling his hand out of Collin's underwear and zipping up his jeans. Collin wouldn't let Eric go, though, pressing his forehead into the side of Eric's face. "I came so fast it's embarrassing."

Eric smiled and kissed him on the jaw. "It's not embarrassing, it's hot."

Collin pulled back far enough to meet his eyes. "From your perspective."

"My perspective's the important one right now."

That made Collin smile. "Okay." He let up on Eric's neck and reached for Eric's groin.

Eric grabbed Collin's hand. "I can wait." He kissed Collin a few more times, then let him loll a minute while he dug napkins out of the door pocket and wiped his hand off.

When he drove the last thirty feet to his usual parking spot, Collin laughed. "Eager?"

Eric couldn't stop smiling at him. "Yeah." Or leaning over to kiss him. "C'mon, let's go inside and see how many times I can make you come tonight."

Collin sucked in a breath. "That sounds promising."

Chapter 13

Eric came around to the passenger side of the car and took Collin's hand when he climbed out, leading him into the house with it. Collin was so captured by the feel of Eric's palm rubbing against his that it didn't occur to him to button his fly and he only caught a general impression of a small house on some rural road.

Hand-holding was new to him. He'd fucked and been fucked, kissed guys, sucked and been sucked, jerked and been jerked, but this feeling of someone's warm fingers wrapping his tightly was completely novel. It set up that flutter in his gut again, and made him wonder what full-body contact with Eric would be like.

If it was anything like holding hands with him, Collin's nuts just might not make it through the night.

They walked through what looked like a side door into a room about the size of a closet. Coats hung on the wall with shoes lined up underneath, and opposite them another doorway led to a dimly lit living room.

Eric turned on the light, and then he turned to Collin, tracing fingers around Collin's neck, and following Collin's clavicles with his thumbs. He stepped forward until Collin's temple brushed his jaw, and Collin rubbed against his scruffy whiskers.

Eric pushed off Collin's coat, hands skating from his neck across his shoulders and down his arms, touching him so lightly it made Collin shiver. He pulled Collin even closer with one hand on his lower back and caught Collin's coat with the other, hanging it somewhere or maybe dropping it on the floor. Eric's nose bumped down Collin's cheek and jaw until their lips met.

"I want to take all your clothes off just like that."

Collin swallowed. "Okay. Anytime. Now."

Eric made a rumbly noise in his throat and finally kissed him again, taking his time and sparking up Collin's nerve endings until

Collin had one arm around Eric's neck, hanging off him in an effort to get closer. Eric's kiss got harder and he slid his hands down Collin's back to his ass, kneading his glutes and encouraging Collin to grind his erection against Eric's thigh while he rubbed his against Collin's stomach.

Collin was hard as hell again already, but he'd had the quick and dirty; he wanted the long and nasty now. He pulled back from Eric's kiss, loosening his hold.

"You're sweet," Eric whispered, kissing his cheek and then his ear, sucking on Collin's lobe.

"What? I'm what?" Was that a compliment?

"You feel good." Eric nuzzled his neck.

Collin pulled in a breath. "Oh, God. So do you. Can I have the tour now?"

Eric stopped the nuzzling and pulled his head back. "You want a tour? Of my house?"

"I want a tour of your *bedroom*."

Eric grinned at him. "You want the clothed tour or the naked tour?"

"I think you already offered me the naked tour."

"I did, didn't I?"

Eric took Collin's hand again to guide him upstairs, into a loft-like room featuring a huge bed covered in puffy blankets. "I need to check the fire," he said. Eric had an actual fireplace, with glowing logs and everything. He knelt in front of it, nudging at the logs with a poker, making sparks fly up.

Collin turned and walked over to look at the bed, impressed. The guys he usually went home with had single beds and multiple roommates. They never had fireplaces and big, inviting rooms in their own homes.

He lost interest in the bed when Eric walked up behind him and reached around to stroke his stomach, then under the hem of his tee, exploring his skin and his line of hair. Eric kissed the back of his neck once before bunching up Collin's shirt and pulling it over his head. Collin tried to help, but Eric stopped him. "No, I get to undress you, remember?"

He shivered when Eric's lips kissed under his ear, and he arched his spine when he felt Eric's fingers on his lower back, dipping under his loose waistband, then into his briefs to circle his tailbone. "Sexy. Did you wear these thinking you might meet someone tonight at the bar?"

Which ones had he put on? The purple ones? "Not . . . exactly." He hadn't really been thinking at all, but at that moment he wished he could say he'd worn them thinking of Eric.

Eric made that rumbly noise in his throat again, and Collin felt cool air on his back. He started to turn, but Eric's now bare arms wrapped around him, and his naked chest slid along Collin's shoulder blades. Collin gasped at the shock of Eric's hair and skin against him and Eric's heart thudding between his shoulder blades. He could feel how fast it was beating and how hard, and he thought he could feel Eric's blood rushing through his body. It was more intimate than Eric holding his hand or stroking his leg in the car. He reached back and gripped Eric's hips, pulling him tighter against his ass.

"I've been thinking about this since two this morning." Eric's hands traced the shape of Collin's pectoral muscles, distracting him.

"Huh?"

"When I had that dream about you."

So fucking fantastic that Eric had dreamed about him. "What was I doing?"

"You were kneeling on my bed between my legs, with one hand on my dick, licking me and about to blow me. Then I woke up."

Oh shit, that was hot. Collin yanked on Eric's hips, rubbing against him, feeling Eric's cock hard against the small of his back. "I can make your dreams come true."

"Later. Right now I'd rather do this." Eric reached into Collin's open jeans and pushed them down, off his hips to his thighs, then did the same with his purple briefs, exposing Collin's dick and baring his ass. It made him feel vulnerable in the best possible way. Collin shoved himself back, rubbing his sensitized skin against denim, trying to work Eric's dick between his cheeks.

Eric spread one hand across Collin's abdomen, and fisted his cock with the other. "Fuck, I wanna make you come again like this."

"No, I want more." Collin could say it, but he couldn't stop himself from wriggling against Eric or thrusting into his hold.

It was the thought that counted.

"Tell me what you want."

"I want you to fuck me."

Eric exhaled suddenly, like Collin had elbowed him in the gut, and then he sucked a breath in. "I'd love to do that."

Collin reached between their bodies to find the snap to Eric's jeans, but Eric pulled away from him. "Get on the bed, I'll do it." Collin let himself fall forward, catching his weight with his hands on the mattress. Was Collin tall enough for Eric to do him just like this, bent over the bed? He wouldn't even have to take off his shoes. Completely naked from mid-thigh up, trapped in denim and sneakers below.

He felt Eric's lips on his back and hands following the curve of his ass, then Eric's thumb resting a split second on the top of his crack before sliding down, working between his cheeks and finding his asshole. Collin rested his head on the bed, arching his back and thrusting his butt up further into the air, wanting more from this man than a tentative exploration. He tried to spread his legs, but his jeans trapped him.

"Just a second," Eric murmured, and then his finger was gone again, leaving Collin's ass in the air waiting hopefully for its return. He heard the sound of lube being squeezed out, and then Eric's thumbs pulling his cheeks apart and his cold, wet finger circling Collin's hole, making him shiver and stroke himself faster.

Eric rubbed his back, long sweeps up to the nape of his neck and back while he worked two fingers inside him. Taking his time until they slid in and out smoothly and Collin rocked back and forth with their rhythm, responding to Eric's touch automatically, like they were tuned into the same frequency. He arched his back more, forgetting and trying again to spread his legs.

"Fuck. You have such a sweet ass. I'd love to do you just like this and watch you take me."

"God, please."

He could feel Eric's whole body pause a second. His fingers stopped, and so did his breathing. Then he leaned over and kissed the nape of Collin's neck. "This isn't how I want you tonight. I want to see you."

He couldn't see from there?

Tonight?

Eric pulled his fingers out of Collin's ass and then nudged him further onto the bed. Urging him to roll onto his back until his legs hung off the edge and he was looking up into Eric's face.

Eric smiled at him and tugged Collin's shoes and pants off, until Collin lay there naked with Eric staring at him. "Just like this," Eric told him. He flicked open his jeans and shoved them down his legs, and his dick sprung up, bobbing while he worked his feet out of his pant legs.

"Do you always go commando, or did you do that for me?" He tried to make it a joke, but he could hear how hopeful he sounded.

Eric grinned at him, leaning over the bed and caging Collin's body between his hands, using his hips to push Collin's legs open, like he belonged there. "I did it for you."

Collin's breath caught in his lungs, but he didn't have a verbal answer for that. Instead, he planted his feet on the bed, wide apart, inviting Eric in further.

With Eric looming over him like this, not trapping him but making himself the current center of Collin's world, staring into his eyes, he felt a little stifled. Except not. More like overwhelmed. He swallowed and tried not to squirm, meeting Eric's eyes, but it was hard when he felt engulfed by him.

Just when he thought he couldn't do it anymore, Eric dropped his gaze and looked farther down Collin's body. Collin could feel Eric's eyes on his shoulders and his chest, then skipping down to his navel to follow the line of black hair there to his dick, standing almost straight and shaking with each beat of his heart.

Collin did squirm then, trying to get Eric's hand's attention, or maybe his mouth's.

Eric stood up suddenly, and for the first time, Collin focused on his cock. He was about normal length, but he was thick, exactly the way Collin liked them. He squeezed his eyes shut a second, wanting Eric to get on with it so he could feel him cram that fat bastard inside him, but unwilling to ask for it because it seemed so obvious Eric was in charge of choreography. At least for tonight.

He heard the condom wrapper crinkle, and opened his eyes. Eric looked up from rolling it on his dick and trapped Collin's gaze again. He took Collin's legs, pushing them onto his chest, until Collin hooked his knees with his elbows and held himself open for Eric to fuck.

Eric pushed into him slowly. Not being so gentle Collin couldn't feel it, but not being too rough. Once he was far enough in, he pulled Collin's legs up over his shoulders and planted his hands on the bed, overwhelming Collin even more.

The whole time Eric fucked him, he looked into Collin's eyes.

Collin would have never guessed he'd like it. Eye contact with the guy fucking him hadn't happened in any fantasies. But with Eric it was the same kind of connection as his thumb circling Collin's palm or fingers stroking the inside of Collin's thigh. The same sensation he'd had when he'd felt Eric's heartbeat against his back.

Every move Eric made echoed through Collin and reflected in Eric's eyes. A drop of Eric's sweat hitting his chest made him gasp. Eric's body hair under his fingertips made his hands tremble. Eric's dick thrusting into his ass made all his muscles tighten up.

Eric shoved an arm under Collin, lifting him farther onto the bed until he could kneel on it. Then he grabbed both of Collin's ankles and pulled them over his head, bending Collin over himself, fucking him harder and gliding over his prostate with every grunting thrust, until Collin's toes curled and his back muscles spasmed and he could hardly stroke his own dick because his fingers wanted to clamp shut and hold onto something. His other hand found Eric's leg, and his fingers dug into the back of his knee, urging him on, until Eric's eyes started to roll up into his head. Eric's dick hardened even more inside him, and the first spasm of Eric's orgasm pushed Collin over the edge. Light and sensation arced through him while he shot cum all over his chest, feeling it dribble down and pool under his chin. Eric ground into him, holding his gaze right through the whole thing, even when Collin's vision grayed out for a second.

Eric let go of his legs and fell on Collin, kissing him even more wildly than earlier, holding Collin's head between his hands. Collin appreciated it—after an orgasm that intense, he needed help holding himself together, and time to come down so he didn't get altitude sickness, or whatever the postcoital equivalent was.

It took a few minutes before their kisses softened. They slowly became more about lips than tongue and tonsils, until Eric was sucking on Collin's mouth with each one, and Collin could stop gripping him so tightly and start focusing on the feel of Eric's skin under his hand. Finally, Eric pulled out and let Collin unfold himself completely. Eric kissed him once more, then rolled onto his back, bringing Collin along with him, pressing Collin's head into his rapidly rising and falling chest.

Thank God the silence was comfortable, because Collin's brain was full of white noise, and he wasn't capable of speech yet. But after a minute or two, his thoughts started to coalesce into something intelligible: a completely random memory from last summer insisted on replaying itself. He'd been almost to his uncle's ranch in Carmel Valley, driving too fast on Laureles Grade, when he'd come around a blind corner and hit a buck. He'd screeched to a halt, worried he'd killed or seriously injured the animal. But it was shaking its head and wobbling around on the road, mouth hanging open and panting until it managed to collect itself enough to run away. Collin knew now what that deer had felt.

Stunned. Eric had stunned him. Rendered him too dizzy to move. He couldn't catch his breath and he couldn't shift off Eric's body to get some distance from the guy who'd blindsided him.

Did he want distance? His hand didn't think so; it looked to be happily twining itself in Eric's chest hair.

"I think I just saw God." Eric's voice rumbled up from under Collin's ear.

Collin couldn't stop himself from admitting it if he'd wanted to: "That was amazing."

Then the most amazing thing of all happened. Eric kissed him on the forehead and said, "It was perfect."

Chapter 14

"You have a perfect body." Eric ran his fingertip down Collin's sternum, then followed the line of his ribs to his obliques.

They lay facing each other in Eric's bed under the big down comforter. Eric had turned out the light and only had the fire to see Collin's body by, but even if it had been daytime, Collin knew what Eric had said wouldn't be any more true.

"No I don't." Collin tried to catch Eric's roaming hand, but Eric grabbed his instead and sucked Collin's index finger into his mouth, slicking it up, then letting it slide out. Another one of those touches that was more than physical.

Eric wrapped his arm around Collin's waist and spread his palm on Collin's back. "I like it," he said, while Collin traced around Eric's lips, then got distracted by the feel of the whiskers on his chin. How did he shave that dimple without nicking it? Collin could fit the whole tip of his little finger in that depression.

Eric wasn't distracted by Collin's wandering exploration. "You're built like a swimmer. Totally my favorite body type."

Well, if they had to keep talking about it. "Yeah? You're my favorite body type. Do you know what they call it?"

He caught a glimpse of Eric's teeth when he smiled. "Square?"

"No, 'yam.'" Collin let his hand drift, running along Eric's muscular shoulder while Eric laughed.

"I'm a vegetable?"

"Mmm, and I'm a fruit. My body type is 'banana.'"

Eric pulled him closer, until their bellies touched. "I like bananas. They taste good."

That deserved a kiss. "You taste good."

Eric kissed him back, lifting his head and searching Collin's mouth with his tongue very thoroughly. "You taste better," he whispered when he was done. "You're a sweet young thang."

This had gotten ridiculously silly, and Collin couldn't help but totally love it. He stretched, soaking in the feeling of Eric's hands on his body, running down his chest and along his sides.

"I like your muscles because they're defined but not too large." Eric had to be flattering him.

Collin felt Eric's biceps, squeezing and then moving to do the same to Eric's pectoral muscle. "You have big muscles. I like."

"I have a gut."

Collin switched his attention to Eric's stomach, rubbing his palm around under Eric's navel and feeling nothing but firm muscle. "Please. You do not."

"Well, I may not have a gut, but I don't have a six-pack anymore."

"Mmm. I don't care, I like this." Collin scratched his nails through Eric's belly fuzz to make it totally clear what "this" meant. "You have body hair. That makes up for a multitude of sins."

Eric kissed him. "From your perspective."

"My perspective is the one that matters right now."

Eric laughed. "Fine. But I still want my abs back. There's this guy at work, Rudy. He's gotta be five years older than me but he's still got them. I don't know how he does it."

Maybe Collin should inquire about Eric's age now . . . But at the moment a bigger part of him wanted to figure out who this Rudy person was and what his relationship to Eric might be.

"Maybe it's genetics," he suggested, trying to figure out how to ask about the coworker. *What in the hell are you doing worrying about other guys for?* He decided to explore that question in more detail later.

"I guess. My genes must have decided that once I hit thirty-five I didn't need the six-pack anymore. I was pretty much down to a four-pack by then anyway. Not fair that Rudy got to keep his; he's married and happy about it. Total waste. Nice to look at though."

The coworker didn't sound like Eric's special friend or anything, then, only eye candy. Collin smiled, and Eric stroked Collin's cheek with his fingertip for a few seconds, while Collin ran his hand over Eric's shaved head, feeling the beginning of fuzz. "Is your hair gray too?"

Shit, was that okay to ask?

"About half." Eric rubbed his jaw on Collin's temple, sounding undisturbed. "I was twelve when my mom found my first gray hair."

"Seriously? Wow, that must have been weird."

"I was pretty freaked out. I thought it meant I was going to die or something."

"Gray hair is a leading cause of death, after all."

Eric leaned down to nip at his earlobe. "I didn't know any better when I was twelve. All I knew was I had gray hair, and so did old, nearly dead people. By high school, I had just enough that people remarked on it. And I could buy alcohol without getting carded."

Collin cupped Eric's jaw, caressing his face. "Did people give you a hard time?"

Eric nodded, but his voice sounded amused. "I was a very sensitive child. I might be permanently scarred."

Collin ran his finger along Eric's brows. He had a few gray hairs there too, Collin had noticed them earlier. "Emotionally scarred people can be healed with enough physical affection. I hear sex is even more healing." He wrapped his leg around Eric and rolled onto his back, hoping to pull Eric along with him. It worked—Eric settled on top of him, not fully hard again, but Collin could get him there. Collin didn't need any help with getting hard; furry legs were his special weakness—almost nothing turned him on more.

Nothing except hairy asses and thick dicks. He massaged Eric's butt cheeks, letting the curls there tickle his palms, and squirmed just enough to feel Eric's chest pelt against his skin.

He'd entered some kind of hirsute, erotic paradise. Bearadise?

"I don't know if I can come again yet, but you will, won't you, Sweet Thing?" Eric didn't let him answer before kissing him.

"You will too," he said when he could talk. "I'll make sure of it."

Eric's weight pressed Collin into the bed, overwhelming him again, but Collin had figured out that yes, he did like that. They made out—more lazily on Eric's part, and increasingly urgently on Collin's—until Eric rocked against him, and Collin gripped his glutes, fingers digging in right where his thighs met his butt, encouraging him.

His mind knew Eric wouldn't stop now, but his body wanted to make sure there were no misunderstandings. He needed that friction and the rough slide of hair across the sensitive nerves of his dick. Eric did it perfectly, a twisting grind of hard muscle and hip action that forced the breath out of Collin's body with every thrust, until his knees were up around Eric's ribs and he came all over both their abdomens. He could still feel the shock of it when he forced his hand between their bodies and used his cum to slick up and wrap tight fingers around Eric's shaft.

"Fuck my fist. I want your cum on me," he panted into Eric's ear. Eric groaned and gave him exactly what he'd asked for.

Chapter 15

About a minute into his conversation with Collin at the bomb scene that morning, Eric had decided he wanted a lot more than sex with him. If it had been all about physical attraction, he probably would have shrugged it off, figuring if they ran into each other again, it was fate. But something told him it could be more, and that's why he'd hunted Collin down at the Slaughterhouse.

He hadn't been prepared for this kind of connection though, not this fast. It hadn't been this way when he'd met Jay, let alone any other guy he'd dated in the past.

He'd definitely never gotten out of a warm bed at 2 a.m. to make spaghetti when any of his previous boyfriends had asked if he had a granola bar or some other snack. He threw on sweats while Collin tried to talk him out of it.

"It's not a big deal. I'm not that hungry." Collin's stomach growled, and Eric laughed before heading downstairs.

Collin followed him, stealing a blanket from the foot of Eric's bed. "Really, a granola bar or, like, toast, is fine."

"It's okay, I'm hungry too." Eric paused halfway down the steps to turn around and kiss Collin. Another thing he doubted he'd ever done. "I'm just going to reheat leftover noodles and open a jar of sauce."

Collin's fingers massaged the nape of Eric's neck. "Let me help you."

"It's freezing down there, and all you have on is this." Eric reached out to touch the blanket to illustrate, but somehow he ended up with his hands all over Collin's ass. They'd spent a lot of time there already, they knew they liked hanging out in that neighborhood.

Collin raised his eyebrows. "You don't want me half-naked in your kitchen?"

"I like the idea of you fully naked, waiting for me in my bed, much better."

Collin chewed on his lip a second. "Do you do this regularly? Pick up guys at the bar, fuck them silly, and make them midnight snacks?"

He pulled Collin closer and kissed his chin, then his cheeks and eyelids, keeping his lips as soft as possible. "I don't think I've ever made anyone a midnight snack."

Collin took a breath; not a deep one, more of a medium yet audible one. "If you cook for me now, I get to make you breakfast."

"Deal."

Less than ten minutes later, Eric was back upstairs with hot food and ice cubes instead of toes. When he complained about it, Collin insisted on Eric propping himself against the headboard while he rubbed warmth back into Eric's feet. Eric let him after Collin had eaten.

Jesus, he could get used to this. He watched Collin's profile—naked to the waist and focused on massaging Eric's feet, illuminated by the light of the dying fire—and let himself wonder what it would be like to have Collin here regularly. He already knew he wanted that, but would it freak out his sweet young thang if Eric told him right now? Collin couldn't be much more than twenty, probably twenty-one, since he hung out in a bar.

"I'm thirty-six," he blurted.

Collin jerked his head up. "Um, that was random."

Crap, he knew he was blushing, he could feel it. Could he blame it on the heat of the dying embers? "It seemed like a good time to say it." He cleared his throat. "I'm not exactly sure why, now."

Collin shrugged, rubbing Eric's feet but watching his face. "I guess that makes you fifteen years older than me. Or sixteen, depending on when your birthday is. I turned twenty-one last April twenty-sixth."

"June twenty-third."

They looked at each other a moment. "Does this matter? The age thing?"

Eric nodded slowly. "I think so. In the long run."

"Okay." Collin crawled up the bed, letting his blanket slip off his back and over his hips, until he lay with one leg thrown over Eric's thighs, naked but not hard. "We should go to sleep. I need my strength if I'm going to keep up with you, old man." But he propped his head up on his hand and twined his fingers in Eric's chest hair instead of settling down.

Eric pulled the comforter over them both, then rubbed Collin's thigh with one hand and his back with the other. General caresses rather than the erotic kind, but he didn't get the impression Collin was looking for sex at the moment. Three times in a night had been enough when he was twenty-one, hadn't it? He couldn't remember, but he thought it might have been. "I think it's me that needs to worry about keeping up with you, Sweet Thing."

"You have plenty of stamina, you're a firefighter." Collin's fingers stroked Eric's throat.

"It's not like stamina comes as part of the benefits package. That'd be cool though, wouldn't it? Besides, I'm not a firefighter, I'm a firefighter paramedic."

Collin wrinkled his brow. "So you do both?"

"No, it means I'm just a paramedic, except on rare occasions."

"If Ricky hadn't broken his leg, I wouldn't have met you."

Eric blinked. That hadn't crossed his mind. "I would have responded to be on-scene for standby, but I wouldn't have spoken to you. Not unless you were injured somehow. Smoke inhalation or something. I would have noticed you, though."

Collin smiled slightly. "I don't know if I would have noticed you. Maybe, but I only sort of did that first morning. I was too freaked out about Ricky and the frat. I noticed you today. I guess it's yesterday, now."

"Maybe I would have figured out a way to talk to you at the bombing scene anyway." He definitely would have.

Collin sighed and laid his head half on Eric's pillow, half on his shoulder. "I'm in the closet," he said, voice muffled against Eric's neck.

He tried to figure out what to say to that. It sucked, but . . . "I was too, in college. Mostly."

"I should have guessed, since you were in the frat. According to my uncle, Brad is the first gay frat member."

Who's Brad? "So, you aren't out to your family, either?"

"I'm not out *because* of my family; mostly my uncle—I don't think my mother or sister will have a problem with it, but Monty will. He's sort of like a father to me, because mine died when I was four."

That was something Eric had a response to. "Mine bailed on me and my mom when I was three. I never really knew him."

Collin kissed up his neck to his ear. "I'm sorry," he whispered.

"It's okay," Eric whispered back, turning to give him a soft kiss. Then he yawned. He tried to stifle it, but he couldn't, and of course it was the huge kind that made his jaw pop.

Collin yawned too. "Why are those contagious?" he asked.

"I don't know. It's not something they teach us paramedics." He looked over at the fireplace. It was mostly out, and he'd remembered to put the screen in front of it. Truth was, he hardly ever used it, but tonight he'd built up a fire and then banked it before going on his Collin hunt. And yes, he could admit to himself it was totally in the hope that he'd have Collin to bring home with him. "Go to sleep, Sweet Boy."

"'Kay." Collin sounded halfway there already.

Chapter 16

F or the second morning in a row, Collin's phone woke him up.
For the second morning in a row, Collin tried and failed to
ignore it. "Sweartagod, if something else burned down or blew up, I
don't fucking care."

"Heh." Eric sounded mostly asleep still.

The dumb thing dinged once more. A text. He could deal with
texting. He couldn't deal with a phone call. Especially not one from
Monty, whom he absolutely had to call today. It was completely unlike
him to not call his uncle immediately and face the consequences once
something happened.

Well, he'd like to think it was unlike him, but he'd done it, hadn't
he? Or rather, he hadn't done it.

The phone dinged again.

Eric rolled over onto his back and snored once.

Shit. Collin scooted to the edge of the bed and peered over,
hoping his jeans were within easy reach. They were. He felt around in
the pockets until he found the phone, turning it on to find out who
had texted him.

Are you alive?

Oops. He'd totally forgotten to check in with Toby, something
they always did if either of them went home with guys they didn't
know.

*I'm hoping for your sake that, should you be dead, it's due to truly
earth-shattering, breath-stealing (literally) sex and not your grisly
murder.*

Well, he had the sex right.

*I'm beginning to worry that you've become the breakfast of champion
firefighters.*

I'm alive, Collin texted back. *And I'm about to have a firefighter
paramedic for breakfast.*

Ah, good to know you survived. And remember, you can perform the Heimlich maneuver on yourself should you get something stuck in your throat.

Thank you for thinking of me.

Is he big enough that choking is a concern?

Nice chatting with you, Toby.

sigh

Collin smirked at his phone and set it on top of his jeans. He turned his head, settling his cheek on his wrist and looking at Eric, still asleep next to him.

Toby would try to get details about sex with Eric later, but for now he'd been thwarted. Or rather, he'd respected the fact that Collin was about to get it again and not intrude. But he'd want details at some point. It was a little game they played. Usually, Collin broke down eventually and told Toby what he wanted to know.

But he wouldn't be sharing any stories of Eric with Toby. Collin rolled over so he was right next to Eric and kissed his shoulder. Eric woke up enough to make the rumbly noise and roll to face him, throwing an arm over Collin's middle. Collin closed his eyes and settled in to go back to sleep.

But the text from Toby kept replaying in his head. Not the actual message, per se, but the reminder that he had a whole world of responsibility outside of this bubble of naked tranquility.

He needed to call Monty.

Oh God, he didn't want to face that reality right now.

Better to face reality now than for reality to come looking for you.

How long could he reasonably make it without someone else telling Monty what had happened? Even Eric was a reminder of the fact that some alumni lived in the local area, and would hear the news sooner or later. What if one of them told Monty? The *Eugene Register-Guard* was a daily paper; the fire would have already been reported in it, and the bomb would probably be a lead story today. The paper was published online, too. Any TAG alumni the world over could find out about the fire and bomb just by deciding he needed to know what was going on at his old college stomping grounds and doing an internet search.

Collin scrunched his eyes, knowing he had to open them, climb out of bed, and call Monty, but wanting those few extra seconds of this. Peace and the unfamiliar sense of contentment lying next to Eric gave him.

Then he took a few more seconds of it.

But finally, he had to face it. The music or whatever.

He forced his eyes open. Eric lay just in front of his face, lips parted, breathing evenly, his arm heavy on Collin's waist. Collin's heart lurched toward him, trying to escape his chest and snuggle in under Eric's chin. He didn't think it was simply because it preferred staying in bed with this man to getting up and calling that other one.

And oh, ick, he'd just drawn a parallel between his uncle and the guy who'd fucked him half the night.

The sooner I deal with this phone call, the sooner I can come back to bed. He forced himself up before he could think about it anymore, slipping out from under Eric's arm. He grabbed his phone and the blanket from the foot of the bed (now on the floor), then went out to sit on the stairs. He was tempted to poke around Eric's house, but it would just be another way of distracting himself. Instead, he stopped halfway down the stairs and sat, purposely not looking out over Eric's living room.

He stared at his phone a few seconds before he called.

Of course the man answered on the second ring.

"Hi Uncle Monty," Collin began. Sounded normal. He took a breath to say more.

Monty beat him to it. "Ah, Collin. How was your meeting with Sparky?"

Collin blinked. He'd forgotten all about that. "Oh. Um, he cancelled at the last minute."

"He did?" Monty's voice rose, as if he couldn't believe Donaldson's gall.

"Yes, sir. He called at about six on Saturday and left me a message saying something had come up but he'd be back in Oregon in a month or so."

"That's odd. He was so eager to meet with you."

"He was?"

"Mmm, yes. Oh well, no matter. I'm sure you'll connect with him soon."

Collin understood the implied message there: he was to contact Sparky Donaldson at his earliest convenience and establish some kind of rapport or something. He stifled a sigh and added it to his mental to-do list.

"Listen, Uncle Monty, I'm afraid I have some bad news . . ."

"Well, what is it?"

Collin squeezed his eyes shut and spit it out. "Theta Alpha Gamma House burned down."

"What? Burned down?"

"Okay, it didn't burn down, per se. Really only the basement was actually on fire. It turns out we had a sprinkler system on the upper floors. Although, there is some smoke and water damage in the rest of the house and w—"

"When did this happen?" Monty barked.

Shit, shit, shit. The question he'd dreaded. "Um, Friday morning, sir."

"Friday? And you're just calling me now?"

"It's just that I was distracted Friday because one of the guys fell and broke his leg pretty badly when the main staircase was damaged and then the fire and dealing with Facilities and getting my—"

"The main staircase? I thought you said the fire was confined to the basement."

"Oh, it was." Collin nodded for emphasis. "But when the hot-water heater took off, it smashed right through the basement ceiling and then took a chunk out of the stairs."

The long pause after that didn't bode well.

"Hot-water heater?" Monty sounded too controlled. Another thing that didn't bode well.

Collin took a breath and consciously relaxed his shoulders. "Something caused it to overheat, possibly the fire, and its safety mechanisms failed for some reason. When the pressure became too much, it took off like a rocket."

"This is ridiculous," Monty said. "Collin, please explain to me why you didn't call yesterday about this. It's going to require a fair amount of money to repair the frat, I imagine, and the insurance deductible is quite high. Is the structure even habitable?"

Collin cringed. "No, sir."

"I'm waiting for your explanation."

For a second, Collin felt like letting his inner twelve-year-old break down and cry so his Uncle Monty would pat his head and fix everything. But he knew exactly what kind of "fix" that would be, and that wasn't an option, so he squared his shoulders and said, "I didn't call you Saturday because of the bomb in the basement."

There was a very long silence. "The bomb," Monty finally said.

Collin swallowed. "Yes, sir."

"Was this a real and actual bomb?"

"Yes, sir. It was defused before it went off."

There was no freaking out, no dissecting of the incident. Instead, his uncle did what he always did. He focused on the meat of the matter. Monty's patronizing sigh clued Collin in to how things were about to go.

"I'm sorry your little experiment with equal rights turned out this way, son. I warned you about the potential for this happening when we allowed you to put that membership policy in place."

Allowed them? "Aren't you jumping to conclusions, sir? We don't know that the bomb and the fire are connected, or that the bomb was planted because of the membership policy. The police and fire department are still investigating."

Monty huffed—Collin could see his nostrils flaring in his mind—then cleared his throat. "Well, perhaps . . . You have a point, but I fail to see what else it could be."

Shit. The weakness in his argument. "There are some people who are very angry about a recent fencing team loss."

"Fencing?"

Good, he'd confused him. "Things are a little different than when you were here. Many people take fencing very seriously now." If one considered twelve "many." "And of course there are personal grudges. Um, our members tend to do very well with the ladies, after all." Okay, he was completely making shit up now. He probably needed to end this call. "Regardless, it seems to me we should hold off judgment until we know more."

Collin heard the familiar sound of the chair in Monty's study squeaking the way it did when he sat back, meaning he was mulling it over. It took him a minute to respond, and Collin held his breath the whole time. "All right, I can accept that. I'm going to have to inform the Alumni Association Executive Committee, but for now we'll hold off on taking any action until you find out more. But Collin, if it is the new membership policy, we'll have to do something."

Collin exhaled as silently as possible. He so didn't want to think about what "something" was, because the Alumni Association could really only do one thing to them. Instead, he forced confidence into his voice. "Of course, sir. Thank you."

"I expect to hear from you with a progress report in two days."

It wasn't an unqualified success, but after Collin had hung up, he stared at the phone in his palm. He felt lighter. Some worry had been lifted from his shoulders, at least for two more days.

He took his phone and the blanket and headed back upstairs, carefully lifting the comforter and scooting close to Eric.

Completely relaxed now, Collin watched his firefighter paramedic sleep for a while. He had even more scruff on his face this morning, and most of it was gray. The now visible fuzz on his head was only about half-gray, and the rest looked dark brown, almost black. Collin hadn't ever realized how sexy gray hair could be, especially on a guy who had gone gray young. Like a daddy without the slightly droopy buttocks. Not that droopy buttocks didn't do it for some people.

And not that Collin needed a daddy.

Besides, daddies had gray pubic hair.

Ohmygod, does Eric have gray pubic hair? And why is that idea hot?

Investigation to answer both of those questions was needed.

Chapter 17

Eric woke up to find Collin under the blankets, kissing and licking his stomach. Dipping his tongue into Eric's navel and breathing on his skin. He smiled to himself and reached down to run fingers through Collin's hair. For a second Collin pushed into his hand, encouraging Eric to pet him. Then he returned to nuzzling Eric's skin, working his way down.

Eric had to swallow a couple of times before he could speak. "What're you doing, Sweet Boy?"

Totally a rhetorical question, but Collin answered it. "I'm inspecting you for gray pubes."

Eric laughed, but it ended on a gasp when Collin placed a sucking kiss on his dick. He gave Eric more of them, working his way along the underside of Eric's shaft until he was fully hard and beginning to ache.

"I found some," Collin murmured, and his breath made Eric shiver. He felt something—a finger—swirl through the sparse hair on his nuts. "Right here."

"Oh, man." Eric shoved the blanket to the side so he could see Collin's dark head between his legs.

Collin looked up, his hazel eyes smiling into Eric's. Eric realized he'd gripped Collin's hair, and he let go, but Collin followed his hand, rubbing his cheek into Eric's palm.

"So sweet," Eric whispered.

Collin kissed the base of Eric's thumb, and it sent a weird thrill straight from his lips to Eric's dick, making it flex in that way penises did when they wanted attention. Collin turned his smile to it, wrapping his fingers around the base.

Then he looked up into Eric's eyes again and sucked Eric's dick into his mouth.

Collin took his time, making Eric crazy for long minutes, until Eric gripped Collin tightly and shoved his hips up and his dick into Collin's heat. "Oh Christ, I'm gonna come."

Collin groaned around him, which sounded like begging to Eric, and his body spasmed against Eric's leg. God, he was jerking himself while Eric fucked his mouth. That was too much. Eric rammed into him while shoving Collin's head down, holding him there while he emptied his nuts into Collin's mouth. He could feel Collin's throat work as he swallowed, and it sent shocks from Eric's ass out through his dick. Shock waves he swore he could feel ripple through Collin, traveling deep into the center of him.

He collapsed, panting and trying to unkink his knuckles from Collin's head. Collin gentled his sucking, but he didn't let go, not until Eric's dick had gone soft and Eric's hands stroked his hair instead of trying to yank it out by the roots. Then Collin laid his head on Eric's thigh and sighed. It sounded like a happy sigh.

Eric *mmm*ed in his throat, because that seemed like the best way to tell Collin how he felt. Well, that and his hand still petting Collin's head. "C'mere, Sweet Thing," he whispered. Collin propped his chin on Eric's hip, smiling at him a few seconds before crawling up his body to settle on his chest. When Eric shifted to be a little closer, his leg brushed the wet spot on the sheets, and just that evidence of Collin coming while blowing him—even though he'd already known—sent waves of feeling through him. Half-physical and half-emotional. He wrapped his arms around his boy and kissed his forehead.

"Was that like your dream?" Collin murmured.

"It was better." He almost didn't add what else he was thinking, but it forced itself out. "Because it was the real you."

Collin smiled wider against his shoulder, then kissed it, pressing his lips against him for a long second.

ΘΑΓ

"I called my uncle this morning," Collin said after a while, breaking the comfortable silence.

"Yeah?" His sweet thing seemed unaccountably concerned about this uncle. "So you broke the news?"

Collin nodded, fingers flexing a second where they rested on Eric, then relaxing again.

Eric stroked his back in long, soothing passes. Well, he hoped they were soothing. "How did he take it?"

Collin rubbed his cheek against Eric's chest, almost as if he were trying to burrow in. "It wasn't good. He's threatening to take away some of the frat's money."

Eric jerked, totally surprised, jostling Collin. "What? Why would he do that?" Fuck, was Collin's uncle some huge contributor to TAG or something?

Collin shrugged, his shoulder bumping into the underside of Eric's arm. "Before, when I said some of the alumni don't like the membership policy, well, he's one of them."

"So, he thinks this fire and the bomb are because of the membership policy?"

Collin nodded. Eric waited. There had to be more to this story, but Collin didn't say anything else. After a few seconds, he tried to hide his sigh—maybe he thought he could tell Collin almost anything already, but that didn't mean Collin felt that way. They'd only met two days ago. He kissed Collin's hair and tried to swallow down his curiosity.

"Did I tell you he's president of the Alumni Association?" Collin asked, twirling some of Eric's chest hair.

He'd wanted to know more, but when Collin said that, Eric got a weird, itchy feeling between his shoulder blades. "You didn't." He couldn't quite put his finger on why that bugged him. "So that's the money he's going to cut off? Alumni funds?"

"Uh-huh. And he has a lot of influence, because he's not only the president, he's also one of the bigger contributors." Collin turned his head, resting his chin on Eric's chest and meeting his eyes. "He's an olive oil importer. Sometimes I tell people that he imports oil, and they think he's a sheikh or something, but he's really just a guy who brings in cooking oil from Europe. It's gourmet oil, but it's not petroleum." Collin smiled at him.

Eric couldn't smile back. He could even feel the look on his face—wrinkled brow and a frown, his neck straining to lift him up enough to see Collin more clearly. The itch between his shoulder blades had become a large mass of unease. "Olive oil?"

Collin raised his head, more alert now. "Yeah."

"Is your uncle J.M. Montes?"

Collin jerked his head back. "You know him?"

Crap. Eric dropped his head back onto the pillow. "He was a senior my freshman year."

Collin sat up, pulling the blanket around his shoulders. "I'm getting the feeling you guys weren't friends."

He had to tell the truth, at least the basic details. "He didn't really like me. And I can't say I liked him much in return. He thought I wasn't 'TAG material.'" Then he held his breath, because there were so many things Collin could say that he absolutely knew he didn't want to hear. Things like, "It doesn't really matter, does it? We just hooked up once," or "Too bad, because maybe we could have had something if you didn't hate my family."

But instead Collin asked, "Is this a big problem for you?"

Eric lifted a finger and traced around Collin's ear. "Um, not really. It's just, I'd like to see you again, but if you're really close to your uncle . . ."

Collin looked away a few seconds, then back. "I'm close to him, but that doesn't have to mean I can't see you again. You knew him fifteen years ago, right? You're probably both different people now." When Eric didn't answer right away, Collin added, "Unless there was more to it?"

Eric shook his head. There *wasn't*, not really. Nothing that meant anything now. "It's not a big problem for me. I don't know about how your uncle will see it, though."

Collin blew out a short breath. "Since he doesn't even know I'm gay yet, I don't know how that could be a problem anytime soon." He worried his lip before adding. "We don't know what's going to happen between us anyway, right?"

"Right." Eric nodded. "Let's just see how things go and we'll deal if stuff comes up."

Collin smiled, his eyes shining and his body relaxing, leaning toward Eric. So Eric pulled him down until he could brush his lips against Collin's and start kissing him, doing it the long, slow way. Soft kisses at first, but he couldn't help but get more demanding, until he had Collin across his chest again and was holding his sweet thing's head between his hands. Controlling how his mouth fit against Eric's, and how deeply Eric could kiss him. He shifted his grip to Collin's hips, pulling Collin on top of him, until Sweet Thing straddled his groin.

Collin crouched over him, asking between kisses, "Are we going to have another therapy session?"

Eric caressed Collin's ass cheeks, kneading the muscles. "Yeah. You remember where I keep the condoms?"

Collin smiled before pushing up on his knees and reaching for the bedside table. Looked like he didn't plan on letting J.M. put a damper on things, either.

Chapter 18

After a lengthy, intense ride—the kind of fuck that should come with its own soundtrack—Collin lay on Eric's luxuriously hairy chest, feeling way less stressed than he had in a long time. At least since his sophomore year. Eric lay half-asleep under him while Collin drifted in his very happy place. He sighed, and Eric's hand stroked his back in response, stilling again after a few seconds.

Coming home with this man had done wonders for his tension. Not even the stuff about Eric knowing but not really liking Monty was a big stressor. His mother hadn't much liked Monty his whole life, and he'd dealt with that fine.

Nothing's going to ruin my morning.

Then his damn phone rang again. "Fucking hell."

Eric rumbled inquiringly at him. Collin ignored the phone as best he could, but every ring increased his anxiety a drop or two, undoing the effect of his last orgasm. Eric seemed to feel his tension, because he reached up to rub Collin's neck. Thank God, his stupid cell only rang four times before going to voice mail. He sighed after the last one and felt his muscles loosen up again under Eric's fingers.

Riiiing. "Fuck. My. Life." He rolled over and reached down to answer the damned thing. Only Kyle would call twice in a row. So, of course his name popped up on the screen—confirmation of who it was made Collin's heart sink. Why couldn't it have been a persistent wrong number? Kyle represented reality—again—and Collin didn't know if he was ready to go back to that place.

"Hello," he snapped, rolling onto his back and covering his eyes with his hand.

"Did I wake you up? It's nearly eleven."

"I'm still in bed."

"With that guy?"

Collin flung his arm off his face to stare at the ceiling. "What guy would that be?"

"Are you with the firefighter Ashley said you went home with last night?"

"How the hell does Ashley know about that?"

"Duh. Toby told Brad and Brad told her."

Okay, he was so going to ignore that for now. Although he might rather deal with bitching out his gossipy friends than with what he had to do next. With a sense of dread, he said to Kyle, "Since you know about that and presumably wouldn't disturb me unless it was important, I suppose you're calling because you have news."

Kyle did have news. The college had found them temporary housing, and it was even a decent deal that wouldn't drain their reserves too fast. "It's the third floor of a residence hall. They're renovating the first and second floors, mostly cosmetic stuff so there isn't any reason we can't live on the third floor. Since the building was going to be shut down anyway, the college is basically only asking we pay utilities."

"Yay. We're moving back into the dorms." Collin twirled one finger in the air, and Eric huffed next to him. Collin looked over and he was smirking.

He stuck out his tongue.

Eric smiled broadly. "Anytime, Sweet Thing."

"You are with that guy!" Kyle crowed, as if he'd solved some kind of mystery. Please. Only straight guys picked up someone in a bar and *didn't* get laid.

Kyle was relatively easy to distract, fortunately. "Are you calling me to ask for help getting ahold of everyone else?"

"Nope. It's under control."

Collin pulled the phone away from his ear and stared at it a second. Kyle had dealt with this all by himself? Carefully, he brought his cell close enough to ask, "It is?"

"Yep, Ashley's been helping me. We're almost done, and Tank's the only real problem."

"Oh." Collin's brain scrambled to catch up. "Um, he's not at Penny's?"

"I didn't have a chance to tell you—since, you know, you've been incommunicado and all with your firefighter—he had some kind of family emergency and had to fly home to Massachusetts Friday night."

Ha! "Okay, in point of fact, I didn't go home with my firefighter until Saturday night."

Eric had been sitting up, as if about to get out of bed, but at that comment he looked at Collin over his shoulder, smile lines crinkling. It made Collin feel strangely bashful, until Eric reached out and took Collin's hand, bringing it to his mouth and kissing Collin's palm. *Gah*, stuff like that made his heart beat funny.

Eric lay back down on his side, facing Collin, so Collin rolled toward him, holding his cell with his shoulder so he could rub Eric's neck and head. Rubbing behind his ears made him rumble like a purring cat.

Oh, that so deserved a kiss.

"Collin, are you listening to me?" The voice in his ear startled him, and for a split second he was shocked to find himself on the phone with someone. *Oh, Kyle. Shit.*

"Not really." He sighed, stroking Eric's cheekbone with his thumb. Eric smiled at him, kissed his nose and sat up again, this time making it all the way out of bed.

Naked.

Yummy. And oh God, he had the smallest of love handles on his lower back. That was surprisingly hot. Collin needed to grasp those and hang on for the ride sometime very soon. He'd never fully appreciated the char—

"Collin! Jesus, how big is this guy's dick?"

Collin shot up. "*What*? What did you say?" He could hear what sounded like Ashley laughing in the background. "Seriously Kyle, I never want to hear those words come out of your mouth again."

"Neither do I," Kyle said. "So maybe, if you'd listen to me, I wouldn't have to say shit like that."

God, he really had horrible phone manners, didn't he? "Sorry. I'm paying attention. Go."

"Okay. I'm emailing you a campus map with the location of the frat—"

"The dorm."

"—marked on it, and when you get here we have to meet with Jules and Plant and refigure the budget."

"I'm not on the Exec Committee, why am I meeting with all the TAG officers?"

"Dude, you know you're like the fourth officer, like a shadow president or something. Don't play stupid."

I've been fucked stupid. He came ridiculously close to saying it. But sharing that with Kyle would be worse than telling Toby. At least he knew Toby wouldn't tell anyone else. Except Toby'd already told Brad about Eric . . . Shit, all his friends were gossips who took an unhealthy interest in his sex life. None of them could be trusted.

Wait, what were they talking about? "Um, okay," he said, agreeing to whatever and hoping agreement was called for.

"You aren't really listening to me again, are you?"

"Yeah, not so much." Collin looked up to see Eric standing in the doorway of another room, the edge of a white counter and the lip of a toilet behind him.

"Shower?" Eric mouthed, lifting his eyebrows.

Collin nodded. "Um, Kyle, I have to go now."

"I bet you do." He had a very sardonic note to his voice. Collin frowned at the phone.

"I'll be home—um, there, soon." Wherever "there" was.

"Okay, dude. Maybe I'll have better luck keeping your attention when you aren't with your firefighter."

"He's actually a firefighter paramedic," Collin said, then nearly slapped himself in the forehead. That was important to Kyle why?

"Uh-huh. Later, dude."

Collin hung up the phone and watched Eric walk toward him, still very naked. "You going to take a shower with me?"

"Just a shower?"

Eric reached the bed and held out his hand. "Well, you got to know my dick up close and personal earlier, I'd like the chance to get to know yours better."

Collin took Eric's hand and crawled out of bed, until they stood face-to-face and chest-to-chest, then slid his arms around his firefighter paramedic. "It expressed a similar desire," Collin whispered.

Eric grinned at him. "Good. After all, I need to be sure my sweet young thang is tasty everywhere, don't I?"

Eric led him into the bathroom by the hand, started the water and pulled Collin in, then pushed him against the wall and sucked him off while stroking himself. It was perfect; hot water and hot mouth and hot guy whom Collin really, really liked, who liked him back. A guy who wanted Collin's cum on his tongue just to find out how Collin tasted.

After Collin had come, Eric stood up and pressed his hard cock into Collin's stomach, saying, "Let me show you how sweet you are." Then Eric kissed his taste into him while Collin squeezed Eric's ass and urged him along until he came all over Collin's belly.

He felt sinuous and sexy and completely sated, wrapping his arms around Eric's neck and holding on tightly. "I've never been into having cum all over me, but yours is different. I might bathe in it if I could."

Eric pulled his head back far enough to look at him, squinting one eye.

"Okay, probably not, but it sounded good for a second."

Eric laughed and leaned forward to bite his neck gently, then rub his whiskers under Collin's jaw, catching them against Collin's own. "C'mon, Sweet Thing." He pulled Collin away from the wall and fully into the spray.

"This has been the best therapy session ever," he said while Eric rubbed suds on his front, turning him to rinse them off. Collin rubbed his back against Eric's chest. "I think I unloaded a year's worth of tension in the last twelve hours."

"So, I'm just therapeutic?"

Shit. What had he just implied? He grabbed Eric's hand—the non-soapy one—and kissed it, then held it to his chest. "No, that's just a bonus. I had a lot of . . ." Collin tried to find the word, but only one applied. "You know, anxiety. You helped me."

Eric rubbed soap onto his shoulders, massaging the muscles as if he wanted Collin to relax even more. "You had a lot of stuff happen in the last few days."

Collin huffed. "And that was on top of my normal stress load."

Eric turned him again, so they faced each other. His hands kneaded Collin's back muscles. "Like what?"

Collin stole the soap from Eric and rubbed it on Eric's chest while he spoke. "Just school and the frat and the Alumni Association and, I don't know, stuff." He shrugged, a little worried about bringing it up. "My uncle."

"Is he hard on you?"

Collin looked up and got caught in Eric's gaze. He had such great eyes. Gray with a dark blue rim around the edge and right next to the pupil. They were soulful—Collin had never figured out what that meant before, but he knew now.

"We don't have to talk about him if you don't want," Eric said. "I'd understand." He looked away.

Collin placed his hand on Eric's jaw to get his attention, then stretched up for a quick kiss. "He just puts a lot of pressure on me. Like, Saturday he expected me to play golf at seven in the morning with an alumnus. He reserved a tee time and everything."

Eric snorted. "Seriously? Why?"

"Seriously. I'm the liaison to the Alumni Association and this guy is supposed to help me plan the TAG Alumni Weekend." Wow, he could really work up some lather on Eric's chest fur. He made little peaks of hair and suds over Eric's nipples, then moved down to wash his abdomen.

"So you went out and played golf before showing up to the bomb scene?"

"No." He snuck a soapy finger into Eric's belly button, twisting it until Eric jerked back, laughing. "Sparky called and cancelled."

"The guy's name is Sparky?"

"Yeah. Look, I can make a little ridge out of your happy trail."

Eric grinned. "Are you playing or washing me?"

"A little of both. You're fun to play with."

"So are you, but the water's starting to get cold."

Hair washed, out of the shower and toweled off, Collin realized he had to get dressed.

Naked fun time's over. For now.

He found his various articles of clothing in their various places, and he'd just managed to untangle his T-shirt enough to pull it on when he heard a clicking noise behind him. He looked over his shoulder to see Eric standing across the room with a camera pointed at him.

"Did you just take a picture of me?"

Eric took another one. "Is that all right?"

"Well, I don't think you just captured my soul with your evil technology . . . but why are you taking pictures of me?" Was this some weird way he recorded his hookups? In spite of Eric saying he wanted to see Collin again, Collin had no problem imagining his photo hanging on some wall, "54" written in sharpie on the corner, surrounded by the pictures of fifty-three other guys.

Eric lowered the camera and shrugged, his cheeks slowly turning red. *Hmmm.* Collin yanked the shirt over his head, then did up his jeans. "Are you blushing?" He had to see something that endearing up close. Eric found something on his camera that needed fiddling with, avoiding Collin's eyes as he walked over. "Eric?"

"It's a hobby."

Collin's breath hitched and he stopped a few feet away. "Taking pictures of guys you've fucked?" Like trophies or something? The tension he'd worked away all night started creeping back into his muscles.

"Huh? No. Just taking pictures."

The sudden tension in his shoulders deserted him. "Oh, so you photograph, like . . ." *What?*

Eric quirked his half smile. "Stuff. Whatever I find that I like. Whatever catches my attention."

His heart banged once against his sternum. "So I guess I caught your attention?"

Eric reached out, taking Collin's hand and pulling him forward. "Yeah. You have my full attention."

Collin took a breath, ready to admit his sin. "Um, I kind of lied to you."

Eric's hand stopped stroking his arm. "How, exactly?"

"I don't know how to cook." He chewed on his lip for a second, until he made himself stop.

Eric frowned. He didn't seem to be making the connection.

Just when Collin was about to explain further, Eric's brows rose. "You can't make me breakfast, you mean." He didn't look particularly annoyed.

"No."

Eric gripped the back of his neck, looking into his eyes a long moment. "Next time, then."

Collin was so caught in Eric's gaze he couldn't avoid asking the question. "Next time when?"

"Next weekend. If you want to come over."

"Yes, please."

Chapter 19

"**O**hthankgod," Collin said suddenly. Eric looked up in time to see Collin's body sag, like all the strength had left his muscles. He stood, one sock on and the other in his hand. "What's wrong?" Collin smiled. "My phone died."

"And that's a good thing?" He sat back down on the bed to finish with the sock thing.

"If my phone's dead, no one can call me, text me, or email me. Except, shit. I didn't get the map Kyle sent me showing the location of the new 'frat.'"

This time when Eric stood up, he was fully socked. "You can get your email on my computer. Print it out and I'll get you there." He reached out and laced his fingers in between Collin's, ready to head downstairs.

Collin bit his lip, looking not quite ready to move. He did it in a funny way, worrying the inside of his bottom lip with his teeth. Someone had to be paying close attention to even realize he'd done it. "I could call Toby. You don't have to drive me all the way to Calapooya. I mean, I'd have to borrow your phone to do it, but I'm sure he'd pick me up."

Eric squeezed his hand. "I brought you out here, I should take you back." And to be honest—with himself at least—he didn't like the idea of some other guy, no matter what their relationship, picking Collin up at his place. It made him feel territorial, and not just because this was his house. "Whenever you need to go."

Collin glanced down at their hands, working at his lip some more. "I should probably go soon. It sounded like Kyle needed me, kind of. And I have homework and stuff that I haven't done all weekend. My car's at Toby's. If you don't mind dropping me there . . ." He looked at Eric questioningly, as if Eric might tell him no.

Not happening. "Of course I'll take you there." He cupped Collin's cheek, bringing him closer for a kiss. While it made him snarly to think of Toby coming here to get Collin, the reverse wasn't true. He liked the idea of Toby knowing he was willing to take Collin home. Looking out his window and seeing Collin in Eric's car. Maybe showering had been a bad idea. If they hadn't, Collin wouldn't have washed Eric's spunk off of him, and maybe other guys' primordial brains would pick up the scent and know to keep away.

Fuck, dude, listen to yourself.

"Let's go downstairs and I'll make you breakfast while you check your email." He tugged on Collin's hand to get him moving.

Eric had it so bad. He was in his mid-thirties and he was a total fool for a twenty-one-year-old guy he barely knew who could do much better than him. Hopefully, Collin wouldn't figure that out anytime soon.

Internally shaking his head at himself, he led Collin into the room he used as an office. It was supposed to be a bedroom, but the first thing Eric had done when he'd bought this place was finish the attic space and turn one bedroom into his studio and the other into this office. "Here, let me put in the password and you can do whatever." He moved out of the way of the screen so Collin could sit down. "Hey, you aren't a vegetarian or anything, are you?"

Collin laughed. "No way. I like meat." He winked, making a big show of it, and Eric laughed with him.

"Be careful or I'll think you're coming on to me and we'll never leave."

Collin sighed. "That'd be so nice."

He didn't know how to answer that, so he rubbed a hand across Collin's back and left the room.

Eric had almost finished the omelet—well, maybe it would be better to call it a scramble—when Collin walked in, kissed the back of his neck, and found the coffee cup he'd filled for him.

"Thank you," he said, coming for another kiss. This time Eric turned around and gave him a proper one.

Eric turned back to the stove, and Collin slipped an arm around him, silently watching. Or at least he thought Collin was watching him, until his sweet thing said, "You have chickens."

Eric twisted his head around to see Collin looking over his shoulder, blinking out the window.

"Yeah, they helped make breakfast. Did you print out the map?"

He felt Collin's forehead rest on his back for a few seconds. "Yeah. And I sent an email to that guy my Uncle Monty wanted me to play golf with, Sparky Donaldson. Guess what his first name is."

"Sputnik." Eric started turning over the eggs, a section at a time.

Collin snorted and bit him gently through his shirt. "Donald."

"Seriously? Donald Donaldson?"

"Yep."

"A name like that's almost child abuse."

"I know. What the hell are those birds doing?"

Eric threw cheese on top of the scramble and covered it. He shifted places so he was standing behind Collin, watching the chickens too. The dumb fowl were doing that thing they did where they found a patch of dirt and rolled around in it. "They're fluffing dirt under their feathers. I can't remember why they do that, but they sure as hell like it." Simple pleasures for simpleminded creatures.

Speaking of simple pleasures, Collin's jeans hung low in the back and his tiny purple briefs peeked out. Eric kissed the base of his neck as a sort of proxy for kissing Collin's spine down there. Collin wiggled and pressed back into him. How much more would he wiggle if Eric pulled down his briefs and dropped to his knees to—

Riiiiing.

"That can't be mine," Collin said, starting to turn.

Eric held him tightly so he couldn't move. "It's mine. I have to at least see who it is."

"'Kay." Collin rubbed his head into Eric's jaw, and Eric reluctantly let go of him to go see who was calling.

The fire department number blinked on the screen when he looked. Crap, he had to answer it. He hit "talk" while turning off the burner under the eggs. "What?"

"Did you wake up on the wrong side of the bed this morning? Well, I don't give a fuck if you did, because I'm working through my weekend, so you can just take your damned attitude and stuff it u—"

"Hello there, Fire Marshal Taggert." Eric grinned, in a better mood now that he knew someone out there was in a worse one. He pulled plates and forks out and set them on the counter. "To what do I owe the honor?" He used hand gestures to indicate Collin should start eating.

"Shut up," Mike grumbled. Eric laughed at him. "Dammit, Dix, you're annoying." Collin hadn't started eating; hadn't even dished himself any eggs.

"Yeah, you're one to talk." Eric covered the phone with his hand and whispered to Collin, "It'll get cold." Then he dished them each some.

Mike sighed. "Guess I did kinda get huffy on you."

"A little. It's okay. What can I do for you?" He leaned his butt against the kitchen counter and started eating. Mike could just live with chewing noises in his ear.

"Did you get any pictures of that hot-water heater on the porch of that frat house the other day?"

"Huh?" It was the best he could do with egg in his mouth.

"If you did, I need them, because the damn thing's gone missing."

Eric swallowed. "Missing? Why the fuck would anyone take a dead hot-water heater?" Collin turned to him, eyes wide. Crap, he needed to be careful. He might not be allowed to tell Collin. Technically.

"I dunno, but this case gets weirder and weirder. When I went back this morning to finish my investigation, the fucking thing was gone. The porch steps were splintered up and bashed in from someone dragging it down them—they didn't carry that sucker. They got it in a vehicle though, 'cause the trail ends at the street. Detective Homes found a possible break and enter too. And the fire's definitely arson unless those frat boys have been scraping the potassium nitrate off of sparklers in their free time and keeping a cache of it under the hot-water heater along with some fuel-soaked papers."

He swallowed his mouthful hastily. "Sparklers? What the hell?" Collin stood in front of him, looking as if he'd perk his ears if physically possible.

"That sound like a frat stunt to you?"

Eric snorted. "Seems unlikely."

"Seems pretty damned smart to me. You can buy the stuff lots of place without even providing your name. It's used for curing meat too. Shit, the arsonist could have made it himself in his kitchen if he wanted."

Eric gave up on his eggs for the moment, setting them on the counter. "Did you find an ignition source?" Collin rubbed his forehead and set his eggs next to Eric's.

"Yeah, that one was easy. This guy didn't even try and hide that, had one of those remote igniters for fireworks you can buy at any big box store."

"You're fucking kidding me."

"Means he had to be within 120 feet to start that puppy up, though." Collin covered his mouth, looking more shocked. Could he hear Mike?

"Have you told the involved parties about any of this yet?" Because one of them was pretty well informed already.

"That's my next phone call. We need to interview all those boys. Dammit, that's going to take forever. I'm not going to have a social life for weeks."

Phew. "Why, Mike, I wasn't aware you *had* a social life."

"Shut up and bring me those goddamned photos when you come in tomorrow morning."

"Yes, sir, Mister Fire Marshal, sir."

"You smart-ass. Just do what I asked."

"I will. See you tomorrow."

After he'd hung up, he and Collin stood there looking at each other for a few seconds. "How much of that did you hear?" he asked.

"I heard how it was started, what fuel they used—not that I can remember—and that someone had to be within 120 feet to do it. So it was arson."

"Yeah."

"And the hot-water heater?"

"It's been dragged off."

Collin stared off into space a second. "I need to go back to the frat," he said.

Chapter 20

C ollin had been nervous on his way to Eric's last night, and he was nervous now on his way back, but otherwise the two trips weren't similar in any way. Well, except that Eric's hand was on his leg again. Last night—which seemed like a few days ago in some ways—it had made him nervous in that apprehensive, skin-buzzing, I'm-about-to-get-some kind of way. Now Eric's hand reminded him that yes, he'd gotten some, but he'd also gotten something more, and his nerves needed to know what would happen next to prepare for it.

Something in his chest (likely his heart) felt warm and languid. He'd had great sex before, and it hadn't ever affected his internal organs like this. Was it possible for him to develop feelings for someone he'd only met a couple of days ago? How did this work? He'd never even really had a boyfriend, and he sort of thought they came in, like, beginner varieties at first.

Ohmygod, I thought the "B" word about Eric.

Clearly, these were uncharted waters for him; he didn't have a clue what exactly he'd entered into with Eric. He stared out the window thinking as they drove back into town, passing the bare trees and farmland that surrounded Calapooya in January. Not that the trees moved away in the summer, but they did grow leaves. The farmland didn't look a lot different then; the vegetation just grew taller. Western Oregon was green almost year round, unless it snowed, and it rarely snowed, and speaking of rarely, he'd never had a boyfriend.

"You're quiet," Eric said, making Collin start. Just a tiny bit, hopefully not enough for Eric to notice. "'Course I guess I don't really know if that's unusual for you."

Oh well, that helped, didn't it? "I'm just," Collin took a deep breath. "I'm nervous."

"About the frat?"

He laughed weakly. "No, not that."

Eric didn't answer right away, and Collin could feel his tension in the air, filling the car. "Is it about your uncle? You never finished telling me about his phone call, because, you know, we got sidetracked."

Collin looked over at Eric, grinning because he remembered what had happened to sidetrack them, but Eric's neck muscles were tensed up. *Oh yeah*. He'd forgotten the other thing that had sidetracked them first—about how Eric knew Monty. Collin took a deep breath. "I know Monty can be a jerk sometimes, but he's always been good to me, and he took over for my father in some ways. I love him, even though I can see why others might not like him." Strangely, talking about Monty seemed to relax him. His back touched the seat for the first time since he'd gotten in Eric's car this morning. Or afternoon, actually. They'd slept longer than he'd thought.

Eric glanced at him, and Collin thought his shoulders had dropped a bit, as if he'd relaxed also. "You don't need to explain it to me, it's fine. He's your family." He squeezed Collin's leg a second, like a mini-hug.

Collin caught himself chewing his lip again, but he didn't stop himself—it helped him sometimes. "I've been thinking, your freshman year was the same year my father died. Dad and Monty were close, and Mom always says he wasn't the same after that. Maybe he wouldn't be such a dick to you now."

Eric smiled at him, not quite getting his eyes into it, but at least trying. "Maybe I'll meet him again and we can find out."

Collin genuinely smiled, because even if Eric wasn't convinced, he'd be willing to fake getting along with Monty. Assuming things got serious between them.

"You gonna tell me about the rest of his phone call?"

Shit. He'd managed to forget it for a few seconds. "Well, I only have two days to start coughing up more information, or he'll take matters into his own hands."

Eric glanced over at him, brow furrowed. "He's not holding you somehow responsible for what happened, is he?"

Collin shifted in the seat so that he was angled more toward the driver's side. It made Eric's hand slide up his leg a bit. Collin only half noticed himself playing with Eric's fingers. "Kind of, I guess. He opposed the new membership policy because he was afraid it would affect Theta Alpha Gamma's reputation." Eric squeezed his leg tighter, and Collin interlaced their fingers and squeezed back. "I convinced him to support it, or at least not block it, by promising we'd deal with any repercussions, but I'm afraid he and I might have different ideas about what that means."

Eric didn't say anything a few seconds, one hand loose on the steering wheel and the other warm on Collin's thigh. "Okay, I getcha, but it doesn't necessarily follow that the fire or bombing reduces TAG's 'standing.' It could be one lone whackjob, not the whole campus, or even a small group."

Collin felt his eyes widen. "Oh my God, I didn't think of that. But I don't know if I can make that argument to him—he'll argue it's indicative of possible disrespect and cut off the frat anyway." For a second there he'd felt a flicker of hope, but by the time he was done speaking, it had died. "I just have to hold my position—that, until the investigation is done, we don't know anything for sure and they shouldn't take action."

"How much does the frat rely on what it gets from the Alumni Association?"

"I don't know exact figures, but because TAG is such a small fraternity, we just don't take in enough per year in dues and living expenses to run, at least not the way we have been. If the association cut us off, we'd have to pretty severely cut back on our living expenses, or we'd have to hope someone gave us a major endowment so we could have the interest. Without that money, we're just a student co-op with a fancy name."

"What are the chances of an endowment?"

"Slim to none. The problem there is that TAG hasn't been around long enough to start seeing earlier members die off. No deaths, no inheritance gifts, etcetera."

"That sucks for you, not so much for the early members." Eric quirked that smile at him. "Okay, so basically you have to convince him there's a possibility that the arsonist has another motive for the crimes."

Collin nodded, staring out the front window. "Really, what else could it be? I'm not admitting that to him, but I don't think it's because of the recent fencing team loss."

Eric lifted Collin's hand, pulling it across the console to kiss his knuckles and then letting him settle back in his seat. "I should probably pay more attention to the alumni newsletter, huh?"

Collin squeezed Eric's fingers on his leg. "God, no. It's nice to know there are alumni who don't give a shit what we do and aren't going to meddle. Like this guy I was supposed to golf with yesterday morning, Sparky Donaldson? He doesn't support the membership policy. How long would it have taken him to steer the conversation away from Alumni Weekend and start pressuring me about that? Oh, turn right at the next intersection."

"I don't know how you deal with all this, Sweet Thing. When I was in the frat, I showed up for the parties, moved things the guys like J.M. told me to move, and played football."

"Mmm, football."

Eric grinned over at him. "You like football?"

"I like football *players*." They laughed together, and Collin had few perfect, transcendent seconds where he believed things could be fantastic with this guy, if he could relax enough to let them.

Then he looked out the window and realized they'd passed the last intersection to Toby's place, and reality slapped him in the face again. "Shit, you need to turn around, I wasn't paying attention and we missed the road."

Eric pulled off onto the shoulder, ready to make a U-turn, but he paused long enough to look over at Collin. "It's okay, I have nowhere better to be." Then he stretched himself across the car, leaning right into Collin's space, looking at him with those gray eyes and smelling like soap and shaving cream. He stopped less than a breath away, and Collin had to move the last millimeters to his lips.

Eric could mean he didn't have anything planned for today, and driving Collin back was preferable to, say, taking out the garbage, but as Collin kissed him, fingers on Eric's jaw, he knew Eric meant he wanted to be with him. More than anything else he could be doing today, Eric would rather be driving Collin home. Or still be naked and in bed with him.

Collin's nerves settled, and he managed to tell Eric how to get him to Toby's without any more weird moments from his nervous system. They sat in the car, parked next to Collin's, kissing for long minutes.

Eric dug fingers into the muscles on Collin's lower back, unknotting the few places that had managed to kink up again, until things got to the point where they needed to stop or find someplace less public.

Breathing heavily, keeping time with Collin's, Eric brought their foreheads together. He held Collin as close to him as he could with a console between them. "You're so easy."

Collin felt like a shard of ice had just slipped into his chest, right between his ribs. From some men he'd been with, it might have been a twisted sort of compliment, but not from Eric. He pulled his head away and tried that single-brow-arch thing. "Aren't most guys?"

Eric cupped the back of his head, making Collin feel somehow incredibly young. "That's not the kind of easy I meant. I meant it would be so easy to fall in love with you."

Collin froze, staring at the neck of Eric's shirt. What was he supposed to say to that? He tried to make it a joke. "No one's ever managed to before."

Eric traced Collin's upper lip with a finger before answering. "Maybe it's that it would be so easy for *me* to fall in love with you."

Oh God. All the ice in his chest melted, and he had to work to take his next breath, and to meet Eric's eyes.

"I'm not saying I'm in love with you. I'm saying if we continue to see each other I probably will be, sooner or later." He paused to lick his lip. "You might need to think about whether you want to see me again."

It was only when Collin took a deep breath that he realized he'd been cheating his lungs of air before. He had to swallow before he could speak. "Okay."

Eric kissed him once more, his thumbs stroking Collin's jaw, then he let go and leaned across Collin to open the door. "Bye, Sweet Boy."

Collin didn't go knocking on Toby's door because then he'd have to talk to Toby, and he didn't want to talk to anyone right now, not about anything, but most of all not about Eric.

And Toby would most definitely ask about Eric.

As furtively as possible, he unlocked his car, got in, and started it—none of which was very furtive. Toby's apartment was in one of those buildings that looked a bit like an old-fashioned rooming house, and it stood at the end of a pretty quiet cul-de-sac—if you could call the gravelly, grassy area in front of the building that—and of course Toby's window looked out over the parking area. But whatever. He left Toby's place driving slowly, trying to give himself time to think.

So . . . Eric didn't have the same uncertainty he had about whether he could develop feelings so fast for someone. *He said he could fall in love with me.* Reflexively, Collin's foot stomped on the brake. He checked the rearview mirror, but the road behind him was clear, thank God. It would really suck if his existential anxieties caused an accident. His other anxieties already had enough control over his life.

By the time he'd rolled through the first stop sign, he'd decided thinking was a bad idea. Thinking made his stomach buzz with nerves, and when his stomach wasn't buzzing, his secondary brain was remembering the sex and diverting the blood supply from his primary brain. What he really needed was to keep busy. He concentrated on driving, making it to campus in a few minutes and parking in the lot Kyle's map indicated was closest to the "frat." He still had to walk a few hundred yards to the brick dormitory they'd be living in for the foreseeable future.

It was pretty much what he'd expected. Something built in the seventies that boasted all the best features of institutional building design from that era.

In other words, it was fugly. Aluminum frame windows, boxy, utilitarian shape, and, worst of all, strange horizontal cantilevers between each story that hinted at balconies but didn't deliver. The tower at one end looked like it had arrow slits in it—that must be a stairwell. It had a steel door that opened at the base of it, and right in front of him, Collin saw the main entrance: glass double doors with a crooked vinyl banner hung over them that read "Temporary home of Tau Alpha Gamma."

Tau Alpha Gamma?

Kyle walked out the doors as Collin stood there trying to puzzle that out. "Like the sign?" he asked.

"No. Who made it?" Collin started toward him.

Kyle exhaled forcefully, puffing out his cheeks. "Housing. It's sort of a welcome gift."

"Some gift."

Kyle shrugged one shoulder.

"Don't worry, if someone from the Housing Office comes by, I'll pretend to be thankful and completely unaware they changed the name of the frat."

"I can't imagine you doing otherwise." Kyle squinted at him questioningly. Collin looked up at the sign again, to avoid the expression. After a second, Kyle did too. "How long do you think it will be before someone crosses it out and paints in 'Theta'?"

"Well, Ricky's in the hospital still, and Tank's out of town. Danny'll do it by evening."

"Remind me to tell him to use acrylic paint. It'll stick better."

Collin nodded.

"Where's your stuff?"

Huh? *Shit.* "It's all at Toby's house or the frat. I guess I'll have to get it if I want to have clean clothes to wear tomorrow." He leaned forward to see below his coat and inspect his jeans. They looked clean.

Kyle guessed what he was thinking. "Uh, no. You need to wear something other than those."

"What? Why?"

"Those are your 'fuck me' jeans. You can't wear those to class. Every time you sit down, everyone behind you will see clearly just how tiny your briefs probably are."

Collin blinked at him. "I find it really disturbing just how much you know about gay mating habits."

Kyle nodded. "Me too. Let's go inside."

About half the guys had shown up at the dorm and claimed their space. There was a bathroom with showers at each end of the hallway, and one big common area in the middle with a TV. Otherwise, it was nothing but a series of small cubicular bedrooms, each with two sorry-looking beds. "There's no kitchen." Of course there wouldn't be—it was a dorm.

Kyle shoved his hands into his pockets and avoided looking at him. "We're on the college meal plan. Our cafeteria is in Wendell Hall. And the laundry room is in the basement."

Collin took a deep breath. Then another. "Okay. I guess it can't be avoided, can it?"

Kyle screwed up his face and shook his head. Then he showed Collin to his room. It was at the end near the stairwell and close to a bathroom, but not right next to either. Collin appreciated it—less noise that way, thank God. "Do I have a roommate?"

"Not yet, and you might not have one at all. Most of the rest of the guys do." Kyle grinned and wagged his brows. "I don't, of course."

Collin snorted, in spite of knowing that the reason *he* didn't have a roommate was because of Kyle. They would have been roommates if Kyle weren't frat president and it was mostly why Collin hadn't had a roommate in TAG House.

"Well, thanks for that." He didn't have anything to unpack yet, so he just checked his cubicle out. "Will they let me in the frat to get some more stuff?"

"Yeah, there's a campus security guard there who'll let you in. They're guarding it because—oh shit, man, guess what happened?"

"The hot-water heater was stolen."

Kyle frowned at him. "How'd you hear that already? I haven't told Brad yet."

"Well..."

"Oooh, your firefighter." Kyle nodded sagely. "So you know it's arson too."

Collin nodded. "Weird, huh?"

"The insurance company won't settle until the investigation's complete, so we might be here a while."

Collin jerked his head around. "But what if they never find the perpetrator?"

Kyle shrugged tiredly. "They said, 'A possible settlement will be determined if such a situation arises.'"

"Fuck."

"Yeah."

"I can't believe this shit," Collin said, sitting on one of the beds. They were as uncomfortable as they looked.

Kyle exhaled and flopped down on the bed across from him. They discussed it awhile, not solving any mysteries and not trying to, just sort of working through what had happened. After a while, Danny peeked in. "There you are. Listen, dude, I can't take that sign out front any—"

"Use acrylic paint, it'll stick better to vinyl."

"Cool. Oh, hey, Plant just showed up and Jules is getting himself all, you know, dithery looking for you two."

Great. The meeting to determine how to budget the frat's limited resources was about to begin. "Oh, I forgot to tell you what Monty said," he told Kyle as they stood up.

Kyle waved him off. "Save it for the meeting."

Chapter 21

E verything that Collin needed to do had been done: he'd gone to the frat for more clothes—currently in a dryer in the basement—and the flash drives he'd need to transfer all his data when he bought a new laptop tomorrow; he'd lived through eating in the dining hall; he'd finished his homework (thank God it was only the second week of the term and he barely had any); and most importantly, he'd made it through the meeting with Kyle, Jules, and Plant.

Plant was a junior, and the past president Eduardo's little brother. It was so obvious he aspired to run for president next year. Overall he was an okay guy, just pompous. A lot like Eduardo, actually. Plant's real name was Fernando, but it had quickly gotten shortened to "Fern," which he'd objected to. Tank and Brad had then started calling him "Plant" as a substitute, and it had stuck. He didn't object again after that, he simply—and very obviously—resigned himself to it. It was kind of amusing to see his nostrils flare that very tiny bit whenever someone used it. His nostrils got a lot of exercise.

As treasurer, Plant had proven himself to be extremely anal about the TAG budget. He dealt pretty well with the concept of using the emergency fund to pay the deductible on the house insurance—"If the investigation ever wraps up and we ever get an insurance payout," Kyle had said—but he had problems with the rest of it.

Plant had something of an obsession with line items, not wanting to delete any. In particular, he didn't want to take the funds budgeted to pay for regular living expenses and reassign them to what Kyle called "emergency living expenses," i.e., paying the college to live in the dorms.

"If we leave all the money budgeted in those categories, we won't have anything to spend it on, and we won't be able to pay to live here," Collin had nearly yelled.

Plant put his nose in the air, looking exactly like Eduardo. "It states quite clearly in the by-laws that we cannot delete a line item without an up or down vote of the entire fraternity."

"We're going to have to have a meeting after this to okay what we decided to do with the budget anyway," Jules had pointed out.

Collin was just about ready to tear out his hair at that point. "Yeah, but if we wait until then to decide whether we can get rid of a line item, we won't have an emergency budget figured out, and we'll have to have another meeting to okay it when we do finally decide on one."

They finally came to the agreement that they would keep all the regular living expense line items but zero them out and move all the money from each into the newly created "Interim Housing Expenses." Creating a whole new line item seemed to please Plant, making his eyes shine, and double bonus, it wasn't prohibited in the by-laws.

Collin stopped himself from asking why.

It was all a perfect example of why he hated committees. Something that should have taken ten minutes took an hour and a half. It was also a great example of his current mental state. He usually negotiated things well, always remaining calm, always being the one who massaged others around to the group point of view. This time Kyle had to do it, looking at him suspiciously during the entire process.

Collin ignored him, walking off to his new room as soon as they were done. His getaway was helped by Julian cornering Kyle after the meeting, expressing his concern over their interim housing not having a proper entryway. "It's important to make the right impression," Collin heard Jules saying just before he closed his door, shutting out the noise.

He'd kept busy for a while with laundry and homework, but now he had nothing to do, unless he wanted to be social.

Nope. Not interested.

Okay, well, great. He could devote some energy to settling into this new mental and physical state he found himself in. Maybe he needed to tack "emotional state" onto the list too. It made sense he'd be experiencing emotional upheaval as well as the other stuff; his whole life had changed in the past three days. Been turned upside down. He'd been traumatically forced to move, and he'd met Eric.

In many ways, meeting Eric—and spending the night with him—was the bigger upset. A positive upset, he thought, but a big one.

Collin felt like he'd lived half a lifetime in the last twenty-four hours. In his sophomore philosophy class (why did they schedule those damn things at seven in the morning? Who really needed philosophy before breakfast?), he'd read something that had stuck with him since: "Each day is a little life." Who'd said that? Schopenhauer, he thought.

The last day felt like it had its own life, that was certain. It had changed his perspective, like one of those photographs Eric had hanging on his wall where the colors had been subtly altered to make things look different somehow, make the viewer see an ordinary scene in a new way. He felt like Eric had done that to his world, and now some formerly unremarkable things stood out while others became more muted.

His heart, for instance. Something he hadn't thought much about before. It beat, it hung out in his chest, it was supposedly red. But now Collin was fairly certain it radiated a subtle luminescence throughout his body that anyone looking at him might see. It stood out, brighter and eye-catching now, going way past that lazy warmth he'd felt this morning in Eric's car.

Was this what Brad had felt after his first night with Sebastian? Collin had been his roommate at the time, but he couldn't recall the dude glowing in the dark. Of course, at the time he hadn't known Brad and Sebastian had hooked up, so he hadn't been looking for it.

But if this was what Brad had felt . . . Brad and Sebastian had eventually fallen in love. Were in love still, if Sebastian's recent jealous behavior was any indicator. Brad had always acted as if they would be in love for the foreseeable future.

Meaning forever.

Collin fell back on his bed, wincing at the thinness of the mattress, covering his face with his hands and gripping his hair with his fingers. If what he and Eric had begun could lead to what Sebastian and Brad had . . . that was terrifying. In a really exhilarating, exciting way.

It would be so easy for me to fall in love with you.

And it was up to Collin to determine if that would be okay. Eric had said so—told him *he* needed to decide whether to let it happen by continuing to see him.

Oh God, what if he fucked this up? What if the warm glow *was* only from truly stellar sex and the release of all that tension? He didn't know if he could live with making one more mistake right now, especially not one that would hurt someone like Eric.

I really, really want to see him again.

Collin's heart faltered. If he didn't know what "this" was, and he didn't know if he could fall in love with the guy, was it fair to continue to see Eric? He slid his hands down, bringing them together in front of his mouth like he was praying, but he didn't generally do that. Instead, he stared at the ceiling, hoping for an answer.

If only answers came knocking on the door when one needed them. Why wasn't it that easy?

Someone knocked on the door. Collin sprang up, staring at it. *Nah, couldn't be.*

The knock came again. "Dude, Kyle wants you to come out here. We have a sitch."

Okay, unless his answer's voice sounded exactly like Danny's, that wasn't it.

And, fucking shit. *Another* situation?

ΘΑΓ

Collin didn't have a clue what the issue was until he got almost to the common area, because he couldn't see over Danny's shoulder. But then he saw Tank, coat still on, arms crossed over his chest and looking at the rest of the brothers from under his brow. He had a few pieces of luggage at his feet. Whoa, how many bags did Tank need to go home for the weekend?

As he got closer, he realized someone was standing on the other side of Tank. Somewhat shorter, shoulders slightly narrower, with lighter hair . . . but with Tank's eyes and chin. Maybe his nose too? This had to be Tank's little brother, but Collin had been certain he went to a not-quite-Ivy-League school somewhere on the East Coast. Didn't he play Division 1 hockey? They were still in season, weren't they?

No one spoke. Kyle bit at his thumb, and most of the guys were looking curiously at Tank. Julian was actually kneeling on the couch, peering over the back of it.

Collin cleared his throat. "Um, hey Tank. Welcome back."

Did he imagine Tank's shoulders relaxing?

Tank nodded at him. "Collin. This is my little brother, Jock."

Collin walked close enough to shake the guy's hand. "Hey."

Jock mumbled something back, not quite meeting Collin's gaze, face pale with dark circles under his eyes.

If Collin thought he'd been through a lot the last three days, this kid—and he seemed like a kid to Collin—had been through worse.

"Jock just transferred to Calapooya, and I want him to join the frat."

"Tank, we can't really—"

"We can." Tank cut Kyle off. "I looked it up in the by-laws. We can vote a guy in early due to special circumstances."

"Yeah, but we have to know what those circumstances *are* and you won't tell us."

Tank scratched the back of his head, pressing his lips together. He glanced at Jock, but his brother just looked at the ground. "Okay, man. Um, can we talk to you and Collin alone?"

Plant stood up. "Tank, I think if a decision like this is to be made, it would be appropriate to include the entire Executive Committee."

Tank glared at him. "I'm including two members."

Kyle sighed. "Collin's not a member. He's the alumni liaison, that's it."

Tank screwed up his face and looked at Collin. "Are you sure you aren't the vice president or something?"

"We don't have a vice president," Plant said.

Tank growled.

"I'm okay with sitting this one out," Julian said.

Kyle turned to Plant. "How about Collin and I go talk with them and make a determination?"

"Like what kind of determination?"

"A determination about whether I'm going to kill you or just kick your ass," Tank snapped.

Plant's nostrils flared and his jaw set, but he sat down. Whoever had the remote turned on whatever they'd been watching. Collin could hear Tim Gunn's voice. Jesus, they were watching *Project Runway* and claiming it was "sensitivity training" again. He couldn't wait until they were sensitive enough to admit they liked it.

As Kyle walked over, Collin offered his room as neutral territory. "Since you haven't even figured out where yours is yet," he added. Tank nodded and dropped a hand on his brother's shoulder, squeezing it. "Does anyone want a beer?" Collin asked.

"Jock's not old enough to drink beer," Tank said.

Collin snorted at him. "Yeah, and when you were underage, you never drank, either. It's just one, and you both look a little worn down."

Tank scowled, but Jock ignored him. "I'd like a beer. Please."

Collin asked Danny if he had any. He was likely to, and he was the only one who wouldn't bitch about it. He nodded. "Um, can I wait for an ad?"

"Aren't you guys streaming this? Watch whatever you miss later."

Danny looked torn, but then he glanced at Jock and stood up. "I'll bring four down to your room."

Walking down the hall behind Jock and his brother, Collin had a few seconds to check him out. Not like "check him out," but get a basic idea of his physical attributes. Like mapping his terrain. Did straight men do that?

Whatever. Jock had the same build as Eric and Brad, but he looked younger somehow, even from the back. Collin loved that build, as evidenced by most of his sexual history. Even Toby had that breadth of shoulder, but he didn't work out enough to be really sculpted, plus he wasn't as tall as any of the guys walking with Collin now.

In Collin's room, no one spoke for a few minutes. Tank rested against the window ledge, Kyle leaned against the door, Jock sat on a bed, and Collin sat on the one he'd started to think of as his. No one said anything. Did they expect him to get the ball rolling since it was his room? He'd just opened his mouth when Danny knocked. Kyle took the beer from him and passed them out. More silence.

Finally Kyle cleared his throat. "So, Jock, I thought Tank said you were a student at Avalon College." Collin tried to remember anything about Avalon, and came up blank.

Jock nodded and picked at his label. "I, um, left."

"He got kicked off the hockey team for being gay," Tank said.

"What? That's totally illegal!" Kyle set his beer down, trying to pace in the tiny space near the door. It looked more like spinning around. "Are you suing? It might have been better, from a legal standpoint, to have stayed enrolled there—"

"Kyle," Collin said. "I know you changed your major to pre-law, but getting litigious isn't the answer to everything." He met Kyle's gaze, trying to tell him to back off of the kid. Kyle nodded and settled back against the door.

"They had a bullshit excuse," Tank continued. "But we know damned well it's because he's gay."

"Tank," Jock said quietly, and his brother shut up immediately. Collin could hear Jock swallow. "Someone put, um, pictorial evidence all over our locker room. The coach kicked me off for unbecoming conduct and withholding pertinent information."

"How is you being gay pertinent?" Collin kept his voice calm.

Jock lifted his head and looked Collin in the eye. That's when it became clear that while the kid felt depressed and ashamed and maybe beaten, he also had a lot of anger. "There's a lot of bloodletting in hockey, you know."

It took Collin a few seconds to get it. "He thinks you're a health risk?"

Jock clenched his jaw and nodded. Then he laughed shortly and looked away. "You can even see the other guy in the photo has a condom on."

"That is the most fucking archaic attitude I think I've ever heard." Kyle said, relatively calmly for him.

Jock shrugged, looking back at the floor. "He's an archaic guy."

"That's illegal." Kyle stood up straight again. "You can't discriminate against someone because of their HIV status, and you certainly can't discriminate against someone because of their *potential* status."

"He said that he needed to know it was possible so he could take the necessary precautions, and that I'd endangered the team." Jock's voice had gone flat, and he took a long swallow of beer.

"The straight guys could have it just as easily," Kyle tried.

"Not statistically," Tank said. "But it doesn't fucking matter, because the coach may be able to twist the words of the ADA to make it sound like what he's doing is legal, but it'll never stand up in court."

"Damn right." Kyle was starting to pace again.

Jock outright chugged his beer.

"You guys, back off," Collin said. "Courtrooms and legalities aren't the issue right now." Jock's pretty obvious distress was. "We need to figure out a way to get the rest of the members to vote in favor of Jock living here without explaining to them what happened."

Jock lifted his head, taking a deep breath. "Thank you."

Collin almost reached across the space between them and patted Jock's knee. He came to his senses in time, though. "How did you get the Admissions Office to let you in the second week of the term?"

Jock's cheeks flushed, and he was back to staring off to the side. His beer was empty, so Collin handed over his own. Jock flicked him another thankful look and took it.

Tank sighed. "Dad did it. He, you know, made a donation."

Collin shrugged. "Sounds like something my uncle would do for me." Although maybe not after finding out he was gay.

"How soon can we call a meeting?" Tank asked.

Collin looked at Kyle. "Well, I'm talking to the chair of the Alumni Association on Tuesday. And we need to call one so the membership can okay the budget changes. I'm thinking Wednesday."

Kyle nodded. "And until then, Jock is our guest, and no one needs to know why. We'll come up with a plan before the meeting for what to say. Don't worry, my girlfriend is really good at this."

Chapter 22

On Monday morning, Eric brought both a flash drive with the images on them and prints of all the pictures he'd taken of the frat as high-resolution eight by tens. He hoped it'd help, and it might because he could see where at least one of the safety mechanisms was supposed to be on the hot-water heater. It had been capped off.

He went ahead and brought the pictures of the tree, too, at least all the ones that included the house in the background. "What're these?" Mike asked. He looked all rumpled, like he'd been sleeping at the station in his uniform.

"The other pictures I took. Probably not useful, but what the hell."

Mike lowered the photo and looked at Eric over the top of his glasses. "Well, aren't you helpful?"

Eric shrugged, unsure of what to say. He'd never really let anyone at the station look at his work before. He rested his forearm against Mike's doorjamb, trying to look unconcerned.

Mike leaned back in his chair, folding his hands over his stomach. "Saw you Saturday talking to one of the kids I interviewed at the scene."

"Oh yeah?" Eric made a show of looking out the window thoughtfully. "That kid with the dark hair, a littler shorter than me?"

"That's the one. How do you know him?"

He totally knew he was walking into a trap, but he didn't see what he could do, other than fake an urgent need to urinate. He scratched his jaw before answering. Mike raised his eyebrows. *Crappity*. "Met him the day before, when I went out on that broken leg. He helped keep the patient calm. Nice guy."

Mike sat forward and eyeballed him. "Are you chasing after that kid?"

He gave up, dropping his arm and slumping against the doorway. "Why does everyone think that?"

"Val told me she thought you were sweet on him."

"He's sweet all right," Eric murmured.

"Huh? Speak up, dammit. Running fire engines for twenty-five years ruined my ears. I don't wear this hearing aid to be stylish, you know."

Eric crossed his arms. "Nothing."

Mike gave him his trademark squinty eye for a few seconds, but let it go. "Well, I just thought I'd let you know he's gay."

"How'd you know that?"

"He told me. It came up in the investigation, but—" Mike glanced around his office, as if someone might be hiding behind his file cabinet or in his wastebasket, then leaned over his desk and dropped his voice to a room-clearing whisper. "He's in the closet, and he asked me not to say anything."

Oh for fuck's sake. "Then what the hell are you doing telling me, Mike?"

He pulled back, poking his lip out infinitesimally. "Well, I didn't think telling you counted, you know. I mean, you like boys; he likes boys . . ." He waggled his brows.

Eric straightened up. "Of course it counts. Let me learn you something about gay guys: if someone tells you he's gay, you don't tell anyone without his permission."

Mike stared at the wall, shifting his jaw as if he was chewing on something. "Huh. That a general rule?"

"It's a definite, nonnegotiable rule."

"Kinda fucked that one up, didn't I?"

Eric sighed and rubbed his hand over his head. "S'all right, I already knew about him."

"So you're seeing him?"

"Well, I mean, I *saw* him."

Mike scrunched his forehead, apparently running that through his circuits. "Getting laid is easier when you're gay, isn't it?"

Eric huffed a laugh. "From what I've seen it is, yeah."

"Well, score one for your team."

"But as far as that 'kid' goes, Collin, I think it's more than just getting laid." *I hope.*

Mike nodded, clasping his hands on his desk. He cleared his throat. "Well, I'm happy for you. I'm not the best judge of man flesh, but that kid seems pretty attractive to me."

He flushed bright red while Eric stared at him. "Mike, you're scaring me."

"*You're* scared? You shoulda heard it from my end." Mike put his glasses back on, rearranging the files on his desk. "Well, anyway, you look old enough to be his father."

Eric rolled his eyes. He liked hearing it from Mike as much as he liked hearing it from Val. "Thanks."

"Welcome. Now, this case, I guess I could say you have a personal interest in it."

That would be the end of his inside track. He sighed, focusing out the windows again. "Yeah."

"I don't really care." Mike peered at him over his glasses again when Eric swung his head back in surprise. "I know he didn't do it."

It was totally possible someone in TAG had started the fire, Eric knew that, and Mike had to have a reason for being sure Collin hadn't done it. "And that's because?"

"Come in and sit down, dammit, I'm getting a crick in my neck looking up at you. And shut the door."

"Yes, sir."

When Eric had sat across from him in the visitor's chair, he explained. "The president of that fraternity gave me a map of where everyone's room is, and indicated on it whether the room's occupants were there when the fire broke out. You know why I wanted it?"

Mike wanted to play brilliant detective, so Eric lifted his hands palm up, shrugging.

"Heh. Knew you wouldn't. I wanted it because whoever's room is right next to the stairs was in the direct path of that water heater, if all things went perfect. I figured those guys wouldn't be stupid enough to send a rocket through their room while they were sleeping in it. Only one guy in that room, and he was there that night. That guy's your boy."

Eric refused to think about the hot-water heater shooting through Collin's bed. Instead, he asked, "How come it took off at an angle then?"

"The tank was on one of those heater platforms. Galvanized steel, which begins to fail at about 900 degrees, but potassium nitrate burns at about 2,000 degrees—it can go hotter depending on the other additives. That stand was a semi-molten lump, and it angled that hot-water heater so it went through the stairs."

Eric shook his head, thinking it over. "Still think it's a strange way to start a fire."

Mike pointed his glasses at Eric, leaning toward him. "Yeah, but what if the fire was a by-product of the arsonist's real intent?"

Something grabbed his lungs and held on tight. "You mean someone was trying to kill whoever was in that room? Collin?"

Mike shrugged and sat back. "Eh, prolly not. Someone just picked a weird-ass place to start a fire." He eyeballed Eric. "At least, that's our official position."

He couldn't get rid of the knot in his chest. Collin might have been hurt, or worse. Eric did what he always did when something affected him at work: he pushed it to the side to be dealt with after-hours. "Can I tell Collin any of this?"

"If you trust him not to leak information. If you don't trust him . . ."

"Then I wouldn't tell him. But I can trust him. You never know, he might even help out."

Mike *hmph*ed.

"So how are things going otherwise?"

"Slow. Lotta fucking college kids to interview, but mostly Detective Homes is taking care of that. I sit in on some of the more important ones. Boring as shit. Every once in a while, one of 'em gets feisty. Those kids watch too damn many police dramas, think we're going to pin it on them."

"Has anyone refused to answer questions?"

"No one yet, but I'm sure someone will, or they'll show up with daddy's lawyer and he won't let them talk. There was this one kid—" Mike interrupted himself, snickering. "He starts blubbering about how he's sorry and he didn't mean anything by it and he'd never do that. Blah, blah, blah. It was the kid that threatened them the day of the fire."

Eric sat forward. "Threatened them?" Threatened who, exactly?

"Eh? Oh, just some jackass from another frat. You can tell your boy that the BLO hard—get it? Blowhard? No? His frat's Beta Lambda— Oh never mind. Tell him that the Cody kid's a big weenie."

Eric snorted, settling into the chair some. The BLO frat had been around when he'd been in TAG, and it sounded like the same kinds of guys were members now as had been then.

"Anywho, I put in a request for a building permit record. The kitchen was remodeled in the mid-eighties, and they must have put that hot-water heater in then."

"Was the tank that old?" That was ancient.

"Well, hopefully these photos will help me figure out what model it was, and about when it was manufactured."

"You think there were any eyewitness when the hot-water heater—"

"For medic twenty-three, engine twenty-three, rescue twenty-three, report of an eighty-seven-year-old unresponsive male—"

"Crap." He had a feeling Mike had more info, and Eric couldn't help worrying he wouldn't be around later. *Why is this so important to you?*

Duh. Collin.

"You better get a move on. I'll keep you updated, don't worry." Mike made a shooing motion.

There wasn't a lot else he could do, no matter what he wanted. He stood up. "Thanks, Mike."

"Welcome. Now go. And don't worry about your boy. I don't think he's in any danger."

ΘΛΓ

The whole time Eric was on the call with Val—the old guy had died in his sleep long before they'd arrived—what Mike said ate at him, so after they'd returned to quarters and restocked the rig, he went to the bedroom he'd stowed his gear in that morning for some privacy—as much as he could get at the fire station.

Instead of texting Collin first to be sure he wasn't in class or something, Eric just called and hoped for the best.

"Hello?" Collin sounded uncertain, his voice going up a little too high at the end for a regular question.

"Hey, Sweet Thing." Eric flinched slightly. He'd meant to not lay on the endearments too much, afraid it would freak Collin out. Because calling less than twenty-four hours after he'd said he was falling in love already pushed plenty of boundaries.

But Collin's voice relaxed. "Hi, old man."

He cringed. "As pet names go, I've heard better."

Collin laughed. "Sorry. I'll come up with a better one later."

That sounded promising. "S'okay. How are you?"

"I'm fine, but the shit going on around me sucks."

"Tell me about it, Sweetness." He could hear that his voice had deepened and slowed, like it wanted to wrap around Collin.

But Sweetness sighed. "I'll tell you later. Can we talk about you? Aren't you at work?"

"Yeah. It's been pretty normal here today."

"What's normal like?"

"We'll have to talk about my job some other time; I called to tell you something else. It's kind of important."

Collin sucked in a breath. "You made a mistake?"

Huh? "A mistake about what?"

"About the falling in love with me thing. Like, you could have been influenced by good sex, good conversation, and sleep deprivation."

"No, I didn't I made a mistake."

"So you still think . . ."

"Yeah," he whispered. He didn't want to kill this moment, but his gut kept nagging at him. "Um, did you hear from Mike today? You know, the fire marshal."

"No."

Crappity. But that meant Taggert really thought Collin was safe. "This isn't something you can spread around, but Mike found something that could be important. That hot-water heater should have gone straight up when it took off, but it didn't." Eric shut the door to his quarters with his foot, sitting down on the cot.

"Okaaay."

He ran a hand over his head. "The way it was situated, it should have gone through the bedroom above it." He didn't think that was enough to figure it out, but it made a good start.

Collin was silent a second. "On the second floor?"

"Yeah. The stairway had enough structural elements to stop the tank, but it would have smashed right through a regular floor, even into the second story."

"Whose bedroom is right above it?" Collin sounded suspicious now.

Eric blew out a breath. "Yours."

He paused for longer this time. "So, you're saying what exactly?"

"I don't know for sure. Mike suggested there's a small chance someone targeted you."

"And you're just telling me now?"

"I only found out this morning, and then I had to go on a call." Eric rubbed his forehead. "I'm, you know, trying to give you space, and the investigation's official position is that no one was trying to commit murder. They thought this over and came to that decision. But it was kind of eating at me, and Mike did bother to tell me. He said I could tell you if I trusted you to keep it quiet."

"Why would anyone want to kill me?" He sounded more doubtful than worried.

"I might be overreacting. I mean, it would be a pretty difficult way to kill someone—how would the killer even know your bed was just above the point the hot-water heater would pass through? And who'd know you were where you'd need to be to get hit by the stupid thing? And for fuck's sake, who tries to kill someone with a hot-water heater rocket? A million things could go wrong. Something did go wrong." Still, it made him nervous.

"It does seem unlikely."

"Yeah . . . but you could be careful, maybe. Not walk around campus at night alone, stuff like that."

"Have someone taste all my food before I eat?" Collin huffed a laugh.

Eric tried to joke back. "Good luck with that one."

Collin sighed. "I'll be careful."

"I'd feel better if you did."

"Well," Collin's voice took on a teasing note. "As long as you feel better."

Eric smiled. "So, it doesn't sound like I freaked you out too much." Dammit, maybe he shouldn't have said that. Maybe he'd get lucky and Collin would think he'd been talking about the hot-water heater.

No such luck. "Because of what you said yesterday? I can't tell you it didn't freak me out, but I don't feel like I need to chew my arm off to get away."

"Well, that's reassuring."

Collin laughed. "It is, really."

"So, I guess you're thinking about seeing me again?"

"Yeah." Collin's voice got so low Eric could barely hear it. The kind of voice he'd use if they were lying next to each other talking. Collin could lie on Eric's chest and twirl Eric's hair on his finger and talk in that voice all night long.

Eric closed his eyes to imagine it more clearly. "That's good enough for me, Sweet Thing." For now.

Chapter 23

Tuesday at lunch, sitting in the student union across from Kyle and Ashley, Collin thought again about his conversation with Eric the night before. Specifically about those few seconds when he thought Eric had called to say he'd made a mistake, and he couldn't fall in love with Collin. Collin's heart had suddenly shrunk in on itself, leaving an uncomfortable tugging sensation. But when Eric said he hadn't made a mistake . . .

I want to see him again.

He wanted the chance to go back to Eric's next weekend, and the weekend after, even if things did get very serious very fast. Even if he didn't feel the same way as Eric in the end. He might even want the chance to reintroduce Monty to Eric and see if they could get along for his sake. But he still didn't know exactly what to tell Eric. What he wanted to say was, "Please don't do anything crazy like fall in love with me until I get a chance to figure myself out." But he didn't think things worked that way. People couldn't necessarily put a hold on their feelings, no matter how fast those feelings had developed.

In the end, wouldn't it be better to know? To follow the relationship to its natural conclusion, or wherever? Ending it now would leave him with this feeling in his chest, and he'd never get rid of it. That seemed so wrong. Unbearable.

But if Collin *couldn't* say he definitely knew he could fall in love with him, would Eric still want to see what they could become together? And how did one go about knowing beforehand who it was possible to fall in love with?

"Kyle, can you go get me coffee?" Ashley said loudly, breaking through Collin's haze. A slice of pizza hovered in front of his mouth, held there by his hands. He hadn't even taken a bite out of it, and he didn't want it now. He set it down and wiped the grease off his fingers and onto his napkin.

"They don't sell coffee here. I'd have to go all the way over to the Beatnick Café." Kyle sounded a bit whiny. And whipped. "Can't we stop by there after lunch?"

"Lovie, I really want one *now*. You wouldn't want me to go without, would you?"

Kyle sighed heavily, and dropped his slice of cheese on his plate, slumping over it. "Okay."

"Thank you." Ashley leaned across the table for a kiss. It seemed to make him move a little faster.

Staring down at his lunch, Collin had begun to slip back into that place where he felt alternately scared and anxious about Eric, when Ashley put her hand over his, drawing his attention again. "Are you thinking about that guy?"

"What? Did you send Kyle away just to ask me that?"

She nodded, not looking the least bit guilty.

"Doesn't that seem kind of, I don't know, unfair to him?"

"Did you want to talk to him about your new man too?"

"I don't even know if I want to tell you."

She let go of his hand after giving it a final pat or two. "You don't have to, I just thought I'd give you the opportunity to talk privately if you wanted." She went back to her pizza, appearing unconcerned.

"You sent your boyfriend off on some bogus errand to talk about it and now you're willing to just drop it?"

She held up a hand, palm out. "I'll have you know I really want that coffee."

Collin gave her a look. She smirked, more with her eyebrows than her mouth.

Shit. He did want to talk about Eric. "Well, I wouldn't want all your hard work to go unrewarded . . ."

She leaned toward him. "We need to hurry before Kyle gets back, unless you want to reveal all your feelings to him also."

Not so much. "How do you know there were feelings involved? It could have been just really great sex."

She arched a brow at him. "Sex so great you're still staring off into space and mooning about it on Tuesday? Brad might have done that if he'd had a slutty period, but not you."

He blinked at her. "I wouldn't?"

"No," she waved a hand in the air. "You aren't the type. You get off and get over it. It's actually a pretty common male response, from what I've seen. It's when a guy is still staring soulfully out a window or ignoring his pizza more than twenty-four hours later that I know it's more than sex. Guys like Brad are outliers—he reads romance into everything."

"Have you ever thought about writing a manual for clueless women?"

"Lots of times. But let's talk about you right now."

Collin picked at his pizza for a few seconds, trying to figure out what to say. "I feel weird talking about it."

"Because it was special or because it sucked?"

"What?" He gaped at her. "It didn't suck."

"Okay, this is a classic example of the male protective instinct being applied to nonmaterial situations. You're protecting those feelings because—to you—they seem fragile and vulnerable to attack by others. It's because, if you told another man about this—well, other than Brad—he'd have a typically male response, usually consisting of mocking the feeling, thereby cheapening it. Now, if you told a woman about it, she'd be happy for you and want to celebrate."

He narrowed his eyes. "Is this some way of making me tell you about it?"

"Oh, sweetie, you already told me enough." She took a bite of her pizza.

"Okay, what about Toby? He wouldn't mock me . . . much. He'd be happy for me."

She snorted. "Yeah, after he stopped warning you about all the ways you could be duped or just plain old fooling yourself. He'd start telling you how it just couldn't be, because, in the area of relationships, Toby gets competitive."

"What? No he doesn't."

She gave him a look from under one raised brow. "Collin, when did you and Toby first start hooking up regularly? The beginning of the school year."

How did she know this shit? He needed to have a serious talk with Brad. "So?" As a response, it could have been stronger.

"What happened right before that between his best friend and yours?"

"Ohmygod." Collin sat up straight. "Brad and Sebastian moved in together and he moved out. Oh! And then Paul and Trevor started seeing each other."

She returned to patting his hand, but he appreciated her half-sympathetic, half-superior expression less. "Now, I'm not suggesting that Toby was only interested in you for that reason. You were already friends, after all. And I certainly don't think he knew what he was doing. But since the opportunity was there . . ."

Seriously, she needed to retire that supercilious eyebrow or some queen would smack it right off her face someday soon. "I'm really not enjoying this girl chat."

Ashley stopped patting and looked up at him, eyes wide. "I'm sorry." Her mouth twisted into a more uncertain line. "That was kind of, I don't know, patronizing, wasn't it?"

"Uh, yeah." He nodded vigorously.

"It's just that I hang around with so many gay guys, I forget you're all male."

"Don't you have any female friends anymore?" And did they like being talked down to?

She shrugged. "Yeah. They just aren't as interesting." She dropped her crust and dusted off her hands, then leaned toward him. "Okay, how about this: if you have any specific questions regarding this guy, just ask." This time her eyebrows remained unmoving.

He worried his lip a few seconds, but she basically already knew his dilemma. "When you and Kyle first got together, did it seem . . ."

"Magical?"

"I was thinking 'different.'"

She bobbed her head to one side, then the other, as if thinking. "I guess different works, if you call it a very good kind of different. Special different. Bordering on perfect different."

He'd never known that different could achieve perfection. Except he knew exactly what she meant. "So, when would you say you knew you could fall in love with him?"

"Right away," she said without hesitation. "It was different—there's that word again—than with any other guy. It just seemed right."

"Yeah, but how does seeming right translate into falling in love?"

She looked at him like he was nuts. "Collin, what is the 'right' it seems, if not 'the right guy'? In both our cases."

Duh. He felt like slapping himself in the forehead. "Okay, but wait."

She did, eyes wide, frozen over her pizza and trained on him. Girls were totally different listeners.

"What if there's an issue? Not a major issue, but one that could be problematic in the future." Collin ended up holding his thumb and finger together, as if indicating the amount of issue, sort of a like a recipe. *Take a quarter teaspoon of baggage, a soupçon of issue, and mix thoroughly with fantastic sex until well blended. Roll into small cylindrical croquettes and stuff up your anus.* Magnifique!

"You want my advice?" He was still weighing out his answer when she continued. "Follow the relationship to its natural conclusion, whatever that might be."

Okay, so pretty much what he'd already figured.

"Like, take Kyle and me. We're going to get married. Some people might think we shouldn't be making a decision like that at our age, and we're kind of young to be so sure. Yet Kyle has already started making payments on a ring."

Collin goggled. "He is? I didn't know that."

"No one knows that; I'm not even supposed to know."

"Then how do you?"

"He left his credit card statement out one month and I saw it, so the next month I checked again. It's one of those jewelry stores that only sell engagement rings."

"Wait, he's charging your engagement ring on his credit card?" That seemed like a horrible idea. He'd buy it three times over in interest by the time he'd paid it off. And what did it say about their future if she was already inspecting his credit card statements?

"His parents pay the bill every month."

Collin decided not to point out that that meant *they* were actually buying the ring. Besides, Kyle came back then. Ashley stood up, took the coffee, and gave him another kiss, a very enthusiastic one. Kyle kissed her back. For a while.

Okay, he had to admit, they looked happy together.

As Kyle sat down, he asked, "What were you guys talking about?"

"Nothing," Ashley said. "Just boys."

"I don't want any part of that conversation." Kyle shoved his pizza into his mouth, as if he had to in order to make sure he added nothing to the discussion.

"We were done," Collin assured him. God forbid the guy should choke.

Chapter 24

Tuesday morning, while walking to class, Collin answered yet another phone call. This time, Marshal Taggert wanted to apologize for not calling the day before, then tell Collin everything Eric already had. "We think it's highly unlikely you were a target, but I figured I should prolly tell you."

"Thank you, Marshal Taggert."

Taggert paused briefly. "You're not having much of a fit over the news. I suppose you've already heard about it from another source."

Collin froze mid-stride, unsure of what to say.

"It's okay, I already said he could tell you. It's all just between us, of course. All of it."

Collin thought he understood all of the "all" Taggert referred to—the part about him being gay, and possibly even about him and Eric. Would Eric tell the fire marshal that? Were they friends?

There was a lot he didn't know about a guy he *felt* like he knew very well.

"That's about what I have right now," Taggert said, reminding Collin he was on the phone. He glanced at his watch. On the phone and about to be late to class. "I'll make sure you and the other guys in your fraternity are kept up to date."

"Thank you, I appreciate that," Collin said, barely getting it in there before Taggert had hung up.

Unfortunately, while he was grateful for being kept informed, it didn't give him a lot to say to his uncle. He waited until right before his evening Lit class to call Monty. At 6:30, he found himself a semi-deserted area of Saklaeth Hall, near the literature professors' offices. It was very quiet; the receptionist had gone home, as had most of the professors.

So there he sat, on the floor with his back against the wall, hiding in a dimly lit hallway. For some reason, calling Monty from here seemed safer than calling from anywhere else. It was semi-anonymous—not his room, not a particularly public area—a good place for secrets and uncomfortable conversations.

Which this next one was guaranteed to be.

Collin closed his eyes and squeezed the phone between his hands for a second, then he just did it. Opened his eyes, unlocked his screen, and hit Monty's name from his contacts list.

It only rang once before his uncle answered. "Collin. Hello."

"Hello, Uncle Monty."

"I was starting to wonder if you were going to call me today at all."

"Yes, well, I wanted to make sure I had all the available information."

"Ah, good. But one thing first; have you contacted Sparky Donaldson?"

Him again? Collin had to think for a second to remember. "Yes, sir. I sent him an email on Sunday, but I haven't heard back yet."

"Understandable, he's a busy man. I'm sure you will soon."

"I'm sure."

"Now, what news do you have for me?"

Collin exhaled, slowly and controlled and hopefully silently. "Not very much more than I had on Sunday. Although it has been determined the fire was deliberately set." He scrunched his eyes shut and balled one fist, waiting for the reaction to that.

"I see." Collin heard Monty's chair squeak, maybe from him sitting forward? "Well, then I'm going to have to call an emergency meeting of the Alumni Association Executive Committee so we can discuss this situation and determine a course of action."

Shit! His eyes flew open, and he stared at the wall opposite him, calculating responses. "What reason would you have for doing that?" As if he didn't know.

"Collin," Monty said in his most patronizing tone. "You did promise there would be no repercussions due to this membership policy change. I think it's rather obvious that that's not the case."

"Because you're assuming the fire and bomb were the work of someone who feels strongly that the membership policy is wrong." He thought again about telling Monty of his possible connection to the case, but his gut kept telling him not to. Probably because then Monty would want to be involved in the investigation. He might even come up here. *Oh God no.*

Plus, he wasn't supposed to tell, right?

"It seems very clear to me. I can see no other obvious conclusion."

"You agreed with me on Sunday that it was possible that there could be another motive."

Monty made his "annoyed" noise, the one where he exhaled harshly through his nose. "Yes, I agree it's possible. However, I find it highly unlikely."

"Wouldn't it be better to wait until we have more information, sir? We both know there's really only one step the Alumni Association can take. I'd urge you to delay the meeting. The police and fire marshal are still investigating, and we're doing all we can to help them."

"It seems to me we have enough information to make a decision."

Collin gritted his teeth but tried not to sound as if he had. "No one knows what the result of the investigation will be. It's possible the culprit will never be caught, and there will never be proof of his motives." Or whether he was trying to murder anyone.

"Listen, son, I know what you're doing. You're trying to stave off the inevitable, but we all know that when the final determination is made and the culprit is caught—"

"If he's caught."

Monty sighed. "Fine, if he's caught, it will be someone who has an issue with Theta Alpha Gamma inviting openly gay members into fraternities, mark my words."

In point of fact, he didn't know why the perpetrator had done this, but attacking it from that angle again seemed counterproductive. Collin massaged his temples as Monty went on. Maybe he should bring up Eric's "lone whackjob" argument, but he was fairly confident Monty would brush it aside.

"Now don't get me wrong, I'm in favor of your friend Brad staying in the frat since he's al—"

"TAG isn't the only frat on campus that has had openly gay members."

"Yes." Monty sounded like he was speaking through his teeth now. "But it's the only fraternity on campus that explicitly welcomes them."

He stared at his hand, propped on his knee in front of him. It had started to shake. "It's a small change, Uncle Monty. We simply went from having gay members to saying we are willing to do it again—to do what we've *already done*. I just can't see anyone being so upset about it that he'd plant a bomb in our basement."

"People do incredibly rash things for reasons that seem stupid to other people, Collin."

"True, but that's just one more reason not to jump to any conclusions and assume this whole incident is the work of someone who's opposed to gay rights."

"Collin, it's the most likely cause. You're grasping at straws. I'm going to have to call this meeting, it's my responsibility as president to do so."

Collin took a deep breath, pressing his back against the wall as if for support. "Can you make a guess as to whether the association will take action?"

Monty hesitated, or possibly he was steeling himself also. "I think it's more likely than not. I'm sorry." For a second, Collin relaxed. He could hear the sincerity in Monty's voice, and he believed it. Until Monty continued. "I'm sorry, but I support taking action."

Collin's whole body went cold. "In other words, you and the other officers will vote to cut off association funds to TAG while we're in the middle of this crisis unless we do what they want. Excuse me, sir, but some might see that as blackmail."

"Collin!"

He'd stopped shaking and now felt strangely calm, and very certain about his next step. "I'm simply telling you what some of the more extreme reactions might be. I also need to inform you that we've also called an emergency meeting for tomorrow evening. We'll be voting on whether to accept another gay member—" a swift intake of breath almost distracted him "—and I'll be suggesting we make a resolution about our intentions regarding the membership policy."

Monty coughed, taking a minute to recover. Maybe he'd sucked spittle into his lungs. "*Your* intentions?"

"In other words, what action we'll take should the Alumni Association vote to cut off funds."

"Ah, I see."

"Yes."

There didn't seem to be a lot more to say, but Collin sat with the phone to his ear for a while before Monty ended the conversation. "I suppose that's that."

"I suppose so."

"Well, then, good night Collin."

"Good night, sir."

He sat in that dead end near the English department a long time, trying to reconcile his inner twelve-year-old's image of Monty with his twenty-one-year-old's reality.

When Collin was thirteen, his sister had a riding instructor who came out to the ranch once a week. He always wore breeches and riding boots, and often carried a crop with him, which he habitually smacked his thigh with. It took Collin a while to figure out he watched Alyssa's lesson not to see how well she could ride, but to watch Ferris Delacourte smack his thigh in those skintight pants, or just walk around in them. When Ferris taught Aly the posting trot, he began by demonstrating the proper seat, his thighs working hard to pull his muscular ass out of the saddle over and over, bobbing up and down while he rode around the arena.

Collin had never missed one of those lessons. Even after he'd realized why he liked them so much. Even after he'd realized how disappointed Uncle Monty would be to find out that he wasn't normal.

Ever since, he'd been preparing himself for Monty's reaction. Trying to excel in other areas to offset that eventual disappointment. But something in his gut knew now that disappointment was the least of his worries.

It kind of pissed him off.

Chapter 25

This was just too weird.

Eric had been trying to schedule some time with this guy for a couple of months. If it hadn't been for that—and how hot he found the dude—he would have cancelled their session. Maybe.

This is your job. Your other job. And if he could swing it, he'd do only this professionally. Plus he'd spent a total of one night with Collin, and in spite of anything he might have said—he squelched the urge to squirm at the thought—Collin had said nothing about love or commitment or exclusivity, so . . . yeah. He could take pictures of a seminude male that interested him.

Artistically. Artistically interested him.

Not that the sexual and artistic interests didn't usually blend, and not that he didn't ever mess around with his subjects. In the past. When he didn't have a boyfriend (whether the boyfriend was faithful or not).

Crap. Okay, that right there was the real problem. He thought maybe, when they finally set up this photo shoot, that he'd given the guy—Marcus—that he'd given Marcus the impression that something might happen between them, if Marcus was into it. And once he'd gotten over his initial wariness of Eric's offer to pay him for seminude photos, he'd sounded like he might consider letting something happen.

And now Marcus was standing here in his small black briefs, perfectly, beautifully imperfect, waiting for something to happen.

"So, you shooting yet? I thought there'd be clicking noises and lights flashing," Marcus said. He shifted slightly, one leg forward, arms loose, sort of a boxing stance.

Great. Eric had stared at him stupidly for so long the guy thought he was a serial killer or something. "Sorry, man. Just thinking about how I want to approach this. I kinda get lost in my head when I do that, I didn't mean to freak you out." *Way to relax your subject, douche bag.* "The lights won't flash because I use continuous lighting, but you'll hear the shutter when I take a picture."

"It's cool." Marcus smiled tightly, but his shoulders loosened up some. When the smile melted off his face, Eric took his first picture almost unconsciously, because that look right there was what he wanted.

Fighter at Home, his brain titled the shoot. Not that Marcus was a prizefighter or that Eric would actually call this series of shots that, but it seemed like the right feel. "Can you kinda ball your fists up? No just, leave your arms down. Yeah. Turn your head to the left. Awesome, man." That would make some great pics—the way Marcus's lower lip plumped up made him look like he expected a lot from the world, but also expected to be disappointed. Perfect in profile like that.

Thank God, he'd finally gotten this shoot going. He'd started to wonder if he really would ask Marcus to leave, tell him it was a bad day or he wasn't in the right frame of mind. But he moved pretty easily into the flow once he took that first shot. He needed this shoot, anyway. He hadn't put anything new up on his site in a while, and he'd noticed a drop in visitors. Plus Marcus was his favorite kind of subject.

"Can you flex your arms and tilt your head down, but look at the camera? Like under your brows. That's fantastic." *Oh, nice angry, sullen look.*

It wasn't that the dude was the most beautiful man he'd ever seen, or the most sculpted, but Marcus had the most complete package he'd ever seen in one guy. Well, not that he'd seen the guy's package—not *that* package. Yet. But if he approached this shoot the way he usually did, he'd at least keep the option open.

"Okay, how about you turn around? You don't need to look back at the camera, just relax, maybe move around like you're loosening tight muscles. Beautiful."

Those shots depended on the guy. If Eric wanted them totally bare, he asked professional models straight out if they did nude work. But with guys like Marcus, who were just average people (with beautiful, expressive faces and very toned, yet not quite perfect bodies—always the best kind), he had to be a little more careful. Marcus had been wary enough just setting up the shoot—Eric had to give him references so the guy could make sure he wasn't a human trafficker or something.

"I'd like to take some profile shots now. Yeah, just like that, stare straight ahead." Eric had planned some shots on the bed he'd set up because Marcus's dark skin would look fantastic against the light sheets, and with that sullen lip and those half-lidded eyes, he'd make the boys (and girls) swoon; but when the time came, he couldn't even suggest it.

Crap. The whole session was off-balance again. Usually he got lost in it, drifting somewhere in a world between his camera, what he saw in his head, and how his subject interpreted his requests, but this shoot had been different. Every time he started to drift into that place, something dragged him out.

"Yeah, so, you did great, Marcus. Thanks a lot, man. Uh, I already had you sign the release, and I'll mail you a check, so if you wanna get dressed you can just go. Home. Or wherever." He sounded like a nervous dork.

Marcus walked over to his clothes, on the wooden chair he'd left them on. "That's it, huh?" He half smiled. "I can get dressed and go? Home?" He quirked one eyebrow and sat down to pull on his jeans.

Eric busied himself with his camera, flicking needlessly through the images. "Yeah, uh, I didn't mean to, like, mislead you, but since we set this up I sorta got involved with someone, and I don't want to, like, start something else."

After a few seconds of silence, he glanced up in time to see Marcus stand and button his fly. "S'okay, man, I have a girlfriend."

Phew.

"It'd just be sex, we wouldn't start nothing."

Not what he'd expected. "Uh . . . is she okay with you messing around?" With guys?

Marcus shrugged and pulled his shirt on over his head. "She knows guys are just play for me."

"Yeah." Eric cleared his throat. "That's not really how it is for me." He started to remove his camera from the tripod.

"Guys aren't just play for you, or your boyfriend isn't okay with you playing?"

"More like guys aren't just play and this one isn't my boyfriend, but I want him to be."

"And you don't want to fuck that up. I get it. But he's cool with you doing photos of dudes?"

Eric grimaced and ran his palm over his head, thinking about that one.

"Guess you have some fessing up to do," Marcus said.

"Yeah, pretty much."

ΘΛΓ

Eric didn't even look at the pictures he'd taken. It didn't really matter what Collin thought about them, *he* thought he needed to explain the extent of his photography activities. The next time they were together in person, he'd tell Collin. Until then, the idea of even looking at Marcus's shots felt wrong. Like cheating, kind of.

He hadn't meant to hide this part of his "hobby" from Collin, he just hadn't even *thought* about it until this morning, when he'd gotten home and Marcus's named had popped out at him from his calendar. He'd been so hot to get that guy into his studio, but once he'd met Collin, it all flew out of his head.

Collin took up most of the space in his head now, if he wanted to be honest about it. As soon as he had the new images loaded onto his computer, he found the idea of looking at the two shots he'd taken on Sunday much more exciting. So he uploaded the pictures of Collin and opened them in Photoshop.

Then he mostly just stared. He tried to fiddle around with them, but other than carefully masking off what he could see of Collin's very sexy briefs, he didn't get anything done. He kept trying things and undoing them, because they kept making the picture, just, *wrong*.

A little after ten, he realized it was because he liked the image without any alterations. He'd been messing with the one where Collin's head was turned to the camera, looking curiously over his shoulder at Eric. He gave up and saved it, then went in search of his phone.

He'd pretty well shown his hand when he'd told Collin he could fall in love with him, so did it really matter if he called now, just to call and not because he had news, right? He stared at his cell, lying on the kitchen counter, thinking about whether this was wise, when someone texted him.

His heartbeat picked up when he saw it was Collin.

Are you still awake?

It was barely ten, of course he was up. Instead of answering Collin's text, he called him.

"Hi," Collin breathed, sounding relieved.

"Is something wrong?"

"No. I mean yes. Everything. Well, almost everything." His voice trembled slightly.

"Tell me about it, Sweet Thing."

Collin sighed, very quietly; it sounded like relief. "I need to ask you something, okay?"

Eric wandered into the living room and lay on the couch. "Ask."

"If I can't say whether or not I'll fall in love with you, would you still want to see me while I figure it out?"

"Yes." *Such an easy question to answer.* In the few seconds of silence that followed, Eric realized Collin must be walking somewhere. He could hear a rhythmic variation in his breathing, and the background noise was clearly from outdoors.

"That sounded definite."

"I'm certain. Where are you?" Eric sat up.

"I'm walking back to the dorm—I guess I should call it the frat—after my Lit class."

Crap. "By yourself?"

"Yeah, but that's why I texted you. I figured if we're on the phone, I'm not really alone, right?"

"I guess not." He'd feel better if someone were with Collin. Like him.

"I called Uncle Monty before Lit and it didn't go well. Maybe if I'd had some more information . . . shit, probably not." Collin blew out a heavy breath.

"Bad, huh?" Not that it surprised him.

"Really bad. I think the Alumni Association is going to cut off funds."

Eric whistled. "Crap. Maybe you should have told him about the possible connection to you."

"I didn't know if I could," Collin said. "Besides, I felt like I shouldn't for some reason, like it was a bad idea. I don't know."

Eric's heart thumped. "A bad idea like he's got some connection to this whole thing?"

"No." Collin snorted. "If he was going to kill me, he'd do it some incredibly symbolic way like poison me with lye, not try to blow me up with whatever that stuff you scrape off of sparklers is."

"Potassium nitrate. But you know he probably just bought it off the internet or at a hardware store. It's used for lots of stuff."

"That. And what kind of person uses that? That's nuts."

"Someone who wants a higher temperature pyrotechnic but doesn't want it to be easily traceable back to them."

"I thought you said you weren't a firefighter, because right there? You sounded like one."

Eric smiled. "I still had to go through the academy and get all the certifications. Besides, that's dinner conversation around the station. While we're talking about chemicals, tell me why J.M. would poison you with lye."

"Because we just have it lying around. It's used for curing olives."

"You guys grow olives, too?"

"We import olives and olive oil from Europe—mostly Spain, because we still have family there with olive farms. Well, and it's the biggest olive oil market in the world. My paternal grandparents came to the US to start the import business."

"That's cool. So you're Spanish." He hadn't realized J.M. was Spanish, but he'd tried to not know anything about the dude. Except for those times he couldn't help himself.

"Half Spanish, and technically I'm American. Anyway, Uncle Monty has this house in the Carmel Valley that's surrounded by olive groves he's planted since he was a teenager. He makes 'special reserve' olive oil and cures olives from them, but the bulk of the business is importing. His groves are more like a hobby for him."

"Huh. Carmel Valley, like near Carmel, California?"

"Yeah." Collin was starting to sound slightly out of breath.

"Your family has money, doesn't it?" Not that he really needed to ask.

"Yeah. I have a trust fund and everything, and a guaranteed position within the company once I graduate, with a ridiculous starting salary." He sounded like he sucked in a breath and held it after that.

"Are you nervous about telling me that? I pretty much already knew J.M. was loaded."

"Well, I mean, I guess I don't feel like the standard rich kid, but once I tell people that, they start treating me a certain way. I don't want you to do that."

"I won't. I promise."

"I believe you. And I didn't grow up like the standard rich kid. My mom inherited her family's cattle ranch, and she made me work my ass off on it when I was growing up. Except she didn't make me ride horses."

Eric started to ask why he didn't have to ride horses on a ranch, but suddenly the sound quality of Collin's phone changed. "Are you at the frat?"

Collin sighed. "Yeah. I have to go upstairs and tell Kyle what Monty said, and we have to prepare a motion for the emergency all-frat meeting for tomorrow night, and then there's this whole other thing going on . . ."

"I wish I were with you so I could give you a back rub." But it would be totally impossible, unless he went and kidnapped Collin. But his sweet boy had just listed all the things he still had to do tonight.

Okay, and it was a stupid idea and he was acting like a lovesick fool.

"And then you'd give me what comes after a back rub?"

"Definitely. I'd give it to you."

He could hear the smile in Collin's voice now, with just a touch of nerves. "I'll need it more tomorrow night, after this meeting."

"Mmm, and what time do you think this meeting will be over?"

Collin sighed. "Really late. And I have a Thursday morning class."

"Are you saying you'd come over if you didn't have a class?"

"Pretty much."

"So, this means you want to keep seeing me?"

"Yeah," Collin said quietly. "I really want to. I don't know what's going to happen or what I feel, exactly, except I really, really like you and I don't want to give that up."

"I'm not giving that up either."

Chapter 26

They had a plan for every eventuality they could think of.
Collin hoped.

They even had a plan to deal with the possibility of the majority of TAG members voting to rescind the membership policy in the face of losing the alumni money. If that happened, Collin and Kyle would resign their posts, and Collin, Tank, Brad, and Kyle would leave the frat, taking along whoever they could convince to join them.

He really, really hoped that didn't happen. It was clear when they had the (secret) pre-meeting meeting this afternoon that no one wanted that. Well, Brad hadn't seemed to care that much.

Fortunately, Brad didn't seem to be upset with Collin either. When he showed up at the bar around the corner from the bar around the corner from the fraternity house (the real one, not the dorm), he sat next to Collin and leaned over to say, "Sorry my boyfriend's being such a douche. I think I've almost got him convinced to apologize. Couple more blowjobs should do the trick."

That had pretty much been that. Except for all the time Collin spent wondering if Ashley had advised Brad to go the blowjob route. He'd finally forced himself not to think about it.

And now the real meeting was upon them.

Collin looked around him at the crowd. He could swear all the brothers were here, even though you'd think a few would have class tonight and couldn't make it. There were so many guys, they packed the whole common area and were spilling into the hallway on either side of it. He sat on the couch between Brad and Jock, with Tank on the other side of his brother. It was a pretty tight squeeze—not so much the butt space, but the shoulders. Collin had to hunch his chest to fit.

Ricky had finally come back today, still in a wheelchair, leg poking out in front of him like a battering ram—a very effective one—but

Collin figured the reason he got a seat up front had more to do with how everyone kept treating him, as if he'd been injured in some kind of battle they'd fought. Maybe vanquished the fire himself with his leg. Their wounded hero.

Kyle called the meeting to order—he used one of Ashley's high heels to do it, knocking it against the window behind him. It was his subtle mockery of Eduardo, who'd had some stupid gavel when he was president. Fortunately, Plant hadn't figured that out.

"All right, let's get started here. Can everyone hear me?"

"Yeah," a few people called out. Collin didn't hear any "nos," but he guessed if they couldn't hear Kyle, they wouldn't know to say anything.

Whatever.

"Okay, you all know this is an emergency meeting. We have three and only three items on the agenda, and I won't be adding anything else to it no matter what, so just shut up if you have something else you want to talk about." He gave the crowd a minute to grumble, but no one did.

It was very different from their usual meetings. No one slept, no one talked in the back and ignored Kyle, no one shot at other guys with water pistols, no one bitched loudly. Collin wondered briefly if they'd invited the wrong guys, but he recognized all these people, so no.

"First item: Tank Gervaise has asked that we consider extraordinary membership for his brother, Jock Gervaise."

"I wanna be an extraordinary member, too," someone shouted. It appeared things were already reverting back to normal meeting procedure.

Kyle ignored whoever it was. "Jock just transferred winter term from Avalon College. Um, does anyone remember Tank talking about his little brother?"

Nods and murmurs met that. Kyle was really asking if anyone remembered Tank saying his brother was gay. Collin couldn't tell from the responses whether anyone had made the connection or not.

Kyle went on. "Jock would be the first member to join under our new membership policy." More murmuring. The guys had to be putting it together now. "And he's asked for membership in Theta Alpha Gamma because we're a place that welcomes all people—"

"All male people," Danny interjected.

Kyle gave him a dirty look and pointed Ashley's shoe at him. "You know what I mean. The point is that Jock was persecuted at Avalon for being gay, and he's looking for a safer, more tolerant environment." They'd decided to just say that and hope for the best.

The room broke out into conversation—something they'd totally expected, and that Kyle would put up with for a minute or two before trying to break Ashley's shoe against something to bring back order. Collin smiled at Jock. He hoped he'd managed a reassuring one, but he didn't feel full of comfort and joy. He was too anxious about the rest of this meeting.

Jock was pale, leaning forward with his elbows on his knees and staring at the floor. It reminded Collin of the time Brad had come out. Collin had probably looked as nervous as Jock did now. He'd *felt* worse than Jock looked. Like a failure, both as a gay man and as a nephew. Meanwhile, Brad had stood up and said, "I'm gay. Get over it."

At the time, Collin's reasons for not coming out were all about his uncle's expectations. Now he'd be just as happy if Monty shoved his expectations up his ass. When had that changed?

Kyle banged the shoe, and once he had silence, he asked for comments. Tank stood up and was recognized. "I have one comment. If you guys don't vote in my brother, I'm out of here." Then he glared around the room and sat down again.

Turbo stood up. "I got a comment. What kind of persecution are we talking about, here?"

Tank jumped back up. "All you need to know is it was bad enough for him to leave school."

Turbo nodded agreeably. "Oh, yeah. That's all I need to know." He sat down.

Tank could teach a Jedi a few things about mind control.

After that, there were no more comments, so Kyle called for a voice vote. There were lots of "ayes" and no "nays."

"Okay, motion passes, Jock Gervaise is now a Theta Alpha Gamma brother and will have conferred unto him all rights of membership . . ."

Collin tuned Kyle's voice out when he felt Jock slump next to him (freeing Collin's left shoulder). He didn't think Jock's apparent relief was so much about getting into the frat as about not having to explain what had happened.

Then Kyle said, "Next on the agenda, the treasurer's going to give the financial report, including changes the Executive Committee planned to meet our emergency needs, then the membership will vote to approve those changes or not." And Collin started paying attention again. "Plant, can you give a brief summary of the provisions we made to cover our interim housing expenses?"

After giving the roundup of the decisions the Executive Committee had made—which no one objected to—Plant sat down in the sea of bodies; up in the front of the room, the options were to sit on the floor or stand.

Kyle asked for comments, and got none. He called a voice vote, and there were no "nays."

Collin's stomach tightened up. Kyle's eye caught his as he stepped up to the podium-slash-coffee table, ready to call the next order of business. It was amazing they'd gotten through the first two items so fast. Collin had been hoping for more time.

But here he was, with Kyle raising an eyebrow at him, beginning to look worried. And since a nervous Kyle was a dorky Kyle, Collin gave him a very small nod. Kyle's shoulders settled.

"All right, moving on, the next order of business is a report on the Alumni Association. Collin, can you come up here and apprise us of the situation?"

When he stood in front of the group, Collin realized they could as easily stone him as listen to him. Or whatever the modern, frat equivalent of stoning was. Pelting with beer bottles, probably. What a way to die. He took a second to look around and remind himself these people were his friends. Mostly. At least good acquaintances.

On a lot of the guys' faces, he saw confusion, and occasionally disbelief. They had to be wondering why they'd been dragged to a "very important" emergency meeting at this point. The first two items had seemed more important than this. So far.

Well, time to elucidate it all for everyone. "I think most of you know that my Uncle Monty is the president of the Alumni Association." There were some nods, but also some bored looks. "You might also know that the association initially opposed the change in the membership policy." Now he had their full attention. "The alumni, including my uncle, seem to think the fire and bombing were the work of someone opposed to gay rights."

"Well, what else would it be?" someone from the back shouted.

Oh no.

Kyle stepped forward. "Well, there was that unfortunate fencing team—"

"I did not throw that bout!" Gomer shouted, standing up.

"It's not the damned fencing team loss," Collin said, raising his hands to regain control.

Brad stood up and gestured to the front of the room. "It doesn't matter what it was, we need to find out what the dude's trying to tell us about the alumni's reaction to all of this, so shut up." It was what they'd agreed should happen if the crowd got offtrack, but Collin couldn't help wishing Brad hadn't done it. Then he wouldn't have to continue.

He took a deep breath, steeling himself. Everyone looked at him expectantly. There was only one way to deal with this: spit it out. "They're probably going to cut off their funds to TAG unless we vote to rescind the membership policy."

No one moved for many seconds, except for the almost synchronized wrinkling of brows.

Finally, Danny sat forward in his seat. "Okay, so how does that affect us?"

Collin didn't know if it was a good thing or a bad thing that someone had asked this so soon after his announcement. If they'd waited, maybe he could have spent some time shoring up support. But wasn't it better for everyone to know what they were dealing with? He looked down at Plant and nodded.

Plant stood up and opened his ostentatious leather-covered portfolio, flipping through pages of handwritten notes while clearing his throat. "After much calculation on my part, I've broken down what we pay for and what Alumni Association funds have allowed us to afford. Between expenses paid by members living in the house—about one-third of us—and the dues all of us pay, we can afford our monthly utilities, house insurance, food, fees to the Greek Council, and regular deposits to the emergency fund."

More brow wrinkling. "That sounds like all we need. What does the association pay for?" Turbo asked.

Plant cleared his throat, flipping to another list. "They pay for our cook—"

Grumbles from the brothers who lived in the frat.

"Our cable and internet connection—"

More and louder grumbles from guys who regularly dropped by to get online and/or watch TV joined those of the guys living at TAG House.

"And the kegerator."

All hell broke loose.

ΘΑΓ

"I'm just saying, dude, I don't need a fucking 'welcoming membership policy,' but I need that fucking kegerator!" The brother shouting in the rear was patted on the back by his neighbors and cheered by people who couldn't reach him.

"Oh my God," Collin moaned to himself, rubbing his temples. It did no good. After—he checked his watch—twenty-two minutes of speeches about every man's right to guts, glory, girls (or guys— they were still equal opportunity, everyone was quick to assure the crowd), and beer, he had a fucking splitting headache. To say the meeting wasn't going well was an understatement. It was all over. He, Kyle, Tank, and Jock would have to pack up their shit and leave. Kyle could go to Ashley's for a while at least, and he'd probably convince her to move into an apartment with him. Tank could go to Penny's with much the same result, and Collin thought he could go to Eric's at least for a while. But where would Jock go? He tried to imagine him on Eric's couch, but that was wrong on a lot of levels, not just because he wouldn't fit.

Of course, Jock would probably be not fitting on Penny's sorority's couch.

"All we'd be doing is going back to the way it was. We'd still let gay guys in," Gomer was saying as Tank stood on the coffee table. It bowed alarmingly.

"Guys!" Tank roared. It got everyone's attention. Sometimes Collin wondered why Tank wasn't president or alumni liaison, but it was probably because he was too smart to take on that much responsibility. "You just voted my brother in after he went through a whole pile of shit at his other college, and why did you vote him in? Because TAG is a safe place, man. It's a place where a guy who doesn't know if he's free to be gay at other frats can come and rush, because he knows he's welcome here, and why? Because of our membership policy."

There was a long silence, and Collin thought that might have done it, but then someone in the back—he thought it might be Zach Wilkerson—said, "Yeah, a safe frat without beer. Are we going to add that to the membership policy?"

Hell ran around that room again like the devil on a motorcycle, inciting useless opinions and shouting.

"Jesus Christ," Kyle muttered next to him. "Do these guys only think about one thing?"

"Uh, yeah. Well, two things, but no one's banning women at TAG. I wish our treasurer had told us that little kegerator detail earlier." Collin sent Plant an evil look, but he hid behind his leather portfolio.

"Well, he kind of tried. Told me this afternoon he needed to talk, but I didn't have time."

Collin turned his evil look on Kyle.

"Fine, my bad. I'm sorry, but at this point it wouldn't have mattered. Nothing other than a beer tax on these guys will get us back the kegerator."

Collin was just trying to figure out how to work the beer tax and having nightmare visions of the Boston Tea Party recreated, but in the Willamette River with him playing the role of "tea," when he noticed Tank and some other guys lifting Ricky—wheelchair and all—onto the coffee table. "Um, I don't know if that table's really sturdy—"

"Hey!" Ricky shouted to the room in general. "Hey, you guys! I have something to say!"

Whether it was because of his leg, or because Ricky was more respected than Collin had realized, the place quieted down.

"Listen, dudes, I know how all you all feel about the porn and the internet and the beer, hell, I feel the same way myself. But there are ways around this stuff if we work together."

A low grumbling started. No one wanted to play that cooperation game, they were past it and had moved on to every man for himself.

"And if you don't think it's worth working for, I got a couple of things to say about that. If the alums are right, and the house was set on fire and then someone tried to blow it up because we're open-minded or whatever, that means I gave up my fucking leg for that policy!"

"He still has a leg," Collin whispered. "I can see it right there." He pointed, but Kyle grabbed his hand and yanked it down.

"Shhh! It's working."

Maybe it was. Guys stood mostly silent, listening to Ricky. Some suspiciously, but some actually looking thoughtful. Not nodding along, but giving the situation another think.

"We all gave up TAG House and our kegerator—'cause I don't see one here—for that policy. So if we vote to change it back, those sacrifices are meaningless." Ricky leaned forward in his chair, gripping the arms, really getting into his speech. "All of that means nothing if we knuckle under and give in to the Alumni Association."

Now guys were nodding along. There were even a few appreciative murmurs.

"And worse than that, you know what it shows them if we give in? It shows them if they want to force us to do something in the future, all they have do is take our kegerator hostage. They're fucking beer terrorists, man. And everyone knows negotiating with terrorists will get you nowhere, 'cause next time they want something from you, they just do the same thing that worked last time—they'll take away our tap until we do what they want, until we bend over and take it. We gotta stand up to those beer terrorists now!"

To Collin's shock, a few guys stood up, pumping their fists in the air, and the rest were looking less sullen and more pissed off.

"We have to nip this thing in the bud, or those keg-stealing bastards will have us by the short and curlies for the rest of our college careers until someone does stand up and say 'no.' Is that the legacy you want to leave your incoming brothers, the future members of TAG? I can't do it. I can't live with that kind of shame. When my grandchildren ask me what I did to end terrorism, no fucking way am I saying, 'Oh, when the terrorists came for me, I just gave them what they wanted and hoped they went away.' What I'm telling you is, I'm not bending over for that. I want my beer and my membership policy too! Now who's with me? Stand up! C'mon, stand up!"

The entire membership stood on its feet and roared. Guys stood all around the coffee table, trying to get close enough to Ricky to pat him on the back, and the whole room had filled with excited buzzing. Collin gaped. He never would have pegged the dude for a revolutionary speaker, before or after the broken leg.

He was still staring at Ricky when Kyle leaned over and said in his ear, "Big mistake the Alumni Association made. You should never threaten a frat boy's beer."

Chapter 27

I t took for-fucking-ever to get everyone settled down enough to vote on a resolution not to change the TAG membership policy regardless of what action the Alumni Association took. It was a unanimous roll-call vote, and Collin had been right—everyone was there. When a group-wide debate about where to get beer money started, Kyle managed to shut it down by suggesting that Plant look over the budget and make recommendations based on his findings over the weekend. To Collin's immense relief, the guys agreed, and people slowly began filtering out.

By 11:30, only the guys who lived in the frat-slash-dorm were left, and even though everyone was amped up and asking a ton of questions, he began to think he could sneak off into his room and call Eric. He owed him a report on how things had gone, since Eric had listened to all his whining, right?

"Hey Collin, can I talk to you for a minute?"

Dammit, someone had caught him. He whirled around to find Jock standing near one of the couches, Tank slouching behind him.

Tank? Slouching?

"Um, sure."

"Okay, uh, I was wondering if you'd like a roommate."

"No." He shook his head to underscore his answer. Why would he want a roommate? Did anyone want a roommate? Roommates were something you suffered through until you got enough clout or money to not have one.

Jock inspected the ground. "Yeah, sure. Sorry." He started to turn away.

Shit, had he meant himself? "Wait, why are you asking?"

He stopped, half turned away from Collin. "It was nothing."

"He wants to move out of my room, and the only people left who don't have roommates are you and Kyle," Tank said sullenly.

Shit.

"I guess I'm the only real option then, huh?" Kyle was the president, and by tradition the president always had his own room.

"Well, yeah," Tank said, talking over a motionless Jock. "I mean, it would be nice if he had a, you know, role model. Other than me." He gave Jock a wounded look.

Jock turned to him. "Beau, c'mon, you were my role model for nineteen years. I need a new one." He punched Tank on the shoulder in a brotherly way, making Tank flinch.

Collin blinked. He'd never see Tank flinch before. But more importantly, "Did you just call Tank 'Beau'?"

"Yeah, dude, he did," Danny piped up. He and everyone else on the couch next to them had their ears perked, blatantly listening. "Why'd you call him Beau?"

Jock rubbed his jaw, hiding a grin behind his hand.

"What's your real name?" Collin asked. He'd held nearly every office in this frat; how could he not know Tank's real name?

Now the whole room was listening. Tank scowled at the floor, hands shoved in his pockets, clearly refusing to answer.

Kyle sidled up to Collin. "Um, his name's 'Beauregard.'"

"Beauregard?"

"It's a family name," Tank growled. He stood up to his full height, all six feet six of it, glowering at the whole room, but Collin thought he'd heard a note of wounded beast in his words.

"It's a lovely name," he said, coming around Jock to speak directly to Tank. He barely stopped himself from petting the dude's arm. "Why don't you just go by Beau?"

Tank scrunched his brows together. "Do I look like a 'Beau' to you?"

"Tank fits you better." Collin nodded encouragingly, and with one last glare for the rest of the room, Tank relaxed.

"You see," Jock said, smirking. "Mom was a Beauregard of the General P. G. T. Beauregards, and she wanted to keep the name in the family even after she married Daddy, who's a Gervaise of the Delaware Gervaises."

"So, what's your real name?" Danny asked him. "It's not Jock, right?"

"It's Gavin Jacques Gervaise." Next to Beauregard, it didn't sound like much of a name. "On one of the teams I played on, there was another Gavin, so the coach called me Jacques, but everyone said 'Jock.' Well, unless they were Canadian. Anyway, the name stuck."

"You've played hockey forever, right?" Jules asked.

"Yeah."

"He's always been around those guys, and you know any of them who are gay, I mean, most of them aren't even out to themselves, let alone a teammate," Tank said. He seemed to have regained his equilibrium. "He's never been around gay guys. I guess that's why he wants to be Collin's roommate. I think it would be good for him, if he just can't stand rooming with me anymore."

Oh God, they were back to the roommate thing.

"Makes sense." Danny nodded. Kyle made a weird, choking noise next to him, and when Collin turned, he could swear he nearly caught him making wild "cease and desist" gestures to the room. Collin looked around. No one would meet his eye.

Weird.

Tank cleared his throat into the silence. "Um, sorry, man." He seemed to be addressing Collin.

"Sorry about what?" About suggesting Jock should move to his room? It did kind of make sense; it would be good for Jock to have someone with a little more experience to talk to about—

Wait.

"Um, why do you think I'd make a good roommate for Jock, again?" He could feel sweat suddenly soaking his pits.

"Uhhh . . . Well, because, you know . . ."

"You're gay too, dude," Danny said. Like it was a known factor.

Collin gaped at him. "What did you just say?"

Danny cocked his head. "It's not like everyone doesn't already know."

He took another look around the room, in between one pounding heartbeat and the next. Oh sure, now guys would meet his eye—a couple were nodding.

He tried to play it off, flinging his hand out as if pushing away the statement. "What would make you think I'm gay? I'm not gay." Except that wrist motion might have been a bit gay. Collin quickly dropped his hand, shoving both in his pockets and widening his stance, trying to project "butch."

Danny stared at him, goggle-eyed, mouth hanging open. "Dude!" He stood up, reaching out to grip Collin's shoulder. "You mean no one told *you* you're gay? Shit, man, I'm sorry, I didn't know . . ." He turned to Kyle. "What am I supposed to do in this situation? They did *not* cover this in that sensitivity training class we took fall term. That's a major oversight, man. Major oversight. Told you that class sucked." He turned back to Collin. "But, I mean, I just figured if I know you're gay, you *must* know."

Collin opened his mouth to explain he *did* know, but Danny wouldn't shut up.

"I'm sorry, dude, but I'm not really prepared to handle outing a guy to himself. Fuck, I hope I didn't, like, traumatize you or anything." He glanced wildly around the room. "Hoy! Billings! Did you role-play this scenario in sensitivity training? What the fuck do I do, man? Is there some kind of, I don't know, comfort I'm supposed to give him now?"

While Danny babbled, Collin turned to Kyle. He had a cringing sort of "I'm sorry" look on his face.

"Maybe he should sit down," Jules said from behind him, and the next thing he knew, he was being forcibly ushered to Danny's former spot on the couch. "Someone get a paper bag, and start boiling water," Jules barked to the room.

"We don't have a kitchen; should I get it from the cafeteria?" Gomer asked.

"Um, I'm not going into labor." He may as well not have said anything.

"Yes!" Jules responded to Gomer, pushing down on Collin's shoulders to make him sit. "And get lots and lots of dishtowels, too. Someone get a footstool, we need to maintain blood flow to the brain. Move!" Collin went ahead and sat down; he felt a little weak anyway. But he wasn't putting his damned feet up.

Sitting there watching everyone freak out around him focused Collin, and he started wondering just how much he really wanted to deny this.

"Everyone just shut up!" Kyle yelled from on top of the coffee table. "And Gomer, get back here!"

Everyone froze in indecision. Collin recognized this moment—he had to gain control now or it would spiral into chaos, just as it had for Brad when he'd come out.

Should I do it? He looked up and met Jock's gaze, feeling for a split second as if he could see into his heart. Jock had been through this, and it had gone horribly wrong. "You can room with me," Collin said. Jock nodded as everyone turned to look at him, then back at Collin. He raised his voice. "And I already know I'm gay, so back off." Jules looked disappointed as he slowly let go of Collin's shoulders.

He stood up as soon as he had the space, and pushed his way toward Kyle. "Okay, just tell me how you guys figured out I'm gay."

Everyone stared at him, until Danny said, "Well, the guys you hang out with socially, they're all gay."

"But Kyle hangs out with the same guys, and no one's asking him if he's gay."

"That's different," Jules said.

"How?"

"'Cause he's not gay."

As a logical argument, it seemed lacking, yet irrefutable. Collin waved a hand for them to go on, not worrying for once how flaming his wrist might appear.

"Um, and you never bring chicks home or talk about them," Billings called out.

Okay, that was a weakness, but he knew other guys didn't do that, either. "Neither does Carson."

"Yeah, he does, just not around you because he's trying to be sensitive to your gayness." Jules whispered in Gomer's ear. "Oh, uh, I mean sexual orientation."

Danny was nodding. "And if someone has a problem or needs to talk about their feelings—"

"Not that we do, ever, this is in theory only," Gomer interjected.

"—they can come to you and you'll help them fix it. Like you just did for Jock."

"You guys don't help each other with stuff?"

Danny wrinkled his nose. "Not unless I have to."

"Oh, and you bet Brad was gay last year when we ran that book," Kyle said. Collin gave him a look and he shut up. He'd deal with Kyle later.

Jules delivered the coup de grâce. "You always put the toilet seat down."

"I grew up with two women. I was trained to put it down from birth."

"Well, I have three older sisters and I was trained to also, but four years after joining TAG, I'm leaving it up without thinking about it. You still don't, man."

"Brad left the seat up!"

Jules *tsk*ed at him. "You know not every gay guy fits the stereotype. What's wrong with you?"

Collin stared at them. He should probably be happy. It was a much less tumultuous coming out than Brad's, but he mostly felt confused. And maybe a little bit let down.

Whatever. He was too tired to deal with it. He turned to Jock. "Can you give me an hour before moving in? I want to call my boyfriend."

As he walked out of the room, he heard someone add, "And you have a boyfriend. That's a big clue."

Chapter 28

Eric had gone to bed, but lay there awake until Collin called. He knew that Collin would call—his boy would be all stressed out and need to talk. Eric planned on listening to and then relaxing him.

The phone rang at 12:03. Eric spent most of the first half of the conversation making agreeable noises, right up until Collin said, "And then I was outed."

Eric's heart knocked on his ribs, wanting him to take some action, and he sat up in bed. "Who outed you? Give me his name." *I'ma kill him*.

"Mmm, are you going all protective bear on me?" Collin sounded something other than anxious, annoyed, or fed up for the first time since they'd started talking.

"Gimme his name. He won't feel a thing, I swear." He could take some of the outdated drugs from the station and—

Collin laughed, then sighed. "It's not like that, it was an accident. They all freaking knew, everyone in the frat, and they thought I knew they knew. Tank just mentioned it naturally in conversation."

Tank. He'd remember that name.

"And don't bother thinking you're going to have a word with Tank. He's huge and mean when you provoke him."

"You don't think I can take him?"

"No. I'm sorry, you know I adore you, but no. He's fifteen years youn—"

"You adore me?" Eric leaned back against his headboard.

Collin caught his breath. "Well . . . yeah. You knew that, didn't you?"

He really shouldn't tease his sweet young thang. Much. "Last I heard, you only really, really liked me. I think adoration is a whole new level of affection."

He could hear a smile in Collin's voice. "Like, what kind of whole new level?"

"Mmm, depends."

"On what?"

"On what you're wearing."

There was a moment of confused silence. "Like, right now?"

Eric smirked to himself. "Yeah, right now. What're you wearing?"

"That sounds like . . ."

"The beginning of phone sex?"

Collin sucked in a breath. "I can't have phone sex."

"Well, you aren't having it alone, sweetheart." He slid his hand under the hem of his tee, working upward on his belly. Collin wasn't much of a nipple guy, but he liked it.

"I mean, because I'm about to get my new roommate."

He slid his hand out of his shirt. "Roommate?" *Crap.*

"Yeah. It's Tank's little brother, Jock. That's why the whole thing about me being gay came up. Jock just moved here and started school because he got outed to his hockey coach at the college he was at, then kicked off the team. Whoever outed him are the guys you should be planning to maim, not Tank."

"What happened?"

"He won't really talk about it. What I told you is pretty much all I know, and it's more than I'm technically allowed to tell."

Eric sighed and ran a hand across his head. That was kind of a mood killer. "What's with outing people? I don't get where the thrill is for the assholes who do it."

"Neither do I, hon."

"Mmm, you called me 'hon.'"

"Yeah, but it's not my pet name for you." Eric could hear the slither of fabric over the phone.

"Are you in bed?"

"How did you know that? Do I sound different when I'm lying down?"

"No, I could hear the sound of you sliding across the sheets. Do you have your hand on your dick?"

"Maybe." Collin's voice got a little higher.

"Did you lock the door?"

"Yes."

"Then I'll assume your hand is around your dick. Tell me what you're doing to yourself, Sweet Thing." Eric slid down in his own bed and spread his legs, tracing fingers lightly across his skin just under his waistband.

Collin's breath was audible now. "I'm stroking myself. What are you doing?"

Eric reached down and fisted his shaft. "I'm doing the same thing, wishing it was you."

"Me too." Collin inhaled. "Want to know what I want?"

"Tell me, Sweet Boy."

"I want you to fuck me."

"You're killing me," Eric half groaned. "Do you have a dildo or a plug there?"

Collin gasped. "Yeah, a dildo. And it vibrates."

"No vibrator, 'cause my dick doesn't do that."

Collin huffed a laugh, then added, "It's got a suction cup on the base."

"Perfect. Stick it to the wall at the right height, then lube it up."

Talking Collin through working himself onto the dildo was so hot that Eric had to stop jerking himself until he could hear how close his sweet boy was. "Wish I were there."

"Me too," Collin panted. "Fuck me."

So Eric did, as best he could by phone, finally stroking himself while telling Collin how fast he could go and when he could touch his dick. Collin came before him, then just about gave Eric a heart attack when he said, "I want to feel your cum all over my back."

As Eric came, he squeezed his eyes shut and imagined it, shooting on Collin's olive-tinted skin till he could see a drop rolling down between his cheeks, like it knew its rightful place and wanted to be there.

That made him open his eyes. Still gasping for breath, he said, "I want to fuck you without a rubber."

"Mmm. We can work on that."

Collin set the phone down while he cleaned up, and Eric grabbed a towel out of the drawer and did the same. When Collin picked up again, he said, "Are you going to hang up now?"

"No, we get to do the postcoital stuff now."

"Like cuddling?"

"Yeah. And talking. Get back in bed and hug your pillow." He sort of meant it as a joke, and Collin laughed softly, but Eric could hear him sliding back between his sheets.

"Okay, now what do you want to talk about?"

"I don't know. Nothing serious."

Collin yawned in his ear. "I haven't learned how to cook you breakfast yet."

"Yeah? I'll still let you come and stay this weekend." Eric rolled onto his side and looked at Collin's pillow next to him. Weird how last week it had just been his extra pillow.

"I'm not really versed in the domestic arts in general." Collin's voice was softer now, and Eric couldn't hear any of the tension he'd had earlier. If he wasn't so sated, he'd try to pat himself on the back.

"Your mom just made you learn how to herd cows, huh? None of that housekeeping stuff."

"Mm-hmm."

Which reminded him. "How can you be a rancher if you don't ride horses?"

"We did most things on ATVs."

Eric all but flinched. He'd seen so many bad accidents on those things. "I'd think a horse would be safer."

Collin was quiet for so long that Eric was about ready to ask if he'd fallen asleep, but then he said, "My dad died in a riding accident. He got thrown off and broke his neck. I guess it killed him instantly, that's what they said. I used to ride with him, all the time. He'd get on and then I'd climb up on a fence rail and he'd pull me up and sit me in front of him. I think it just . . . those are my strongest memories of him."

"I'm so sorry, Sweetness." Eric closed his eyes and imagined wrapping Collin in his arms, holding him tightly. Maybe, if he imagined it vividly enough, Collin would feel it, or at least feel comforted. "I'm sorry I brought it up." Hopefully it hadn't undone all his therapy.

Collin sighed. "It's okay. It feels good to talk about him sometimes. Especially when I'm telling someone who really cares about what I'm saying. It's sort of like I'm bringing small pieces of him back to life for a few minutes." Collin still sounded relaxed. Eric could almost feel his sweet boy's warmth in bed next to him.

"Remember I said if we saw each other again, I'd probably start falling in love with you?"

"Yeah." He was pretty sure he heard Collin suck in a breath and hold it.

"I guess I don't need to see you to get the ball rolling, I just need to talk to you on the phone."

"I don't know what to say."

"Tell me how that makes you feel."

"Happy. Scared but happy."

Eric's heart skipped a beat. "Good."

Eric still felt half-buzzed from being with Collin (without actually *being* with him) the next morning when he got to work. For once, he barely made it on time because he'd slept too long after the phone sex and the postcoital activities, so it was a surprise that Lincoln was still there, waiting for him.

Lincoln normally went home when Val showed up, and TimTam did when Eric arrived, but this morning Lincoln had told Tim to go.

"Hey, man. What are you still doing here?" Eric asked when he walked into the station kitchen to find Lincoln reading the paper.

Lincoln folded it and laid it on the table, grinning at Eric. He started to get a funny feeling. "Mike tells me you met a *boy*."

Eric groaned. Figured.

"That's the word he used, too: 'boy.'" Lincoln tilted back in his chair and rested his hands behind his head, smiling like a big stupid loon.

Eric turned to the fridge and opened it, looking inside as if he had an actual reason to. "Just tell me you haven't told Mandy."

"Not yet. I'll do that when I get home. You should expect a call from her at, oh . . ." Lincoln made a big show of looking at his watch. "Yup. About five seconds after I tell her. Just after she stops squealing and jumping up and down."

Eric slammed the refrigerator door shut. "Seriously? It's that big a deal?"

"Yup. Let me refresh your memory: the last time you dated anyone was a year ago."

"Bullshit! The last guy I dated was that optometrist, Gary."

Lincoln crossed his arms and lifted one eyebrow. "And when was that?"

Crap. "About a year ago."

"This is serious, isn't it?"

Eric blew out a breath. "Yeah."

Lincoln sat forward, letting his chair legs drop. "And is he really a 'boy'?"

"Mike just said that because he's a senior in college."

Lincoln's eyebrows flew up, but he didn't lose the smile. "When did you meet him?"

"Mike didn't tell you that?"

"Well, he might have told me you met him on a call, but that he wasn't a patient."

"It was at the bombing. It was at my old college fraternity, Theta Alpha Gamma."

Lincoln didn't say anything, just smirked.

"Shut up," Eric said anyway.

"You know, a lot of people meet their destined mate on calls."

Eric gaped. "'Destined mate'? Have you been reading the horoscopes in the paper again? Besides, you're the only one I know who married someone they met on a call."

"Oh, so you're thinking marriage already?"

Eric grabbed a roll of gauze sitting on the counter and flung it at Lincoln. He ducked, laughing. "Go the fuck home already. Tell your wife and you two can giggle like girls about it all day, just leave me alone."

Lincoln stood up. "All right, since you want me to."

Eric picked up a jar of peanut butter and held it threateningly, cocking his arm to chuck it too.

Lincoln smirked. "You know what's about to happen, don't you?"

Eric dropped the peanut butter on the counter. *Crap.* "Yeah."

"My wife's going to start trying to get you to bring this boy over."

"His name's Collin."

"Good, she'll want that information."

Eric scowled at Lincoln, who stood grinning, arms crossed over his chest.

"Eric Dixon! Where are you, goddammit? I don't have all the time in the world to sit around waiting for your lazy ass to—"

"Mike's looking for you," Lincoln said, picking his car keys up from the table and heading toward the exit. "I forgot to tell you."

"So I hear."

ΘΑΓ

Mike was kind enough to update him on the investigation, little as there was to say. "Homes interviewed all the Theta Alpha Gamma guys, and all the members of the other frats that are known to be hostile to TAG, and got nowhere. Then she started talking to the sorority across the street, and got one possible lead. A sorority girl in Nu Omicron Mu has some kind of a thing for a guy in TAG, and she keeps a telescope in her room trained on the frat at all times."

"She admitted that?"

Mike smiled. "Nope, her roommate did, though, then she fessed up. The night before the fire, she saw someone lurking around the fraternity. She thought it was some guy named—" Mike picked up his notes and peered through his glasses at them "Huh. Name is Tank."

Tank again.

"Not the guy she's interested in, I guess his name's Jules or something. Anywho, she was just about to stop watching when this guy walked through a pool of light and she saw he had light hair. I guess this Tank person has dark hair."

"Did she keep watching?"

Mike snorted. "No such luck. She shrugged it off and went to bed."

Mike steepled his fingers on his desk, and Eric steepled his between his knees. "That's all you got, huh?"

"Yup. Sucks, doesn't it? What we need is a break on this case. I've done everything I know how, but I can't trace the specific seller of the potassium nitrate without a bar code or a receipt, and our guy wasn't nice enough to leave me one. There are no fingerprints, no eyewitness that we've found—not even the night he took the hot-water heater. How in the fuck did someone thump something that heavy down four front-porch steps, then drag it along a concrete walkway to the street without someone hearing the god-awful racket he had to be making and looking to see what was going on?"

"Not even the chick with the telescope?"

Mike waved him off. "She stopped spying once this Jules guy wasn't there to see."

"What about my pictures, did they help?"

"Told us the hot-water heater was about ten years old and was tampered with. That's pretty much it."

"What are you guys doing now?"

"We're casting a wider net. Looking at non-suspicious frats and sororities, for beginners—Homes has started talking to them already. But I gotta tell you, this might be one of those cases, you know? Might go cold."

Eric jerked his head back.

Mike held up a hand. "I'm doing everything I can. I even got a copy of that damned building permit from when the kitchen was remodeled and an auxiliary hot-water heater was originally installed, but that's not telling me shit." He picked it up from his desk and looked at it in disgust. "All I know is it's from 1985 and the guy who signed the thing has a last name of Donaldson. Can't read the first name."

"Donaldson?"

"That mean something to you? But you graduated in the late nineties."

"1998. But Collin's been trying to get ahold of some guy named Donaldson who's in the Alumni Association that doesn't support the membership policy. Nicknamed Sparky because the rumor is he was a firebug in college."

Mike perked up, then looked down at the copy of the permit. "First name starts with . . ." He screwed up his face.

"Starts with a D. Donald D. Donaldson."

Mike whistled. "Well, well, he musta been one ugly baby. Excuse me, I need to make a phone call."

Eric didn't move. "That seems kinda thin to start looking at him as a suspect."

Mike focused on him a second, mid-dial. "Dix, all I fucking have is thin."

Chapter 29

"I'm afraid to even turn my cell phone on," Val's patient wailed, sobbing. Eric stood in the corner, putting all of his twelve years of experience and training into keeping a straight face. "I'm telling you, someone's been doing it in my sleep!"

"Ma'am, as a medical professional I can assure you that it's impossible for anyone to wire your breast implants to explode. They're filled with a certified nonflammable material," Val assured her for about the fourth time. "Also, unless you're being drugged into unconsciousness, you couldn't possibly sleep through it."

Eric winced. *Big mistake.*

"I'm being drugged into sleep," the woman wailed. "And they're *definitely* doing it, I can prove it. Look!" She yanked her shirt up, and Eric barely stopped himself from flinching back at the sight of a huge pair of knockers. But then the open wound in her left breast with half an implant hanging out of it registered.

"Jesus Christ." Fortunately neither Val nor the patient heard him.

"Whoa, whoa, whoa," Val half shouted. "Okay, you got your ride to the hospit— Oh my God, don't stick your fingers in it!" She lunged to grab the woman's hand, but it was too late. She was already done shoving the implant back through the laceration, along with who knew what germs.

"Did you see them? Did you see the wires?" she demanded. "I'm telling you, someone's trying to turn me into a walking human *bomb*!"

A couple minutes later, as Eric shut the rear doors on the ambulance, he heard the patient telling Val, "I don't think you need to worry about a billing address. I do a lot of volunteer work for the CIA, so I think they'll be picking up the tab."

That's a new one.

Finally, he escaped the crazy for the front seat of the rig, where he could reflect on all the bombs in his life lately. First the TAG bomb, now this. Not to mention Collin, who was totally explosive.

ΘΛΓ

Back at the station, Eric wasn't planning on calling Collin—okay, more like he was thinking he shouldn't call him *every* night—but when he checked his email, Sweetness had forwarded him one.

snort Guess I can't expect any help from Sparky. Read below. Call me later if you have time.
Hugs-
Collin

---------- Forwarded message ----------
From: **Sparky Donaldson** <bigfish.bigpond@genericmail.com>
Subject: Sorry to Have Missed You
To: Collin Montes <coliveoil@calapooya.edu>

Collin-

Sorry I didn't get back to you sooner, but I left Oregon and immediately went to conduct some business with a client in Miami. I'm sure you can imagine how difficult it is to make oneself devote what little free time one has to extraneous projects while in Florida. My hotel room overlooked a topless beach. ;-)

I'm not sure when I'll get back to Oregon—my client there has been satisfied with the way things are progressing, and this next week I'll be in New York City. As you suggest, we can communicate by email, but again I'm unsure how frequently I'll be able to respond to your requests. However, please let me know what you need from me in regard to coordinating Alumni Weekend and I will endeavor to meet those needs.

Best-
Sparky Donaldson

What a loser. Beyond that, Eric forgot about Sparky; mostly he thought about Collin asking him to call.

ΘΔΓ

After dinner, Eric shut himself up into his chosen night-cubby, first giving Val the "if I find you out here listening at the door I'll skin you alive" look. She smirked and wandered off, whistling, toward the kitchen. Probably to find a water glass to better hear through the door.

Couldn't be helped. Eric called Collin anyway.

"Hey," Collin said, and Eric could hear him smiling. He'd never figured out how that could come through in someone's voice.

He lay down on the bed with the phone. Too damn bad it couldn't just be next to Collin instead. "I might have to go on a call, but as long as the tones don't go off, we can talk."

"'Kay. How was your day?"

"Busy, we had a crazy patient."

"Mmm," Collin said.

"You sound happy."

Collin's voice softened. "I am happy. You called me."

"I had to, didn't I? You're my sweet young thang. Isn't that what sugar daddies do after a hard day at work?"

"I don't know, you're my first sugar daddy."

"You're my first sweet boy, so I guess we'll have to feel this one out."

Collin laughed. "Tell me something."

"What?"

"About your mom."

So Eric did. About how his mom had been sort of a hippie and she'd hooked up with a guy in college who knocked her up, married her under (her father's) duress, and then left her with a toddler and no money. "We had to move back to her parents' place while she finished school, but it ended up all right. By the time I was five, she met her boyfriend, Nick, and they've been together ever since. He's a photographer."

"Is that who taught you about it?"

"Yeah. Nick was really good to me. They've never been married or had any other kids, but I always felt like I had a father figure, you know?"

Collin sighed. "Yeah. That's what Uncle Monty was for me."

"I'm sorry you're going through all this crap with him, Sweetness."

"So am I, but . . . I don't know, what else do I do?"

"Nothing," Eric said, even though he had a feeling Collin hadn't really been asking.

"Do you think family is more important to us because we didn't have traditional ones?"

"Maybe. I've never thought about it before."

"I think about it a lot. I guess because of the family business."

"Tell me about it." Eric rolled onto his side, snugging the phone up next to his ear with his shoulder and settling in. Closing his eyes so he could concentrate on Collin's voice. The sound of it made him feel like he'd been wrapped up in something—some private space just for them.

"Weeeell . . ." Collin began. "A long time ago in a small town in Andalusia, my grandfather *didn't* inherit the family olive farm. Instead, his older brother did, and they fought about it so much that Carlos— that was my grandfather's name—took his new wife to America, to settle in this golden land called California and start a company. He didn't know for sure what kind of company, but he knew about one thing only—olives and olive oil. When he got here, though, in spite of having believed America was the land of opportunity, he couldn't buy a grove, or find a farmer who grew what he wanted, so times were hard. Then, one day, he got a letter in the mail from his brother, offering a business deal. He would sell his olive oil to Carlos, and Carlos could turn around and sell it to Americans. And that's how Montes Imports began. The end."

Eric smiled and stretched, rolling onto his back again. "And everyone lived happily ever after?"

"More or less. My father and his brother had very Spanish first names—my dad was Juan Carlos Montes and Monty is Jose Maria Montes. People started calling him Monty in college, and it stuck."

"Some people in college called him J.M. At least if they weren't part of his inner circle." Crap, he shouldn't bring up how well he and J.M. didn't like each other. "Sorry, forget it." Eric felt like much more than a phone and geographic distance was separating them now, and it was all his stupid fault.

Collin didn't respond right away, and the silent seconds had Eric sweating. The ache in his chest ran all the way through him, settling between his shoulder blades, knotting up the muscles there. He opened his mouth, probably about to say something stupid, but Collin saved them. "We have to figure out how to talk about him without it being an issue."

"It'd probably help if I didn't say anything about him."

"So we'd have a taboo subject between us? No thanks. Not for my uncle's sake."

"But he's your uncle and you love him." Dammit, had he whined that? If Lincoln had said something that way, Eric would've totally busted him for whining.

"I don't really *like* him right now though." Collin huffed. "I know what you meant when you said that about his inner circle. He's a snob. It's something that I've always known, but I guess I've never been on the wrong side of it before."

"You're on the right side of it," Eric said.

"Well, that's how I feel. But, I mean, it's not easy to defy him. For *me* to defy him. I tried so hard for so long to make sure he *liked* me. Loved me too much to ever reject me when he finds out . . ."

"That you're gay."

"Yes." Collin paused to take a deep breath, and Eric bet that his boy was worrying his lip. He closed his eyes and listened to Collin speak. "But lately, I just care less. Or maybe it's that I care in a different way. When I don't feel kind of guilty, I feel mad. Why can't he view this the same way I do?"

Maybe he shouldn't have closed his eyes, because he could see Collin's voice in his mind—long strings of doubt, maybe backlit with some fear, but also anger. Eric sighed. "Sweetness, the only answer I can give you is that he doesn't know why he should. But since I know the guy, and based on what you've said, I don't know if he'll have a good reaction. Not the one you'd like."

"Maybe he'll surprise us," Collin said. But his voice didn't have the faith his words did.

"I hope so, Sweet Thing," Eric said, and he truly meant it.

Collin's voice completely changed, all the angles softening in Eric's mind's eye. "We just did it. Talked about Monty without it being a big problem between us."

Because J.M. was a big enough problem already. Eric almost opened his mouth and said it, but he stopped in time. "Good, 'cause I'm not giving you up for his sake."

"I want to keep seeing you. My uncle has nothing to do with us."

"I'm so glad you feel that way, Sweetness. How about tomorrow night?"

Chapter 30

I n spite of feeling like there might be worms in his stomach, Collin couldn't stop smiling the whole way out to Eric's house. The farther he got from Calapooya, the lighter his life seemed, and he could swear the clouds thinned a little, but that had to be his imagination.

Buoyant. He felt buoyant.

He needed directions, because he hadn't been paying enough attention last weekend to remember how to get back there. He glanced down to make sure he knew the street number, then looked up just as the house came into view from behind a stand of oak trees.

It was darling, in a very mountain man kind of way. A true craftsman style, low to the ground, sided in natural wood shake with some trim boards picked out in a very dark teal. Smoke curled out of the chimney, and a lamp glowed through a large side window. It was the next best thing to a log cabin. A very stylish man cave. He pulled up next to Eric's car by the side door, even though the front porch was one of those totally awesome ones that were big enough to fit a small dining table on and he really wanted to explore it.

But Eric was standing in his side doorway, and, given the chance, Collin would rather explore him. He looked good enough to eat—his head had a quarter inch of fuzz on it and his face had more. Plus he was just plain old hot.

"Hey, Sweet Thing," Eric called as soon as Collin was out of the car. His smile looked like Collin's felt. Collin grabbed his bag out of the backseat and kept himself from running to Eric, but it was a near thing.

When he got close enough, Eric grabbed him and pressed himself into Collin's chest until it felt like their hearts were beating in the same space, right next to each other. Maybe with some snuggling.

"I've been waiting for you," Eric said in his ear, then kissed it. He started working his way to Collin's mouth, rubbing their cheeks together, making them rasp against each other, then nuzzling along Collin's jaw to his chin.

"Kiss me." Collin's lips brushed Eric's when he spoke. They were getting chapped, and it made them more sensitive.

"Anything you want." Eric grabbed his head and held him still for a serious, tongue-twining kiss that made Collin's stomach turn back into the tight pit of excitement it had been most of last weekend

When he was done, Eric held his head right there, near his mouth. "Let's go inside, Sweet Boy. I have plans for you."

Oh God. Plans. That sounded so promising. And hot.

It wasn't quite what Collin expected, though. Eric took Collin's bag and Collin's hand, and led him into the house, through the living room, dropping the bag on the couch, and then into the room Collin had guessed was another bedroom. But it appeared to be a studio, with white walls, and what looked like powerful lights on tripods.

On one side of the room was a mattress pushed up against a wall paneled in rough wood, with more of Eric's fluffy bedding—or maybe he'd stolen that from upstairs—and opposite it was a camera on another tripod.

Collin looked over to Eric, and he had that totally endearing blush on his face. Collin squeezed his hand. "What's this?"

Eric cleared his throat. "I thought you might let me take a couple of pictures of you. They'd be just for me, I wouldn't sell them or anything."

He turned to face Eric, who didn't quite meet his eyes. "You sell your photos?"

"Sometimes. Online. I don't really make any money at it."

"Photos of what?"

His blush got darker. "Guys. I kind of need to talk to you about that . . ."

Hmmm. "Naked guys?"

Eric ran his free hand across his head. "Well, you know, mostly naked. Most of the time. Sometimes they're, you know, completely naked. Is that all right with you?"

Collin blinked. "Why wouldn't it be?"

"Not everyone I've dated was okay with it."

"I trust you."

Eric heaved a sigh, looking around, still not quite at Collin. "We don't have to do this if you don't want."

"Would the photos you take of me be mostly or completely?"

Finally Eric looked at him, but Collin chalked that up to confusion. "Mostly or completely what?"

"Naked."

Eric swallowed. "Whichever I can talk you into, I guess."

That so deserved a kiss. Collin cupped his face and kissed one corner of Eric's lips, then the other, until they parted and he could work his way into Eric's mouth while Eric slid his arms around him, palms moving on Collin's back. He took his time, until he had Eric breathing in tandem with him, and then he let him go.

"Is that a yes?"

"Yes." Collin kissed him quickly again. "Where do I put most of my clothes?" He had a little surprise for Eric, and he had a feeling he'd keep at least one thing on for a while.

"All over the setup. I'm taking pictures of you undressing too."

Collin looked at him carefully. He didn't seem embarrassed anymore; now he seemed like a man with a plan. "What else are you taking pictures of me doing?"

"We'll see how far we get, Sweet Thing."

Chapter 31

E ric wouldn't say he was nervous (anymore), but he was definitely excited. Collin might have had a problem with Eric's pictures. He could have said no to the pictures of him—he'd had boyfriends do it before, and a couple thought it was sort of perverted that Eric wanted nude pictures of them. He couldn't figure that out; wouldn't they rather he was jerking off to them than to anonymous porn when they weren't around?

And none of them had ever understood that it wasn't just Eric wanting to have nudes of them, it was also him wanting to take the pictures of them.

But Collin was a little different. Everything with him was a little different, from midnight snacks to phone sex to this. Eric could never quite explain his relationship to his camera, and he hadn't fully fathomed his relationship to Collin, but having the two of them in the same room with him, about to engage in this exchange together, was enough to make him hard before Collin had removed any clothes. It was like having a threesome, except his dick liked the idea better than any three-way he'd ever been in.

Eric turned on the lights, then checked the levels and the setup and the LCD screen, until finally he had to look up at Collin, standing there with his hands poised on his waistband, ready to unsnap his jeans as soon as Eric said "go." His eyes were bright and he had an almost-smile on his face, as if he were looking forward to this. Eric swallowed. "Can you take off your shoes and socks first?"

Collin looked down and toed his sneakers off, revealing bare feet. The shoes were still in the frame, but Eric didn't want them in the pictures. He went to move them, kissing Collin while he was there to calm his nerves—his, not Collin's.

Fine, his nerves got the best of him.

Collin's brow wrinkled. "You want me to throw my clothes off to the side?"

"No, I want your clothes on the floor in front of the bed, just not the shoes."

"'Kay." He kissed Eric quickly. "Let's start."

Eric wanted this, but his feet wouldn't leave Collin and go back to the camera. *You can rub all over him later.* He didn't move. Instead Eric got another kiss. *It's not that far.*

He still didn't move. Then Collin leaned into him, kissing along his jaw, petting his chest through his shirt. "Save it for the pictures, Sexy Man," he whispered.

Dazed, Eric walked back to the camera, wondering if Collin meant what Eric thought he did. Another thing he could only see himself doing with this man. Not that the thought hadn't crossed his mind before, but he'd never done it because the idea of being the guy in front of the camera had never been part of his fantasy.

Before.

"Okay," he said when he had turned around and grabbed the remote. Did his voice sound as low to Collin as it did to him?

Collin unsnapped his jeans, staring at Eric, not the camera. Only the professionals seemed to figure that out, but before Eric could say anything, Collin stopped, brow wrinkling. He refocused, and this time his eyes connected with Eric's through the screen, sending a cascade of prickles along Eric's skin.

Oh yeah, Sweet Thing gets the program.

Collin could have been reading his mind. He smiled at Eric's camera, pulling on his lower lip with his teeth—Eric hit the shutter button reflexively—then turned around, back to the camera, but glancing over his shoulder. He pulled his shirt up from the hem, revealing a slice of his brief's waistband above his jeans, then the skin of his lower back. The light hit the little dimples next to his spine perfectly, shadows sliding and dripping along the contours, making Eric catch his breath. He'd crop that shot, make it monochromatic. The denim of Collin's pants just peeking above the frame, then that slice of his briefs slanting above it. With the combination of Collin's shirt angled opposite them across the top of the image, it would frame that sweep of shadowed skin, making it pop. The smoothness of it would make the fabric look rough by contrast.

In Eric's mind, all the action froze right there, and his body pulsed in time with the sound of the shutter. Then the scene moved on as Collin bared more of his back. Stretching his whole body, rising onto his tiptoes, erector spine muscles flexing. Eric's thumb worked independently of his brain, taking pictures of it all—he could hear the shutter, and every time he did, he had a moment frozen in time—but the rest of him was totally absorbed with what he was watching on the camera's LCD screen.

God, he's good at this. A natural. Totally comfortable with the camera.

Collin balled his shirt, bending to the side and dropping it in front of the bed, showing a flash of nipple.

"Stop."

Collin froze. Eric did too, staring at the screen, feeling his heartbeat in his eardrums and his blood pump into his dick. Then Collin turned to look over his shoulder, eyes half-lidded, meeting Eric's gaze through the lens somehow, and Eric's lungs started working again. He focused on the motionless figure framed on his screen and could already see the end result—the image he'd see on his computer later.

Collin's waistband gaped more in this pose, showing a hint of some designer's name, then a bit of pink fabric. *Sexy pink ones today.* Another perfect contrast shot. All the trappings that made his boy sexy when he was clothed also highlighted the profile of that one, nude nipple. The lines of Collin's back and arm were long and fluid and solid, but that nub poked out like it would ruin the curve, yet it didn't. Like it knew it was the prize the strength of Collin's body protected.

Eric caught himself swaying closer to his camera. He swallowed down whatever it was that made it hard to speak. "Turn around."

Collin did, resting his hand on his sternum, then following the centerline of his body with his fingertips, down to his navel. He circled around it and began riffling the hair below it, playing in it. Another shot he'd crop—Collin's fingers and the way some strands curled around them, catching the light and flaring with paler brown and reddish highlights. Collin laid his palm flat on his abdomen, caressing himself as he slid closer to his unbuttoned fly, teasing both him and the camera, until Eric could almost feel his skin.

"Do it."

Collin smiled and worked his hand under his waistband, pulling the zipper down with his other one as he reached into his pink briefs to stroke himself. Eric could see his knuckles pushing against the fabric, and a small spot of darker pink that had to be pre-cum. Another image popped up in his mind, and he thought fleetingly about what he'd do to make that bulging pink cotton the visual focus of the shot.

Then Collin gasped, barely audible. His lids had gotten heavy again, and his lips had parted.

"I want to see it." Collin visibly pulled in a breath, and Eric's lungs echoed his. "C'mon Sweet Boy, show me what you did for me on the phone the other night."

Collin pulled his hand out of his briefs, eyes clearing. "Not yet."

Eric stopped himself from demanding it. Or begging. Sweetness wanted to put on a show, and he wasn't about to ruin that.

For the first time, Eric wasn't running the shoot.

Collin pushed his jeans off his hips, but not his underwear, which disappointed Eric but also made his gut tighten up in excitement because that was a sexy image—Collin's dick almost bursting out of his briefs and his thighs wrapped in denim, thumbs hooked into the waistband.

He stopped for a second, smiling while biting his lower lip, and Eric felt himself sway toward the camera again, holding his breath, waiting for the rest of it. Collin's smile grew—he knew he'd captured his audience, didn't he?—then he shoved the jeans down, palms rubbing along his thighs, lifting one leg and then the other to pull off his pants. His whole leg flexed as he pushed them away, and Eric had another mental flash—a vision of Collin as a modern-day Roman sculpture, slim and defined, looking down to watch his body perform some common chore, caught in the calmness of the moment before activity that those marble figures were so good at expressing.

Then Collin stood, letting the camera capture him.

Eric took a difficult breath. "Turn around." It was a request rather than a command, and they both knew it.

Collin smiled and did it.

A jock. Eric groaned—he couldn't help it—and grabbed his own dick at the sight of Collin's ass exposed, except for those straps cutting across under his cheeks, framing him perfectly. That was pure porn-art, the images he got then. Beautiful shots of Collin's muscles tightening up between the elastic bands. All just for him. This whole shoot was just for him, wasn't it? He'd said that in the beginning, but Collin was the one who'd really understood it.

Eric's mouth had gone dry. Could Collin hear him breathing from across the room? He licked his lips. "What are you going to do for me now?"

Collin gave him one last look over his shoulder before putting one knee on the bed, then his hands, and lastly the other knee, giving Eric a stunning series of images—he just held down the button once Collin started moving and let the shutter run continuously—a progression from standing sculpture to pure sex, on the bed on all fours, ass open to the camera. Eric could barely breathe, watching Collin unfold in front of his lens.

Then Sweetness turned around, situating himself so he was facing Eric again, stretched out on the bed, butt cheek just peeking over his shoulder, smiling. He held out a hand. "C'mere, sexy."

Eric read his lips—he couldn't hear Collin over the pounding in his ears. His head only just cooperated, not able to think straight from lack of blood. Using his last few functioning brain cells, he brought up the menu on the LCD screen and set the shutter to capture an image every sixty seconds.

Then he went to join Collin in front of the camera.

Chapter 32

When Eric came over to the bed, he was already barefoot, and his jeans were open. All Collin had to do was angle their bodies right—he couldn't help but be aware of the camera and their relative position to it—and get his sexy man naked. He knelt on the mattress again, this time positioned sidelong to the lens, and reached to pull Eric's shirt over his head as soon as Eric was near enough.

"This is the closest I'll ever get to making a porno," he said.

Eric laughed. "Let's hope so." He didn't wait for Collin to pull off his jeans, but climbed on the bed with him, forcing Collin to make way for him, until he lay on his back with Eric on top of him. Eric was crazy hot, too excited to kiss him properly but not willing to stop trying, pulling on his own jeans and reaching into Collin's jock to rub his dick at the same time. Collin helped him with the pants, and he heard a click just as he was shoving them over the curve of Eric's butt. That would be a sexy picture, Eric's ass in the air, Collin's hands all over him, the rest of their bodies hidden in the puffy bedding.

Once he had Eric naked, he grabbed his head, trying to kiss him into focus so Eric would get what he wanted out of this. It was beyond obvious that Eric was really into doing it in front of the camera—he was freaking incoherent. Collin wanted him to get it right, the way he envisioned it. Not that he wouldn't be willing to try again as many times as Eric needed him to. Because it made Eric crazy, but also because it touched on that place inside of him that was both afraid of and titillated by exposure.

Weird, he'd never found that remotely interesting before.

Suddenly Eric was off of him, straightening out blankets and throwing pillows behind them. Staging a better scene? The camera clicked again while he was arranging stuff. He stopped to lunge down and kiss Collin, saying, "It's okay if we have a couple ruined shots, I wanna get this right."

Collin didn't care, but Eric seemed to find it reassuring to say.

"You on top." Eric lay down, looking untamed against all that perfectly pillowy bedding. He grabbed Collin's hand, pulling him over his naked, hairy body. "I want to see you in those pictures, not me."

Collin straddled Eric's pelvis. "You're my mountain man," he whispered, resting his weight on top of Eric from chest to legs. He lined their dicks up next to each other, separated only by the fabric of his jockstrap. "And this bedding is tumescent."

Eric laughed. "Our cocks are turgid, too." He had to suck in air to speak.

"Mmm, yeah. Turgid." Eric kissed him, probably to shut him up, but Collin's sexy man couldn't stop laughing. Laughing kisses were the best. Eric tasted bubbly when he laughed, and Collin could get an angle on his mouth he couldn't any other way. He needed to make Eric laugh more. But Eric wasn't laughing now; he was kissing Collin deeper, tongue-fucking Collin's mouth while his hands slid down Collin's back. Collin jerked when Eric's finger stroked around his tailbone, making goose bumps crawl up his spine.

He pulled away. "Why does that spot feel so good?"

"You have a lot of nerve endings there," Eric said, then pulled on Collin's earlobe with his teeth. "Here too. Mmm." He pushed farther into Collin's crack, until his finger just rested on his asshole. "This is another nerve center."

Collin gasped. "Yeah. I knew about that one." He swiveled his hips, but Eric pulled his finger away, kneading Collin's cheeks and exploring further. He dug under the jockstrap and found his balls, stroking the back of them. He gathered the straps that ran under Collin's ass into his fist, knuckles rubbing against his taint, and why was that so hot? Collin was grinding against him hard, frustrated by the fabric between them but not willing to stop thrusting.

"You're beautiful," Eric murmured.

Collin looked down at Eric, who was smiling at him and watching God knew what on his face while Collin rubbed himself crazy against Eric's cock. "I am?" No one had ever called him that before.

"I think so." Eric tugged on Collin's jock, pulling it down enough that his dickhead tangled in the hair on Eric's abdomen, making Collin gasp.

He forgot all about being beautiful.

Eric worked his jock down, without a lot of assistance from Collin, but he couldn't help himself. This had gone from being Eric's show to Collin having this driving need to come all over his boyfriend's belly. Finally, Eric worked it around Collin's upper thighs, and he went back to rubbing Collin's ass again, gripping and pulling his cheeks apart—something that had always completely flipped Collin's switch. Collin pushed himself up on his hands for leverage, and he kept up an urgent rhythm, even when Eric stuck fingers in his mouth, saying "Get them wet."

Collin licked and sucked and worked up as much saliva as possible to lavish on them, and when Eric pulled them away, his eyes flew open and met Eric's gaze, holding it the entire time Eric worked his fingers into Collin's ass, filling him up and stretching him wide.

"Oh God." Something about that was the final thing he needed. His reward for making Eric's camera fantasy come true.

"C'mon, Sweet Boy." The most satisfying ache shot down his legs and into his dick, his nuts and ass throbbing and shuddering as he came on Eric's hair and skin, leaving plenty of evidence he'd been there. This was his man, and only Collin could do this for him.

He kept twitching with aftershocks while Eric thrust against him, sliding in Collin's cum, which made Collin twitch more and his elbows give out, so he was deadweight on Eric, which hopefully helped. He couldn't do much else right now. Something worked, because Eric came within a minute of him, shooting out more cum to mix with Collin's, until they couldn't tell one from the other. Then they both lay there gulping air, until they quieted enough to hear the camera click.

Collin started laughing, and Eric snorted before nipping his neck; something he kept doing until Collin rolled off of him. Collin laughed harder when he realized there was probably a very nice picture of Eric crawling out of bed, dick half-hard and covered with cum. He wanted it for his Christmas card.

Chapter 33

They were still on the bed in the studio, cuddling. Eric loved this almost as much as the sex. Well, almost almost.

Collin burrowed further under his chin. "Mmm, you're so snuggly. You're my snuggle bear."

"Oh God, please don't tell me that's your pet name for me."

He felt Collin smile against his neck. "Says the man who calls me sweet whatever, including sweet baby."

"Sweet baby's just for sex, and even then only on rare occasions."

"Well, snuggle bear is solely for postcoital situations."

Eric expressed his annoyed acceptance with a throaty growl.

"Would you prefer snuggle bunny?"

He couldn't help it, he laughed, but it died when he felt Collin lose his smile.

"Shit," Collin said, "I forgot I need to talk to you about tonight." He didn't sound happy about it.

Eric sighed. "I forgot the same thing."

Collin pushed up on an elbow to look at him. "You need to talk to me about tonight?"

"Yeah. Do you have somewhere you have to be?"

"Well, I'm under a lot of pressure to be somewhere, and I'm under even more to bring you with me."

Eric made a face. "Same here, on both counts."

"Grrr."

Interesting. "Sweet Thing, you might want to leave the growling to me."

Collin stuck out his tongue, but before Eric could turn it into an invitation, he said, "Okay, you go first."

"My friend Lincoln and his wife want to meet you and invited us over for dinner tonight. We can blow it off, but I'd be in trouble for a while. And I actually like them. Okay, your turn." Eric nudged him. "What do your friends think we need to do?"

"My friend Brad and his boyfriend Sebastian are having a sort of impromptu party to welcome Jock to the frat. To tell you the truth, I think it's an excuse for Brad to force Sebastian into apologizing to me. I don't really need him to, but I think Brad does."

"What is he supposed to apologize for?"

Whatever it was, Collin didn't want to tell him. He looked away, inspecting the wood paneling on the wall. Eric could see him chewing on what to say. After about ten seconds, he looked back. "Okay, roughly a year ago, I figured out Brad was gay. He's in the frat too, and at the time, he still lived there. He's a good-looking guy, he's built a lot like you, actually, and I already told you how much I like your body type."

Eric nodded and combed his fingers through the back of Collin's hair.

"So, I guess I kind of had a thing for Brad. I don't think it was that serious, but maybe some people do, including Brad. We weren't really friends then, so I'm not sure he's a good judge."

"But you don't think it amounted to anything."

Collin shook his head. "Not really. I was sort of lonely—I didn't know any other gay frat brothers, and I wasn't out, and I tried much harder to hide it then. I didn't have many gay friends. Actually, I don't think I had any. The guys I hung out with back then just aren't in my life anymore."

"So now you have gay friends?"

"Yeah. Brad, for one, and Toby; they're the ones I'm closest to, but I'd say I'm friends with Sebastian and even Paul and Trevor now."

Eric nodded, not knowing who any of them but Toby were, but understanding, regardless. "So what happened?" Because obviously something did. He had a wild guess about what it was.

Collin dropped his head, hiding it in the bed. "I ambushed Brad in the shower one morning and blew him. He'd already been with Sebastian a couple of times." His voice was muffled but easy enough to understand. Even though Eric kind of wished it hadn't been.

Still. "Seriously?" Not as bad as he'd thought. He rolled toward Collin, but his boy stayed hidden.

"If I'd known he was seeing Sebastian, I never would have done it," he said into the sheet.

"He could have told you. He wasn't the one with a dick in his mouth."

"Well, he'd never had a blowjob before."

Eric screwed up his face. "How old is he?" Was he fugly?

"No, he'd never had a blowjob from a *guy* before. And actually, he and Sebastian weren't exclusive yet."

"Sweetness, that doesn't sound that horrible."

Collin turned his head toward Eric, skin a little pale and worrying his lip. "It was bad. Brad had just figured out he was gay, and he was still trying to get the hang of things. He wanted to be exclusive with Sebastian. I think he was already in love with him. If he'd had a little more experience, he might have been able to turn me down. I'm pretty sure he wanted to more than he wanted that blowjob; his dick just got the upper hand before he could get a handle on what was going on."

Eric touched Collin's lips with his fingertip, tracing the seam. "So what did Sebastian do that he needs to apologize for?"

"He just made some snarky comments about it recently. Actually, it was the night of the fire and I was supposed to be staying at their place. He knew all about the blowjob about ten minutes after it was over, and supposedly it wasn't an issue, but all the sudden that night he got weird about it. So Brad went off to bed with him, and I went off to bed with Toby."

Eric caught Collin's almost imperceptible wince. "Toby. I'd kind of figured that out already, sweetheart. It was just a friend thing, right?"

Collin nodded. "I couldn't even do it that night anyway. I really just needed someone to comfort me."

"Can I tell you something stupid?"

"Of course."

"It makes me more jealous that he was the one who comforted you that night, not me."

Collin grabbed his hand and kissed the palm. "If I'd had a choice, I would've rather been comforted by you."

Eric pulled him close again with an arm around the waist. "Yeah, and if I'd comforted you, you could have done 'it' that night too."

He grinned. "God, yes."

Eric hugged him closer, tucking Collin's head under his chin. "Um, since we're confessing..."

Collin yanked his head up, hitting Eric's jaw and making Eric's teeth snap together. "What?" He stared down at him with wide eyes.

Crap. "It's just, you know how I said I take pictures of guys?"

"Yeah."

He spit it out, like ripping off a bandage. "I had a photo session on Tuesday with a guy."

Collin stared at him a second. "And?"

"Well, I mean, he was nearly naked and . . ." he took a breath. "It felt a little like cheating."

"Cheating?" Collin's gaze drifted away from his, and Eric cringed internally. But then Collin looked back. "Because you were with another guy like that, or because you hadn't told me?"

It was Eric's turn to stare. How did Sweetness cut directly to the heart of the matter like that? "I guess just because you didn't know. I felt like I should tell you, not like the photography was wrong."

Collin kissed his chin. "Then it's not cheating."

Eric felt like he had to make this very clear. "But sometimes, in the past, after sessions with models, things kinda got, you know, hot."

"Are you trying to tell me you might hook up with one of these guys?" Collin had his head propped on his fist, smiling slightly. "Nothing happened Tuesday, right?"

"No!" Eric lifted his head, then let it drop. "Nothing's ever happened with any of my subjects when I'm seeing someone."

Collin shrugged. "I trust you."

"Good." Eric brushed his fingers through Collin's hair, relieved. Until a little thing inside him prodded him and reminded him he hadn't been entirely truthful about *everything*. But Collin had taken this so well. *Maybe when the time comes to tell him, he'll laugh off my stupid thing for J.M. twenty years ago.* It had been so long ago, and so minor, he didn't see it being a big deal, anyway. "I wouldn't do anything to hurt you, not if I can help it."

Collin's fingers traced across Eric's cheekbone, then his jaw. "In my head, I call you my boyfriend."

Eric grabbed his hand and kissed each of his fingertips. "I'm your boyfriend outside of your head, too." *And I'm hopelessly in love with you.*

"I'm yours." Collin wiggled a little nearer and rested his forehead on Eric's, eyes closed and a smile on his face. "I love it here with you."

Eric's heart stretched in his chest, trying to grow bigger or something. Like one of those tiny sponges that came in a capsule but grew hundreds of times their size in water. "Me too, Sweet Baby."

Chapter 34

R*iiiing.*
The damned phone just never wanted them have any peace, did it? Collin sighed and started to get up, but then he realized it wasn't his ring. "That's you, Sexy Man."

Eric huffed. "I know, I'm just wishing I didn't have to go find it." But he pushed himself up and off the bed, padding out of the room naked and barefoot. Collin watched his ass flexing the whole time, then lay back and stared at the ceiling. Eric had painted it with clouds. His man kept surprising him.

He listened to the distant sound of Eric's voice and started to drift, thinking a nap might be nice, but then Eric was standing in the doorway, saying something. Collin pushed up on his arm, rubbing his eyes with his other hand. "What?"

"Sorry, Sweetness. I have Mike on the phone and he needs to talk to you."

"Mike?" Collin blinked a few times, but he still couldn't remember who Mike was.

"The fire marshal. I told him about Sparky Donaldson, and he started looking into it, and things aren't adding up."

"Why did you tell him about Sparky?" Collin tried not to yawn but it forced its way out, so he went ahead and stretched too while Eric explained about the building permit.

"And since he's rumored to be a firebug, it started making sense to give him a second look, I guess. They weren't getting answers anywhere else." Eric held out his hand, and Collin finally climbed out of his nest, sighing and pulling on his jeans.

"You don't need to do that for me," Eric smiled at him.

"I can't talk on the phone to someone while I'm naked."

"You were naked the other night on the phone with me."

Collin grinned, walking to Eric to wrap his arms around him and give him a kiss. "Except for you."

"Mmm." Eric pushed his hands down the back of Collin's jeans and squeezed one cheek. "I like you naked." He started kissing him, and Collin knew this pattern. He started with short ones, just dipping his tongue between Collin's lips, teasing him until he built up to the more explicit kisses, where he twined his tongue around Collin's and pulled it into his mouth. But this time he stopped after a couple of the preliminary ones. "You need to talk to Mike."

Collin groaned, but let go of Eric and followed him into the living room.

"How did he know I was here, anyway?"

Eric glanced back at him a second, cheeks pink. "He said he had to call you next, so I told him he didn't need to."

Collin grinned at him and grabbed his hand, holding it even after they sat on the couch.

"Hello, Fire Marshal Taggert, what can I do for you?"

"Call me Mike. Okay, kid, I'm going to tell you what we have, and this is not for general consumption, you understand?"

"Yes, sir."

"'Sir,' huh? Dix rubbing off on you?"

Collin started laughing, then tried to smother it, which made him laugh harder.

"What did he say?" Eric asked, grinning.

"They call you Dix at work, right?" Collin sputtered.

"Yeah."

Collin took a deep breath and managed to spit it all out. "He asked me, 'Dix rubbing off on you?'" Then he lost it again, the whole thing made funnier by how hard Eric laughed.

It took a while, but finally Collin managed to keep himself confined to occasional giggles. "I'm sorry, s—Mike. Please excuse me." He wiped at the tears on his face, avoiding Eric's eyes. He'd bust up all over again if he looked at him.

"Goddammit, I was going to tell you guys I didn't want to know what that meant, but I think I figured it out. Mental image and everything. Jesus."

Collin giggled, then stifled it. "Please, go on."

"Hell, where was I, anyway?"

"You told me not to tell anyone anything you say. Other than Eric?"

"That's right, you can tell Di—Eric. Anywho, this guy Donaldson, his wife filed a missing person's report on him in New Jersey. She says he never came back from a business trip to Chicago three weeks ago."

"What? But he was in Oregon a week ago." Wait, was he? "Except I never saw him, and I don't know anyone who did."

"But you've had communications with him, correct?"

"Yeah, a phone message and an email. Sparky said he was in Florida and headed to New York in an email he sent me yesterday. And I guess my uncle must have had contact with him too."

"I don't suppose you'd be interested in sharing that phone message and email with us to further this case?"

"Of course. How do I get them to you?"

"Shit, I don't understand this electronic fuck-whatery. Can you meet me at the police station in a half hour? I have more news, but we'll wait until then."

Collin ended up agreeing to meet Mike in an hour. They could be there in a half hour if they didn't clean up, but Collin thought it would be considerate to the rest of the world if he and Eric had a shower first and didn't smell like a bathhouse.

Weird that they had to take a shower to not smell like a bathhouse.

ΘΑΓ

"Hurry up, Sweetness, the water will get cold."

Obediently, Collin rinsed his head. "If we're going to continue seeing each other, you need more hot water." After the obligatory orgasms—not that it was exactly some horrible chore to let his boyfriend suck him off and then come all over his stomach—*and* actually cleaning up, they simply needed a longer shower than normal. Better that the shower adjust than them.

Eric smiled. "I guess I'll get a bigger hot-water heater, then." He was rinsing soap off his belly, so Collin reached to help him with that. His fingers may have strayed a bit low.

"It's so weird how much of my life revolves around hot-water heaters right now."

"Mmm." Eric kissed him and turned off the water, pulling Collin out and wrapping him in a towel. "You're so sweet."

"What makes you say that?"

"Your taste. There weren't any frat boys as delicious as you when I was in college."

Collin grinned and leaned to kiss Eric's shoulder while drying his legs. He nearly lost his balance. "You were there, so that's one."

"I'm not as yummy as you."

"I thought we agreed to disagree about this?"

Eric turned him around so he could dry Collin's back. "Oh yeah. Fine." He finished, and Collin turned and started on Eric's. They had this sort of figured out, and it was only their second shower together. If they were together for years and years, would they keep this up, or would they someday take separate showers all the time?

Years and years. He could imagine it, but it made his stomach feel achy too. "Did you hook up much in college?"

Eric snorted. "No, I was pretty sex-starved. I hadn't really figured out the bar scene, and I definitely never hooked up with any frat boys. None of them even knew I was gay. I still talk to a couple of those guys, and they know now."

"You really weren't that into the frat, were you?"

"Not so much." He led him out to the bedroom.

"Eric?" Collin didn't know why, but he decided it was time to probe the sore tooth, so to speak.

"Yeah, Sweetness?" Eric was digging through his underwear drawer. Was it normal for Collin to already know what drawers he kept different clothes in?

He took a second to marshal his thoughts. "I know Monty can be pretty snobby, but I really don't see why he'd think you're not TAG material."

When Eric glanced over, he was holding a pair of boxer briefs in one hand, studying Collin. "Because my major was art and all I wanted to do when I finished my degree was take pictures."

Collin stopped digging through his own underwear pile. "Really? I guess that makes sense, but how did you end up a paramedic?"

He smiled, pulling on his shorts now. "I minored in anatomy and physiology because someone told me it would help me understand the human body, and I liked it so much I started thinking I might want to go into medicine. Getting my paramedic certification was sort of an experiment, and it kind of got out of control."

Collin laughed. He was always laughing around Eric, it seemed.

"Anyway, my freshman year . . . sorry, but it sucked because of J.M. I guess he had stuff to work out, since your dad had died." He stood there, holding Collin's gaze.

Collin took a deep breath. "Yeah."

Eric took a couple of steps toward him, until he could grab Collin's hand and kiss it. "If it makes it any better, knowing it was your father—I mean, knowing J.M. was a dick for a reason makes it easier for me not to hold it against him."

That so deserved a kiss. Collin stretched up and kissed his jaw, then the corner of his lips. "I prefer my method of working out stress." He couldn't help feeling like they'd hit some new milestone, being able to just talk about Monty.

"Me too." Eric said, nodding once. Collin expected a kiss after that, but Eric dropped his hand and turned to his dresser.

It was probably just nerves from them getting through a decent conversation about exactly why Eric didn't like J.M. He'd been nervous about that from the beginning, almost more than Collin had.

Collin focused on his own clothes. "I guess it might not be the norm, but we certainly have guys like you who aren't planning on making six or seven figures a year." Hmmm, put on sexy underwear now in front of Eric or just semi-sexy ones and surprise him later?

"Yeah, maybe it's just when I was there. My freshman year, it seemed like there were a lot of guys that thought the way J.M. did."

Definitely surprise him later. He stuffed the lime green ones back in his bag and pulled out the purple ones Eric had already seen. "I think there are a lot of guys who don't think it's this amazing brotherhood thing. I don't think Brad does. Although if it wasn't for Brad, I'm not sure I'd be very happy to be in TAG either. When he came out, everything just seemed different, and all the sudden I could see ways to change the frat to something I liked more. Now it's what I want it to be. Kind of."

Eric walked up behind him and kissed his neck. "Makes sense to me." He patted Collin's butt, then sat down to put on socks. "So, are we going to meet each other's friends tonight?"

Collin blew out a breath. "We may as well get it over with. It's going to happen sooner or later."

Chapter 35

G oing to the police station wasn't exactly an ordeal, but it took a while, and Eric felt like he needed to keep a hand on Collin the whole time or his sweet young thang would start tensing up again. If he had to, he could "administer therapy" to Collin in the car between the station and Lincoln and Mandy's place.

But Collin was still pretty relaxed by the time the officer who dealt with technical stuff had copied the phone message and got whatever he needed from Collin's email. Then they spoke to Mike a few minutes, and his further bit of news was that Sparky had been let go from the brokerage firm over a month ago because, as Mike put it, "I guess they don't like you much when you stop making money. He was fired before that business trip to Chicago, but he pretended to go on it anyway."

"Did the police in New Jersey know anything else?"

Mike shook his head and poked in his ear a second, looking annoyed and curmudgeonly. "The detective who's looking into the details hasn't returned Homes's call yet. He should soon, but until then no one knows much but that."

Collin spent a lot of time in the car on the way to dinner thinking hard, judging by his silence and the wrinkle in his forehead.

"Watcha thinking, Sweetness?"

Collin tilted his head, still frowning at the dashboard. "I don't know. It's just weird . . . the guys in the Alumni Association, Mom always refers to them as 'the good ol' rich boys,' and really, that's what they are. If Sparky lost his job because he wasn't making any money and Monty knew that, he never would have let him take over Sooty's job as the TAG liaison."

Eric raised his eyebrows and stared steadfastly ahead, biting his lips over the comments he was dying to make about elitist douche bags.

Collin sighed. "I know what you're thinking."

Eric glanced at him. "Yeah, but I didn't say it. That's progress, right?"

Collin laughed and rested his hand on Eric's thigh.

Phew.

When they got to his friends' house and he'd parked the car next to the curb, Eric found himself glued to his seat.

"Um, is something wrong?"

He turned to Collin, and he couldn't swear the twinkle in his eye was just the reflection of the street light. "Okay, listen, Mandy's kind of..."

Collin raised his brows. So that hadn't been enough info.

"If she squeals and claps when she meets you, it's just, I don't know, she has kind of a thing for, you know, my boyfriends."

Collin laughed. "C'mon, it'll be fine."

And it was. Mandy answered the door and thankfully managed to restrain herself from gushing too much, although she seemed really overdressed—she even had on pearls. Or what did he know? They could be fake. Lincoln stood behind her, smiling and offering to take their coats.

Collin seemed to adjust to it all faster than he did. Until Eric placed his hand on Sweetness's back to guide him to the kitchen and he felt the tension there. Eric took advantage of the opportunity to rub his muscles.

When they all walked into the kitchen and Mandy offered them wine, Eric could see that split second of indecision in her face, when she wondered if Collin was even old enough to legally drink. Hopefully, Eric was the only one who saw it.

"I'd love some wine. What do you have?" Collin asked.

"Well, we're having pot roast at Eric's request, so I'd planned to open a red, but Lincoln and I have already opened a local chard if you want white." She lifted up a half-full bottle to illustrate.

"Red would be fine," Collin said.

She started pulling out other bottles from their little rack under the cupboards while Lincoln went back to making something on the stove. Mandy was a horrible cook, so Lincoln did most of it. "Okay, we have this 2012 Pinot from Hogue, or this 2007 Bodegas Landaluce

Capri-blah, blah, blah. I can't pronounce all of that. Someone gave it to us as a gift, and I'm not very familiar with Spanish reds."

Eric was looking at Collin, so he saw his eyes light up at the mention of the second one. Of course Sweetness would know all about Spanish wines, wouldn't he?

"Wow, someone must like you guys. If you don't mind wasting the Bodegas Landaluce on pot roast—"

"Hey." Eric prodded him in the side.

"That one would be fantastic." Collin turned and smiled at him, catching his hand and hanging on to it, lacing their fingers together.

That's my boy. But while Mandy was busy opening wine and Lincoln was stirring something that sizzled like mad, Collin leaned toward him. "You didn't tell them how old I am?" he murmured.

Crap, so he had noticed that look. "Not really, not your actual age. I didn't think it mattered."

"I think it matters to them." He squeezed Eric's hand, and Eric could imagine Collin's back muscles knotting up.

"Did you tell your friends?"

"Yes."

"Here you go," Mandy interrupted them, handing out glasses of wine. "I have to go check on the baby and see if Greta finished her dinner," she said as she walked out of the room.

"Eric tells me you're a senior at Calapooya," Lincoln said. "What are you going to do when you're done with school?"

The wine and small talk seemed to loosen Collin up, thank God. They chatted until a three-foot tornado with red hair ran into the room and straight at him. "Uncle Eric's here!"

"Hey!" He grabbed Greta and swung her up into his arms. "How's my girl?"

"You have hair," she told him, poking at his head.

"She's been waiting for you." Mandy smiled. "Greta, this is Uncle Eric's friend, Collin."

She half turned in Eric's hold to look at his boy. For a few seconds, Eric's own stress mounted. "I can't call you Uncle Collin until you've been seeing Uncle Eric longer. That's what Mommy said."

Lincoln spewed his wine across the counter, and he and Collin started laughing.

Phew.

That was the point at which everything really loosened up. Mandy had planned to put Greta to bed, but she refused. No one seemed to mind when she sat herself at the table during dinner with crayons and a stack of paper.

By dessert—apple pie, *yum*—Mandy was picking Collin's brain about Spain because "we've been talking about going there for a of couple years now."

"You guys like to travel, I take it." Collin had relaxed even more, but to Eric he still sounded a little formal. This was the same guy he got when they were alone, but more self-contained somehow.

"We do, although I didn't so much before I met Lincoln. Oh, but don't try and get Eric to go to Europe. He hates leaving home. He's never even been out of the country." In his opinion, Mandy had just officially had too much to drink.

Collin turned to him. "You haven't?"

What was he going to say? "No."

Collin leaned toward him and kissed his cheek. "Lots of people haven't, honey." When Collin straightened up, Eric's eye caught Mandy's. She had the look of a woman about to squeal with the cuteness of it all. He got the impression from the way she winced and glared at her husband that Lincoln had kicked her under the table.

At least she didn't clap.

They stayed longer than he expected to. Right up until he was on the couch, talking to Lincoln and letting Greta climb all over him, when he overheard Collin say to Mandy, "That's so cute how much Greta likes playing with Eric."

"Isn't it? He's so good with kids. He'll make some lucky man a great househusband."

Eric cringed. Seriously, could she be any more obvious?

"Someday he'll be the jolly rotund dad at the playground that all the kids love."

Rotund?

"Except, you know, he won't molest them." She and Collin laughed over that, as if it was actually funny. He tickled Greta, hoping her giggles—man, he'd never noticed how much her squeals had in common with her mother's—would drown out the rest of their conversation.

It worked, but only long enough that he missed the next thing Collin said. He totally heard Mandy's response, though.

"I'm so glad you think that, because his last serious boyfriend thought it was too 'heteronormative' for him to want a family. Not that I'm suggesting you'll give him that family, I'm simply glad you're supportive." She giggled again, but Collin didn't.

Crap.

"I think it would be nice to have a family someday," Collin said after a second. Their entire conversation had made him cringe inside and feel embarrassed, but it was all made better by that one comment. He could forgive Mandy's househusband-trolling, her spilling the beans about him wanting his own kids, and even the giggling. It was all better.

Except he wouldn't forget that "rotund" thing anytime soon.

Chapter 36

"**S**eriously, I heard her say it. I'm *not* going to be rotund," Eric grumbled. Collin let himself smile, since it was dark in the car. He rubbed Eric's shoulder, feeling relaxed and languid. He didn't think it was just the wine.

"What else did you hear her say?"

Eric cleared his throat. "Nothing."

Uh-huh. Collin smirked down at his lap, but turned toward Eric. "Maybe she just meant you'll have a little bit of a gut."

"Crap," Eric grumbled. He tilted his head when Collin's thumb worked up under his ear.

"I'll still be attracted to you with a beer gut, don't worry." Eric flinched, but Collin couldn't tell if it was because of what he'd said or if he'd hit a nerve, literally. He switched to rubbing with his palm.

"How fancy was that wine, anyway? It was pretty good."

"It costs about fifty bucks a bottle in the US." Collin had a feeling Eric didn't often drink wine at all.

"Seriously?" He gaped at Collin a second, then turned back to the road.

"Seriously. You think Mandy knew that?"

"She probably did, but Lincoln didn't, otherwise he would have been hoarding it in the basement for a special occasion that would never arrive."

"Mmm, I'm glad he didn't know, then." The dumb console was in the way, but Collin leaned over to kiss Eric's cheek. The perfect finish to a vehicular neck massage. He laid his hand on Eric's leg now.

Eric picked up his hand and kissed it. Who did that as a random gesture of affection anymore? In the good old days—the days Monty claimed had ended with General Franco—people probably did it all the time, but not two guys, not to each other. Yet Eric did it, and he didn't seem embarrassed or overly sentimental.

Sigh.

Eric, however, was focused on different things. "Okay, we're almost to campus, tell me how to get to this party."

ΘΔΓ

Collin had told his friends Eric was a lot older, but he'd forgotten to tell the rest of the frat. Danny made that clear about a minute after they walked into Brad and Sebastian's place and he greeted them with, "Hey Collin, I didn't know you were bringing your dad!"

He felt Eric jerk behind him. He reached back and took Eric's hand, pulling him forward enough for Danny to see. "Actually, Danny, my dad died when I was four. I'd like you to meet my boyfriend, Eric."

Danny's mouth fell open, and he flushed. "Oh, man, I'm sorry! My bad. Shit, you don't look that old, the lighting in here sucks. Uh, I think I'll go hide now." As he passed Collin, he said quickly, "I'm pretty sure they didn't cover this in sensitivity training either. I *told* Kyle that class sucked."

Collin turned around, standing very close to Eric. "I'm so sorry." He couldn't stop himself from biting his lip.

"It's okay, I've been expecting it, Sweet Thing."

"I really need a pet name for you. I wanted to say 'I'm so sorry, sweetie,' but that's one of your names for me."

"You can't use it too?"

"Is that allowed?"

Eric quirked a half smile, and Collin suddenly realized he hadn't seen one in a while. Eric gave him full smiles now. "Yeah, it is." Eric leaned forward to kiss him, but stopped himself. Collin guessed because he didn't know if it was okay in front of all these people.

So he leaned forward and kissed Eric instead. "That was my first semi-public kiss," he whispered.

Eric kissed him back. "And that was your second."

Collin found his friends in the kitchen. How did these parties always get segregated into gay guys in the kitchen, straights in the rest of the house? Well, Kyle and Tank were in the kitchen, as was Ashley, but she fit more into the gay guy category than the straight guy one.

He intended to quietly do the rounds, introducing Eric to a couple people at a time, but of course everyone stopped talking and looked at them as soon as they came in.

Shit. "Um, this is Eric."

Everyone smiled at them. Ashley gave a little wave as a bonus.

Collin smiled back. When he looked at Eric, he was smiling too, but not his normal, natural smile.

Collin added a nod to his smile.

Now everyone was nodding and smiling back.

Only one thing could save them now. Collin stacked one hand on top of the other and started circling his thumbs. "Awww-kward."

In the ensuing laughter, Eric asked him, "What the hell was that?"

"It's the awkward turtle. I'll explain later. Come and meet my friends."

"I thought I just did," he muttered.

Things got better. Collin started by introducing him to Kyle, Tank, and Ashley because they were closest. Ashley managed to contain herself to only one, "Oh my God, I've heard so much about you!"

"She has?" Eric murmured in his ear.

"Not from me."

Toby was talking to Jock, and Collin could tell where that was headed. "You remember Toby, probably," he said to Eric. Eric nodded and shook his hand. "And this is Jock, my new roommate. He's Tank's little brother." He tried not to make the emphasis on that too obvious, but clearly Toby hadn't picked up on it, because he'd turned The Smile back on Jock.

They made small talk a few minutes before Collin managed to work in, "Yeah, it's amazing how protective *Tank* is of his *little brother*."

Jock gave him a pleading, puppy dog look—man he was good at that—and flicked his eyes to Toby. Collin shook his head minutely. When he looked back at Toby, he could tell the message had sunk in. Probably assisted by Tank joining them and glaring at Toby.

When Collin turned to Eric to move him along, his boyfriend was smirking. "Your friends are entertaining," he said in Collin's ear.

Brad, Sebastian, Paul, and Trevor made up the last group. For a second after the introductions, Collin thought he'd have to do the awkward turtle again, until Eric saved him by saying to Trevor, "Aren't you the new girls' softball coach?"

The question ultimately led to Collin discussing sports with Brad, Trevor, and Eric, while Paul and Sebastian talked about whatever they liked to talk about. History?

To be honest, Collin wasn't that into sports. He'd played soccer occasionally, but he didn't follow any teams. He liked running, and he'd started lifting last year when he'd wanted to catch Brad's attention. He kept doing it because it gave him a nicer body. Seemed as good a reason as any.

"Sebastian wants to talk to you privately," Brad said in his ear.

Collin turned to him. "Okay, he wants to talk to me, or you want him to want to talk to me?"

"Little of both, seems like."

"Uh-huh."

"I'm serious, dude. He said he had something to say to you."

"Oh, I bet he has something to say to me."

"He promised me he'd be nice. Besides, you can totally take him."

What kind of fight would he and Sebastian have? A relatively butch fist fight, or would they roll around on the ground and pull hair? It could go either way. And anyway, what kind of boyfriend was Brad to encourage it? Maybe he harbored secret fantasies of Sebastian fighting for him. Shit, that meant Collin would have to let Sebastian win. The things he did for his friends.

Eric took his hand, recalling Collin's attention while saying to someone, "Yeah, we were late because we had to go to dinner at the house of some friends of mine."

"Doing the rounds tonight, huh? Lucky you." Trevor didn't sound envious, though.

Eric pulled Collin closer and smiled at him. "Yeah, but once we're done, we get to go back to my place, lock the doors, and hang out naked in front of the fire all weekend."

"Oh my God, that's so sweet," someone said. They all turned to see who it was.

It seemed to be Paul. He blinked at them, then looked over his shoulder to the cupboard behind him. "Who said that?"

"You did." Trevor smiled at him. "We all heard you."

Paul straightened his spine and sniffed, looking away. "I'd never be caught dead saying any such thing."

"Well, technically we didn't catch you, but the evidence overwhelmingly points in your direction." Sebastian was such a helpful guy.

"Oh, don't try to pretend you aren't a closet romantic," Trevor said, sauntering up to his boyfriend.

"There's no need to *pretend* I'm not, because I'm simply *not*." Paul refused to look at him, even when Trevor stood in front of him with his hands on Paul's waist.

"Yes, you are. We all heard you say that was the most romantic thing ever."

"That's not what I said!" Paul whipped his head around, gaping at Trevor.

"It's not? Then what did you say?"

"I fail to see how it is that you keep outsmarting me."

"Because I know all your weaknesses."

Collin wasn't sure what Paul said to that, because by then they were murmuring to each other, and Paul had given in and put his arms around Trevor.

"I give it ten minutes, tops, before they bail on the party," Toby said next to Collin.

Collin turned. "I can't believe you were hitting on Tank's brother."

"I wasn't to the hitting-on-him stage. I was still seeing if he was interested."

"Of course he's interested. He's nineteen and you're reasonably attractive."

"Thanks for the ringing endorsement. By the way, Brad's looking for you."

"Oh my God, you know how I meant it. Tell me that, when you were nineteen, you were looking for more than that."

"Unfortunately I can't, because reasonably attractive and willing was more than good enough for me. Did you hear what I said about Brad?"

Collin sighed. "Yes. I'm just ignoring it."

Toby smirked.

"Shut up. Where's my boyfriend?" Seriously, had he said that enough tonight? Was it becoming obvious to others that he just liked to remind himself he had one?

Toby raised an eyebrow at Collin's word choice, but he didn't say anything about it. "He's talking to Tank and Jock. Oh, look, they're right next to Brad, who's clearly waiting for you."

"Shit. I guess I should get this over with."

"Have fun. I'm going to go talk to your boyfriend."

Collin plodded across the room, stopping a second to kiss the back of Eric's neck as he passed. "I guess I have to go talk to Sebastian now," he whispered.

Eric's smile was much more sympathetic than Toby's had been.

"Do we have to do this?" he asked when he reached Brad. "I'm seriously okay with pretending nothing happened."

"You have to do it."

"Why?" Collin nearly whined.

"Because it's important to me."

There was no reasonable argument to that. He couldn't say, "I don't care what you want," and Brad knew it.

"Fine."

"Okay." Brad nodded once and stepped to the side, revealing the back door behind him. He turned the knob and held it open, grabbing Collin's coat off some handy surface Collin hadn't noticed.

"Plan ahead much?" he grumbled while putting on his coat.

Brad didn't answer, just shoved him out the door with a palm on his back and shut it behind him.

Some host.

Sebastian stood on the back porch, hands stuffed in his coat pocket and kicking at something until he heard Collin get pushed out. "Hey."

"Hey," Collin returned. "I guess we both know why we're here."

Sebastian nodded, then stared up into the sky a few seconds. At what, Collin didn't know, because it was too cloudy for stars. Sebastian took a breath. "I'm only apologizing because Brad is making me, but I do want to thank you."

Thank him? "For all the blowjobs?"

"Well, that also."

"That wasn't my idea."

"It seems like something Ashley would advise him to do."

"I thought so too." Collin shoved his hands in his pockets. Brad might have included gloves if he'd wanted them to do this in comfort.

Sebastian kicked a few times at whatever he'd been looking at before going on. "I'm trying to finish my dissertation this term, and sometimes I get so stuck in my head I forget I have a heart. It's hard on Brad. Last Friday, I'd had a difficult time with some research I needed to get done, and I wanted to just relax, if you understand my meaning."

"I know exactly what you're talking about."

"But you were there, I let it get to me, and I lashed out. The quandary for me is that if you hadn't been there, I would have taken Brad for granted. Again. But you were there, and—through a lot of conversation with Brad later that I don't particularly want to relive but that we needed to have—it came to my attention that I don't want to lose what I have with him, and since that's the case, I need to make certain that he knows how I feel. Is this excruciatingly embarrassing for you, too?"

"Probably not as much as for you."

"I also want to tell you—well, 'want' may be a bit of an exaggeration. Let's say I feel compelled to tell you how angry I was with you for what happened between you and him, even before Friday." He looked out into the night, so Collin couldn't really see his face, but he could still hear him. "I got Brad's every first experience except that. He'd never kissed another guy before me. I felt like—" Sebastian had to stop to clear his throat. "I felt as if you had stolen that one thing from me."

Now it was excruciating. Collin fisted his hands in his pockets, nails biting into his palms. "If I could give it back, I would, I swear." He started worrying his lip, and freely allowed himself to.

Sebastian glanced at him, then away again, but Collin could see his profile now. "Yes, well, that's something else I learned the other night. Those firsts weren't my experiences to have; I just got very lucky and he shared them with me. Chose me to share them with."

"He would have chosen you for that, too, if I hadn't jumped him. I'm sorry."

"If you hadn't done it, I wouldn't have figured anything out the other night, and I can't help but think I'd have lost him someday. So, maybe you can see why I don't want to apologize, yeah?" Sebastian looked at him again, holding his gaze a few seconds this time.

"Yeah."

"Now." Sebastian blew out a breath. "I'm going to go back inside, and we'll never speak of this again."

"I'm more than fine with that."

He turned to the door, then stopped. "Oh, by the way, nice firefighter."

"Thank you. He's actually a firefighter paramedic."

Sebastian shrugged. "Either way, he's hot."

Chapter 37

After they'd (finally) left the party, Collin offered to give Eric roadhead on the way home for "valor under fire," but Eric knew for a fact that it could lead to some nasty and/or embarrassing accidents, so he had to turn it down. Besides, the dumb console would make it seriously uncomfortable for Sweetness.

When they got to his place, Eric lit the fire he'd laid in the bedroom while Collin checked his email downstairs. He didn't know what the deal was with Collin checking his email, but he'd seemed to think it was important.

Well, what the hell, Eric thought the fire was important. He was pretty sure that this time he had the kindling and logs set up into the perfect tepee so he could light it and it would just get itself going. He'd thought that before, though. The regular way he lit a fire was to sit in front of it for ten minutes (minimum), feeding it less and less frequently, until it got to the point where he could walk away and ignore it for fifteen minutes to an hour.

He'd really like to perfect the art of laying it out so all he had to do was strike a match, then watch it burn. Or rather, wander off for an hour until he had to throw a log on it. He'd heard it was possible, but he'd become increasingly sure that was a myth.

It turned out that his newest attempt wasn't the mythical one-tepee-wonder either, and he had to light the fire the regular way, so he was still feeding it when Collin walked in and stood behind where he was crouched in front of the damn hearth. Collin stroked the week's growth on Eric's scalp, knees pressing against Eric's back.

"Mmm, Sweetness, that feels good. Gimme a couple minutes and I can leave this thing awhile."

Collin's hands and knees left, replaced by his lips on the very top of Eric's head. "That's okay. I want to brush my teeth."

Eric had thrown on an actual log—one that would burn awhile all by its lonesome—and was mostly undressed and lying in bed waiting for Collin, wondering what kind of underwear his sweet thing would have on, when it hit him how tame this all seemed. They'd been seeing each other for only a week, yet they were at the point where Eric was waiting in bed for Collin to finish in the bathroom: way past the ripping-clothes-off-as-soon-as-they-got-home stage. He'd been obsessing about the fire in the fireplace while he should have been stoking the fire in Collin's micro-briefs.

Seriously, dude, is this how you show a college guy a good time? When he'd been in college, if he'd gone on a date with a guy like him, he would have thought it was lame. Boring.

Fuck, he'd even turned down roadhead.

Oh God, I am *domesticated.*

He'd just started to feel really insecure when Collin walked in and said, "We need to talk about something."

Eric's heart did a weird double-pump thing that just had to be anatomically impossible. He straightened up from the headboard and nodded. "Okay." If his sweet young thang wanted something more exciting, they could go back out to the car just like this and Eric would drive up and down the highway all night while Collin sucked his dick if that's what he wanted. Or he could rip off clothes, do it on the stairs, hang from a light fixture: whatever it took.

But Collin just stood there, naked except for a pair of sweats (and whatever he had on underneath them, which, in spite of everything, Eric couldn't stop wondering about), and fidgeted, pressing his fingertips together and worrying his lip.

"I'm sorry," Eric blurted. "I should have been paying attention to you instead of the fire. I mean, I think it's romantic, but I'm not all about romance. I can do passion." He stood up, looking for his jeans. "We can go back to the car and you can blow me while I drive."

"What the fuck are you talking about? And what do you mean, blow you in the car? You were totally right, the console would get in the way."

Eric looked up into Sweetness's eyes, torn. He didn't want to sacrifice Collin's life, and if it came down to choosing between keeping him safe and losing him or spicing things up and killing him, he'd have to go for safe.

He sat down heavily on the bed, rubbing his head. His heart knocked, wanting to know what was going on.

You're about to get very, very broken.

But he couldn't just give up. "I can trade that car in. I'm sure there's some vehicle out there that comes with a bench seat." Would there be any dealerships open this late?

"What?" Collin's whole face screwed up in confusion. "You seriously think . . ." He walked to the bed and cupped Eric's face. "Sweetie, what's wrong?"

Eric wrapped his arms around Collin's hips and pulled him close, so he could rest his cheek on Collin's stomach. "You want something more, right?"

Collin's breath caught. "I thought you were the one who wanted something more."

Eric turned to look up at him again. "Huh?"

Collin licked his lips and looked off to the side for a second. "Can I ask you to explain first?"

He let his chin rest on Collin's tummy, thinking about what to say. It would be so nice to say he'd rather Collin went first, but he couldn't do that. Collin needed him to speak. "My ex-boyfriend Jay is right, I'm domesticated."

Collin ran light fingers around Eric's ear, scrunching his brow. "So?"

"You're fifteen years younger than me, Sweetness. You want excitement, not a guy who's ready to settle down. Someone who'll let you give him roadhead and rip off your clothes when you get home."

"That's one of my favorite shirts, and I really didn't want you to rip it."

"You know what I mean."

Collin sighed, but he smiled while he did it, and tilted his head too. As if he thought Eric was unbearably cute. "I've given roadhead, and other than wanting to do it for you—if you wanted it—I had no burning desire to do it again."

"Oh, I feel much better now. Thank you." And seriously, had the guy he'd been blowing cared nothing for Collin's safety?

"What I'm saying is that I've had that crazy, gotta-have-you-now stuff. When we got together, I had that with you. You couldn't wait to pull all the way off the road the first time. But seeing you today was better, because you'd planned out that photo shoot. I've never done *that* with anyone else, and it was freaking hot. Coming home tonight was the best because I realized something when we walked in and you turned up the thermostat—you don't need to build a fire at all, you just do it for me. You did it for me that night you came to find me at the Slaughterhouse, right? When we got here and there was a fire already, that's because you planned that, isn't it?"

"Yes." He was pretty sure he was blushing, but he took it like a man. Hopefully.

"Do you think anyone but you has ever gone looking for me— and at the bar I hang out at which isn't the one you hang out at— with the intent of taking me home, *and* bothered to do something romantic beforehand?"

"No?"

"No. Guys in college are looking for one thing, mostly. You know that; you've been there. Falling in love is incidental. Even Brad and Sebastian—they've been together nearly a year, and Sebastian just figured out this week that he needs to show Brad how he feels or he might lose him. I'm babbling, I know, but I don't know how else to—"

Eric yanked him down onto the bed. He got it, the whole thing, and now he needed to kiss Sweetness.

It was a while before Collin could say anything again. Then he just managed, "See? Totally passionate." before Eric was kissing down his sternum and across his stomach, and dipping into Collin's navel with his tongue. And yes, he was partly obsessed with getting to see what tiny little briefs Collin was wearing for him—would he have on an itsy-bitsy, teeny-weeny yellow polka-dot bikini?—but Collin's words kept echoing somewhere in the back of his head, about falling in love. Because whether Collin realized what he'd said or not, Eric did. He'd admitted that they were headed that way, sooner or later— now for Eric (if he was honest with himself) and possibly later for Collin, but he'd get there. This relationship was on the love-track, not the oops-just-lust-track or the FWB-track. And thank fuck, because Eric's heart really would have self-destructed if Collin had dumped him. The list of ass-making things he would have done to keep Collin was potentially endless.

And crap, he was nearly to Collin's pajama pants. Eric slowed down, nibbling the exposed upper corner of Collin's hip bone, making himself wait a little before pushing down Collin's waistband enough to see at least the color. They'd definitely be a color. Collin's underwear was all about color and minusculality. If that was a word. Oh God, if it was another jock, he wouldn't waste the opportunity to make Collin wear them the whol—

Collin shoved him off and stood up, panting and resting his hands on his waistband.

"Wha...?"

Collin grinned at him, and Eric got it. Sweetness had planned another little show. Eric lay back on the bed, head propped in his hand, breathing hard and ready to be an attentive audience.

Collin pushed down his sweats to show lime green briefs with dark purple around the legs—definitely not a jock, but still hot. "Nice. Turn around, Sweet Thing."

Collin smiled and did, looking over his shoulder.

"Holy shit." It was a thong, and the way that tiny triangle of fabric at the top of Collin's ass disappeared down between his cheeks made Eric want to dig it out with his teeth.

Collin smirked. "You like? I got it to wear for you."

He held out a hand. "I like. C'mere, Sweet Thing." That was probably more growl than voice. Collin turned back around, taking ahold of Eric and ready to climb back into bed.

Eric didn't give him a chance; he yanked Collin forward to the edge of the mattress while he stood up, then knelt behind him.

Collin felt Eric drop to his knees behind him, then spread Collin's cheeks and pull the string of the thong out of the way. He was startled enough that he didn't realize what was happening until Eric's tongue slid down from his tailbone into the valley between his glutes. He sucked in a breath, holding it until Eric reached his asshole and began circling it. Then he exhaled shakily.

Eric pulled back far enough to tell him, "Spread 'em wide, Sweet Baby. I want to be able to see everything I'm about to eat." Oh God, hearing Eric talk like that sent a bolt of lust through his gut. Collin spread his trembling legs as wide as possible, then bent over the bed, grabbing onto the sheets with one hand, shoving his other hand into his briefs and gripping his cock. He didn't stroke himself yet, because it would be over too fast. Instead he held on, massaging himself carefully, scrunching his eyes shut and simply feeling.

He'd not had a lot of guys do this—it seemed like something you should know someone pretty well for. Not even Toby had done it. And right now, feeling Eric's tongue lick up from his taint to his hole, probing gently at the opening, he realized that the few times anyone had rimmed him, he'd never really been able to just let it happen, not like this.

He trusted Eric.

The realization made him gasp, and Eric rumbled at him in answer, which Collin could feel as vibration in his nerve endings, making him very nearly bite through his lip. He pried his teeth open, and a moan escaped him. Eric stopped for a second to say something, his breath blowing against everything he'd wetted, and Collin shoved his hips back. His hand had started stroking his cock, and as Eric continued to eat his ass, he tried to burrow his head under his arm, unable to stop rocking his hips, up on his tiptoes and nails digging into the sheet until he thought he would tear right through it.

When Eric pushed his tongue inside Collin's asshole and stroked in and out, Collin lost it. He could hear himself moaning, and his hand was jacking his dick like crazy. It was too obscene to resist, that feeling of Eric inside him in such an intimate yet dirty way. His ass muscles rippling around Eric's tongue pushed a noise out of his lungs Collin had never heard.

Collin's eyes centered on his shaking arm holding him up when he came, gasping out moans. A hot, burning sensation rushed all through his balls and inside his dick, filling him up and radiating out into the rest of his body. So intensely good it streaked down his legs, and for a split second Collin thought he was coming out the soles of his feet too. Every muscle from his back down spasmed and shook, then suddenly let go of him, and Collin nearly fell, held up only by the bed and his fingernails anchoring him to it.

Eric stood up and bent over him, whispering sweet things—literally—and thrusting between Collin's ass cheeks until he came too, hot and slick on Collin's back and groaning into his shoulder. He kissed the back of Collin's neck, then lay on him, panting.

"You've never made that much noise." Eric bit his trapezius lightly, as if he were hugging it with his teeth.

Collin shivered. "I don't know if I've ever come like that."

"While someone rimmed you?"

"That too, but I meant that intensely."

Eric kissed where he'd bitten. "Not even when I fuck you?"

"It's not the same. I'm expecting you to fuck me. I'm expecting to come when you fuck me. I wasn't expecting that."

Eric rumbled at him, and it echoed into Collin's back. When Eric stood up, Collin shivered from the sudden loss of heat. "Come back."

Eric laughed, wiping Collin's back off with something.

Collin unkinked his hand from the bedding, stretching out his fingers, trying to ease the muscles and keep them from cramping. He pushed himself up with his hands until he was standing next to Eric, then leaned against his chest, kissing his whiskery chin. While Eric held him up with an arm around his waist, Collin shoved halfheartedly at his cum-soaked thong, until he got it far enough down that he could kick it off.

Eric kissed him. "Get into bed."

With Eric's help, Collin climbed in. He could have made it alone, but it felt so good to be touched like that. Lovingly, not sexually.

Eric went and poked at the fire a minute and threw on a log, then came back to bed. "Scoot over, Sweet Boy." When he lay down, he held out an arm so Collin could rest his head on Eric's shoulder.

Collin took full advantage, draping himself over Eric. The fire kept the room warm enough that they didn't really need a blanket, so Collin watched the way the light flickered on their skin, and zoned out.

"Sweetheart?"

"Mmm?"

"What did you want to talk about earlier?"

Collin's whole body stiffened up. "Shit, I forgot about that."

"I guess I should have let you forget."

"It's okay, I would have remembered eventually." He rolled onto his back, covering his face with his hands. He could feel Eric shift on the bed—rolling onto his side to see him, Collin thought.

He took a minute to figure out what to say. Whatever words he'd meant to use when he came out of the bathroom were long gone.

"We don't have to talk about this if you don't want."

Collin slid his hands down his face, looking at Eric. He needed to just get it over with. "I was checking my email earlier to see if I got the results of my HIV test from the Student Health Clinic. I took the ELISA test because it's more accurate." Eric nodded. Of course he'd know that. "The guy there also said that since it's only been six weeks since I was with someone else, I should wait another six and get tested again." Collin had had to ask—he'd never taken an HIV test with the objective of going bare with someone before.

"Did you get the results?"

Collin swallowed. "Yeah."

"And it was negative." Eric looked so sure.

Collin nodded. Then he stared at Eric, worrying his lip.

"I'm negative too. I get tested every year through the department, and then I try to go in every six months on my own. My last test was a month ago, and I haven't hooked up with anyone for three months. I have the results, if you want to see them."

Collin slid his hands back into his hair and gripped it, looking at Eric from between his arms. "Maybe we should wait that extra six weeks."

"It seems like an acceptable risk to me." He laid a hand on Collin's stomach. For comfort, possibly.

Collin took a slow breath. "I might need time to, I don't know, adjust. Maybe. Something. I'm scared."

He looked for signs of hurt feelings on Eric's face, but he didn't see any. The light in here sucked, though. "Scared of being that close to me?"

"It's so personal," he whispered. Of course, what they'd just done was very personal, wasn't it? Collin bit his lip.

Eric glanced down at his hand, rubbing across Collin's stomach, then looked back up and met Collin's eyes. "I can wait. We don't have to, sweetheart."

Did he really deserve this much understanding? Collin gripped his hair harder, shaking his head and his fists with it. "I don't understand. I was a halfway devoted slut before I met you, but now things are totally different." Why couldn't he do it with the guy he was pretty sure he was falling in love with?

Just the thought of falling in love made his heart bump around erratically in his chest a few times. *Maybe that's a clue right there.*

Eric was tracing designs on Collin's abdomen. "Would you have not used a condom with anyone else you've ever been with?"

"Ohmygod, no!"

"Even if you saw him a while and you both got tested?"

It took Collin a minute to decide, and his hands eased up on his hair while he thought. "Some of those guys I didn't really know, but my gut keeps telling me that even if I had, I wouldn't have been willing to go bare with them. It's so . . . intimate." He finally dropped his arms back onto the bed. "But I want to with you, I just don't know. This is happening so fast."

Eric traced Collin's lips with his finger. "I understand, Sweetness. It's a big step." He met Collin's eyes again, finally. "I can't tell you I'm happy about it, but I *am* okay with this."

Collin rolled, pushing Eric back on the bed so he hung over him. "Are you sure?"

"I'm sure." He met Collin's eyes steadily.

He felt lighter all at once, because he knew that Eric would give him time to adjust and not resent him for it. "Thank you." Collin kissed him and laid his head back on Eric's chest with a sigh.

Eric stroked his hair. "We're all good, Sweet Boy."

Chapter 38

"You have a pretty prick."

Eric laughed. He'd thought Collin had dozed off until he said that out of the blue. "A pretty prick, huh?"

"Yeah."

Eric looked down at his dick. It was doing its famous impression of a dead slug. "I think it's still sleeping."

Collin kissed the base of his throat. "I bet I can revive it." He gently bit Eric's skin. "You have a sexy neck."

"You have a very sexy everything."

"Right now we're talking about you." He pushed up on his elbow and leaned close. "I like this divot at the base of your throat. What's that called?" He put his finger on it, sliding from the top of one clavicle around to the other.

"It's the suprasternal notch, but it gets called the jugular notch pretty commonly."

"Mmm, anatomy turns me on."

Eric laughed and pulled Collin half on top of him, until Collin straddled one of his thighs. "Anatomy doesn't turn anybody on, Sweet Thing," he said against Collin's temple. He traced across the small of Collin's back with his thumb. "This is sexy."

"Shhh, we're focusing on what I like right now."

"Fine, what else do you like?"

He rubbed his leg across Eric's. "I like thighs."

Eric slid his hand down to cup one of Collin's buttocks. "What do you like about them?"

Collin lifted his head and looked down at him. "Aside from how muscular they are? I like them when they're hairy like yours, and I like when a guy with nice thighs—"

"Like mine?" He grinned.

Collin smiled back. "Like yours. I like to feel them on mine."

"Between yours, rubbing against you?"

Collin caught his breath and nodded. Eric could feel him getting harder against his hip. "And I like to lie on my stomach and feel them flexing against the backs of my legs while someone fucks me. Rubbing me inside and outside and all over me."

Eric gripped Collin's ass tighter, pressing him into his thigh and encouraging him to ride it. "Are you telling me you want me to fuck you like that?"

"Yes."

Eric took a minute just to look into Sweetness's eyes. Everything he'd said about them being good and it not being a problem was true. Except a small part of him didn't like waiting for Collin to work it all out. That part of him wanted it all now. That part of him needed this—Collin on his knees, body begging for his, being his sweet boy.

That part of him was very possessive. That small part of Eric wanted it a little rough, and a little dirty. Eric let that part of him have it.

"On your knees, Sweet Boy." Collin did it immediately, watching Eric the whole time. His sweet thing was so obedient. Eric traced a finger down Collin's jaw. "You're *my* boy."

Collin's eyelids went heavy, making him look so sultry. "Every time I spread my legs for you."

Eric caught his breath and started moving. Kneeling behind Collin, doing everything he needed to show his sweet thing just who could really do it for him. Even with a condom on. He started slowly, but kept pushing the tempo, speeding things up until they had a bed-shaking rhythm going. Until he could hear Collin gasping for breath because he kept losing the air in his lungs. Then Eric pressed on his lower back, following him down when he lay on the bed. He stopped to wrap his legs outside of Collin's, pushing Collin's thighs closer together and trapping them under his. "This is what you like?"

Collin moaned and tilted his hips, which Eric took as a yes. He grabbed Collin's wrists, pinning them against the bed and thrusting steadily until his sweet boy was writhing, pulling against Eric's hold. "Please."

"Please what?"

"I wanna stroke myself."

Eric let go of one hand, and Collin shoved it under his hips. He'd turned his head to the side, eyes closed and mouth open, making those small noises with each breath.

Eric worked very hard to draw louder sounds out of him. Moans and even a short cry about a half second before Collin came. His eyes flew open and his breath hiccupped, then his ass muscles started spasming, rippling around Eric's cock. Eric dropped onto his elbows, feeling Collin come under him, until he couldn't hold on anymore and he came too, making all the noise Collin didn't, his dick held so tightly by Collin's ass that Eric's eyes rolled up into his head and he shook.

He fell onto Collin's back, breathing in gulps and feeling Collin's heart beat like crazy under him. Collin shifted his legs, rubbing against Eric's thighs, then reached back and held onto Eric's hip, fingers digging in for a second.

Eric kissed across his shoulders before rolling off him onto the bed. He took off the condom and dropped it on the floor, excavated the lube bottle from under his right buttock, and pulled a mostly limp Collin to him to settle under his chin. "Mmm, Sweet Boy. You're mine."

He felt Collin nod against him.

Eric woke up early but let his sweet boy sleep, kissing him on the cheek before easing out of bed. He'd been getting up at 5:30 for too many years to be able to sleep in himself. Well, 7 a.m. was kind of sleeping in. He made coffee and started something for breakfast, then went to his office go through the images from yesterday's shoot.

Watching the movie-like progression as each image flashed on the screen while they downloaded, one in particular caught his eye. The glimpse he'd gotten showed emotions all over Collin's face. It felt voyeuristic, the thought of reading emotions from a picture instead of hearing about them from the source.

But who knew when he'd hear about them from Collin?

Maybe he shouldn't look at these right now. Yesterday and last night, so much had happened—more than he'd expected by far—and maybe he just needed to let things lie for a while. Wait for Collin to work this out for himself and hope for the best.

Yeah, right. He knew he was going to look at those pictures. He took the mouse in his hand, ready to scroll through them, but he didn't select anything.

Okay, so look at the picture.

Stop nagging.

Taking a deep breath, he clicked on the viewer, ready to open that file, but the image he'd glanced at wasn't the picture he got stuck on. The one that grabbed him and held him to the chair, finger hovering over the button, was one where Collin lay on his stomach naked except for that jockstrap, at an angle to the camera, peeking over one arm, the other one held out like an invitation. He was looking straight into the camera, and on the visible half of his mouth he wore a Mona Lisa-esque smile. Sort of a mixture of knowing he was sexy and not being sure he truly believed that.

His eyes were what really got Eric, though. They looked huge, larger than normal, and they were shadowed in just the right way to be extra dramatic and beguiling. The camera had picked up more of the brown than the hazel in his irises, and with Collin's dark hair and long lashes, he looked exotic. A harem boy from the Mediterranean, tempting the viewer to bed.

It was the last picture Eric had taken before he'd put the shutter on a timer, before he'd gone to join Collin in the bed. The next shot wasn't a very good one, but it showed Collin kneeling in his pink jockstrap, looking into Eric's face, reaching to help him undress. In the next few, Eric was barely visible and still clothed, and Collin didn't even appear in them because Eric had him pinned to the bed, as if he were smothering him. Then came an image Eric hated—his ass in the air, jeans half off of it, Collin's hands helping his pull on the waistband.

At least it provided evidence that Eric wasn't just passionately humping a bed for the camera.

Things got better after that. There was a shot of Collin's head and shoulders rising up off the pillows and blankets, Collin holding Eric's face in his hands and kissing him, mouth sealed around his. He looked dark and smooth against Eric's whiskers and hairy chest.

The picture of Eric throwing pillows off the bed and shoving blankets out of the way wasn't a ruined shot at all—Collin's face had been turned toward the camera but watching him, his lips curved up in amused affection.

After that, things got amazing. Collin on top, leg muscles straining and corded, glutes taut, working himself against Eric. The series of those showed him in various stages of thrusting, from ass up to fully stretched out. The shot that made Eric's skin tingle with excitement was the one where Collin had Eric's fingers in his mouth, watching his face, legs fully extended.

But the last picture was amazing. It must have been from just before Collin came. His jock was tangled around his thighs, and his ass was pushed up, tilting for Eric's hand. Eric had his thumb on Collin's butt cheek, digging in, and fingers buried inside him while his other hand gripped Collin's back just where it had begun arching up. Collin held himself over Eric, looking down into his face. His eyes were half-lidded and his mouth hung open, but something about his expression, even in profile, was indescribably emotional. All those tiny cues humans could read in someone's face but not explain were there, and it created an electric, almost visible connection between his eyes and Eric's in the image.

Collin wasn't just about to come, he was about to come with Eric. Maybe even *for* Eric.

After staring at that image forever, Eric closed his eyes. He could remember the look on Collin's face just before his orgasm. He'd seen it before, when people were dying and conscious of it. Sometimes, those patients had this look of rapture, and he always felt that if he stared at them hard enough or long enough, he could follow them into another, more enlightened world.

That's how Collin had looked yesterday.

Collin loved him, he'd bet money on it.

Eric pulled the biscuits out of the oven. He'd burned them, so engrossed in those photos that he hadn't heard the timer. Upstairs, Collin lay in bed still asleep, probably partly because Eric had kept the blackout shades down. It barely looked like predawn in the bedroom. He opened the one on the landing, and in the alcove next to the bathroom, just to give the room a little more light. Then he climbed back into bed with his sweet thing, pulling Collin's back against his chest, holding him tight. He told himself not to wake Collin, but his hand didn't get the message, and it felt Sweetness up. Stroking up and down Collin's back, and then his side, down to his hip and across his buttocks, palming each one.

"Mmm."

Oops, woke him up. He slid his hand around to Collin's stomach, riffling fingers through his trail of hair.

Collin stretched, nearly hitting Eric in the chin, then rolled onto his back, eyes heavy still but smiling. "Hey, Sexy Man."

Eric kissed him, ignoring any morning breath and sucking Collin's lips inside his, then running his tongue along the seam to feel the soft undersides. The tip of Collin's tongue met his, and Collin's hand pushed on his shoulder, until he'd rolled Eric onto his back and Collin was on top, straddling his stomach. Eric couldn't stop running his palms up and down Collin's body.

For a guy his age, Collin really knew how to kiss someone. Actually, he kissed better than most of the guys Eric's own age. Collin liked to start slowly, teasing, and he actually used his lips—he didn't seem to think they were just fortress doors that swung open or shut depending on whether his tongue might want to ride out that day. And his tongue—he was a tickler, the kind of guy who used the tip to feel things out before really plunging in and rolling around in sensation.

"Did you know your tongue's a muscle?" Eric asked when Collin gave him a breather.

"I figured that out, since I can move it and all."

"I really love your muscle."

Collin laughed.

"I love the way you trace things with the tip and the way it twines, and how hot and wet it is."

Collin slid his hand under Eric's neck. "I'd tell you to keep talking, but I really want to kiss you more." He used his fingers to cup the base of Eric's skull, controlling the movement of his head. Eric knew that trick; he used it on Collin when he really needed him a certain way. When he needed to run the show.

The next time Collin let up on his mouth—to use his teeth on Eric's earlobe, pulling it, then biting Eric's neck—Eric asked, "Do you always bottom?"

Collin stopped what he was doing—totally not Eric's intent—and pulled back. "Usually." He frowned. "Do you prefer to bottom?"

Eric traced his lips. "No." Collin's frown relaxed. "But I'd like to with you."

Collin's eyes lit up, the same way they had when Mandy had offered him that Spanish wine, except maybe more. "Now?"

"Yeah. Except . . . I need to take a shower first."

"Be fast."

ΘΑΓ

It took him longer than he would have liked—well, actually, he would have preferred not having to shower at all—but when he walked out of the bathroom, wrapped in a towel, Collin was lying naked on the bed in the uneven light, looking very composed. He didn't look like Eric's sweet young thang; he looked more like a sweetly wicked thing. Maybe an incubus that had popped out of Eric's hearth and lain in wait for him. Collin had one arm crooked behind his head, propping it up on some pillows, and his legs crossed at the ankles.

His dick lay on his belly, but it looked solid—turgid, even—like it might levitate up at any second. Eric could imagine it, Collin staring at the door and lazily stroking his cock, thinking about drilling him with it.

Then Collin sat up, and the shadows on his face that had made him look a bit sinister slid off. He looked like Eric's sweet boy again, holding out a hand for him.

His sweet boy, about to pound his ass.

"Pound" was such a hard-hitting word.

"Are you nervous?" Collin asked. "We don't have to do this." He dropped his hand, and that was the action that prompted Eric to move toward the bed.

"Of course I'm nervous. I haven't done this in forever." He stood in front of Collin, who reached for his towel, looking up at Eric questioningly—Eric nodded—before pulling it off of him.

Not surprisingly, he was completely flaccid.

Collin kissed his stomach. "It's okay. I know how to make it good." The mating cry of tops the world over, but coming from Collin, he believed it. Collin ran his hands up Eric's thighs, holding his hips, fingers splayed across his butt, rubbing little circles in his hair. "Why don't you lay down on the bed and I'll give you a backrub?"

Ah, the Backrub Maneuver. A proven classic. Eric cleared his throat. "Okay. Um, I need to tell you something." Collin looked up at him, eyebrows lifted. "I don't really like fingers. I mean, inside me."

Collin didn't seem to think that was weird; he just kissed Eric's stomach again, and (unnecessarily) helped him assume the position.

Okay, thinking about it that way isn't a good idea. He took a deep breath and slowly let it out, imagining himself sinking into the bed, loosening up all over. Being receptive to his sweet thing.

A few minutes into the massage, lying on the bed while Collin straddled his pelvis and kneaded his muscles, Eric began to appreciate the full benefits of this strategy. It wasn't just to relax him, it was to tantalize him with the way Collin's cock felt on his lower back, and the way Collin's nuts rested on the end of his spine. As Collin moved, reaching to work on one side or the other or maybe Eric's neck, he could feel the shifting weight of Collin's scrotum and the drag of Collin's dick across his skin. Pretty soon he didn't give a flying fuck about how loose his muscles were; he just wanted Collin lower so he could feel the tease of Collin's cock along his crack. He gave in to total fantasy, imagining Collin's balls hanging down, bumping against his taint. He'd have to spread his legs for that, the thought of which sent little shivers all over his body.

Collin leaned forward and kissed his neck, pushing his dick further up Eric's spine, that bend he had pulling it right and lifting his balls so that Eric's skin tingled at the absence of them. "Mmm."

"Feels good?" Collin whispered.

"Yeah. Go lower."

Collin did, working down his spine and finally shifting position so Eric could feel his scrotum pressing right above his asshole. He swiveled his hips, and Collin *hmmm*ed appreciatively. One of Collin's hands gave up on the massage and instead held his dick just at the seam between Eric's ass cheeks, thrusting lightly across it. Eric pushed up against him, and it wasn't long before they were rocking together, working out a rhythm. He shoved his hand under his body to grab his own dick, and Collin stopped.

Eric groaned and let go of himself, pulling his hand back out from under him.

Collin lifted himself off of Eric. "Put a pillow under your hips." Eric did, and hugged one to his chest also.

Using his knees, Collin guided Eric's legs open until there was room for him between them, and then he lay down. His face hung right over Eric's ass; Eric could feel his breath. And his hesitation. His fingers caressed Eric's skin, running across his cheeks. It felt good, but wasn't enough, so Eric lifted his hips. Collin met them with his lips, kissing him up and down his crack, but not going any farther, not pulling him open. Eric wiggled—that always spurred him on when Collin did it—and got rewarded. Collin's tongue gently probed, worming its way between Eric's glutes just below his spine.

Then—*finally*, thank fuck—Collin's fingertips dug in and pulled his cheeks apart. "Yeah. That."

Collin huffed a short laugh around his tongue, which was doing that thing he did, tracing things with the tip, like he had to draw the outline first so he knew where to color in. Down from Eric's tailbone, then carefully around his hole, getting tangled in hair and pulling on it, breathing rapidly. Eric gripped the sheets in his hands and held very still, all his muscles quivering. It felt like Collin carefully mapped each pucker with his tongue, then finally, gently probed the center, pushing on the opening and making Eric gasp.

Collin lifted his head just enough to speak. "How am I doing?"

Oh Jesus, Sweetness had never done this before? So fucking hot. Eric groaned, his blood pounding through his body. "Awesome. Need more."

Collin gave him more. Wet swirls of his tongue and sucking kisses. Sinuous explorations, nudging Eric's sphincter muscle until it relaxed and Collin could worm his way inside, and eventually thrust into him.

Eric's back had frozen into an arch, holding his hips up at a perfect angle for Collin, and he couldn't stop moaning and making other noises he didn't want to name, because he'd have to call them things like "whimper" and "mewl." He dug into the pillow to keep his hands from going for his dick. If this was the pregame, he absolutely needed to hang on for the kickoff.

Then Collin stopped and pulled himself up to lie on Eric's back, panting and gasping in his ear. "No condom?"

He should totally say something like, "Is this a decision you should be making now?" but fuck, he wanted it so badly; Collin inside him without anything between them. He nodded. He was totally willing to dwell in regret later for this moment.

Collin grabbed the lube. Eric heard the cap flip open, then Collin slicking up his dick, and Eric shoved his hips up a little higher, holding his cheeks open with his hands.

It felt like a kiss, when Collin first placed his head against Eric's asshole, and it sent a shock through him. Collin felt it too—he gasped and froze. But they couldn't stay like that forever, even if for a moment Eric felt like he might want to. He wanted the other stuff too; the feeling of being opened up and the pressure of Collin's dick filling him.

Collin went slowly, and although Eric had expected some pain, he got to the point where Collin's groin was up against his ass with only a little discomfort along the way.

"All right?" Collin whispered, propped on his elbows. He nuzzled Eric's neck.

Eric nodded, then lifted his head for Collin's kiss. It didn't work that well—Collin was too short, and their aim was off and they couldn't line things up quite right. But the rush it gave him ran through his whole body, and the flavor of the two of them mixing together on Collin's tongue felt like reassurance. Exactly what he needed then.

"Here we go," Collin said, rocking his hips. He stayed pressed against Eric, barely moving until Eric pushed back into him. Then he picked up the pace.

Eric had either forgotten a lot about what being fucked felt like, or Collin was extremely good at it.

Or it was just that it was Collin.

Sweetness could really hit a target. Eric had never been that impressed with the sensory abilities of his prostate, but Collin plumbed untold depths, propped up on his hands and rhythmically massaging it with his cockhead, until Eric felt that insistent edge of orgasm with every stroke. Losing his breath each time Collin glided into him, and thrusting into the pillow but unwilling to touch his dick because then it would all be over.

"How close?" Collin gasped, and Eric knew he couldn't last much longer.

Eric shoved his hand under his hips, and it took seven strokes before he was coming, toes curling and eyes squeezing shut. One of those orgasms that felt like everything inside him had contracted toward his center, then expanded explosively, all that tension he'd built up while Collin had fucked him pinging around inside him until it found its way out. Draining through his dick.

Collin came just after him, and Eric felt Collin's cum rushing inside him while those little, uncontrolled noises Collin made spilled out of his throat and right into Eric's ear, pulling one more moan out of his own lungs. Collin's whole body jerked, and then he lay on Eric, heart pounding on his back, occasionally kissing his skin.

"Oh, Sexy Man, that felt so amazing."

"Uh-huh." Ah, his fine motor control was returning.

Collin recovered faster. He lifted his head, kissing across Eric's shoulders. Then he squeezed Eric as well as he could with his arms. "I wish I'd let you do me bare last night."

"Oh God," Eric groaned, and while he couldn't possibly get hard again right now, his gut tightened in excitement. He grabbed Collin's hand in front of his face and kissed it. "No regrets?"

"I've never felt this close to someone in my life," Collin whispered.

Chapter 39

Collin sat in his boyfriend's office, checking his email on his boyfriend's computer while his boyfriend made him biscuits and gravy. Collin had never had biscuits and gravy before. It wasn't something the housekeeper had ever made. Fortunately, his boyfriend would correct that oversight.

Boyfriend, boyfriend, boyfriend.

Boyfriend.

Hopefully that got it out of his system for a while.

At first, looking through his inbox he didn't see anything interesting. Sixteen emails from Kyle, probably all one to two sentences, half of which would be semi-frantic questions about how to do something frat-related, the other half of which would be telling him to disregard the previous email, Kyle had figured it out. Four solicitations from offshore pharmacies. A long one from his debate partner in his Advanced Verbal Communications class, which he should totally read but he'd save until tomorrow when Eric had to go to work.

Then Collin noticed an email from Plant. It was intriguing because Plant rarely emailed him in the first place, this one was to the entire TAG email list, and most importantly, it had the tantalizing subject line "Budget Recommendations for Funding the Kegerator and etc."

Collin clicked on it, feeling nervous. This email could literally—in effect—kick him out of Theta Alpha Gamma. If Plant couldn't find the money somewhere, the guys could go back on their vote. Collin didn't *think* so, but the possibility was still there.

Plant was just as pompous as usual, and he used about a thousand more words than necessary, but the gist of his email was that he'd found the funds, contingent on another frat-wide vote. Collin groaned. They'd have to call another emergency meeting for that. He kept skimming, trying to find where Plant explained his budget plan.

If it was really lame, they could dispense with the emergency meeting and start looking at other options. One thing they'd never discussed was reaching out to the alumni who did support the policy, and Collin knew there had to be some. Like Eric, for instance.

Just then, Eric came in with coffee for him. That so deserved a kiss.

"You look excited," he said, standing up again after Collin pulled him down and kissed him.

"I do? What do I look like when I'm excited?"

"Your eyes get sort of bright, somehow, I don't know exactly. And you get this specific smile that you don't get at any other time, just the corners of your lips." Eric studied his face, cocking his head. "There may be more, but I can't tease it out."

"You're so observant."

"I like watching people." Eric shrugged and sipped at his own coffee, flushing slightly. "Why are you staring at me?"

"I don't know. You're just so . . . I don't know." Collin stood up and kissed him again, wrapping his arms around Eric's neck.

Eric only let him have one kiss, though. "I have to go check on breakfast—I already burned one batch of biscuits this morning."

Collin sighed, but let go. "Okay. I need to read this email anyway." He sat back down.

"You have so much email, Sweetness," Eric said before walking out of the room.

God, he did, didn't he? It was ridiculous. He looked at his inbox—over forty emails, and he'd checked it last night. Crazy. How much of it was truly important? *Very little.*

Oh, but the email from Plant, that was important. He needed to get back to it. He sipped his coffee and looked at it, skimming less and reading more as he got further in because it got very, very interesting.

Plant's suggestion was to cancel their Alumni Weekend. They'd drain the money from that single line item and use it for the kegerator and the cable internet. They'd even have funds left over—not enough to pay a cook, but a lot. Enough to start replacing the common property items in the frat that were ruined, including all the TVs. Insurance wouldn't pay for those because they essentially had a community housing policy.

At first, Collin had very mixed feelings. As alumni liaison, at least half his purpose was to plan that weekend.

I never wanted that job in the first place.

Shit. He'd been forced into it by Monty, of course. So Collin could impress the other alums. So they'd see how put together he was, how well he could organize something like that, and that he *got* them. Knew what men like them wanted and needed out of a weekend like that.

I totally shouldn't have shot down Danny's call girl suggestion.

But Collin had started to see it slightly differently when the membership policy issue came up. Their arguments over it during fall term had hinted at something Collin didn't like that much. His uncle wanted him to shine in the alumni liaison position, but not only because of how it reflected on Collin; he wanted it because of how it reflected on Monty just as much. And by extension, their business. The membership policy had threatened that, hadn't it?

Collin had always thought Monty's view of TAG was a little skewed. He focused on the elite membership, the guys who'd come through it with aspirations of six-figure salaries. But seriously, had he met the other 90 percent of their members? Guys like Gomer would be lucky to make enough to survive, although he was a trust fund kid just like Collin, so not the best example.

Brad. Brad was a great example. He was on scholarship, and while he had aspirations and dreams—good, solid, respectable ones—the amount he brought in a year fulfilling those dreams played no part in the formation of them. Collin knew for a fact he'd enrolled in his first business class this year just so he could figure out how to make a market garden work, financially. That'd be his last business class too.

Or Eric. He'd had aspirations of being a starving artist when he'd been an active TAG member.

Seriously, they were as motley a collection of frat brothers as the guys in *Animal House*. If slightly cleaner.

If Plant had this figured right, Collin could be free not only of his position, but of some of Monty's expectations. His heart picked up a little speed as he went back to Plant's email. He didn't know whether it was anxiety or excitement.

He found the important detail almost right away. "The Theta Alpha Gamma Alumni Weekend festivities are funded entirely by a 10 percent surcharge on *active member* dues."

It was a very high tax on current brothers, in essence. None of the money came from the alumni, not through the association or through direct donations. No one could accuse them of misusing funds if they reallocated it—its use wasn't specified in their by-laws. And under the circumstances—their frat house was uninhabitable, for God's sake— they could fully justify that reallocation.

Quickly, Collin scanned to find the specific motion Plant was proposing they would vote on. There it was—Plant moved that if the Alumni Association voted to cut off their funds to Theta Alpha Gamma, TAG would cancel all their planned Alumni Weekend activities and divert those monies to the budget items that were shorted when the alumni ended their financial support.

Collin stood up to go find his phone, but a wave of giddiness made him grab the desk a second. *I could be free.* For a short period, and only from some of Monty's expectations, but he could be. He could decide what would happen, not take directions. He'd even continue as liaison, but he'd do it his way.

As he ran past the kitchen, Eric stared at him. "Sweetness?"

"I have to make a phone call. I'll be ready for breakfast in ten minutes." He stopped and backtracked to throw his arms around Eric and kiss him. Not messing with any of the preliminary stuff, just insinuating his tongue into Eric's mouth—*mmm*, coffee and mountain man—and entwining their muscles (*giggle snort*) until they were both breathless.

"Good news?" Eric asked, panting slightly.

"The best. Ten minutes."

Then he ran upstairs and called Kyle.

"When's the meeting?" he asked as soon as Kyle answered.

One thing about Kyle, he checked his email religiously. "As soon as we get enough votes."

"Huh?" How could they vote before the meeting?

"I knew you wouldn't read the whole email before you called me." He sounded smug, but Collin's mood was too buoyant to bitch him out.

"So what else did it say?"

"It's freaking brilliant. I think we've been underestimating Plant, dude. He's really got a good head for strategy. Now if we could just get him to stop being so verbose, we might be able to really work wi—"

"Um, hello? Pot, meet kettle. Just tell me what the email said."

"Oh, sorry. Okay, he said that to delete the line item altogether, which is what he's suggesting for a bunch of reasons you can read later, we need a majority vote of active members. But si—"

"I know that."

"Shut up and stop interrupting me. But since calling another emergency meeting would be 'cumbersome'—that's the word he used—he suggested everyone designate him, Jules, or me as their proxy and send in their vote."

Collin blinked. "So, that means as soon as you guys have a majority of 'yes' votes, the Executive Committee can meet and do it. Fuck, that *is* brilliant!"

"I told you."

"Okay, you're my proxy. I vote yes. Now go check your email for more."

"No, dude, you have to copy and paste the wording Plant put in the email and send it in that way. We have to have this by the book."

"Consider it done." He started down the stairs, back toward Eric's office. "What's a majority of votes?" He waggled his fingers at Eric on his way past again.

"Forty. But it's a little early for a Saturday, and not all the guys have checked their email yet. I made everyone who lives here that's around this weekend get up and vote, but that still only brings us to twenty-one, including yours."

Collin swung into the office, hand on the doorjamb, and nearly ran to the desk. "Okay, I'm doing this now. When do you start calling guys and harassing them?"

"Noon. I figure that's late enough. Tank will go door to door if necessary."

Collin brought Eric's sleeping computer back to life. He found and copied Plant's very legal-sounding wording, pasted it into a reply, and filled in his name and "yes" vote. "Okay, done. I replied to Plant. Keep me updated and let me know when you guys meet."

"You really don't have to be there, you know. You aren't actually part of the committee."

"Oh, my little boy's all grown up now and can handle things all by himself?"

"Asshole."

"Douche bag."

"Talk to you later."

"'Kay."

He felt short of breath. Not from running up and down stairs, but from the adrenaline. He should get up and go tell Eric, but he couldn't do anything at the moment but stare off into space and blink.

Forty votes and his life would change. It seemed too simple, but every way Collin looked at it, that's how it ended up. Forty votes and Monty's entire reason for forcing him into being alumni liaison would be null and void.

"Sweetness?"

Collin jerked his head up to see Eric standing next to him, brows drawn together and mouth turned down. He launched himself out of the seat and into Eric's arms, hanging off his shoulders and burying his face in Eric's neck. His breathing sounded ragged, echoing back to him in this little space.

Eric's hands ran up and down his back, occasionally pressing Collin closer. "Sweet Thing? Can you tell me what's going on?"

Collin hugged him tighter. "Just a minute. I need a minute."

Eric kissed his temple. "Just tell me it's a good thing."

"It's a very good thing."

Chapter 40

"It seems ridiculous, doesn't it? That I'm so excited over something this simple, but seriously, my whole life will be different, at least until the end of the school year." Collin's eyes were shiny to the point that Eric started to wonder if he had tears in them. He looked down at Collin's plate. Sweetness held a fork in his hand, but he hadn't taken a bite.

Honestly, Eric didn't quite get it. Collin seemed to feel this was revolutionary, but all he could see was that Collin would have less responsibility (and hopefully less email). He swallowed his food before saying anything. "I don't really understand." He felt almost like he'd let Collin down by admitting it, but Collin just smiled bigger.

"Monty has directed my academic life since I started school. He decided what prep school I'd go to, what activities would look best on my college application, what classes I need to take." Eric's horror must have shown on his face—how could it not?—because Collin held one palm out. "I mean, not that I couldn't make any decisions for myself. He didn't pick my friends or stop me from doing something I wanted. He just guided my development."

"Did he pick your major?"

Collin looked down, finally poking at his food. "Well, yeah. But I don't hate it. I like it."

Jesus. If someone had tried to do that to him, where would he be? Not Eric: the guy that tried it. Because Eric thought he'd have had a pretty bad reaction. And if it was J.M. doing it, his reaction would be worse. He didn't know how to react now. He didn't want Collin to feel bad. "Um, so what's your major?"

"Communications."

At least it was something Eric could imagine him choosing. He set down his fork, not hungry anymore. "So, this frees you from being the alumni liaison?"

Collin had finally taken a bite, and he spoke around it. "No, I'll still be the liaison, but I'll get to decide what I want to do. It will totally fuck with Monty's plans for me when I became liaison."

J.M. sounded more and more like a mammoth prick every second, not that it surprised him. Eric took a calming breath. "He decided you'd be the liaison, and then he decided your agenda?"

"Pretty much." Collin was deflating before his eyes. Eric knew it was his reaction—he couldn't be happy about Collin having this tiny bit of freedom now that he'd gotten a picture of how much control that douche bag had over Collin. It made him sad enough to want to punch something. Or someone.

Instead, he reached across the table and took Collin's hand. "I'm sorry."

Collin pulled it away. Gently, but still. "What do you have to be sorry for?"

"For not being happy for you. It's just . . ."

Collin lifted his chin. "You think I'm weak."

What? "No I don't. I didn't say that."

"You weren't thinking it?"

"No. I was thinking you were a kid and J.M. indoctrinated you into thinking he had this right."

Collin shrugged, stabbing his biscuit with his fork. "Dad died and Monty was there for me. I thought his involvement in my life was normal." He gave up on his biscuit and carefully set down his fork, lining it up next to his plate. "It *was* normal, right up until college. All the other guys in my prep school were under the same pressure, and a lot of them had it worse. I could at least pick my own sports." Collin took a drink of orange juice, focusing all his attention on it.

"Did you pick your own college?" Crap, he never should have asked that. *Way to calm things down.*

Collin's nostrils flared. Eric was going to take a wild guess and say that meant he was angry. "Lots of fathers want their sons to go to their alma maters."

"He's not your father." Fuck, why had he said that? It had just slipped out before he'd thought.

Finally Collin looked at him, and his eyes were still shiny but his face had tightened up. Even his forehead had developed a wrinkle.

"How did this turn into an argument? I was happy and you can't just be happy for me, you have to turn this into an indictment of my uncle?"

Eric closed his eyes for a second and tried to mellow out enough to explain. He took a breath before looking at Collin again. "I'm sorry. I like seeing you happy. I want to be happy for you. But I feel like, I don't know, like J.M. is taking advantage of you."

"I already told you, he's guiding me. It's not unreasonable since I'm going to work for the company after I graduate. He's helping to prepare me for that." Collin picked up his fork again, like he might take a bite now that he'd settled this so completely.

Eric couldn't not say it, because someone had to point it out sooner or later. Better now. "And who decided you would work for the company?"

Collin slammed down his fork and leaned toward Eric. "He was an asshole to you; I get that. But it was nearly twenty years ago, can't you just get over him?"

"I *am* over him. I was never that *in*to him."

Oh fuck me.

Collin froze and stared at him. "What?"

Eric planted his elbows on the table and rested his head in his hands a second. "Nothing."

"You had, like . . . a thing for him?" Collin's voice sounded scratchy, but Eric couldn't even look at him.

He looked at Collin's hand, reaching out take it. "Sweetness, I'm—"

"Do *not* call me that." Collin stood up, the legs of his chair screeching on the floor. "And do *not* try to tell me again you're sorry." He walked across the kitchen and out the back door, wearing nothing but socks on his feet. He didn't even have a coat, just sweats and a T-shirt.

Eric managed to wait fifteen minutes—the amount of time it took him to clean the kitchen while mostly looking out the window at Collin, sitting on the back deck, arms and chin resting on the mid-rail and feet in the grass. It looked like he might be watching the chickens. But probably not.

He should give thanks that Collin hadn't gone farther. Like back to town. Back to his life before last week.

God, I hope I haven't fucked this up. Eric couldn't help but remember all the uncertainty between them—Collin didn't know how he felt, and things had moved so fast, and he was so young.

And now Eric had announced he'd been attracted to J.M.

He didn't know what to do about any of it, except try to explain, so he stepped out the back door, bringing Collin's coat with him. When he walked up, Collin took it, wrapping it around his shoulders.

"You're lucky it hasn't rained recently or your feet would be soaking." Eric sat next to him, trying not to spook him and make him run.

Collin glanced at his feet. "They're sort of damp."

Well, his boy was speaking to him. "I should have told you before. It wasn't that big a deal, Collin, I swear. It just drove me nuts because I was attracted to him even when he was such a dick to me. I didn't think about him for years, but then when I met you and after a while we figured it out . . . I don't know why I didn't tell you then."

Collin closed his eyes a long second, slumping slightly. He took a breath and opened them again, turning to face Eric. "The night you came looking for me at—"

"I wasn't thinking that you looked like him and I could get a piece of what I never had. The first time I saw you, I thought you had eyes just like J.M. Then I had that dream, and I knew it was you. I never thought once about him again until we started talking about the frat."

They sat silently and for a long time, Collin watching chickens and Eric watching him. Until his butt got damp from the deck boards under his jeans, and the damn birds had clucked him nearly crazy with waiting.

"If you had told me in the beginning, I would have believed you."

Eric's heart dropped into his stomach. "I know."

"But you didn't and now it seems so weird and I don't understand and . . . I don't know, Eric." Collin shook his head. "How do I trust you really feel the way you say you feel about me?"

Eric didn't know what to say. His first reaction had been "You said you trust me," but he couldn't say that. Collin had given him that trust, and it was up to Collin to continue to believe in it.

"How would you feel if you dated a guy who'd gone to college with your father, and then found out that he'd had a crush on him? It wouldn't cross your mind that you could be a substitute for your dad?"

"You aren't a substitute."

"I know you believe that, and it's true *now*, I know that. But would you have even looked at me twice that first time if I didn't look like a guy you wanted to fuck twenty years ago?"

"It's not that simple. I disliked him, but I was still attracted to him. It was like, I don't know, popcorn that gets stuck between your teeth and you can't get it out even with dental floss. But eventually it works its way out and you forget about it, until the next time you eat popcorn."

Collin huffed. "So what, I'm popcorn?"

"No, you aren't popcorn, you're something much better. You're what I was really craving every time I had the stupid popcorn. This is the worst example ever and I'm losing you, aren't I?" He could feel his voice going hoarse and trembling in his chest, shaking its way out of him.

Collin sighed. "It's not the worst analogy ever. It's weird, but I understand it. I just don't know how to feel . . ."

Eric cleared his throat, but that didn't help him say what he needed to say. He just had to spit it out. "I'm in love with you, Collin."

Collin swung his head up, eyes wide, and met Eric's gaze. He licked his lip. "You are?"

"It's the truth."

Collin looked away again, but Eric swore something in his face had eased. His jaw or something around his eyes. "I still need to think about it."

"I'll give you all the time you need." He took a chance and picked up Collin's hand, holding it carefully. Collin allowed it, but didn't respond otherwise, just let it lie there in Eric's, limp.

"I know you're at least partly right about Monty." Eric could barely hear Collin's voice at first. "But that company belongs to our family, and I've always wanted to work for it. It never even occurred to me to do anything else, and no one ever encouraged me to think otherwise. He just told me that was my future. And right now I'd say that I don't want to do anything else."

"Well, then that's what you should do." But did that mean he had to move back to California after graduation? *One problem at a time.* Right now Eric didn't even know if Collin wanted to keep him.

Collin deflated a little, looking down toward their hands. "Maybe it should have occurred to me I could do something else."

Eric reached for him, rubbing the back of his neck. "If you tell me he's got your best interest at heart, I'll do my best to remember that."

Collin snorted, but didn't say anything right away. He turned his head back toward the chickens. "Since I met you, I've been scared he'd ruin this for me somehow. I just never would have guessed it would be this way."

He went cold all over, everything inside him shrinking in. "So, that's it? We're ruined?"

It took long seconds, but Collin looked down, maybe at their hands, and said, "I don't know."

Before Eric could figure out how to ask anything else, something that would give him another clue to how badly he'd fucked up, a phone rang inside the house.

Collin sighed. "It's mine. It could be Kyle, I need to get it," he said, standing up and heading in. Eric watched him leave sock prints on the boards, leading away from him.

Chapter 41

H e should have checked the display before he answered his phone. Or he should have a special ring for his uncle, so he'd know before he even got up to answer the damned thing.

"Hello Collin," Monty said when he answered, and Collin's heart slunk off to hang out somewhere in his intestinal tract.

Eric walked in the back door just as he said, "Uncle Monty. Hello." Eric lifted his eyebrows, tipping his head toward the office. Collin shook his head and grabbed Eric's hand. Boyfriend or not, he felt like he needed support.

"I thought I should inform you that the Alumni Association Executive Committee met last night. I think talking about this over the phone is better than email."

Interpretation: he hadn't liked Collin sending him a summary of the TAG meeting. "I see."

"I'm sorry, but after much debate, we were forced to vote to cut off alumni funds to Theta Alpha Gamma unless that membership policy is rescinded." God, was that satisfaction in his voice? It sounded like it. Or was he imagining it?

He had to let go of Eric's hand to rub his forehead, but Eric stayed right there next to him, loaning his body heat. "And when do you have the general meeting for the membership at large to vote?"

"According to our by-laws, this motion can be voted by email. However, the restriction is effective immediately, only to be rescinded if a majority of the association members vote against it."

"Can you do that?" he blurted. Dammit, he had to keep calm. Think out every word.

"I assure you, we followed our by-laws carefully." Collin heard Monty's chair squeak in a familiar way. He'd just leaned back in it. God, he was probably smiling too. "We *can* do that."

He drew himself up very straight. "Well, since things have gone this far, it's my duty to inform you and, through you the association, that we're about to hold a vote on whether to cancel the Theta Alpha Gamma Alumni Weekend activities and divert those funds to replace what we're losing from the Alumni Association." Verbal poker, that's what he and his uncle were playing.

"What?" Collin thought he heard a thud, as if Monty's fist had hit his desk. "You can't do that, that's misuse of funds."

"Actually, we *can* do that. Not only is it allowed for in our by-laws, but Alumni Weekend has traditionally been financed through a 10 percent surcharge on all TAG dues. The money comes entirely from current, active brothers, not donations from alumni."

Were those Monty's teeth grinding? "I would urge you not to take this step. Once that money is spent, you won't be able to reverse this decision."

"What reason would we have for reversing it?" *Please give me a reason.*

"What if this investigation concludes the arsonist was motivated to act by that membership policy?" Not the reason he'd been hoping for.

He turned it back around on Monty. "Has the Executive Committee determined it will repeal their motion if the arson *wasn't* motivated by the membership policy?"

Another familiar squeak—this time Monty turning to look out at his olive groves. *Uncertain.* "I can't promise that. We didn't feel it necessary to make any such provision."

"But you want us to make such a provision?" Collin took a deep breath in through his nose. He didn't care that his uncle could hear it; he wanted him to know he was pissed off. "What the Alumni Association action suggests to me is that this is only an excuse. You were just looking for a way to force us to rescind this policy."

Monty's small cough gave him away. He was about to try to pass off bullshit as the truth. "I know it must seem like that, but the association has come to the conclusion that even if this isn't a result of the open policy issue, future attacks may be."

"Based on what? What evidence did you find to bring you to this conclusion?" Collin paced across the kitchen and back, stopping in front of Eric. "I can't imagine what might make you think that, unless you all came to realize that's what you would do if you were able to, in order to force us to revoke the policy. Maybe we should start looking at the Alumni Association for our perpetrator. Maybe I should talk to Detective—"

"Collin!"

"What? What, Monty?" He threw his hand out, asking the ether. "Did I hit a little too close to home?" He opened his mouth to say more, but just then Eric grabbed his hand out of midair, catching his attention. He shook his head. Collin scowled at him and yanked his hand away. Annoyed that Eric was right: he'd been damn close to bringing up Sparky Donaldson.

"Collin, I believe you're speaking thoughtlessly, coming to conclusions based on your emotions rather than logical thought. I'm going to end this conversation now, and call you later, after you've had time to cool off—"

Oh that was just *it*. He pulled his hand out of Eric's and started pacing again, stabbing the air with his finger. "The problem is that your emotions *aren't* involved. You're totally unconcerned with what's right and only thinking about what it means for your image and the damned company. What do you stand to benefit from this? You do a lot of business with some of those guys."

"I'm doing this for you!"

"Well, don't! It's not what I want. Do you ever think about what I want, or only what you want for me? Do you ever try to see things my way?"

"Being persuaded to see things your way is how we got into this mess." Monty's voice shook, probably with anger, but who the fuck really cared?

"You don't know that, not yet! The investigation isn't even completed, but you've forced the Alumni Association to make a decision based on the outcome you expect. The only reason we have any sort of mess at all right now is because you're trying to push your moral values on a system that's grown beyond them, and you've convinced your cronies to see it the same way."

"I'll speak with you later, after you've had time to calm down and think clearly."

Collin opened his mouth to say more—he didn't even know what at this point—but it was useless. "That motherfucker hung up on me." He blinked at the phone, shaking in his hand, and listened to the blood pound through his ears and head. He couldn't fucking understand what had happened, and he couldn't think straight, could barely see straight. *Straight, that's a funny word.* How had everything gotten this fucked-up?

He felt Eric's hand on his back, and barely stopped himself from flinching away. He needed to be alone, away from all people and email and this goddamned phone.

So he flung the fucking thing against Eric's wall and watched it break into pieces, then said, "I'm going for a run," and fled upstairs to get his running shoes.

ΘΔΓ

He didn't stretch before he took off down the road. Stupid maybe, but he didn't have the patience for that. He ran too hard at first, also not surprising. He turned back toward Eric's at about a half mile. He hadn't worked out a damned thing or even had a clear thought by then—couldn't even make himself think calmly. But he felt better, so he just went with the not-thinking thing and hoped for the best. Hoped he'd have some answers sooner or later.

Except he already had a lot of them, didn't he? He knew how TAG would handle the response from the Alumni Association; he knew Uncle Monty was, in fact, a douche bag; and he knew what he was running toward: Eric's place. Eric.

Because he believed him. Because he trusted him. He could see sincerity in Eric's eyes when he said he loved Collin. Collin didn't know much else right now, but he knew that.

Am I choosing Eric over Monty? Collin nearly twisted his ankle, his feet stumbling a second, feeling like he'd put his shoes on backwards.

No thinking. His feet and mind sorted themselves out somehow, and eventually his mind wandered on to his father.

Collin had quite a few memories of his dad. He remembered riding in front of him on his horse, which his mother said he'd done a lot. When he thought about it, he could feel his father's palm planted on his abdomen, so big his thumb rested by Collin's heart and his little finger could poke into Collin's belly button and tickle him. But his dad never did that on a horse, because Collin hadn't been allowed to squirm if he wanted to ride with him. It felt more secure than a seat belt, sitting in front of his father and holding onto Tonto's mane.

Those were the strongest memories, not anything his dad ever said to him. He had a little kid's view of what he'd looked like. Dark hair and tan skin and a very angular nose, which (of all the ridiculous memories) Collin could remember looking into. Holding his dad's hand and looking up his nostrils while Daddy talked to someone. He'd seemed so tall, taller than Monty. Shit, his mother was taller than Monty. Collin was taller than Monty, which said a lot.

But the thing he couldn't remember, and that he'd never realized until this week was even lacking, was his father and mother together, interacting. He knew his dad had loved his mom, and she loved him. As Collin got older she'd dated some men—she was attractive, even he could see that—but never seemed serious about any of them. He'd never asked her about it; he just assumed she still loved his dad. That she'd always love his dad.

If he couldn't remember what his parents' relationship was like, how could he recognize being in love? It would have been the only model he had for love. Monty didn't date often, and he'd never been serious about anyone as far as Collin knew. Actually, Collin had begun to suspect he paid for what he needed physically. That sounded like a really bad approach to love.

He slowed to a walk, cooling off for the last few hundred yards. Was it even possible to fall in love when he knew so little about it? Other people managed to, didn't they?

Just like that, out of the blue, his brain supplied him with another answer: he needed to talk to his mom. He had a lot he should have told her a long time ago. He probably needed a working phone first, though.

Eric opened the door when Collin walked up the porch steps. He looked somewhere between worried and relieved, leaning his weight on the doorjamb and not quite smiling at Collin. Keeping his distance, arms crossed over his chest.

Collin didn't want distance. He held out one hand toward Eric, coming closer.

Eric stood straight, reaching for Collin's hand and pulling Collin into his arms.

Ohthankgod. He leaned his head on Eric's shoulder and held him tight around the waist, squeezing until Eric grunted softly. Then he let up a little. "I'm sorry," Eric whispered.

"So am I." The hairs on his head caught in Eric's whiskers as he spoke.

Eric leaned them both against the doorjamb, like he needed the support. "We aren't ruined?" he asked, running his palms up and down Collin's back.

"No," he said with a sigh.

Eric's scruff rubbed against the side of his face, and then Eric pressed a kiss on his temple. "I'm going to try to think of him as 'Monty' and not 'J.M.' Whatever he may have been to me isn't important anymore, and what he is to you now *is* important."

Relief rushed through him, easing his muscles from the neck down. He didn't have to choose anyone, not now.

"I built you a fire."

Collin couldn't help but smile. "Is that like your version of making things better with a cookie?"

"Probably. Do you want to come inside and lie on the couch with me?"

"Mmm-hmmm." Collin kissed his neck. He was so close to saying it in that instant, the big "L" word, but he stopped himself. Eric may know he loved Collin, but this had happened so fast and Collin had so many other stressful things going on, and, yes, he could admit he was scared.

And yes, it still felt like choosing one person over the other.

But then Eric took his hand and led them to the couch and the words subsided, back to lying in wait in his chest for the right moment. Collin was secretly certain they'd get their chance.

"Here you go," Eric murmured when they reached the couch, kissing Collin's temple again.

Collin lay down and held his arms up to Eric. "Be my blanket."

Eric did it without question, just a smile, placing one leg between Collin's and bringing them chest-to-chest. "What am I supposed to use for a blanket?"

Collin pulled the blanket off the back of the sofa and over them. It couldn't be the most comfortable position for Eric; he was up on his elbows, looking down at Collin, but it would only be for a few minutes. Collin may not be ready to say everything, but there were still things he needed to tell his boyfriend. He cupped Eric's face between his hands and looked into his eyes. "I feel like I've learned more about sex in a week with you than in the previous five years."

Eric's brow furrowed, and Collin realized that probably wasn't the best way to start. Except he didn't know what exactly he wanted to say next.

"You started having sex when you were sixteen, even in the closet?"

He nodded, still at a loss for what exactly he was trying to communicate.

"I didn't start that early, and I was out, at least to my mom and a couple friends in high school."

Collin looked down between them, trying to figure out what he was doing. "I'm sorry."

"Sorry I didn't have sex until I was eighteen?"

When he looked back up, Eric had his half smile, but it didn't look like a happy one. "Sorry I said it that way."

Eric sighed. "What exactly are you trying to say?"

"I'm not sure."

"Sweetness," Eric whispered. "I need to tell you this isn't going well."

Collin nodded. "I know."

"But it's still better than what I told you earlier."

About Monty. Collin shook his head slightly, dismissing the whole subject. They looked at each other a few seconds before something popped into his mind, something he knew he meant to say. "You taught me about intimacy."

The line between Eric's brow softened. "I guess that means you care about me some, huh?"

Collin wrapped his leg around Eric's, trying to snug him closer. "I care about you so much. This is hard for me. I started liking guys and that was something only I could know about, then I had sex and that meant more secrets I had to hide. I don't really know how to unhide. My feelings, or something. It feels—it felt, I don't know, dangerous."

Eric turned his head enough to kiss one of Collin's palms. Collin's eyes prickled in answer, like he had a tear or two wanting out. "You're safe with me."

Collin nodded. "I know."

"Did you feel ashamed?"

Collin felt as if Eric had just dropped his full weight on his chest, denting in his ribcage and making it harder for his lungs to expand. "No."

Eric kissed his other palm.

"Shit. Maybe. Why would I feel ashamed?"

"I don't know. For not being what your—what people wanted you to be."

Oh God, now he felt nauseous. "That's so unfair."

Eric smiled sadly. "It's unfair that you felt that way?"

Collin swallowed, nodding. He couldn't blink, because tears had filled his eyes and if he blinked they would run down his face.

Eric leaned down and kissed his eyes closed. "I love you, Sweet Boy," he whispered.

Collin choked on a sob and wrapped his arms around Eric's neck, hiding in his chest because he knew more tears were on their way. Eric rolled, bringing Collin with him, turning them sideways and holding Collin in his arms. Keeping him safe.

He didn't know how long they lay like that, Eric letting him hide for as long as he wanted while he rubbed Collin's back. More sobs leaked out, fewer than Collin had expected, and more than a few tears, enough to soak Eric's T-shirt and create a wet spot on the couch. It should have been embarrassing, but Collin didn't feel embarrassed, he just felt very, very cared for.

Loved.

Chapter 42

Collin seemed all right now. Eric had worried he'd feel embarrassed over crying, or still wary about Eric's feelings, but judging by the way Sweetness was melted all over his chest, he felt plenty relaxed and unconcerned. Eric kissed him on the head and Collin wiggled closer, mumbling something that sounded suspiciously like "snuggle bear."

He ignored that. "Are you falling asleep, Sweet Thing?"

Collin sighed. Was that his answer? "I wish I could. I need to send out an email to the frat, amending that motion now that we know what action the Alumni Association has taken."

Lovely. Again with the email. Which reminded him. "I don't know if your phone's broken or not. You smashed the hell out of the screen, but it still turns on. I thought you broke it in half, but that other piece was just the case popping off."

"Dammit," grumbled Collin. "I was trying to kill it. Has it rung?"

"Nope." Because he'd turned it off. Eric smiled to himself.

"That's weird. You'd think if it still turns on it would still take calls. Did you turn it off?"

Crap. "Yeah."

Collin started laughing, except it sounded like a giggle. Eric had never heard that noise from him, and it made him laugh, until Collin fell off the couch.

He peered over the edge. "Are you all right?"

"I'm fine." Collin grinned at him, pushing himself up. "I do need to check my email, though." He lost the smile.

Eric sighed. "Go ahead. I'm going to make us sandwiches since we didn't really have breakfast."

While he was in the kitchen, his phone rang. For a second, he thought it was Collin's phone, and he was about to throw the goddamned thing against the wall again, but then he realized it was the ring he'd programmed for his mom, "No Woman No Cry." She kept track of his work schedule, and if he didn't answer it when he wasn't at work, she'd worry.

"Hey, Mom." He tucked the phone between his ear and shoulder so he could spread mayo on the bread.

"Hi, honey. How are you doing? What's new?"

He could totally go with the standard reply, but he didn't. "I just told my boyfriend I love him, and now I'm making him a sandwich."

She squealed in his ear and clapped, then suddenly stopped. "Wait, is this guy anything like Jay?"

"Nothing like him. Physically or otherwise." Jay had been tall and blond. He probably still was, actually.

The squealing continued, although less piercing this time. He was so glad they were on the phone and not video chat—then she'd go on about how cute his blush was. And she'd probably harass him until he let her see Collin.

"Should we video chat?" she asked. "Then you could introduce him to me."

"You just want to see what he looks like." Eric had spread mustard on the other slice, and now he started piling on the good stuff. Well, and lettuce. Sweetness probably didn't get enough vegetables.

She motorboated her lips. "Duh."

"He's using the computer anyway. So, how are you doing?"

"You seriously think I want to talk about me? Tell me about your boyfriend."

Eric exhaled heavily. "Well, he's fifteen years younger than me. Actually, it's closer to fourteen."

Silence—she was probably doing math. That always took her a while. He'd added the tomatoes, pickles, and cheese before she said, "He's twenty-one?"

"Yup."

"Oooh, a younger man."

Eric laughed—that had been about the reaction he'd expected. "Yeah."

He was putting turkey on top of the cheese when she asked, "So, can he just fuck forever?"

"Mom!"

"Dammit, I knew you wouldn't answer that one. Okay, tell me this: is he likely to provide me with grandchildren?"

Probably, if things work out. "We've been seeing each other a week. I really don't know." He got out plates and napkins.

"You've been seeing each other a week and you told him you love him?"

"Yeah. Listen, I should take him his lunch. Love you—"

"Don't hang up yet!"

"Mom, c'mon, I have a guy here. I'll call you later." He could tell she'd let him go if he just pushed it a little more. He cringed, but added, "You know, he's got quite an appetite." Had he added too much innuendo to his voice?

"I knew it, he *can* do it forever! Okay, you go, honey. Love you."

"You too."

He carried the phone into the office with him when he delivered Collin's sandwich. Collin typed away busily, then he clicked on something and turned to Eric. "Done. I'm just going to check a couple of new ones and then turn this off." He clicked on something else.

Eric didn't mean to look, but as he came up behind Collin to set the plate down, a picture loading on the screen caught his attention. "Who's sending you porn?"

"It said it came from Jock, and it went to everyone in the frat."

"That kid I met at the party, the hockey kid? He's sending gay porn to everyone?"

"Uh-huh . . ." They both stared at the image of a guy sucking another guy's cock, taken from the perspective of the guy being sucked. The guy doing all the work was looking up at the camera, and was clearly recognizable.

"That's him, isn't it?" Eric asked.

Collin inhaled audibly, holding it a second. "Yeah, that's Jock." He turned to Eric. "I need to use your phone."

Eric handed over his phone, then leaned forward and clicked the mouse to close the email. He didn't trash it—for all he knew it was evidence. He just didn't need to see it.

"Kyle, it's possible no one recognized him—they might have seen a guy sucking a dick and deleted it without figuring out who it is. They're probably still puking."

Kyle's strident tone carried clearly across the room.

"Shit." Collin rubbed his forehead. "Okay, how bad are things? Do I need to come back?"

Whatever Kyle said was not good. Collin slumped against the desk, shoulders drooping. "Are you sure? Brad's there, right?"

Wah-wah-wah-wah, wah-wah-wah-wah. Kyle sounded just like any adult in a Charlie Brown cartoon.

"Well, can I talk to Brad?" He rolled his eyes at Eric. Then refocused on the phone. "Okay, seriously, is Kyle overreacting? How much?"

He went back to massaging his forehead.

If he and Collin stayed together, how much of his own life would be taken up by watching Collin deal with problems on the phone or put out fires by email? Could he live with that? Eric sighed to himself. He knew he could, and would.

It was one of the main skills of househusbandry, after all.

For now he grabbed his coat and went outside to make sure the chickens had food and water. Collin found him a few minutes later, while he was scattering some cracked corn around for them, watching them all but kill each other to get to it. He kept the dumb rooster away with his foot long enough for the hens to get a reasonable share.

"How come I'm the college student and you're the firefighter paramedic, but I'm always the one on the phone dealing with emergencies?" He stood right against the chicken wire, fingers gripping the loops.

Eric smiled at him and rolled up the feed bag. "You'll get your turn." He latched the door to the coop, and when he turned around, Collin was right there, sliding hands up his chest and stretching for a kiss.

"I have to go back to the frat," Collin said against Eric's lips, then kissed him. Nice tactic. Give him bad news, then keep his mouth too busy to react.

"I'm going with you," Eric said when Collin started to pull away, and kissed him in return.

Collin was smiling when Eric let him go. "Yay. I was hoping you'd say that."

Chapter 43

A s Eric drove them to campus, Collin gave him a quick briefing, trying to hit the major points. "Some of the guys looked at the picture long enough to see who it was, and they got all worked up about it and told the others. I guess the big problem now is that all the brothers are trying to be 'sensitive' and offer their support. No one thinks Jock sent it out himself, they think it was some kind of joke or something."

Eric shook his head at the road. "College is totally different now."

He rubbed Eric's leg. "I think it's just TAG. These guys are kind of freaks, you know?"

Eric glanced at him, widening his eyes. "Uh, yeah."

"Anyway, Brad offered to let Jock and Tank stay at his and Sebastian's place for the night, just until Jock feels a little more, I don't know, even-keeled?"

Eric nodded.

"Kyle thinks I can help somehow."

Eric picked up his hand and kissed it. "You probably can, Sweetness."

When they got to the frat/dorm and took the elevator up to the third floor, the doors opened just in time for Collin to hear someone saying, "Okay, but dude, I want to know what our response is gonna be."

Kyle was standing on the coffee table, hands in the air, palm out. "For the last fucking time, there will. Be. No. Response!"

"Response to what?" Collin asked loudly, even though he knew the damned answer.

Everyone turned around, and Danny spoke up. "Oh, hey! Collin's here with his boyfriend. This is his *boyfriend*, everyone."

"See what I mean about them being freaks?" he whispered, squeezing Eric's hand. Louder, he said, "I think everyone met my boyfriend last night at the party." Had that only been last night? How come every time he stayed with Eric, it seemed like forever? In a good way, but still. He tried to drop Eric's hand, not wanting to drag him into this, but Eric wouldn't let him go.

His sexy man was so sweet.

As he led them up to Kyle, Collin looked around, assessing the situation. Jock was nowhere to be found, and neither were Brad or Tank. Maybe they'd already taken off for Brad's place. "Did Jock go yet?" he asked Kyle quietly.

Kyle rolled his eyes. "He's in your room with Brad and Tank."

"Why are they still here?"

"Because," Kyle said raising his voice. "These guys want to talk to him first, instead of just leaving him the fuck alone."

All the guys started yammering at once. There were about fifteen to twenty of them, all making comments about things like revenge and showing their sensitivity.

"This is insane," Eric said, looking around. "The frat I belonged to was nothing like this." He looked at Collin, raising a brow. "You have a lot of support here. They're fucking nutjobs, but very concerned ones."

It took a few minutes to sort out, but after listening to the guys' comments and a quick consultation with Kyle, it became clear they had two core groups of nutjobs. First there were the guys who felt some sort of response was necessary, as in, they wanted revenge. Like it was all just a frat prank gone too far, and now they needed to go out and return the favor.

Second were the guys who wanted vengeance, but also felt it was important to offer "acceptance" to Jock. "Acceptance of what?" Collin asked Kyle.

Kyle looked as if he were at the end of his rope. His hair was all standing on end like he'd run his fingers through it over and over, and most of his statements now involved him throwing his hands up in some way. "Of his dick-sucking activities," he nearly yelled.

Collin blinked. "You didn't explain to them that Jock wanted to have that dick in his mouth?"

"What do you think?" Kyle threw out his hands, spreading all his fingers as if that could make his meaning clearer. "Of course I explained that—they even get that. The problem is that they want Jock to *know* that they get it."

"For fuck's sake," Eric muttered behind Collin.

Someone please save me from straight, sensitive frat boys. Collin counted to ten before speaking. "Did you explain to them that Jock would find that not only unnecessary, but condescending?"

"Yes! Some of them even got *that*. It's the reason there are guys who *only* want revenge now."

Collin looked at the group again, picking out faces. Danny, Gomer, Billings, Turbo, Ricky... in other words, their standard cadre of idiots. Well, Danny showed real intelligence at times, but most of the others were just dense. "Did you define 'condescending'?"

Kyle rolled his eyes. "Of course."

"Okay, let me try talking to them."

Kyle waved him to the coffee table with a flourish and a scowl. "Be my guest."

Collin glanced back at Eric, who was looking at the table dubiously. "Can you stand nearby? Then if it goes . . ."

"I gotcha, Sweetness."

Collin stood near the corner supports on one end, for added security. "Guys!" he yelled. He got some attention, but it took a few seconds before the room was quiet enough for him to speak.

"I know you're all pissed off about this photo going around—"

"Goddamned right, and whoever did it's going to feel the pain!"

He held up his hands, waiting for the yelled agreements to stop. "Okay, let's start with that—how are we going to figure out who did this?"

Silence. Then Turbo asked, "You mean Jock doesn't know?"

"No. Listen, this is how he got kicked off his hockey team and why he left Avalon—"

"What? That's discrimination, man!"

"Exactly!" Kyle yelled. Collin gave him a look and he subsided, staring at the floor. No wonder they were still stuck on the revenge thing. It took a few minutes and a piercing whistle from Eric before Collin could get their attention again. "Okay, now let's think about this a minute. If Jock doesn't know who the guy is, why do you think the dude would have sent it to all of us?"

"To shame him," Flounder pointed out reasonably.

Collin took a calming breath. They'd deal with the shame thing in a minute. "But what do you think the dude who sent this thought the reaction of the frat would be?"

The atmosphere in the room was thick with ruminations, but not a lot of conclusions. Like, none. Clearly, they needed to be led to the obvious. "If Jock had joined pretty much any other frat in the country, and his brothers saw this picture, what would they do?"

"Kick him out!" Jules said.

"Yeah, probably," Turbo nodded. "But no one would think we'd do that."

"But whoever did this is from Avalon College—they don't know who we are," Kyle called from behind him.

Lots of "ooohs" filled the room. A sophomore Collin could never remember the name of—Nolan? Norris?—said, "So by not kicking him out, we're already taking revenge." He sounded a little exasperated, as if maybe he'd been trying to explain this for a while. Collin made a mental note to figure out his name—he was clearly destined for a leadership position in Theta Alpha Gamma. Before Collin could lead them to the next obvious conclusion, Noah (that seemed right) added, "And he'd expect us to spread it around, so if we don't, that's even more revenge."

"Hot damn, we got him!" Danny shouted, jumping up. After general agreement, some guys wandered off, as if their work was done. Great—less of them to massage around to the right point of view.

"Okay, but what about, you know, showing him our acceptance?" Ricky asked, swinging his wheelchair around and nearly decapitating another semi-anonymous sophomore sitting in front of him. "I really want to do that, man. I mean, I thought with all you gay guys around I'd be doing it, like, all the time, but I hardly ever get to let my sensitive side show."

Eric seemed to be having a coughing fit behind him. Collin refused to look at his boyfriend, or he'd start laughing, so the dude was on his own with that. He thought he heard Kyle thumping him on the back.

"I think what you guys are thinking of as 'showing your acceptance' could be seen as being, well, insulting." He pressed on, speaking over the denials and objections. "Just look at it this way: if a picture of one of you, uh . . . "

"Eating out your girlfriend," Kyle supplied.

Okay, gross. "Of one of you eating out your girlfriend, or just any girl, what would you all think of whoever the guy in the photo was?"

"That he's a stud!"

"And lucky," Gomer added.

"So why don't you think those things about Jock when you see this picture?"

Silence.

Then Ricky ventured, "'Cause, you know, he had to suck dick. I mean, I know you guys like that shit, but that's gross, man. You guys seriously expect each other to do that? See, that's why I'd never be gay."

Deep breaths. "From my perspective, dick is a hell of a lot more appealing than what the average woman has between her legs. Jock feels that way too, I guarantee you. He'd way rather be sucking on dick than—" *gag* "—pussy."

Stunned looks—except from Noah, who smirked. *Hmmm.*

"I already told you guys that," Kyle complained.

Danny squinted at him. "Yeah, but you aren't gay. We didn't think you knew what you were talking about." He turned to Collin. "So, like, you're saying he's happy he's got that dude's thing in his mouth?"

"Uh, yeah."

"Yeah, *some* of us understand that, but he *knows* we think it's gross that he sucked dick." Jules pointed out. "None of these guys would think it's gross if I had a picture of me doing that to my girlfriend. 'Course, I'd have to kick the ass of whoever exposed her like that."

"You don't have a girlfriend," Turbo pointed out.

Flounder nodded. "And I don't really see you kicking anyone's ass unless we get you a step stool to do it."

Jules glared at him. "Someone get me a step stool!"

Flounder ignored him and turned back to Collin. "Yeah, if someone shames your girl like that, you can't just let it slide. Like, doesn't Jock need to, I don't know, get all protective about his boyfriend?"

Shit. How to explain this? "It's a little different for guys, right? I mean, if that was you getting your dick sucked by a girl—not your girlfriend; pretend you can't even see her face—you wouldn't feel shamed, right?"

Billings looked at Collin like he was the dense one. "Well, no . . . but my girlfriend would kill me, dude."

Jesus H. "Okay! Imagine this—a picture of Jules goes around the internet of him getting his dick sucked—" Collin held up his hand, stalling the questions he could see coming. "I don't know how we know it's Jules. Pretend he has his name tattooed on his dick, whatever, but it's Jules getting his dick sucked. What would you guys think of Jules?"

"That he's a fucking dork for getting his name tattooed on his dick. What's he gonna do, misplace it?" Flounder asked.

"I don't have my name tattooed on my dick!" Jules stomped on the floor.

Collin ignored that for the good of his stress level.

"I'd think he's a fucking stud," Gomer yelled. "And lucky."

Finally! "Do you get it, now? Jock doesn't need to look for revenge, okay? He just needs to be left alone about this for now. And he needs you guys not to be total douche bags and make him feel like a freak because he likes to suck dick and not, you know," Collin waved his hand in the air. "Do that other thing."

"Eat pussy," Turbo supplied helpfully.

Gag.

"So . . ." Danny began, clearly thinking. *That can't be good.* "Shouldn't we, like, congratulate him for getting some?" When Collin just stared, he went on, beginning to look faintly green. "I mean, tell him that that guy's dick looked—" He paused, swallowing. "Uh, juicy, 'n' all . . ."

"For fuck's sake, no!" Collin said.

Danny looked hurt, lower lip poking out. "Man, I'm just trying to be sensitive the best I can. This sensitivity shit is hard." He looked at Kyle. "And that fucking sensitivity training class—"

"Danny," Collin snapped. "Whenever sensitivity is called for in the future, I think you should ask yourself, 'What would Tim Gunn do?'"

Comprehension—or something—dawned, and slowly Danny began to nod. Collin glanced around, and other guys were nodding too. Shit, he should have started with the Tim Gunn thing.

"Okay, so we're clear here? What would Tim do in this situation?"

Danny straightened his spine and cleared his throat. "Well, I'm pretty sure Tim would try to give Jock his space until he's ready to talk about it. Right guys?"

A chorus of "yeahs" filled the room. Thank God, because all Collin had left in his arsenal was jumping up and down on the coffee table until it broke to distract everyone while Kyle snuck Jock out the back.

As he and Eric headed back to his room, Collin heard Danny asking, "Hey, anyone want to watch *Project Runway*?"

ΘΑΓ

Collin pulled Eric along toward Jock's room—Collin's also, he guessed—but Eric couldn't help wondering if he really needed to go. He tugged on Collin's hand to get him to stop. Collin turned back, lips parted in surprise.

"Do you really think it's a good idea for me to come along? That kid doesn't even know me."

Collin shut his mouth and took two steps toward him, until he was looking directly up into Eric's face. "I guess me wanting you to isn't really a good reason, huh?"

"Jock might not see it that way, no. Regardless of what you said to those guys out there, I don't think this is something that makes him feel like The Man, is it?"

"Not so much, no."

Eric gave him a quick kiss. "It's fine, Sweetness. Go do what you need to do. I have something to do out here, anyway."

Collin tilted his head. "You do? Will you tell me what it is later?"

"Yes. Sweet nosy thing."

Collin smiled, and then Eric's phone rang.

When he checked it, they both saw Mike Taggert's name. Collin looked at him curiously but only said, "Okay, I'll go. You get that."

Eric hit talk. "Hey, Mike." He watched Collin walk down the hall, then knock on a door.

"Hey, I have some news I thought you'd be interested in. Your boy said that Donaldson character couldn't have planted the bomb because he was on a plane, right?"

"Yeah?" He stepped to the side of the hall, halfway between where all the guys were watching *Project Runway*—WTF?—and the room Collin had disappeared into.

"Well, he wasn't on any plane that we can find. That flight announcement in the background of Collin's voice mail message isn't from that Saturday morning, or any Saturday morning, and it's not from either the Portland or Eugene airports. No such flight number leaves from either of them. That flight number belongs to a little airport outside Chicago. Dammit, I forgot the name, just a minute here." Eric could hear him shuffling papers.

Eric hadn't ever listened to the message in the first place, so he'd take Mike's word for it. "It doesn't matter, I don't need to know the name of the airport. So you're saying Sparky recorded that and played it back while he was leaving Collin a message?"

"Can't imagine how else it'd get on there. Flight doesn't even leave in the morning; he'd have to have recorded it. We're trying to get a warrant to have the phone company release the location of his cell phone at the time, but he may not even have used it. Although I guess Collin's phone showed it as coming from his number. The tech guy here says there's some way to fake that, but my eyes glossed over about ten seconds into that explanation."

"What about the email?"

"Gotta get a warrant on that one too. Came through some internet site or something. Can't remember how the hell that worked, all I know is we have to ask the mail hosting company to pretty please tell us where the email originated, and they won't do that without a court order. You know, all this goddamned technology is supposed to make our lives easier, but I'll tell you what, this is a helluva lot more complicated than when I was—"

"Mike, I've heard this rant already."

"Dammit, gotta find someone who hasn't, and they're getting pretty thin on the ground. Well, anyway, that's all I've got. You got anything for me?"

"Nothing related to the case, but you remember that girl that kept the telescope trained on TAG House?"

"Eh? Oh, yeah. Wacko."

"Is that her name?"

"Hang on, let me look through my notes, here..."

"You know, if you put your notes in the computer, like everyone else, this would be easier."

"Well, aren't you the smart-ass? Just shut the hell up, you're distracting me."

"Yes, sir."

"Dix, I'm warning you, you want this information you'll be nice."

"Calling you 'sir' isn't nice?"

"Not when you do it. For all I know, it's got some kind of kinky sex meaning, too. Oh, here we go. No, I didn't write down the girl's name—Homes did the interview, so I was cribbing her notes. All I have's that she's in Nu Omicron Mu, and the guy's name is Jules."

"That's enough. Thanks."

"All right, Dix. You in tomorrow?"

He sighed. "It's C shift, so yeah."

"I'll be at the station in the afternoon. See ya."

It took Eric a minute to find Jules. He had a feeling what he had to tell the guy would be appreciated, though, so he made the effort. He found him near a side table by the elevator, about halfway through turning a big messy stack of mail into many small, perfectly aligned stacks of mail.

"Hey, Jules, right? I'm Eric." He held out his hand, and the guy took it, but he looked a bit weirded-out.

"Um hi. You're Collin's boyfriend."

"Yep."

Jules nodded, moving kind of like a nervous rodent. He looked at his orderly little stacks, then back at Eric, then to the big messy pile. "Yeah, the guys like their mail organized. If I don't do it, no one will, so..." His fingers twitched.

Neat freak. Collin had mentioned that. "You don't have to stop doing that on my account."

He fell on the rest of the mail like a rat on cheese.

"So, you know I work for the fire department?"

Jules nodded, efficiently sorting through the pile.

"And I hear things occasionally about this investigation—nothing important, just random things."

A line appeared between Jules's brow, and he glanced at Eric, then went back to his mail.

It felt kind of surreal to continue talking to this little rodent-man when Jules had made it pretty clear he'd rather be playing with his envelopes, but Eric went on. "So, one of the things I heard was that one of the girls in that sorority across the street from TAG House—"

"Nu Omicron Mu?" Jules looked at him, somewhat less interested in his sorting task.

"Yeah. One of these girls keeps a telescope trained on the frat, watching for you."

Jules gasped and dropped the mail in his hands, falling against the side table and promptly hyperventilating.

"Okay, man, let's just sit down right here, how does that sound?" Eric took his arm and sat down on the floor with him, keeping track of Jules's respirations. Jesus, just his luck. Try to do a guy a favor and end up giving him CPR.

But Jules recovered fast. He grabbed the front of Eric's coat and pulled him closer. "Which girl?"

"Well, I didn't get her name, but . . . no offense, but does it really matter?"

Jules let go of him, nodding. "You're right, it doesn't. What do you think I should do? Go over there?"

"Well, yeah. I mean, you aren't going to figure out which girl it is by staying here, right?"

Jules sprang off the floor. "Right! You're right! I'm going now. Oh! But this shirt, it's kind of —" He sniffed at his pits. "I should take a shower and change, don't you think? Yeah, you're right, I'll do that." He scurried down the hall, still talking. Hopefully to himself, because Eric wasn't going to follow along.

He started to get off the floor, and a hand appeared in front of his face.

Sweetness; offering to help him up.

Eric took it, even though he didn't need it, and let Collin pull him up and directly into his arms. "What you just did for Jules was the nicest thing ever," he whispered into Eric's ear.

Eric felt heat flood his face, so he changed the subject. "Um, how's your friend?"

Collin smiled at him, like he thought Eric was just so cute. *Gah.* But he answered Eric's question, at least. "Jock, Tank, and Brad went out the back. He's okay—as far as anyone knows, the guy doing this only sent the picture to active Theta Alpha Gamma brothers, and Jock got the message loud and clear that they aren't going to turn on him over this. Even if they are a bunch of nutjobs. He still doesn't want to sue or anything, though. I think he's hiding something. Not anything, like, nefarious, but some detail he's too embarrassed to admit."

"Probably. Don't worry, Sweet Thing, this will all work out eventually."

He chewed his lip a second. "I feel like I'm not being as supportive as I should. Like I should be the guy he brings all his problems to, but you know who he went to first this morning? Brad."

Eric shrugged. "So Brad's got it under control. You don't have to be the go-to guy for everything, you know."

Collin made a happy-sad face—that weird mouth shape that was both frown and smile. On him it looked like disappointment and acceptance.

"Let's go," Eric said, tugging him toward the elevator.

"What did Mike have to say?" Collin asked.

"Oh yeah." Eric pulled him in across from him, hitting the "1" button. "He said Sparky recorded that flight announcement, so it was totally bogus. He was trying to cover his tracks for some reason."

Collin worked his lip again and looked at the floor numbers pass by on the display. "He looks kinda suspicious, doesn't he?"

"He does." He took Collin's hand and leaned to kiss his temple.

Collin sighed and shrugged. "Monty's not going to like that." He rested his head on Eric's shoulder, then stood up again as the elevator dinged and the doors slipped open.

"No, I imagine not." Eric would admit to enjoying that Monty wouldn't like it. Collin looked over his shoulder, giving him a look that Eric could only interpret as half smirk and half scold.

Heh.

For some dumb reason, he'd thought Collin wouldn't think to try checking his voice mail on his broken phone, but on the way back to the car, he had the damn thing out, turning it to try to see his shattered screen from different angles. "I think I have messages, but I can't tell for sure because of that crack right there." He pointed at one of the hundreds of cracks across the glass. It looked like a standard eggshell fracture to Eric, but those were supposed to be confined to eggs and skulls. He didn't know if there was a term for that kind of injury to a phone. Except FUBAR.

"I thought you wanted to kill that thing. Ignore it."

Collin looked down at his cell, steps slowing. "I sort of feel . . . I don't know, guilty. I mean, I like my phone."

"Sweetness, your phone is an inanimate object. It has no feelings of fondness for you."

Collin frowned at him. "But it must like me. It's trying to communicate with me, see? There's the little bubble with a number in it, telling me I have messages."

"I'm not going to talk you out of checking your messages, am I?"

Collin shook his head. "It's not likely."

"Fine." Eric waved at the phone. "I'll just hope it doesn't work."

But after a couple of attempts, Collin managed to get his messages. Eric kept herding him toward the car the whole time. Collin snorted when he got the first one. "Kyle, telling me to check my email." The delete icon was under a particularly nasty set of fracture lines, so he had to listen to the whole thing.

By the time they were at the car, Collin was silent, slightly pale, and very composed—back perfectly straight and face blank. Eric opened the door for him when he didn't do it for himself, and Collin got in with jerky, automatic movements. *This can't be good.*

When Eric got around to his side, he found Collin staring out the front windshield, phone in his lap. Eric laid a hand on his leg.

"That was Uncle Monty." Collin lifted the phone and poked at the screen until he got the message to replay, then held it to Eric's ear.

"—just contacted by a Detective Homes, who is apparently overseeing the arson and bomb investigation, and had a very interesting phone conversation with her. Since you apparently felt it necessary to share your baseless accusations about someone from the Alumni Association being the perpetrator of these crimes, I feel it's best if I come up there and speak with the detective and this Fire Marshal Taggert in person. I'll be arriving first thing in the morning, and I've made my usual hotel arrangements. I've also made a 7 p.m.

dinner reservation at the Water Station, and I expect you to meet me there. Please don't keep me waiting."

He squeezed Collin's leg, giving himself a second to get over his own knee-jerk desire to call J.M.—*Monty* a douche bag. "Are you going?"

Collin focused on something out the windshield. "I kind of have to."

Eric took his hand so Collin would look at him. It worked, but whatever Eric had meant to say slipped out of his head when he looked into Collin's eyes. They were so beautiful—he could swear Collin's lashes hadn't been that dark nor his irises that swirlingly colorful when they'd first met. Then Collin blinked, and Eric realized his boy was trying to keep it together. His eyes looked so big because he had so much turmoil inside. Now all Eric wanted was to comfort his sweet thing. He wrapped his other arm around Collin's shoulders and pulled him as close as the stupid console would allow. "You can do whatever needs to be done, Sweetness. You're strong. Look at what you just did with the frat guys."

Collin sighed and fell a little farther into him, then lifted his chin for a kiss. When Eric had given him what he seemed to need, Collin said, "I'm going to have to tell Monty I'm gay."

Eric had thought this might be coming. He nodded. "Okay."

"This isn't personal for him, and if I tell him, it makes it personal." Collin leaned his forehead against Eric's. "But not just that, I need to know how he's going to deal with this for the rest of my life, you know?"

Eric choked up, thinking about what "the rest of his life" might include. So he kissed Collin instead, over and over, and when he finally pulled away, he realized the edge of the cup holder was digging into his solar plexus. "I'm going to get a new car, swear to God. One without a console."

Collin laughed.

Heh. He'd made his sweet thing smile.

"Let's go home," Collin said.

Chapter 44

Collin was convinced every possible stressful, unnerving thing that could happen in a day already had, until Eric said, "Sweet Thing, there's something we need to talk about."

Collin jerked to a stop just inside Eric's side door. He hadn't even taken his coat off yet, and they "needed to talk"? He turned to face his boyfriend, feeling his spine straighten automatically. "Just tell me."

Eric's expression wasn't upset or grave or any of the things Collin expected. He looked excited. With maybe a nervous edge. "Uh, after I start the oven." He held up the unbaked pizza they'd stopped for on the way home.

Collin all but stomped his foot. "No. I want to know now." It was either that or run from whatever Eric had to say.

But Eric was edging around him, using the pizza as a sort of prod to get Collin to move father into the house. "Let me set this down first."

"You can't just start something like that, especially on a day like this has been, and then stall before finishing. It's not fair." Oh my God, he was whining. He'd sunk to a new low.

Eric stopped maneuvering him and reached for Collin's wrist, pulling him closer. "It's nothing bad, Sweetness. At least I don't think so." Then Eric kissed him quickly, leaving Collin in the living room, staring after him as he walked over to the table and set down their dinner. "You know I have to work tomorrow," he said as he walked back.

Collin nodded. "You told me already."

Eric came to stand in front of him, in his personal space, and took Collin's hand. "Yeah. I was thinking you need your sleep and I have to get up so early, so you should just stay in bed when I get up." He half smiled. "You could even stay here tomorrow."

This was what they needed to talk about? Collin leaned back an inch, as if the distance might give him a better perspective on what Eric wasn't saying. "'Kay . . ."

Eric glanced down, squeezing Collin's hand. "So I need to give you a key to the house."

Collin swallowed. "A key?"

Eric met his eyes again. "Yeah," he whispered.

Oh God, he felt faint. They were conveniently next to the couch, and Eric followed him down onto it, or possibly he was pulled there by Collin's sudden death grip on his hand. "That's like . . . that seems significant." Oh shit, maybe he was overreacting. "Unless you mean it's just for to—"

"I'm not loaning it to you." Eric rubbed the back of Collin's neck with his fingers, pulling him close enough to rest their foreheads together. "I'm giving you a key to my house. That I want you to keep."

Collin's mind could only focus on one thing. "Why does this seem more overwhelming than when you told me you loved me?"

Eric took a breath, as if he could finally breathe right. "Because you aren't thinking about dumping me this time?" The smile he'd been working on slipped away. "It's overwhelming?"

"In a good way," Collin rushed to say. He pulled his hand out of Eric's to wrap his arms around his sexy man.

Eric swallowed. "So, you want the key?"

"Yes." Collin kissed him, trying to calm Eric's nerves for once.

"Thank God."

Collin grinned. "You know what? This so deserves impromptu sex on the couch."

ΘΑΓ

A few hours later, Collin lay in bed naked, warm, and full of pizza, and watched his mountain man in front of the fireplace, poking at the fire with his naked self all exposed. He'd squatted down, ass muscles flexed, quads working to hold him up. "You're so sexy." Had he said that loud enough to be heard?

Eric looked over his shoulder and grinned. "Thank you."

Collin grinned back. "Thank you for not arguing with me about it."

When Eric came to bed, instead of crawling in next to Collin, he went around to the other side, then lay down and surrounded Collin's body with his own. His groin cupped Collin's ass, and his half-hard-and-getting-harder dick lined up almost perfectly between Collin's cheeks. Collin arched his back and rocked his hips, encouraging things along, *hmmm*ing when Eric rumbled at him.

"Collin?"

The fact that Eric had used his name and not an endearment grabbed Collin's attention. "Yeah?" He tried to turn and see him, but Eric held him too tightly.

"I want to talk about condoms again."

Shit. He didn't know what to say, so he worried his lip.

"What happened this morning doesn't mean we have to stop using them."

He grabbed Eric's hand from where it was rubbing his thigh and held it between his. "You'd still wait?"

"Of course I would." Eric's lips brushed the back of his neck, then his whiskers rasped against Collin's skin, making him shiver.

That cleared everything up in Collin's mind. "I don't want to use them, though. I want to feel you inside me."

Eric rumbled again, this time pressed so tightly against Collin's back that it vibrated through to his fingertips. Eric untangled his hand from Collin's and started a slow journey down his chest. "Do you want to not use condoms now?"

Collin pushed his hips into Eric's, feeling the heat of his cock rub against him. "Yeah, I don't want to now." He sucked in a breath when Eric's fingers stroked his lower abdomen, making him feel ticklish even though he'd never been that way before. Then Eric found Collin's dick, caressing it too softly. Collin tried to spread his legs to give Eric more room, but Eric's thighs trapped his, holding them close together until he let go of Collin, trailing his hand around Collin's hip and kneading his ass.

Collin started to reach for himself, but Eric said, "Just wait awhile. Make it last." Then he pushed Collin half over onto his stomach, arranging him so he had one knee bent and he was wide open for Eric to explore.

Eric reached over him, getting the lube he'd pulled out earlier and flipping the lid. Why was that such a sexy sound? Because it only meant one thing, of course. He watched Eric pour some out into his palm. *Those fingers are about to slide inside me.* Collin shivered, and Eric tossed the tube aside and his hand disappeared, to be felt seconds later against Collin's taint when Eric's slick fingers rubbed against him. Collin let out a slow, shaky breath. Sucking it all back in when he felt Eric's thumb pressing against his asshole.

When Eric first pushed inside him, Collin's body had the same reaction it always did: he made one of those small, unstoppable sounds in his throat while his spine curved and elongated, unfurling for Eric and pushing his hips closer. His body welcomed Eric's, opening more, his knee sliding farther up the bed.

"Love the way you respond to me," Eric whispered, kissing across his shoulders. "So sexy."

That Eric could see and appreciate Collin's subtle signals made it all better. It filled him with that kind of liquid heat he only experienced during sex. He reached back and caressed Eric wherever he could reach, along Eric's side and back. "I want more."

Eric pushed closer to him, kissing the curve between Collin's neck and shoulder and rubbing his chest hair along Collin's back. He worked his thumb deeper inside until he could massage Collin's prostate and had Collin writhing on the bed, gasping, and he'd trapped Collin's wrist to keep him from reaching for his dick.

"Want me to fuck you now, Sweet Boy?"

"Please," he gasped.

Eric slid across his gland, making Collin twist and jerk. "That feel good?"

"Yeah." If "good" meant turning him into one large, sweating, quivering nerve.

"It's going to get better," Eric whispered. Then he slid his thumb out, still holding Collin's wrist and knee in place, keeping him open and pinned to the bed the entire time Eric worked his dick into Collin's ass. When Collin could feel Eric's pubic bone right up against his tailbone, Eric stopped a few seconds, breathing heavily into Collin's ear.

Collin pushed back against him, signaling he wanted Eric to move. But Eric only kissed his neck. "Hang on, Sweet Thing." Then he let go of Collin's knee and clamped his hand on Collin's hip, gripping tightly as he rolled them over, Collin on top, back to Eric's chest. He blinked at the ceiling until he felt Eric's dick pushing up into him and his body caught up with the program, automatically planting his feet on the bed for leverage.

"Put your arms over your head." Collin did, shivering when Eric slid a hand down his chest, passing over his nipple. Not stopping until his fingers were hooked around Collin's hipbones and he could hold them while he rocked his, thrusting up into Collin and beginning that prostate massage all over again.

Collin let it all happen, enjoying the feeling of being fucked with no immediate goal in sight, just pleasure. Arching his back and pushing down into Eric, noticing the way Eric's body undulated under him, and how Eric's furry chest rubbed against his back. He ran his feet up and down Eric's legs, the hair rasping his soles and sexy shivers traveling up to his groin.

Eric's thrusts got rougher and faster, and Collin began to feel like Eric was building a fire inside him. "I want to jerk myself," he panted.

Eric let go of one of Collin's hips and clamped his arm across Collin's neck and upper biceps, keeping Collin from reaching for himself. "Just wait, Sweetness."

Collin groaned, the feeling of Eric's dick rubbing inside him getting more and more insistent. He was working up to a serious explosion, one he desperately wanted now. He needed a hand on his dick as Eric pushed him closer to it. "Touch me. Please."

Eric kissed his ear, panting in it. "Not yet, Sweet Baby. Hang on a little."

Fuck. "I need to come."

"You can come any time you want." Eric spoke in time with his rhythm, barely intelligible. Collin groaned, partly in frustration and partly because every time Eric's cockhead passed over his gland, it felt like the beginning of orgasm, when his muscles crossed that thin line from voluntary movement to involuntary, forcing Collin into that space where he had no control and he had to just let it happen.

Then Eric stroked inside him just the right way a few times in a row, and Collin couldn't stop himself anymore, his cum gushing out onto his abdomen. For a few seconds he lost all ownership of his body—his existence began where Eric slid inside him, coaxing one more spasm out of him, spreading that ache everywhere from the palms of his hands to the soles of his feet. But it wasn't the ache of wanting; it was the ache of getting.

He choked out Eric's name, then he felt him coming too, and that was hotter and more emotional than he could have imagined. More than coming inside Eric had been this morning, and he floated somewhere nearly perfect, totally senseless. He didn't think he passed out, but he definitely lost touch with reality. When he became aware again, Eric's hands were rubbing up and down his body, and Eric was shuddering under him with aftershocks.

"Holy fucking shit," Collin panted.

"Good?" Eric asked, kissing his ear.

"I think I saw God."

Eric laughed breathlessly. "That's my line."

"I'll move in a few seconds." When he had some muscle control.

"I like you here." Eric wrapped arms around his chest. "Be my blanket."

"That's my line."

Eric rumbled at him. He was like a big cat sometimes.

"I didn't know I could come that way."

"I had a feeling you could."

"So you pushed me? What if I hadn't been able to?"

Eric's lips touched his neck just under his ear. "I was just about to give in and stroke you myself. I wasn't going to last much longer."

Collin rolled off because he wanted to be able to kiss Eric. He ignored his cum soaking into the sheets and rubbed his palm all over Eric's furry chest and pressed his lips under Eric's jaw. Mmm, damp skin and that yummy musky smell. *Rrowrr.* "I'm glad you didn't give up."

Eric turned his head and lifted Collin's chin. "I would have tried again until we got it right."

"Tell me again." He shouldn't ask for it, since he couldn't seem to say it back, but Collin couldn't help himself.

"I love you."

Collin sighed and snuggled up under Eric's chin. It was a happy, sappy kind of sigh, and he couldn't even feel like a geek for being that mushy about his boyfriend. It was all just too good.

I must love him. What else could this be?

"We should go to sleep, Sweetness. Or at least I should. I have to get up really early. You have the key I gave you?"

Collin wiggled closer, trying not to cut off Eric's airway. "Yes, on my key ring."

Eric kissed his head. "You can stay as long as you want tomorrow."

"I wish you could sleep in with me."

"I can't really sleep in; I've been getting up too early too many years. I got up at about seven this morning and let you sleep for a couple hours before I jumped you."

Collin lifted his head. "You didn't get up early last weekend." Eric's eyes were half-closed. He really should let his man sleep.

"Someone kept me up all night."

Collin huffed. "I told you not to get up and make me spaghetti."

"Spaghetti was only a fraction of the reason you kept me awake."

"If you think I'm apologizing for the sex, you're smoking."

Eric grinned. "Well, neither am I." He pulled Collin's head back down to his chest. "What are you doing tomorrow? I mean, before you have to meet Monty for dinner."

"I was going to do a bunch of homework, then I need to get a new phone to replace the one I maimed but didn't kill. It's time to put it out of its misery."

Eric sighed. He seemed to have an unreasonable hatred of Collin's phone.

Collin tried to explain. "I need to call my mom before I talk to Monty."

"Yeah, that would be good, wouldn't it?"

"It seems like it." Collin closed his eyes and let his boyfriend massage his scalp, making patterns on Eric's chest with his fingers.

He may not be able to say he loved Eric, but he could totally draw hearts in his boyfriend's body hair.

Chapter 45

*Y*ou *have a new phone, now call Mom.*
   He didn't want to give himself any more time to think about it—he'd managed not to think about it for most of the day by doing homework, and just the fact that he didn't have a fully functioning phone had prevented it from entering his mind often.

Now he had a shiny new smartphone that he'd even synced to his laptop (a delay tactic, probably) and a very pressing need to talk to his mother, but he just stared at her name on his preferred contacts list instead of selecting it.

He looked around Eric's house a minute, feeling strangely and suddenly out of place. Well, not out of place, exactly, more like it was his last moment before he introduced this world to his other world. He could have gone to the frat/dorm after driving into town to buy the phone, but he'd come back here to be alone while he talked to his mom.

Just do it.

She answered on the third ring. "Collin!" She sounded happy to hear from him—a nice reminder to himself that he probably didn't call her enough. "How are you doing?"

"Hey, Mom. I'm fine. How are you?"

"Good. We're moving cattle up to the spring pasture already." She talked about the ranch a while, and Collin found himself interested. He'd never been that into it as a kid, that was more Alyssa's thing. She continued to be the heir apparent to his mother's empire, just as he was to his father's—which was Uncle Monty's now. After Collin's father had died, the company-held life insurance policy had allowed Monty to buy his brother's widow out almost completely. The few shares Collin held had all been gifts from his uncle, and for graduation he would receive a full 10 percent with the understanding that he'd devote his life to Montes Imports.

Assuming Monty didn't force him out after tonight.

"I suppose you called to talk about your uncle," she said, surprising him. "You know, it might have been nice to call your mother after your frat house burned down to tell her you were all right. I had to find out from Monty."

He winced. "I'm sorry. I didn't even think you'd know about it, honestly. And since I wasn't hurt . . . I would have mentioned it eventually." *Weak.*

She sighed. "It's okay, the only reason I did find out was because he called me. He also called me yesterday, wondering if I'd heard from you and saying you were acting strangely."

"Great," he muttered.

"When I asked him what 'strangely' meant, he said you were being 'unaccountably defiant.' I told him I thought it was about damn time."

Collin shocked himself by laughing. It hadn't exactly been a secret that Monty wasn't his mother's favorite person, and it had always made Collin uncomfortable before. Not that she ever tried to influence or even end Collin's relationship with his uncle. He couldn't help wondering, though: if he examined his past, would he see that Monty had tried to manipulate Collin's relationship with his mother?

"Mom, do you remember what I told you when I was home last summer about the membership policy changes we were planning?" He pulled a throw pillow from the couch onto his lap, tracing the patchwork on it with his fingers. Where had Eric gotten these?

"I remember. I still think it's a good idea. I thought you guys went through with it?"

"We did, but I had to work pretty hard to convince some of the alumni, including Monty."

"Ah. That's not surprising."

"What? Why?" Was there something he didn't know about Monty's past? He sat forward, gripping the pillow in his hand.

"No reason, really, he just likes to err on the side of caution if it might affect his business interests, and I know he does a ton of business with the others in the Good Ol' Rich Boys' club. If any of them didn't support it, he wouldn't either."

"So it's not personal for him?"

"Not that I know of. Is this 'unaccountable defiance' due to that policy?"

He couldn't relax back into the couch yet, but he managed to let go of the pillow, petting it to soothe where he'd been so hard on it. "Sort of, in a way. The thing is, Mom, it's, um, personal for me."

"Personal."

Collin didn't realize he'd been holding his breath until he had to speak again. "Yeah, very personal. Mom . . ." *Shit. Just say it.* "I'm gay."

She was silent so long he had to ask, "Are you still there? You didn't, like, faint or anything?"

"I'm still here. I'm sorry. That was just—" He could hear her swallow. "Shocking."

He collapsed back into the cushions. He'd sort of been hoping for Brad's experience, where his family had figured it out a long time ago. Brad was way more butch than him too, without even trying. Why couldn't Collin's family have known it already if Brad's had? "So, you didn't have any idea at all?"

When she didn't answer right away, he clutched the throw pillow to his chest to protect his heart. "I don't know," she said. "I guess I should have, huh? It's just that you're so much like your father. You're very private, so I didn't worry or even think about it when you never brought any girls around in high school or mentioned any . . . Did you have a boyfriend?"

"In high school? No. I've never had a real boyfriend, until, um, now."

"Did you date guys in high school?" His mom asking questions seemed like a good sign.

"Well, I'm not sure you could call it dating, per se."

"Ah." She sounded amused, and Collin suddenly knew it was all right. He nearly fell over on the couch in relief.

"So, this is okay? That I'm gay?"

"Well, I can't change it, so I have to accept this, right?"

That was it? "I guess I was hoping for a little more."

She sighed. "Collin, I've barely known three minutes. Give me time to adjust, then we can figure out how I feel. Except I already know I want to meet your boyfriend. Have you told Aly?"

"No, I wanted to tell you first. Before I told anyone else."

"You're planning to tell Monty, aren't you?"

He swallowed and nodded, then realized she couldn't see. "Yeah. Tonight."

"He said he planned to go up there. Dammit, I wish I could be there with you."

"That's what Eric said too."

"That he wanted your mother to be there when you told your uncle?"

He laughed. She was really good at making him laugh when he was stressed out—a lot like Eric, actually. "No, he wants to be there, but he has to work."

"Eric is your boyfriend?"

"Yeah. Um, he's fifteen years older than me." Collin squeezed his eyes shut, waiting for her reaction.

"You think I'm going to care? Look who you're talking to."

"Oh my God, I forgot." She'd been ten years older than his father. It had been mildly scandalous when the rich, twenty-two-year-old son of a prominent family had married a local cattle rancher in her thirties.

"Your father wouldn't have cared, either."

"About Eric being a lot older than me?"

"About you being gay. I'm certain of that."

Oh God. He had to cough something out of his throat before he could say, "Thank you."

"I love you, baby."

"I love you too, Mom," he whispered.

"Dammit, just a minute." He heard her set the phone down, then the back door squeak open. She had a hollered conversation with someone before coming back. "I told the guys to go ahead without me. I'll ride up later. It's not like they need me to move a few hundred cows, anyway."

He knew her well enough to know she wanted to go, though. He should say good-bye, but there was something he needed to ask her. "Mom, how soon after you met Dad did you fall in love?"

He heard her sipping something, probably coffee, before she answered. "I think right away. But he was so much younger than me,

I just couldn't imagine it happening, so I didn't admit it to myself for a while."

"How long's a while?"

She snorted laughter. "A couple days. It took him longer, though. He was so cautious, just like you are."

He was back to exploring the contours of the pillow with his fingers. "Did it scare him, that you knew so fast?"

She laughed again. "Well, I wasn't stupid enough to tell him until later."

"Do you think if you'd been stupid enough to tell him, he would have been scared?"

"How long have you been seeing Eric?"

Of course she would know what he was really asking. "About a week."

"Hmmm. And he knows, but you don't. This is what I think about your father: he could look back later and see that he knew from nearly first sight—he said as much to me after we were married—but he couldn't admit it to himself right away. He was too careful with his heart by nature. But he never would have let me go, I know that."

"I don't want to let Eric go."

"Well, that should tell you something right there. But give yourself time. If this is real, he'll wait for you to figure it out."

Collin didn't know what to say to that. He'd never imagined having this conversation with his mother. He knew he'd have to tell her about being gay someday, but he'd never imagined asking her about the love stuff. It made him feel mildly embarrassed, and glad he'd told her by phone.

"I should go soon, but there's something I have to say."

She seemed to be waiting for a response from him. "Okay."

Still his mom hesitated. "It's just that, I wish you'd felt like you could tell me earlier—"

"Mom, I didn't—"

"Collin, I know what expectations Monty has put on you your whole life, and I've tried to mitigate them, but I guess my big disappointment in finding out you're gay is realizing that he had more influence on you than I thought."

"What? Why do you think that?"

"It's just I don't think you were really worried *I'd* reject you, I think you were worried *he* would. I can't even imagine what it must have been like when you were a teenager and keeping this secret . . ."

Dammit, she was getting choked up. Mom tears were the worst. "Mom, please, it's not your fault."

"I feel like I failed you."

Shit. "You didn't fail me." *Please, spare me from parental guilt.* Was there one of those painted saint candles he could light to avoid this?

"You know, it really doesn't matter how many times you say that, I'll still feel like it. It's just the way it is. If you ever have kids, you'll get it. For now, just accept it, okay?"

He sighed. "Fine."

"I love you."

"I love you, too," he responded, wondering if he'd ever said it to her twice in one day before in his life.

After Collin hung up, even with the damned dinner looming, he felt good. Relieved. When it came down to it, between Eric and his mother, most of his world had aligned perfectly.

Chapter 46

Collin was ten minutes late, on purpose. It was a petty, immature thing to do, but he did it in the hope that he could conduct himself calmly and rationally after having his small show of "unaccountable defiance."

When the maître d' led him to the booth—good, the booths were high-backed and offered a little more privacy than the tables—Monty raised his brow at Collin but didn't stand up.

Yeah, he'd noticed Collin's tardiness all right. Five minutes might have been excusable, but ten was clearly deliberate. He sat while his uncle watched him silently.

"Thank you so much for joining me," Monty said in his normal tone once the maître d' had left them.

"Thank you for inviting me," Collin returned, picking up the wine list.

"I've already ordered a bottle," Monty said.

Of course, because Collin wouldn't want to pick out his own damn wine. "A whole bottle? That seems excessive."

Monty's glance flickered away and back. "I anticipate being here for an extended period while we discuss this issue."

Collin didn't respond to that. Instead, he asked, "Did you order dinner for me, as well?"

Monty looked appalled. "I would only make such a presumption about what my dinner partner wanted if I were on a date."

Jesus, no wonder he had to pay for sex. Collin picked up his menu, surreptitiously watching his uncle. He hadn't changed much since Collin had been a kid: shorter than average, broad-bodied and muscular. He looked more like a farmer than a wealthy businessman, and in some ways that was the truth. He was a very wealthy businessman farmer, who wore his rustic Spanish ancestry all over his features.

When people saw the two of them together, did they look alike? Collin had an inch or two on his uncle, but his body didn't have the tote-that-barge build Monty's did. They shared the same dark brown hair color, but Collin couldn't honestly judge how similar their features were—he felt too close to get a decent perspective. According to his mother, Collin looked more like his uncle than his father, and the only resemblance he had to her was in eye color.

The sommelier brought the wine, and they had to go through that whole ritual—Monty inspecting the cork, swirling a little wine in his glass and so forth. When that was finally over, the waiter came around to take their order, and Collin picked something random from the menu. He probably wouldn't eat much anyway. He hadn't touched his wine yet.

"How did your meeting with the detective and fire marshal go?" Collin asked, sipping his water.

Monty frowned at him. "They seem to be making a big deal out of these irregularities with Sparky Donaldson. I'm concerned they're barking up the wrong tree."

"Really? And what irregularities are those?" Collin had no idea how much information they would share with someone else. His special source had never told him what was public information and what wasn't.

"Well, this missing person's report is obviously bogus. I spoke with Sparky on the phone after it was filed, and he clearly wasn't missing."

Collin stared at his uncle. He had to be kidding, right? Except Monty didn't make jokes. "Um, he doesn't actually have to be literally missing. Someone who can reasonably expect to know where he is—like his wife—can file the report if he doesn't show up when he should."

"Well, yes." Monty admitted. "That's what the detective said. The point is, it can't have been him, because he called and cancelled your golf game Saturday morning. Didn't you say he'd left a message?"

"Yes." He decided not to point out that Sparky could have planted the bomb before that, not to mention started the fire the day before. He and Monty could argue about this all night, but Monty clearly had his mind set against thinking it was possibly Sparky. "I gave them a copy of it, and of the email I received from him last week."

"Good, I'm glad to hear you're cooperating, Collin. I'll admit I doubted you after that conversation yesterday afternoon, but my understanding now is that you never made the suggestion that Sparky was involved."

"No, sir, I didn't." *My boyfriend did.*

"Now, let's talk about this membership policy. You've demonstrated that it means a lot to you, and while I support the sentiment behind it, I think it's time for you to accept that it's failed the test."

Collin took a deep breath and looked away, around the restaurant, as if thinking, but really he needed a moment to steel himself for this. "Let's say I did accept this as a failure—which I don't, just to be clear—but if I went ahead and told you for some reason that I'd withdraw my support, what good would that do you? There are seventy-eight other active members of TAG, and every single one of them voted not to rescind the policy no matter what the Alumni Association chose to do."

Monty picked up his wine, swirling it, giving Collin a smug "boys' club" smile. "I think it's reasonable to assume that you're a TAG brother with considerable influence over what the other brothers choose to do. I'm quite sure that if you changed your vote, many would follow."

Collin sat back, giving his uncle the same smile, rotating his wineglass on the table by the stem. "I wouldn't count on that."

Monty's smile melted right off his face, leaving behind it a split second of alarm before he covered it up with his frown.

Collin went on before his uncle could begin his next volley. "I consider the membership policy a win. Other than the reaction of the Alumni Association, it's been surprisingly successful." Well, except for Beta Lambda Omicron, but they'd been quiet since Cody had his little freak-out.

Monty sat forward, leaning over the table and poking it with his finger to underscore his words. "How can you say that? TAG House was *set on fire* because of this policy."

"As I've told you repeatedly, that's nothing but a theory so far, and the more this investigation drags on, the less I'm convinced it's the correct one." Collin made a show of picking something off his cuffs, listening to Monty huff and sit back. "You know," he said, knowing full well he shouldn't go here. "Maybe it is Donaldson, and he has some kind of grudge against the alumni that he's taking out on the frat, or even the current frat brothers."

Monty didn't say anything, and when Collin peeked, his uncle was nearly gulping his wine.

Hmmm. He was about to push it a little farther, but their salads came just then, and he had to suffer through that ritual. "Sir, would you like some pepper?" Blah, blah, blah.

Collin pushed his salad aside as soon as it wouldn't be insulting to the waitstaff.

"You've become quite good at this—verbal sparring," Monty said, stabbing at his lettuce and shaved Parmesan.

Collin blinked. He had, hadn't he?

His uncle nodded, looking satisfied. "College has been excellent for you." He took a sip of wine and began on his salad again. He didn't even seem to notice Collin wasn't eating.

"I think I probably learned most of what I know about negotiations from you." But nothing about diplomacy. That he had learned mostly at school and in the frat.

Monty wiped his mouth and sat back, measuring something about Collin with his eyes. "I'm going to lay it all on the line for you." He pushed the rest of his salad aside, then rested his elbows on the table, as if they were now in the boardroom and not a restaurant. "There are some things that, if the police knew, might throw more suspicion on Sparky. However, I've known the man a very long time—he was my broker—and I just can't see that he'd be capable of these crimes."

Collin felt his jaw drop open, but Monty didn't notice; instead, he returned his attention to his salad. "Wait, you're telling me you intentionally kept information that could be pertinent from the police?"

Monty's head jerked up, quickly followed by the straightening of his spine. "I wouldn't call it withholding pertinent information—that makes it sound altogether criminal."

"What would you call it?"

"I call it protecting a friend—a member of the Theta Alpha Gamma community, mind you—from undue scrutiny that has no bearing on the reality of the situation."

Collin had to blink a few times to reengage his brain. "Are you telling me you think he's incapable of committing a crime because he was a TAG member once upon a time?"

Apparently he'd spoken a little too loudly, because Monty looked at him pointedly and gave him the quelling, keep-it-down hand gesture. Collin leaned forward. "If you'd omitted information like that in court, you could be convicted of perjury. There's a crime I can imagine a TAG man committing."

"Collin!" Monty hissed, leaning forward also before sitting back and looking carefully around, as if he might discover that someone in the booth with them had overheard. "My point," he said, setting his fork down and folding his hands on the table, "is that he would never hurt TAG House. He's one of us."

When all Collin could do was stare, Monty seemed satisfied and went back to eating his salad and sipping his wine, ignoring his completely fucking dumbfounded nephew.

Jesus H., Eric had been so right. Monty was a complete and utter elitist. Had this really escaped Collin's notice before? "If he's innocent, how could telling the police whatever it is you know be an issue?"

Monty sighed and set down his fork. "Because it's simply something they wouldn't understand." Monty leaned forward again, in a confidential rather than confrontational way this time, hands on the table and open as if he were holding something between them—maybe a small, invisible world populated by elitist pricks. "There are some men, those of us of high finance, who do business together. Our friendships are founded on that premise, and each of us understands that the business we do is the primary focus. So, if something happened and one member's financial situation changed, and that change affected the other members' investments, they would divert funds from that single member's business. To people—like the police—who aren't accustomed to the way these relationships work, that may look like the group turning on the single member, when that's not the case at all."

Everything—a whole story he'd bet was the real one—unfolded in Collin's head. Between what Monty had said and what Collin knew about his uncle and the details of the case he already had, he *knew*. "You guys all pulled the money you had invested through him, didn't you? Let me guess—he was doing badly in the market and you were losing money so, by the rules of the Good Ol' Rich Boys' club, you basically bankrupted him."

"Your mother's influence is showing. You know I don't like that name she uses."

Collin ignored his comment. "Am I right? Did you all bail on him?"

Monty's eyes flicked away and back. "Well, that's one description, but it's a bit harsh. I'm sure it didn't amount to bankruptcy—the fees alone from us leaving would keep him going for a while. We all believe Sparky will recover from this earnings slump, and then we'll—"

"So these rules you have about the money being the number one priority, they're written? Everyone understands them?"

Monty's eyebrows pulled together. "What? We don't need to do that, certainly."

"How do you know that Donaldson understood this, or even that if he understood, he didn't resent it? I bet you had millions invested through him, and I bet others in your club did, too. He might very well want revenge." Collin had to literally bite his tongue to keep from adding, "Especially after being fired."

Monty's frown grew, affecting not only his eyebrows, but turning down the corners of his mouth, now. "He's not the kind of man who would commit such a crime."

Collin looked toward the window, giving himself a second to get control. He didn't want to start shouting. Yet. "His nickname in college was Sparky because, as you told me, he was a bit of a firebug. But you don't think he could have set the frat on fire?"

Monty sat back and shoved his empty salad plate away, picking up his wine. "This discussion is over."

That very nearly did it. Collin nearly started ranting—about not being twelve or seventeen anymore, and deserving some answers and if Monty wanted to end this fucking discussion then it was *all* over— but at that moment the waiter sidled up to the table with their main courses. Probably sensing the mood. He didn't even offer pepper or anything else, simply said, "Enjoy, gentlemen," and fled.

Collin ground his teeth and ignored his plate, staring sightlessly at other diners, trying to compose himself yet again, wondering why he didn't just let it all go. Let Monty have to put up with a screaming tantrum.

Because I was programmed not to question him.

The thought made him want to puke all over Monty's perfectly cooked steak. Dammit, he should have eaten some salad so he'd have something to regurgitate.

"I'd like to revisit why you're taking this membership policy so personally," Monty began, paying as much attention to his wine as to Collin.

"Because it's personal," he said, without thinking first, and suddenly he was very certain about where he wanted to take this conversation now. "Because I'm gay."

Monty jerked his head toward him, eyes so round they bulged out, fumbling his wine glass and spilling a drop of Bordeaux on the perfect white table cloth. "What?"

Collin leaned back and realized he was shaking. Nerves, anger, or both? Who knew? "I said, I'm gay." He carefully folded his hands in his lap and waited for Monty to respond, feeling incredibly calm. Completely unable to eat, but calm.

One of Monty's eyelids twitched. A seizure?

"You might like my boyfriend, actually. He's a TAG alumnus. I believe you know him. His name is Eric Dixon."

"Eric *Dixon*?" Monty gaped, but within a second his face twisted into a truly ugly expression, and he leaned across the table, finger poking practically in Collin's face. "He's using you. He's using you to get back at me."

Amazing. Collin laughed shortly. "Are you fucking delusional? Let me give you a little life lesson, Monty: it's not all about you." He pulled his napkin out of his lap, ignoring his sputtering uncle, and stood up. "This time, it's about me, and let me tell you a few things."

"Collin," Monty hissed. "I forbid you—"

He spoke louder to be heard, attracting the attention of some nearby diners. "You know what the difference is between us? You live, eat, sleep, and breathe the company. You'd give up anything for it. You'd sacrifice anything for it."

"Shhh!" Monty pushed down with his palms, as if that would stifle Collin. He was only half-listening, looking around at the people starting to stare.

Collin spoke louder. "I don't know if you've always been that way, or if it developed over time, but I remember Grandpa well enough to know he didn't devote himself to Montes Imports the way you do. That's what I want for my life."

Monty leaned toward him, not quite raising his voice, not completely unaware of the people watching them, but just pissed enough to not care so much. "You can't have a normal life in this business if you're dragging a husband along with you."

Collin threw his hand in the air, done with speaking and not yelling. Done with Uncle Douche Bag. Just done. "For fuck's sake, yes I can! Someday soon, Eric and I will be able to get married anywhere in the country and it will be a legitimate marriage in every freaking state. I promise you that as soon as it is, we'll start planning the wedding." He was on a roll, getting into Monty's face and stabbing his index finger into the table to make his point. "What I'm telling you is, I will always be gay, and if you can't deal with it, I guess I won't be joining the company." It felt awful saying that—like ripping something out of his gut and handing it over to Monty to do whatever he wanted with it. Collin *did* want to keep Montes Imports in the family, but he also wanted to have children to pass it on to someday. Ten years down the road, he wanted a househusband named Eric with completely gray hair and no abdominal muscles.

And if he had to choose between those things? He'd give up the company and take the kids and the husband and the beer gut.

As he straightened up, satisfied he'd said it all and covered everything that needed covering, he realized just how silent it had become in the restaurant. Almost the only sound was Monty's harsh breathing. Then a piece of cutlery clattered loudly onto a plate, as if someone had dropped it. Collin turned away from his uncle and looked around.

Everyone was staring at him. Mostly agog, although when his eyes met those of one waiter, he got a small smile and a very quick thumbs-up. He didn't know how to respond to that—it wasn't as if he'd been performing for their benefit—so he ignored it and turned back to Monty. "I think that's pretty much all I have to say to you. Thank you for dinner."

Monty had finally composed himself enough to speak. Even enough to stand up in order to say whatever he thought needed saying, meeting him toe-to-toe. "Collin, you'll need to find a very good lawyer, because you'll be hearing from mine in the morning."

Collin nodded once. "That's pretty much what I expected from you." Then he turned and walked out.

ΘΑΓ

Collin passed through the foyer of the restaurant while people stared at him—oh yeah, he'd made a scene, hadn't he?—including the maître d', who looked horribly confused. The damn front doors were glass, and the restaurant had a million windows, so Collin had to keep walking, head high, completely confident, through the entire, extremely well-lit parking area.

He finally made it to his car, in a relatively dark part of the lot, convinced he could relax, maybe drive just far enough to pull over for a private little breakdown before calling his boyfriend so he could finally tell him what he'd figured out—he loved Eric.

But as he stuck the key in his door lock, someone came toward him, between his car and the one next to him. Collin tried to ignore him, but whoever it was said, "Collin Montes? It's nice to finally meet you. I'm Sparky Donaldson."

What the fuck? Collin jerked back to see a man in a rumpled suit just as Sparky held out his hand to shake. Automatically, Collin reached for it, looking down, and that's when Donaldson pushed the hand right into his gut, just below his ribs. Poking into Collin's flesh.

It was a distinctly gun-like hand. So much so that he wasn't surprised to figure out it definitely *was* a gun.

"Don't move," Sparky growled.

"Okay," Collin said on autopilot, not having a clue what else to do.

"Good. Now get in the car."

Chapter 47

In the late afternoon, Eric and Val went out on their second call of the day—seventy-four-year-old ground-level fall at the local big box store—and when they got back to quarters around seven, Mike was stomping around the station, hollering Eric's name.

"Didn't anyone tell you I was on a call?" he asked, following Mike back to his office.

"Yeah, I just thought that would help."

Help? Help what? "Well, did it?"

Mike grinned over his shoulder. "You're here, aren't you?" He reached his office and unlocked the door. "Shut it behind you," he said to Eric.

He did and shoved his hands in his pockets. "I guess that means you have more news?" He felt unaccountably nervous. Gut feeling.

"I do, a lot." He sat down, his chair squeaking as he turned it toward his desk. "Have a seat."

Eric took a breath. "Okay." Still feeling a little antsy, he sat. "Did you get those warrants?"

"Yeah, but we don't have any answers yet. Homes got through the flight information, and we can't find evidence of Donald D. Donaldson on any flights into or out of either Portland or Eugene in the three weeks prior to the fire or since."

"What if he drove?"

Mike nodded and perched his glasses on his nose. "Or flew under a false identity. Lots of options. And I'm more convinced than ever it was him."

"What else do you know?" Eric shifted in the seat, looking for a more comfortable position.

"Guess what ol' Sparky told his roommate in college? He got himself all liquored up one night and explained his detailed plan to make the hot-water heater into a rocket and send it through the room of the guy he viewed as his personal enemy, while burning down the frat and destroying all evidence in the process."

Eric shot up. "So he *was* trying to kill Collin? I need to find someone to work the rest of my shift." He started out of the room.

"Hold on," Mike called, chair groaning as he stood up. Eric stopped, hand on the knob. "I didn't say that. What motive would he have for killing Collin? How did he even know who slept in that room anymore, or if the bed was in the path of the hot-water heater? I think he wanted to burn the place down, and just used his already thought-out plan."

Eric turned around, not convinced but willing to listen. Mike was right—there was no reason or guarantee the hot-water heater rocket would have touched Collin. It was unlikely, but . . . "Why did he try to burn down the frat in the first place? You don't even have a motive for that."

"Well, we might, but hold your horses, dammit, I'm not to that part of the story yet. You know if I really thought your young man was in danger, I'd be all over it. Be patient, goddammit."

"Fuck me," Eric muttered, rubbing his forehead.

"Anywho," Mike continued. "Turns out the Alumni Association sent out an email newsletter this weekend with all the details they had on the fire, and that's when Donaldson's former roommate came forward. Says he always remembered his old buddy's plan, because for something he claimed to have said as a joke, it was incredibly detailed and thought-out. "We also know where he got the bomb." Mike paused to huff. "Excuse me, we know where he allegedly got it. The bomb tech thought he recognized the work, so they dragged the guy in, and he says he sold 'something he had lying around' for cash to a large, blond-haired man in—get this—a suit and tie. Claims the guy told him he just wanted it for 'personal, recreational use.'"

"What the fuck?"

"Yeah, still illegal as hell, and the bomb-maker's being charged with a bunch of stuff. FBI's looking at him for abetting terrorism. See, a guy like Donaldson, who knows his pyrotechnics? He could figure out how to build a bomb on his own pretty damned easy. But if he was short on time because Plan A failed, and he just happened to have the name of someone who could provide him one, he might go that route."

Eric threw out a hand. "Okay, but what about motives? Do you have any?"

Mike looked at him a second over the top of his glasses. "You gonna come and sit down again?"

"No." Eric leaned back against the door. Not that he was actually relaxing or anything.

Mike sighed. "You know motive's the least important thing, right? We really just need means and opportunity before we start looking at someone seriously, and he had those. He knew how to start a fire, he knew the frat house pretty well—it hadn't changed that much, except for that sprinkler system, bet that was a surprise. No one knows where he's been for weeks, so that's all kinds of opportunity right there. The thing with motive, that's subjective. Guy might be mad enough to burn down a frat house just because someone jaywalked in front of his bicycle if he's really a screwball."

"Yeah, but you said earlier you might have one."

"We might. According to the guys in New Jersey, Donaldson took all the remaining cash out of his and his wife's joint accounts, leaving her with nothing. And 'all the remaining cash' isn't much—he was nearly bankrupt."

Eric crossed his arms. "Mike, I'm trusting you to get to some kind of point, soon."

"Well, from what I gather, Donaldson started losing money on investments in 2011 and never recovered it, and he blamed it on bad advice from members of his college fraternity's alumni association. This is according to the wife and coworkers."

Eric shoved off of Mike's door, walking around his office a few seconds. "So there's a link to the TAG Alumni Association, but not specifically to Collin's uncle?"

"Yup, far as we know."

"So it probably doesn't have anything to do with Collin."

"Nope. But you're worried, aren't you?"

"Yes," he admitted.

"Well, hell. Doesn't Tim Tambo owe you a shift? Tell you what, I'll do you a favor and call him for you."

Eric felt most of the tension leave his spine. Even though he really should find his own replacement, if Mike wanted to offer, he'd take it. "I'm going to go talk to Val, warn her TimTam might be coming in."

Mike grunted. "Yeah, that idjit oughta come with a warning label." He waved Eric out of the room as he dialed.

But just as Eric opened Mike's door, the worst possible thing happened.

The tones went off.

"For engine twenty-three, rescue twenty-three, medic twenty-three, report of unknown injury, car versus tree accident on McKenzie Highway, cross of Buck Point road. For engine—"

"Not now," Eric groaned.

"Just go. I'll have TimTam waiting here when you get back. Hey, isn't that accident near your place?"

"Not far," Eric called over his shoulder on his way out of the room to the bay. Val was already in the rig and had it running when he got there.

Chapter 48

"Don't move. Now get in the car."

Seriously, that should have been his first clue. He'd been too wrapped up in the fact that someone was holding a gun to his liver and he was actually being *kidnapped* for it to sink in that his kidnapper was a giant, fucking buffoon. How could he both not move and get in the car? He had, somehow—that part was all blurry. He knew he'd parked in one of the dimmer parts of the lot, but he couldn't remember if anyone had seen them. He had a flash of memory—getting in the car, struck by the normalcy of sitting in the seat and buckling on his seat belt, yet doing it all at gunpoint—but not a lot else once Sparky had tied his hands together in his lap.

But after five or so minutes of hair-raising, death-defying driving, wherein the moron who was kidnapping him tried to both watch the road and keep his gun pointed at his captive's midsection, the fear factor had worn off some. Collin came out of the white noise of terror and focused on the faint glow of the dashboard lights reflecting off his knuckles, clearly defined under his skin. His heartbeat had slowed down enough that it didn't fill his head completely, and he began to notice things other than "gun" and "kidnapper." Things like, "When's the last time this man took a shower?"

Of course, considering the cold sweat he'd broken out into and the scent of his own fear, he didn't smell any better. Besides, Donaldson was a fugitive, so where would he take care of personal hygiene? Did fugitives think about their personal hygiene?

It was only one of many things he'd started to wonder. He finally cleared his throat. "Isn't it customary for the kidnapper to make his captive drive?" he asked while they waited at a red light. And that was another thing—did criminals wait at traffic lights while committing crimes?

"I play by my own rules, kid," Sparky growled. Then he coughed a few times. "Dammit, I can only talk like that for so long. Hurts my throat," he said in a much higher-pitched voice. When he floored the accelerator, it seemed like he'd left Collin's brain back at the last intersection.

"Um, I guess it takes a while to cultivate a good villain voice."

"Shuddup." Sparky was back to the growl.

"Just trying to make polite conversation."

Sparky forgot about the growly voice. "I'm kidnapping you!" He turned to Collin in outrage, the gun and the car waving wildly. Collin watched the road for him, afraid to blink or he'd miss seeing them pass over the bright yellow centerline into oncoming traffic. "There's no polite conversation in kidnappings! I knew I should have thrown you in the trunk."

Collin shut up, irritation ratcheting into fear again, his elbows squeezing his ribs reflexively, trying to make himself smaller. Less of a target. He didn't want to visit the trunk. Or get into a car accident.

I don't want to die. I want to live with Eric. So much so, he nearly cried with it. Terrified he'd never see his boyfriend again, and never tell him he loved him and never get to make love with him again or get married or learn to make breakfast or feed chickens or gather their eggs or decide what to do with his life now that he'd told his uncle to fuck off or—

"Quit sniffing over there! You're making me angry." Sparky poked the gun into Collin's upper arm to make his point.

Collin bit his lip and breathed in a conscious rhythm, trying to make his heartbeat slow down.

Sometime later, he didn't know how long, they were outside of town, and Collin's pulse had settled down again. Sparky paid more attention to the road and less to him, which did wonders for his adrenaline levels. He was still plenty scared—he was tied up in a car and being held at gunpoint by a driving madman who had clearly gotten all of his criminal expertise from TV. Yet scared was less than terrified, and he'd begun to think about things once more.

Sparky did not appear to be the sharpest tool in the shed, or the sanest. Collin looked down at his hands. His abductor had only tied his wrists; Collin could totally grab something if he wanted. Or rather, had to. But what would he grab? Not the gun—he'd have to turn sideways for that, and he didn't know handguns from water pistols. Not Sparky, because, yuck.

Without moving his head, he tried to cast his eyeballs around, looking for things to help him out of this. The gearshift was on the steering column, so that was no good—the steering wheel would impede him, and if he were going to grab something, he'd need to do it quickly and in a direct path to maximize the surprise factor.

The steering wheel.

Oh no. That was a horrible idea.

Sparky went around a corner on two wheels, and Collin nearly screamed. *Never mind, not a bad idea at all.* He had a better chance of steering this car safely than Donaldson did.

And if he was going to do it—his heart revved up at thought, convincing him it might redline for a second before slowing down again—he needed to do it soon, right? Before they were too far from town. He furtively watched out the window to figure out their location. A green and white road sign flashed by. Millican Road. To his shock, they were headed toward Eric's house. "Where are we going?" he blurted.

"Waterboard Park. After I shoot you, I'm going to dump you in the river there."

He jerked his head toward Sparky. "What? You're going to shoot me?" Instead of having the effect he'd expected—gibbering fear—it kind of pissed him off. Although with a healthy dose of gibber.

Sparky nodded, not even looking at him, gun hand sagging more toward Collin's hip. He could totally survive with a bullet in his hip, right? *Please God, not the groin.* He tried to swallow, and for a split second his throat stuck closed like it had been glued shut, but he got it working again. "So you've really been trying to kill me all along?"

Sparky—that bastard—smiled. "No, that was just a happy accident. I'd had that plan since college, the hot-water heater, and I didn't really care if it killed anyone, I just wanted to burn that place down and get revenge on those bastards. It wasn't until afterward that I figured out I could kill you. Monty *loves* you, talks about you all the time; I knew killing you would be the best way to pay him back."

Shit. Collin licked his lip, trying to think through the fear that was filling his head again. "But, don't you want to get all those guys back? Not just my uncle? The others won't care about me, you know."

"He's the one who pulled his money out first. They all were waiting for someone to go first, and he did. And it's all his damned fault I was losing money in the first place. Olive oil futures! That bastard!" Sparky slammed his hand—the one with the gun—on the steering wheel, making Collin jump and the car lurch. The lurching didn't stop, as if Sparky had decided he enjoyed swerving all over the road.

Jesus, this guy will kill us with his driving. Collin almost started laughing hysterically. That was the point, wasn't it? If he let Sparky get to Waterboard, he'd die. If he got Sparky worked up enough to crash, he'd probably die. If he took control of the car and made them crash . . . well, death was still an option.

He took a chance on looking over at Sparky. He looked like a giant blond bully in a bum's three-piece suit. Brows lowered over his eyes, both hands on the wheel, swerving all over the road.

Both hands on the wheel.

He didn't think, he just did it. Lunged forward, noticing in that last split second before he grabbed it that Sparky didn't have a seat belt on. *Air bags, please fail me now.*

"Hey! Get the fuck—"

The *whump* of the car hitting the dirt shoulder, a headlight kaleidoscope of shadows, sticks and leaves hurtling at him like he was wearing 3-D glasses at a poltergeist movie, and then a screeching, metal-rending crash, then something punching him so hard in his chest that it ripped his fingers off the steering wheel. Collin reeled back into his own seat, heartbeat drowning out everything, only vaguely aware of the headlights cutting through the night at crazy angles, picking out tree limbs and bark and black space. His heart beat so fast and hard he thought it would shake him apart.

"Jesus." He wasn't sure if it was a curse or gratitude. The wind had been knocked out of his brain, making it gasp and sputter. He blinked, trying to clear the blurriness from his head. "Uhhh . . ."

The blinking, or maybe just time, smacked his thoughts back into gear, and after a couple of attempts, he managed to find the seat belt release. Then he grabbed the door handle with his bound hands.

Bound hands. Sparky had done that. Collin looked over in befuddled interest.

Huh. Sparky was out cold. And there was the gun, resting against Sparky's hip.

Ohmygod. He probably needed to grab that, get it away from his kidnapper while the guy was out. Carefully, he picked it up by the grip and set it in his own lap, and finally he could think about getting out of this fucking car.

After the second try, he unlatched the door, but only got it open by shoving hard against it with his shoulder. Unsteadily, moving through a world that looked suddenly surreal and way too sharply focused for night, he lifted the gun off his lap and turned and placed one foot on the ground, then the other. He hauled himself upright on the door frame with his elbows, took a deep breath, and sagged against the car, shaking.

Suddenly a light shone in his face. Collin raised his wrists ineffectively, trying to block it out, and it was lowered immediately.

"Dude, are you all right? Why are your hands tied? Is there anyone else in there? I called 911."

Ohthankgod. The ambulance. Eric.

"Whoa, wait!" his good Samaritan yelled. "Is that a *gun*?" He backed off, staring wide-eyed at Collin.

Collin dropped it on the ground. "It's not mine." He sounded horribly out of breath, didn't he? His lungs were working like he'd run a mile, and his chest ached like crazy. When had that started? "It's the other guy's."

The man stopped retreating, but he didn't come any closer. "There's another guy in the car? Is he all right?"

"I don't know." Collin started to move away from the door at the memory of Sparky, toward the back of the vehicle, leaning against it for support. "And honestly, I don't fucking care."

Chapter 49

A few minutes out from the scene, dispatch contacted them again. "Caller advises of a possible hostage situation. One victim is unconscious inside the vehicle, the other is ambulatory and appears to have a weapon. Police are en route and request you stage."

Eric's heart slammed into gear, because he had a very bad feeling about this. "Get close enough to see the scene." They shouldn't get that close without law enforcement, but Val didn't even argue.

They arrived on the scene of the accident, and Eric recognized Collin's car before Val had pulled over behind another vehicle.

"Stop!" He jumped out and ran. To a huddled shape crouched beside the rear fender, hands tied together and head buried between his arms. He didn't know how he was so sure it was Collin, but he knew it.

Then Eric had him and held him so tight, and Collin was gasping and possibly crying, trying to burrow into Eric's neck, under his chin. Eric calmed himself enough to cup Collin's head right there, holding him against his skin, listening to him babble while untying his wrists with his other hand. It didn't work—he shook too much, so he fumbled in his cargos until he got the bandage sheers and then he just cut through the bond.

For a surreal second as the fabric fluttered to the ground in the ambulance lights, it looked like a tie—small foulard designs on a pale ground.

"—he did, Eric, he wanted to kill me. Not the first time, not the rocket thing, but this time. That bastard was going to shoot me and throw me in the river. I don't want to be in the river, the water's cold this time of year, and I had to stop him—"

"Shhh, Sweetness." Eric gathered his boy closer, ignoring Val next to them with the pack, trying to check Collin for injuries. He stroked Collin's back until Collin calmed down enough to breathe regularly, if fast, and only the occasional shiver wracked him. At some point Val gave up or was satisfied, and she went to check on the other guy in the car. Eric had seen the police arrive, he'd thought.

Donaldson.

He kissed Collin's hair. "Was Sparky driving?"

"Yeah." Collin sounded much steadier now. He took a shuddering breath. "I yanked on the wheel and made us crash. He wasn't wearing a seat belt. I had to. He was going to—"

"You did have to. Fuck, I'm so glad you did." He didn't need to hear again about Sparky's plans.

"I thought I was going to die."

He wanted to say, "Don't think about it," but it was better if Collin got it all out now, or as much as he could. He was still shivering, and Eric finally remembered he was a medic and he could do something about that and other things. He began by taking off his jacket and wrapping it around Collin, over his own coat.

"Can you walk to the ambulance?"

"Yeah."

"I should get the stretcher."

Collin shook his head. "I want to be with you."

Fuck protocol. He helped Collin up, then supported him to the ambulance, carefully searching his pale profile in the headlights for bruises or other damage. "You have a red mark on your jaw." He nearly stopped in alarm. "Do you remember the accident at all?"

Collin glanced at him a second. "I don't remember hitting anything." His eyes were huge and dark. Eric pulled him even closer and kept walking.

He should have put a C-collar and a backboard on him and kept him still and they shouldn't be doing this—

"Dix!"

Mike. Eric stopped at the back of the ambulance, hearing Mike walk closer, already talking as Eric pulled open the rear doors.

"I brought Tambo out with me. I had a feeling this might be the dealio." He eyed Collin critically as Eric guided him up into the ambulance. "Right after you left, we got the location on that email— Donaldson sent it from the Eugene Public Library. We started thinking he might still be around to finish the job."

"Figured that out, thanks," Collin said, dropping onto the stretcher. "He's in the car."

Mike's eyes went wide and he took off, leaving an equally wide-eyed Tambo in his place. "Man, you know you shouldn't be—"

"TimTam," Eric interrupted him. "I'm no longer on duty now that you've arrived. I'm just here with my boyfriend while you check him out." He sat in the jump seat next to the head of the stretcher and held Collin's hand (unless Tambo made him let go) while the medic examined him.

"No headache. No signs of concussion, broken bones, or internal injury," he recited when he was done. "I suppose you're going to tell me he shouldn't go to the hospital?"

Crap. "You're the lead medic. I'm just the boyfriend."

"I don't want to go to the hospital," Collin said, sitting up straight and pulling the blanket Tambo had given him tighter around his shoulders.

Eric sat on the stretcher next to him and bit his tongue. Tambo raised his eyebrows but didn't comment; instead, he turned to Collin again. "You may not be having a lot of pain right now because of adrenaline, and it's not like we have full diagnostic equipment out here. No X-rays—just because I can't find any sign of broken bones or internal bleeding doesn't mean it's not there."

Collin looked at Eric while speaking to Tambo. "But if I stay with Eric tonight, he can keep an eye on me?"

Eric nodded.

Tambo snorted. "I'll get the damned paperwork."

When he'd left the back of the rig, Collin asked, "That's all right? Do you think I should go to the hospital?"

Eric swallowed. "Well, you should . . ."

Collin worried his lip. "But I had my seat belt on, and my car has air bags."

"Air bags sometimes cause their own injuries, and so can seat belts."

"I want to go home with you," Collin whispered.

Eric knew better. He really did. But he picked up Collin's hand from his lap and kissed it. "I want you to, also."

Collin signed the paperwork, and they were free to leave, except neither one of them had a car there. "Another ambulance showed up for the other guy," Tambo said, once he had the paperwork all right and tight. "You two can hang out here until Mike's ready to take you back to get your car."

Then he even shut the rear doors on his way out.

It took work, but Eric managed to lie down with Collin on the little tiny stretcher and hold him. Slowly, Collin calmed even more. The very slight tremble from the leftover adrenaline eased, and so did his muscles. Eric didn't try any massage, just general caresses.

"I'm so glad you're here."

Eric kissed him on the forehead. "Me too." He ran his hand up and down Collin's back.

"You know what I was thinking about when you showed up? I had finally figured out that you might not be the paramedic to respond to the accident. I don't know why, but right then that seemed like the worst thing that had happened all night."

That even sent a shiver through Eric's heart—to have Collin in that much trouble and not be there for him. He couldn't think of much worse. "You could have just asked for me. I would have come for you."

"I know. I'm just so glad it was you." Collin snuggled a millimeter closer. "Dinner was so awful. You're right—he's such a douche. He thinks being gay is bad for business. It's all about him, he doesn't give a damn about me."

"Sweetheart, I'm sure he does."

He thought he felt Collin smile against his skin. "You don't believe that."

"I do. Kind of."

"I feel like such an idiot. I let him run my life, and he's . . ." Collin shook his head. "I was a kid and I never challenged him before, so I never saw this side of him." He struggled up, supporting himself on his elbow. "I needed him when Dad died, and, I don't know, I feel like he took advantage of that. I feel used." Collin's lip curled in disgust.

Eric didn't say anything, just petted him more.

"He told me I need to find a good lawyer, because I'll be hearing from his."

Eric stopped his soothing strokes and gripped Collin's side a second. "He's going to kick you out of the company?"

"I guess." Collin lay back down. He seemed to be taking it very calmly. "It won't be hard, I only own 2.5 percent."

"You don't care?"

"I do. But . . . Do I even want to work with him? He's not only a bigot, he's a self-serving jerk. I feel like he corrupted the company my grandparents started." He snuggled up close again, back to tucking himself under Eric's jaw. "I care a lot," he said finally, voice choked up.

Eric kissed his head. "It's okay," he said. "It'll be okay, I promise."

"When?"

"Eventually," Eric murmured in his ear.

"Am I weak?" Collin asked.

Eric squeezed him tight a second, until Collin squeaked, then loosened his arm again. "You're one of the strongest people I know. You can handle anything. Look what you just did. You're my hero."

Collin kissed his neck. "You're my hero too. And I'm not weak."

Chapter 50

It seemed like they lay there forever, until Collin asked, "How long does it take to clear a scene?"

"It depends," Eric said. "This one will take longer because a crime was committed." He seemed content to just hold Collin, but Collin kept thinking they needed to get out of there. Didn't they need this vehicle for something? And he was feeling strangely normal, and a little antsy. Over being weak and shaky, and ready to move on from this.

"You don't have to stay here with me," he said. Not that he wanted Eric to leave, but because he needed to signal to Eric that he was better now.

"Just let me hold you a little more."

Collin suddenly understood that Eric needed this as much as he did. "I know you love me," Collin said, propping himself up again and looking into Eric's eyes.

"I know you do." Eric didn't quite meet his gaze.

"But you don't know I love you, do you?" he asked.

"It's okay." Eric lifted his hand and kissed the palm. "I can wait for you to figure it out."

Collin cupped his face. "I already did, at the restaurant. And I don't want you to wait. This is a stupid place for it, but I want to tell you now."

Eric finally met his eyes, swallowing. "It does seem kind of . . ."

"Lame? For me to tell you I love you the first time right here, in the back of this ambulance, and when we can't, like, ride off into the sunset?"

"On a white steed?" Eric asked. "The ambulance is white. Not that you can ride in it now, since you signed that paperwork. Not without getting injured for real." He smiled slowly, as if he were fighting it but it wouldn't be contained.

Collin leaned down to nuzzle his cheek, keeping their faces close together and recreating that little space just for them. "I don't want to be injured when I tell you I love you, and I don't want to have to do any more paperwork. I just want to say it and have you know, so you can stop worrying."

Eric's cheeks flushed, although Collin didn't think it was with embarrassment. Some other, happier emotion. "You really don't want to wait? I could build you a fire when we get home and we could get naked and lie in bed, and you could tell me then."

"I can tell you *again*, then. I want to tell you for the first time now," Collin whispered, kissing him softly, letting their lips cling together for half a second. "I love you, Eric."

Even though he'd known it was coming, Eric's breath still caught, and something about that small hiccup made Collin tear up. He took his other hand out of Eric's grasp and held his face, kissing him again, harder and deeper, rolling partway onto him and losing track of time and what they needed to do and where they were.

Until someone knocked on the ambulance door. "What are you two doing in there?" Val asked, just loud enough for them to hear. "You know you can't do that in the ambulance, Dix."

Eric pulled back—the few millimeters he could—trying to straighten his uniform and adjust his dick. Collin grinned at him, feeling like a studly debaucher of firefighter paramedics. Eric was trying not to laugh, he could tell. He wouldn't meet Collin's eye, and he had his lips pressed together.

"We aren't doing that in the ambulance," Eric finally called back.

"Better not be. It's not fair to rest of us. It's bad enough you're getting off shift early to go home and—"

"C'mon Val, give me a break," Eric said. She actually did.

He leaned down and kissed Collin one more time, quickly. "We better get moving."

Collin couldn't stop smiling at him and checking his sexy man out. Eric was still hard, it looked like. "'Kay."

"Stop it," Eric whispered. "You're distracting me."

"Sorry." Collin grinned. He so wasn't.

Collin wanted to go back to Eric's place and have sex all night long—he felt like he could. All that adrenaline and the events of the evening right up to telling Eric how he felt had him worked up.

But he'd forgotten a few details. Like that they had to go back to the fire station to get Eric's car. And that Mike would drive them back and spend the whole trip telling him how much better it would be if he gave his statement to the police tonight.

"You don't have to do it tonight," Eric whispered in his ear while Mike was going on. They'd both sat in back, which Mike seemed to think was cute but also to find annoying.

"I kind of want to get this over with," Collin murmured. So they did—Eric and Mike went to the police station with him while he gave a statement.

If anyone had told him how long giving a statement would take, and how many times his boyfriend would ask him if he had a headache, or if anything had started to hurt—and fine, his arm and shoulder had, and his wrists felt a little raw, but he didn't have a freaking headache—he would have done it in the morning.

By the time he and Eric were in Eric's little car, Collin was half-asleep and desperately wanted to climb over the console and sit in Eric's lap with his head on Eric's shoulder. If he did that, he had a feeling the warm happy glow in his chest would expand, maybe enough to light up the whole car, and people would have to cover their eyes to protect them from the brilliance of it when he and Eric drove by.

When they got to the house, Eric took him upstairs, helped him undress, and then took a shower with him. No sex, just washing and warmth and being held. And only the occasional suspicion that Eric wasn't so much washing him as checking him for injury. It was still comforting either way.

"You feel better?" Eric asked when they did their drying-off routine.

Collin smiled and nodded. Then he swayed in exhaustion, and Eric all but carried him into bed.

In the bedroom, Eric built a fire while Collin crawled into bed, blinking at his sexy man and trying not to fall asleep.

Then his stomach growled

Eric glanced at him. "You didn't eat anything when you met your uncle, did you, Sweetness?"

Shit. "No," he admitted.

Eric stood up from the fireplace and came to the bed, leaning down to kiss Collin, one hand caressing Collin's stomach. "You rest while I make us something to eat. I didn't have dinner tonight, either."

Collin reached up and caught Eric with arms around his neck before he could move. "I love you." It wasn't part of any plan he'd been hatching—he kind of thought sleep was more likely than sex at this point—but he couldn't not say it. Eric did so much for him.

Eric's cheeks flushed just like they had before, and his breath got short, lips parting. It was amazing the way saying that made his eyes brighten up. Collin fell just a little more in love with him, which he hadn't thought was possible.

That so deserved a kiss. He pulled Eric nearer, until he fell into the bed. Collin rolled to face him, lining them up so he could press his body against Eric's, getting as close as two people possibly could be. When their skin met, Eric sighed and Collin shuddered. "That's . . ." Something had changed since the last time they'd touched each other like this, and now it felt as if they could communicate directly from body to body.

"Yeah," Eric agreed, tracing Collin's muscles with his palms, making Collin feel like an instrument Eric was playing.

He gripped the back of Eric's head with his hand, guiding Eric's lips to meet his. "You mean everything to me." It seemed like an incredibly inadequate thing to say, but it was all Collin had.

Eric took a breath, drawing Collin closer, and kissed him. It felt like every stroke Eric's tongue made in Collin's mouth echoed inside him. Every little tiny movement reverberated around, and he could feel it happening to Eric too. He kissed him incessantly, tongue wrapped around Eric's, undulating against him. He could feel Eric's groan in his own throat when Eric held their cocks together. Collin wrapped a leg around Eric's thighs, so there was hardly any room to move, and thrust in and out of his grip, skin pulling and tugging and sliding with sweat.

Collin came within minutes, at the same time Eric did. It surprised him—the orgasm felt like it started everywhere at once, and when he opened his eyes and looked into Eric's, he saw that same surprise. Like it was just one big release they'd both shared in.

Afterward, still as close as possible, Collin felt that same communication between them—they didn't need to talk because he could sense Eric's emotions, and he knew Eric could sense his in return.

Eventually it faded, though, and while it did, Collin faded out, too.

"If I don't get up and put another log on, the fire will go out," Eric said, waking Collin out of his half sleep.

He sighed and kissed his boyfriend's neck. "That was perfect."

"It was." Eric lifted his head and kissed Collin. "I love you."

"Mmm, I love you, too."

Eric rubbed the muscles along Collin's spine, working down until he cupped Collin's ass. "I'll go make us something to eat."

"I should help you," he said while he yawned.

"You had a hard day."

"You did too. You went to work before all this stuff happened."

Eric rumbled at him. "Yeah, but what you went through was way more stressful. I want you to lie here naked while I make us something to eat. It'll give me something to look forward to."

Collin wrapped his arm tighter around Eric. "I really should help you."

"Sweetness, you don't know how to cook." Eric kissed his ear, as if Collin might be insulted.

"Well, there's that. Fine, I guess. Go cook. I'll be right here."

"Naked."

"Almost naked?"

"Mmm, that sounds even better." Eric kissed him one more time before getting up.

Chapter 51

E ric had just finished heating something up for them to eat when his phone rang. It was Val, texting him the basics on Sparky.

Pretty major concussion but no other serious injuries. Stabilized. Police guard on room. Tim Tambo driving me nuts. Please send reinforcements.

Well, there was something Collin would probably want to know. Except for the bit about TimTam.

But when Eric came back upstairs with soup—why did soup always seem comforting?—Collin was asleep, only his head poking out from under the blankets. Eric abandoned the soup on the nightstand and climbed in too, spooning him. He could swear neither one of them moved all night, until he woke up and slipped out of bed at six.

After watching Collin a few minutes, thinking about waking him to make sure he was all right, Eric decided to just go make coffee. He'd wake Collin up soon and check him out, then let his boy go back to sleep. A day of rest (with some gentle exercise, mostly involving bed sports) and coddling was in order for Sweetness, as far as he was concerned. Collin needed sleep. And Eric needed something really major to distract himself from waking Collin up for a couple hours.

Like cleaning out the rain gutters. How could he regularly go out on all kinds of maimings, maulings, and various misplaced body parts but find rotting leaves gross? It was a mystery.

He was outside on top of a ladder an hour later when he heard the back door. Eric glanced down to find Collin standing in the doorway, hair sticking up, eyes still heavy and blinking, wrapped in the blanket he seemed to like wearing as a robe. "What are you doing out of bed, Sweetness?"

Collin yawned. "Couldn't sleep. How come you let the chickens out?"

Eric looked on his other side, where the chickens were scratching through the muck he'd thrown down, generally having a field day. "They like to look for bugs and larvae and stuff in the gunk I'm cleaning out. They don't get a lot of regular entertainment, I guess."

"Gross. So do you have to catch them all to put them back?"

"Nah, I just wait until dark and they go back in by themselves, then I close up the coop." Eric pulled more crap out and threw it down, which served the dual purpose of not only delighting chickens, but also giving Collin something to watch. *Heh*. Who said he didn't know how to show a guy a good time? When he glanced back over at his boy, Collin was leaning against the door. Eric climbed down and stripped off his gloves, joining Collin on the porch. Reaching out to rub his neck.

Collin shrank away from him, shivering. "Your fingers are cold."

"Want me to come inside and I'll build you a fire?"

"You just think that's the cure-all for everything, don't you?"

It must be, because it made his boy smile. "Are you saying it isn't?"

"I'd never say that."

Collin sat on the couch while Eric built the fire, and whenever Eric glanced back, he could see the wheels turning in Collin's head.

"Why'd you wake up again?"

"I couldn't sleep." Before Collin said any more, some damn phone rang. It had to be Collin's because Eric wouldn't have given anyone he knew and/or loved a "Single Ladies" ringtone.

"That's Aly," Collin told Eric as he stood up. "My sister. I better get it."

Eric finished with the fire and went off to work on his computer, trying not to completely hate Collin's phone this time.

Chapter 52

After he'd hung up with his sister, Collin found Eric on the couch, totally absorbed in his laptop. As Collin sat down next to his boyfriend, he saw the screen completely filled with an image that Eric was working on. Collin didn't know what he was doing, but he could see that Eric had already done something to it, subtly muting and maybe blurring the background, which made the figure in the picture pop out.

The mostly naked male figure.

Collin looked over in interest, figuring it was one of Eric's models, until he realized *he* was the figure and those were his glutes inside his purple briefs that drew the viewer's eye right to them.

"Ohmygod, does my ass really look that good?" He slapped his hand over his mouth. *Yeah, I said that out loud.*

Eric smirked at him. "It looks so much better in real life, Sweetness," he said, reaching behind and underneath Collin to cop a feel.

Collin hid his eyes in his hand. "I'm such a dork." With his vision blocked off, he could feel Eric's fingers trying to find the line of his underwear through the blanket. They were hampered by Collin's weight on them. He reached back and grabbed Eric's wrist. "Wait, before you get me all hot and bothered, I have something to tell you."

"Okay," Eric said, pulling Collin closer and kissing his jaw. "What did your sister say?"

Collin ignored the feel of Eric's lips and teeth. "Alyssa just wanted to bitch me out because I didn't call her and tell her I'm gay myself, and then she demanded a good explanation for why I hadn't. So I gave her one."

Eric had figured out that Collin actually intended to talk and sat back, still right next to him, though. "You had a pretty good one."

"Yeah, she agreed about that." Collin turned to more fully face Eric, tucking one leg under him. "Then Mom got on the phone and I told her about what happened." He couldn't kill the small smile thinking about that gave him. Or the slight pang in his chest. "She got really mad at Monty."

"But not Sparky?"

Collin eyed Eric sideways. "Well, I didn't really tell her that part. Yet."

Eric smiled. "What did she say about what your uncle said?"

"She thinks Monty's bluffing, and he'll come crawling to me around graduation time, asking me to work for the company. I guess he already called her, asking about me, and she's certain he wants to keep the company in the family. Montes Imports means everything to him, for whatever reason." He worried his lip a second. "She said she thinks he really does care about *me*. He just doesn't deal well with things he can't control. And I haven't heard from his lawyer, so . . . I don't know."

"So maybe you don't have to give the company up."

"But do I really want to work with him? I feel like the scales fell from my eyes or something. He's not exactly what I thought he was. And besides, I might have another option . . ." He peeked at Eric to see his reaction, but his boyfriend just looked interested. And content. Collin took a breath. "What I really want to tell you about was what woke me up so early this morning."

"Yeah?" Eric's fingers rubbed his neck, his other hand holding one of Collin's.

Collin nodded, staring at the fire, turning it over in his mind again. "I had this idea, and I don't know . . . I think I could do it." His heart skipped a beat, but in a positive way, because really, it was a great idea if it worked. "It's possible. I know the import market, and my cousin Fermin knows olive growing, and between us, we have the money to buy the land and invest in the startup. Seriously, I think we can do it, Eric." He turned to his boyfriend, taking his hand. "I haven't talked to Fermin yet, but—"

"Sweetness, you haven't told me yet, either." Eric smiled at him.

"Huh? Oh, sorry." He blinked, trying to let his tongue catch up to his brain. "When I went to Spain this year to inspect the harvest with Monty, my cousin Fermin—he's really like my fifth cousin once removed or something, who knows—and I went out for tapas a couple nights. He's a few years older than me, and he's finishing an advanced degree in agriculture this year. Anyway, he was bitching to me about how he's the third son, and he has no influence on farming practices in the family, but he'd like to change some things. They use a lot of pesticides and machinery, you know? But that's not the traditional way to grow or harvest the olives, and there's a movement to get back to the old way. It's more labor intensive, but I think we'd end up with a really high-end product if we did it his way. He wants to go organic, and once you stick the organic label on something, people will pay more. That's good, too, because it costs a hell of a lot more. It would be a few years before he can produce anything, I think about four. Although maybe we could buy a place with already established groves. There are some older farmers in the area that just want out—"

Eric pulled on his hand again, like he had to get Collin's attention. "So what you're saying is that you want to start your own olive oil import business."

The pulse in Collin's neck fluttered just at the thought of saying it, and he wanted to worry his lip, but, "Yes. I do. I want to do it differently, and I don't need to be as big as Montes Imports, but I want to. Maybe. If Fermin is interested. Is it crazy to start a business like that at twenty-two?"

Eric lifted his hand and kissed it. "You can do anything, Sweetness. I believe in you."

He let himself worry his lip, because it helped him think. If Eric thought he could do it, and his mother and Aly did . . .

Eric rubbed the back of Collin's neck, and Collin realized he'd been staring off into space. "When I said you're the strongest person I know, I meant it," Eric said.

"I still have to talk to Fermin, and it means breaking into my trust fund."

Eric kissed him.

"But it also means I could—maybe—start a company more like what my grandparents had." He shivered at the thought, because that would make up for so much that had gone wrong in the last twenty-four hours.

"It does." Another kiss.

"You know what else my mom said? When I said the company was all I had left of Dad, she reminded me of Grandpa leaving Spain and his legacy because he couldn't live the way his family wanted him to. She said Dad would understand if I did that same thing."

"Anyone who loves you would."

When Collin met his eyes, Eric looked happy. Excited even. "You really believe in me, don't you?"

Eric nodded, squeezing his hand. "You can do this. That doesn't mean it'll be easy, but I'll support you."

Collin cupped Eric's face, his heart thumping with exhilaration and fear and love. "You know what this means, don't you?"

Eric quirked his endearing half smile. "No."

"It means you have to get a passport. I'm not leaving my househusband here every time I go to Europe."

Eric sucked in a breath. "Are you asking me to marry you?"

"Someday, will you marry me?"

Eric's breath caught, just the way it had last night. "Yes. Someday I will."

Collin figured that covered all the important stuff, and he needed to kiss Eric. His boyfriend smiled the whole time Collin kissed around his lips, like he was too happy to stop, but when Collin started tracing the inside of Eric's mouth with his tongue, things got serious. Until Eric pulled away. "Someday our grandkids will tell the story of how their grandfather started the family business."

Chapter 53

O n Thursday night, Collin went back to Eric's after school so they could watch Donald D. Donaldson taken to the courthouse for his arraignment on television. He'd stayed at Eric's since the night of his dinner with Monty. He'd thought about making up a list of excuses for doing so, but he didn't. The reality was, when he woke up in the middle of the night after the latest dream of Sparky driving him over a cliff, or of floating in freezing water with bullet holes in his stomach, he needed his boyfriend there. Eric had even taken the week off work for him.

Eric made them a nest on the living room floor in front of the TV by dragging the mattress from the studio in, blankets and all. "I don't want to pollute the bedroom with a television," he told Collin.

"You're so sweet," Collin said on his way upstairs. He changed into pajama bottoms but no shirt, and came back down to find Eric in bed, mostly naked and all hairy. *Yummy*. He snuggled in next to him. "Okay, so tell. He must have confessed or something, right? Otherwise would they arraign him yet?"

Eric shrugged, one arm tucked under his head and the other wrapped around Collin. "Yeah, he confessed. He still claims he wasn't trying to kill you until that night, that the thing with the hot-water heater was an accident. It was what you said he told you—Sparky used the plan he'd had in college."

Collin nodded, trying not to shiver. He changed the subject. "No one at TAG can believe what happened. They all mostly thought it was a guy with a grudge about the policy." Collin snorted. "Ricky's still talking about sacrificing his leg for the rainbow family. But everyone else seems to be catching up with the program." He settled onto Eric's chest, making designs in his fur. Hearts again. He was all about the hearts tonight.

"What a freak," Eric muttered, but he sounded close to laughing. They both focused on the TV again a second when the newscaster mentioned the local arson case, but it was just a teaser before they went to commercial. Eric turned to Collin. "Here's something weird—they figured out he'd been hiding in TAG House."

"Seriously?"

"Yeah, in one of the bedrooms in the back, where no one would see light at night. He was building another bomb. Detective Homes seems to think he planned on taking himself with the house this time. That's part of why it took so long to get all the info—the bomb techs had to clean the place up, and they put off completing questioning him. Not to mention the two days in the hospital."

"That's crazy." He made more designs, then started running his feet up Eric's legs, rubbing his soles against Eric's body hair. "Mmm, you feel good."

Eric rumbled. "So do you. Are we done talking?"

Collin turned his head up to see Eric, right there above him, gray whiskers and gray eyes and gray stubble on his head. Eric leaned down to kiss him, and then smiled at him a long moment. Collin dragged him close for another kiss, combing fingers through the head fuzz Eric still hadn't shaved. "Would you grow this a little longer for me?" he asked. "I want to see what you look like with hair."

"I look old."

"I bet you don't. I bet you look distinguished and sexy." He wrapped his leg around Eric's thighs. "I love you, so much."

"Mmm, show me," Eric whispered.

So Collin did, but just when it was getting serious, his ear caught "Donaldson was arraigned this evening . . ." so he pulled away and propped himself up against the couch to watch. Eric propped himself against Collin, playing fingers across the skin of his abdomen, skirting close to his waistband.

"I don't think he's right in the head," Collin said when they showed Sparky. He was cleaner, and had traded his three-piece suit for a less rumpled one, but was still unshaven (in that not-intentional way), with unkempt hair.

Eric hugged him around the middle. "You all right?" He kissed Collin's shoulder, then his neck.

"Yeah. You know, he really is corpulent. That's what I thought about him the first time Monty mentioned him."

Eric nuzzled under his jaw. "You aren't corpulent."

"Nope, I'm not." He was starting to think Eric wasn't interested in this at all. And starting to wonder why *he* was.

"You're succulent." Eric bit his earlobe, tugging on it with his teeth.

Fuck this. That was old news; this was now. Collin shut the TV off and turned to face his boyfriend again. Eric tried to kiss him, but Collin had something to say, so he traced Eric's lips with his finger. "It's kind of not fair that we didn't get to play detective. Especially since I had to go through, you know, that scene with him."

Eric kissed his fingertip. "That stuff only happens in books, Sweetness. Besides, you gave them the clues to start looking at the right guy. And then you outsmarted the villain." He sucked Collin's finger into his mouth and swirled his tongue around it.

It made Collin feel a little squirmy all over. "And I did get to fall in love."

Eric rumbled at him. "Yeah, there's that. Not such a bad consolation prize." He tugged Collin down, until he was flat on the mattress facing Eric. "I'm pretty happy with just that, actually."

"Me too," Collin whispered, wiggling closer to his sexy man, until Eric's lips were right in front of his. "Maybe we can do our own private investigating."

Eric rolled over on top of him, pressing Collin into the bed with his weight and reaching for his waistband. "Yes, we can. I have a very important investigation to undertake in here."

"Mmm, I'd love to assist you with that investigation. I'll give you your first clue: I bought them just for you."

They had hearts all over them.

Acknowledgments

Thanks to all the usual suspects: Thorny, mc, LC, Taylor, Alec, Will, Shawn, Justin . . . I hope that's everyone. This time, there are also unusual suspects to thank: Denise, Edmond Manning and Joe (even though he'll never know it), and the Eugene Public Library. Special thanks to my editors, Rachel Haimowitz and Sarah Frantz.

Author's Note

If you're in emergency services, or are familiar with them, the way I depicted some things in this book may seem different to you. That's because things can vary widely from one region of the United States (not to mention the world) to another. Budgets, land use planning, protocols, laws, philosophies, and administrators (shhh, no one tell the chiefs I called them that . . .) can mean big differences. The way Station 2, Eric's station, is organized and functions is as accurate as I could make it for Oregon, the city of Eugene, and Lane County specifically. That said, the real Station 2 in Eugene bears no resemblance to Eric's station, other than accidental. And, of course, all mistakes and inaccuracies are on me.

Also by Anne Tenino

Task Force Iota series:
18% Gray
Turning Tricks
Happy Birthday to Me

Whitetail Rock
The Fix (Whitetail Rock, #2)

Theta Alpha Gamma series:
Frat Boy and Toppy
Love, Hypothetically
Good Boy (Coming soon)

Romancelandia series:
Too Stupid to Live

About the Author

Raised on a steady media diet of Monty Python, classical music, and the visual arts, Anne Tenino rocked the mental health world when she was the first patient diagnosed with Compulsive Romantic Disorder. Since that day, with her trusty psychiatrist by her side, Anne has taken on conquering the M/M world through therapeutic writing. Finding out who those guys having sex in her head are and what to do with them has been extremely liberating.

Anne's husband finds it liberating as well, although in a somewhat different way. He has accepted her need for "research," and looks forward to the benefits said research affords him. He thinks it's kind of cool she manages to write, as well. Her two daughters are mildly confused by Anne's need to twist Ken dolls into odd positions. They were raised to be open-minded children, however, and other than occasionally stealing Ken1's strap-on, they let Mom do her thing without interference.

Anne's thing is writing gay romance and erotica.

Wondering what Anne does in her spare time? Mostly she lies on the couch, eats bonbons, and shirks housework.

Check out what Anne's up to now by visiting her site, annetenino.com.